RED:

BURNING DESIRE

By Allison White

RED: BURNING DESIRE

Limitless Publishing, LLC
Kailua, HI 96734
www.limitlesspublishing.com

Formatting: Limitless Publishing

ISBN-13: 978-1-64034-531-7
ISBN-10: 1-64034-531-0

Dedication

To all my readers who love the craziness of these books. <3

Prologue

College had never meant much to me. Not the way my parents wanted it to. I was taught from a young age that your alma mater controlled your life, your career, and how society perceived you. I never understood why. Wouldn't it be smarter and more progressive to base someone on their personality and talents and their morality, rather than passing a few classes and possessing a piece of paper?

I ignored my mother's strictness and relied on art, like music and painting, drawing passion from deep down. I didn't want to sit in a lecture hall and listen to some old guy ramble on and on about history when I could make the best of the present. Let him teach *that* to his students. Instead of doing what is the normal thing nowadays and going straight to college after high school, I travelled.

I went to Greece, Paris, the Mayan temples, Egypt—everywhere you could possibly imagine. I did this for one year. The past year was the happiest, most well spent year of my life. I didn't have to wake up at a ridiculous time to hoard into a classroom. Didn't have to stress over tests and lose all of my hair as a result. I said screw it and lived life how *I* wanted. We only have one shot at living. Why waste it?

Who would have known that when I stepped foot on a college campus, I would actually want to stay? Rot away my young years when I could be living my absolute best life? And all for a girl. Red Sylvetti. She was spontaneous and witty and a bit of a firecracker, but she was that magnet pulling me to something I'd loathed. Where I was cool, she was a flame that didn't know how to control herself. Nothing, and I mean *nothing,* could have ever prepared me for her. She hit me like a freaking craving, out of nowhere, making me greedy for more. She was my sweet-tooth.

She was an inferno, but I didn't mind stepping into the flames for her.

If you'd asked me if I could, would I have traded it all for traveling and having fun, my answer would have been I honestly didn't know. Would you regret finding a fiery passion that it almost consumed you with hunger and fulfillment? Or would you want a watered-down flame, so small it didn't excite you? Red was my flame. And hell if she was excitable. I think about the clear difference between us, the obstacles that hit us from left to right, the excruciating pain. But like a whisper, I remember the good times, the laughs, the passion—the *everything.*

All I know is one thing: after her, she made me see Red.

Chapter One

"Oh, Noah," the dark-haired girl beneath me moans. But she hasn't been only moaning for the past hour. Several curses in her Italian tongue have been thrown at me. And a few concerning threats that I presume are effects of her natural language, passion mingling under her tanned skin. She is quite the looker with her curvaceous body and hazel-brown eyes.

But it isn't what drew me to her on the dance floor on the street downstairs last night, not the desire to fuck her, at least. Not just that alone. But also, the desire to paint her body, replicate these light honey eyes of hers.

I know I probably sound like a creep, but I swear I'm not. I'm an artist. It's more of a hobby than a proper title for me, but I take it seriously, and I like to paint the girls I sleep with. Geez, not really helping the creepy vibe, am I? To put it simply: I love art and how it takes nothing but passion and a drive to create something magnificent. Something that just makes you stop and stare. Like the lovely girl beneath me, whose name I forgot, but I blame that on the insane amount of liquor I drank last night.

Trust me when I say it's incredibly easy to get drunk in Italy. They basically start pouring drinks for little kids at eight, and they don't stop there.

"*Perché non ti riposi, amore mio?*" I ask her softly, kissing her neck. (Why not get some rest, my love?)

She giggles. "*Hai bisogno di una pausa per il secondo round?*" (Do you need a break for round two?)

The main objective is to paint her. I would have asked her straight away while she was dancing with me last night, but the alcohol kind of blurred my intentions, and I couldn't stop staring at her in her short skirt and her slender, tan legs. Okay, maybe the painting was a *bit* of an afterthought.

I smirk and run a hand along her exposed thigh. "*Magari dopo che ti avro 'dipinto, se me lo permetti? E 'per un progetto...*" (Maybe after I paint you, if you'd let me? It's for a project...)

"*Vai pure, amore mio.*" She pushes the satin sheets that are covering her body down and winks at me. (Go right ahead, my love.)

Someone's obviously *very* comfortable in her skin.

I admire it, admire her. Not many girls are confident like her. People, in general, don't understand how that confidence goes a long way. It pushes you to only better things in life. You don't get to be a supermodel by being modest and not pushing yourself. Nor do you get to be on the top of the business world by not opening your mouth and thinking the worst of yourself. When I notice someone with confidence practically spilling out of their relaxed postures and the way they carry themselves, I absolutely melt.

Kissing this gorgeous, confident, Italian girl, I thank her for pushing her boundaries.

I leave her on the bed and walk over to my easel and canvas in the corner of my hotel room. I've been staying here, in Venice, Italy, for about three weeks now. This room has been the base of my artworks. I glance at my past works, reflecting on the different skin tones and unique marks, all within the three paintings. In my present work, I will inflate her confidence between her relaxed curves and broad posture.

I pull up the easel in front of the queen bed and begin working. I begin with the outline of her curvy body, making sure to add everything I see and not embellish anything else. Most people want their portraits to be altered to appease what they wish was different in reality, but I don't do that when I paint. What's the point in art if you're going to make what isn't already in eye view? Both figuratively and literally.

I focus thoroughly on the afternoon sky of Italy as my brush swipes across the canvas, behind her body. The sky is a breathtaking canvas itself, with its arctic blue splashed over horizon to horizon, blush pink layering the blue, while a sunrise orange mingles in between. The colors swirl, and I can't help but appreciate where I am and doing even more.

I'm a nineteen-year-old guy who, instead of going directly to college like the rest of my graduating class, traveled the world. The minute I hit eighteen and walked across that graduation stage, I booked a ticket to China and left. It wasn't because I hated my parents and couldn't get away from them fast enough. I did it because I didn't have any desire to continue school. In previous years, my parents drilled into my brain that college is extremely important: *job-wise and world-wise.* But it never interested me. I have to be interested in something to pursue it. Otherwise, what's the point?

I graduated as top valedictorian in high school. Aced all my classes with ease. I just didn't want to sit behind a desk when I could be traveling the world, learning more about life and hardship, and real things you can only experience and grasp outside of brick walls.

I tried repeatedly to explain this to them, but they just cried out that I'd have no future and dismissed me. Especially when I expressed my love for art and how I had a natural talent and infatuation for it. I always had and, I believe, I always will. But the moment I entered high school and professed my passion, I knew I lost my parents.

A lump forming in my throat makes me pause in filling in her light brown eyes. I swallow it away and expel the thoughts about my parents and how they will never see eye to eye with me. I don't need their negativity invading my mind. Especially not when I am in the middle of doing what they despise so much but what I live and breathe like it's air.

I begin to draw in different shades of her sun-kissed skin when there's a knock at the door. "Just a minute," I call out. It's most likely the room service I ordered: a few sandwiches and drinks. I'm setting down my brush when there's a harsher knock on the door. "Coming!" Geez. This worker must be in a rush to get to other places.

"*Spero tu abbia ordinato delle fragole...*" the girl croons with hooded eyes. Something tells me she has a special trick up her sleeve that has to do with strawberries. I send her a wink and receive a giggle. (I hope you ordered strawberries.)

"*Grazie per essere venuto...*" I begin with a smile as I twist open the door. But I stop short when I look into the eyes of the last person I expect. (Thank you for coming...)

My father.

Neither of us says anything for a minute or an hour. I can barely tell time since he's in front of me. I haven't seen him in a year. Since I left New York, my home state, and began traveling. I didn't expect him or my mother to check up on me, so consumed in their rage when their only son ditched them without much of an explanation. Even though I genuinely conveyed my ardor for both art and traveling many times, I can't even recall an exact number. They called maybe two times out of the twelve months I've been venturing out in the world.

Except they had me in Miami for two months, but since then, since a tragedy, I resumed traveling and thought I wouldn't expect to hear from them again.

But here is my father, who doesn't look very different from the last time I saw him. His green eyes are darkened and almond shaped, contrasting to my similar, but brighter, more vivid, rounder green eyes. There are still wrinkles and laugh lines from age and networking: laughing and befriending tycoons in the business industry he currently dominates. He's tall—where I get my height from—but he doesn't have anything on my six-foot, four-inches.

Dressed in a pressed suit and gray tie, he looks like he's here to conduct business, not reunite with his son. Which brings the question: how did he find me? And what's his purpose for coming after all the time he spent clearly despising me for my decision of what to do with my own life?

"Well? Aren't you going to invite me in?" he asks, a faint smile working on his thin lips, those laugh lines from tycoons gaining momentum.

I don't say anything, because I haven't found my voice or the reason for his sudden appearance in his eyes. I used to be able to detect bullshit after watching him bullshit other businessmen on his long climb to the top. But now…I see nothing but a blank smile.

"Noah?" A sweet whine sounding behind me snaps me into reality, and I shift uncomfortably on my feet. No matter how silently upset I am at him for shutting me out when I chased after my dreams, I can't just slam the door in his face. He is still my father.

"Hold on," I tell him in a low voice.

He nods. "Of course."

I give him one last look over before stepping back into the room. I walk over to the glowing

Italian and groan internally. Her posture is so open and inviting, and her eyes are dark, lips flirty. It's taking everything in me to not hop onto the bed and go for round two, but my father is a few feet away, and something tells me fucking this lovely girl would be very, *very* awkward. "*Dammi qualche minuto. Puoi prendere quello che vuoi dal frigo.*" (Give me a few moments. You can take whatever you want from the fridge.)

She looks disappointed but blows out an, "*Va bene*," and waltzes over to the mini fridge that stocks fruits and sweets and other things. I nearly combust when she bends over and rummages through it. (Okay.)

Just walk away, just walk away, just walk away…

I reluctantly shut the thick, wooden sliding doors that close off the bedroom to the rest of the suite. Turning on my bare feet, I find my father sitting on one of the white floral armchairs. His back is straight as a pencil, his gaze on me casual, a technique taught by him to me that is supposed to intimidate anyone you speak to.

I scoff in my head before sitting on the matching sofa in front of him, imitating his pose. There's no way he's going to manipulate me into doing whatever he wants. Not when he showed me the game of manipulation. But to be fair, he was prepping me to take over his business, which he may be here to remind me is going to be mine one day.

He smirks. "It is so nice to you see you, son."

"Right," I murmur, then speak up. "What do you

want, Dad? Because if you haven't noticed, I'm a little busy at the moment."

His smirk grows into a smile, then a little chuckle. "I can see that. Saw a peek; I'm very proud of you."

For once in your life? Mind saying that again so I have it in documentation?

"Thanks."

A moment of silence passes as he bounces the foot of the leg that overlaps the other, another intimidating technique. I kick up my leg over the other and arch an eyebrow. He smiles, and I keep my face straight. Isn't he going to tell me how and why he's found me? If not, he is wasting my time. I could be painting and fucking a beautiful Italian girl.

"Father, why are you here?" I ask. If he's not going to cut to the chase, then I will.

"Straight to the point, aren't you?" he says, subtly teasing me.

I offer him a deadpan expression.

Chuckling condescendingly, he leans forward, green eyes trained on me. "I'm here to tell you that you need to go to college."

Not this again.

"What?"

"You heard me, son." He sits back and runs a hand down his sleek tie, as if he's bored out of his mind. "Your mother and I have arranged for you to attend our alma mater—John Hopkins University."

He has to be out of his mind.

"You're not serious." I laugh nervously.

They've been strong advocates for my college

education, but they wouldn't dare enroll me in a college without my permission. Can they even do that? Surely, they can't and he's just bluffing, waiting for me to fall for his deceit so I fly to wherever the hell John Hopkins University is, and he locks me in a dorm room *then* enrolls me, like the psychopaths he and Mother are.

"Oh, I am very serious." He snaps his fingers, and the hotel room door jars open. Two men dressed in bellhop uniforms open the doors connecting to the bedroom, and I jump to my feet.

The Italian girl screams and curses.

"Hey! What the hell are you doing? *Metti giù la mia merda!*" I scream and storm over to one of them; he's hauling one of my black suitcases out of the room. (Put down my shit.)

"What is going on? Noah! Noah!" she cries, and I try to shush her, but her screaming is too much, too fast. I explode at her in Italian, and she curses one final time before storming into the bathroom, slamming the door shut behind her.

No! I need her to finish the painting! What the hell is going on?

"Father!" I storm back over to my father, who is striding to the door in a calm manner as my shit is being hauled out of the room. I stamp myself inside of the door before he can leave without answering me. "What the hell is going on? You can't do this!"

"I told you, sending you to where you're supposed to be—*college*," he answers around a cloud of annoyance and brushes past me. I let him, holding in the rage that's filling my clenched fists at my sides. It's taking everything in me not to swing at my own father. I hate the thought and wish for it to go away, but it grows and grows as he leisurely walks to the elevators.

"I already told you and Mother that I'm not going to college!" I shout after him, following him. He presses the down button and stares straight ahead, as if I'm not talking to him. "Hello! I am right here, and I'm *staying* here!"

"No, you aren't." His voice fluctuates, rising.

"Yes, I am!" I scream in frustration. "I'm taking some time to myself to do what I love! College is not my passion or what I want to pursue! Art is! Traveling is!"

He snaps in my direction, seething with each word he spits. "And how do you expect to pay for hopping from country to country? Buying expensive art supplies? We've been leaving money in your account, just to entertain your ridiculous dream to travel from coast to coast. But you've been wasting precious time that should have been spent furthering your education. Your mother and I have decided to cut this shit right now. Effective tomorrow, you will be attending college, whether you like it or not."

Silence lingers in the air between us, and the tension is thick. I keep my mouth shut and my hands clutched in fists at my sides. I want to hit him. I want to hit the world that believes going to college to be stuck inside four walls with your head stuck in a book is more important than creativity and pursuing what makes you happy. I want to hit everything in sight. But most of all, I want to hit myself, because without their funding, I won't be able to afford anything. I won't be able to buy paint and easels and drinks for girls to use as muses. I won't be able to be myself.

The negatively charged air becomes so intense that when the elevator dings and opens its door and he climbs on and tells me, "I'll be waiting downstairs," and the doors shut—I snap and punch the wall.

Chapter Two

If you ever want to know what hell on earth feels like, take a plane ride from Italy to America—an eleven-hour trip—with a wailing baby on board. Want to really feel the sizzle? Make the mother new, having no idea how to soothe her infant. I'm usually an upbeat, positive person, but being ripped from my content life and being crammed between a sweaty overweight man and a sick woman who constantly sneezes on me can suck every optimistic cell out of a person.

I still can't get over what my father did, even though I doubt he was the sole master behind this wicked decision. My mother can be even harsher, stricter, more overbearing. He's usually the middle man between her and me, ready to jump in when the fight gets too hot and heavy. But she's either pushed him over the edge or he snapped himself and got fed up with his only child actually enjoying how he were living and went through this course of action. Forcing me into school.

I would say it's sick and unforgiving, but I

wouldn't want to raise the bar too high and jinx myself. I have no way of seeing into the future. I can only brace myself for it, and even then, it will never be enough for me to survive their one-track minds. Once they have something made up, they will not deter from it for even one inch, especially my mother. Where my father is a Pomeranian that barks a lot, my mother is a vicious shark once she gets a whiff of blood or a disobedient child; they mean the same to her.

"Mr. Wells, we're here," the chauffeur my parents hired to drop me off like a little boy being taken to his first day of pre-school announces. Is he going to hold my hand as he walks me up to the class too?

I stop my witty thoughts before they can grow. This isn't his fault; he's just doing his job. I shouldn't act like a dick to him, even if it's just in my head. I sober up from my train of thought and smile at him through the rearview mirror.

"Thanks for the ride, sir." I slide out of the black town car and grab my suitcases from the trunk. Shutting it, I tap it for him to leave, and he waves shortly inside the car before driving away. I watch the car drive down the block before jogging onto the curb. I finally take in my surroundings.

I'm standing in front of what I can only assume is a fraternity house, my references being shitty teen movies I've had the *pleasant* experience of watching. I'm more of a horror film kind of guy, so I expect Jason to come clambering down the white-painted porch, wielding his famous machete as I walk up the path of the house. The house itself has dark blue paint and bushes with colored Solo cups hidden in them. Greek letters are printed above the open door. I notice the A is crooked and wonder if it will set the tone of my staying here. I hope not. I *pray* not.

My plan is to serve my time here then fly back to Italy to resume my painting. But it doesn't even have to be Italy. I can go to Seoul, or Dubai, or London. I haven't been to London in a while. Overall, it doesn't matter where I end up. I could throw a dart on a map and be satisfied, whether it means I'll spend a month sailing the Red Sea or camping in Iceland...as long as I am somewhere that I have never experienced. I want knowledge of other cultures. I want a wide variety of food I never knew about. I want what this place could never offer me—not in a million years.

But until I find a plan to have an unlimited amount of money in my hands so I can travel the world without my parents nagging me about school, I will have to stay put and continue being their little boy puppet for a while.

Inside, I let out a whopping sigh and run a hand over my hair. The foyer is ordinary, and I can see the open layout of the house. It seems like a mini-mansion. There are loads of framed photos of group pictures of guys in khakis and t-shirts with the fraternity name printed in capitalized letters. I pass the living room, where a large group of guys are laughing and playing some shooting game. I peek into the massive dining room, then head into the attached kitchen. Corian countertops, wooden floors—pretty normal for an area I was expecting to be overflowing with beer cans and condoms.

Guess I just have to wait for the first party. Which, according to teen films, are weekly.

Yay.

I'm walking back into the open area in the middle of the house, looking around aimlessly in an attempt to familiarize myself with the place, when something hard and fast hurtles into my chest. I throw my arms out to stabilize myself and whatever flew into me, my head spinning. I work quickly to re-adjust myself before I can bust my ass and take a step back.

"Watch where the hell you're going, prep!" I hear her before I see her, but when I do, my jaw slackens and I feel woozy all over again.

A girl a few inches shorter than me glares up at me. She has untamed blonde hair that she pushes back with black-painted fingers. They're chipped and curl into little fists at her sides. I quickly look down at her attire: a ripped black tee, dark jeans, rugged combat boots, and a leather jacket with lots of zippers and pins, so I can focus on her face. She has these naturally reddish, puffy lips. On the right side of her lower lip is a lip ring, and she has the most breathtaking blue eyes that nearly take up her entire face. They each have a massive ring of eyeliner, and above her left eye is a piercing. With her heaven-high cheekbones and dusty pink cheeks, she looks like a Barbie doll got a bad-ass makeover.

I try to speak, but it's hard for some reason. It feels like a brick is sitting prettily on my chest. And I frown because this isn't me. I can make a girl swoon just by looking at her from all the way across the room. I never have any problems striking up a conversation about anything. Ever. Yet it feels like my tongue is a cherry and it's tied up like a dainty pink bow.

She leans forward and snaps her fingers up at me. "Hello?" She waves her hand, then steps back and gives me a look that electrifies my organs and makes me melt. "I think you've got another slow one this year, Mikey." Who is she talking to?

"Who's the first one? And I keep telling you: it's *just* Mike." A guy with dark brown skin and a charming half-smile sidles up next to her, passing me. He gives me an apologetic look.

"That little kid who got lost going to his room. You know the one. And your name is whatever I say it is." Then she nudges his side harshly, her eyes never leaving mine. Her lips tip upward in a slight smirk. She's messing with me; she has to be.

Then why don't you speak, dummy?

"To be fair, it is a large room—" Mikey or Mike sighs.

"It's the first one upstairs; the kid's a dope!" she exclaims. "And this one's the next in the crazy-bin lot."

"I thought he was slow," Mike says. I'm going with Mike. The Mikey thing sounds like it's their thing.

"He can be both; get with the times, Mikey," blonde beauty scoffs, glancing at him. And when those eyes of hers shift over to meet mine, my breathing kicks up a notch and I find the ability to speak. Only after a freaking eternity.

"Are you guys gonna keep talking like I'm *not* a

foot away?" I squish my eyebrows together in a joking manner, shoving my hands in my khaki shorts.

They stare at me, look at each other, then back at me.

"Maybe," they say in unison.

I crack a nervous smile. "Great. Not weird or anything."

"Sorry, man. We're just messing with you." The guy laughs and reaches forward. I meet his hand halfway and give him a firm handshake, unable to take my eyes off of her. Her smirk grows, and she tilts her head. She slips her tongue out of her mouth and plays with her silver lip ring. My eyes stare at the action for a beat too long, and she's full on mocking me with a smirk.

"I'm Mike Freeman, and this is—" he begins, gesturing to the girl as he steps back.

"Someone who doesn't give a fuck," she cuts him off with an oversaturated grin. She's obviously pissing with me, and I laugh lightly, nodding. Even though she called me slow and crazy, I kind of dig this girl.

"Well, Mike and Someone-Who-Doesn't-Give-A-Fuck, I'm Noah. Noah Wells," I tell them, and Mike chuckles, but mystery girl merely stares at me. Her gaze is intense and looks like she's analyzing me from the inside out. I should fidget under a seemingly rude stranger's gaze like this, but all I can do is the same. And smile. Smile fondly. She snorts, and I don't know if it's because of me or the loud clambering sound thumping behind me.

"Red! Red, Red—*RED!*" a voice screeches.

"What's the rush, buttercup?" Mystery Girl has her eyes fixated on something, or someone, behind me.

I look over my shoulder. A tall girl wearing a golden sequined top and a matching hijab comes clambering down the tall steps, almost falling because of her seemingly slippery flats. Luckily, Mystery Girl grabs her wrist and pulls her upright before she can face plant.

"Brandon just texted. We've gotta go!" says the girl with wide brown eyes, yanking her friend toward the door. I wonder how much she likes this Brandon to risk tumbling down a set of stairs and breaking her neck.

"Him again?" Red, I'm assuming, spits with a disgusted expression as she lets her friend drag her to the door. "Really, Majesty?"

"Yeah. Now, pick up the pace!" Majesty—a unique name, though I'm not too surprised it belongs to her—cries. Before they disappear out of the massive house, she throws over her shoulder, "And don't forget you totally owe me, dickwad!" Then the door slams shut and the obnoxious sound of automatic guns and cheering from the living room fills the house without the girl's squawking.

"And that, my friend, was Red Sylvetti and her insane friend, and your roommate Tyler's adopted sister, Majesty. National Treasure, the both of them, don't you think?" Mike smiles at me.

"Sure are." I smile back, and he chuckles, nudging me and nodding to the stairs. I follow him to the top and let my burning curiosity shine through me. "So, Red…is she usually that mean?" I ask in a joking manner, shoulders hunched and teeth bared.

He chuckles the ideal way, in a way that tells me he's used to being asked that. "I could lie and say no, but I'd be lying." Looking back at me as I glide my suitcases along the polished wooden floors, he says, "She's a real fireball. Rude and crude and…punchy when she gets mad. But she's a good person up close, that is if she lets you that close…" He trails off, and I sense muffled words on his tongue. There's more to it, to her, but he stops in front of one of the many rooms and knocks, even though it's cracked open slightly.

"This is you and Ty. He can be a bit of a douche at times, a major slut most of the time, honestly, but he's the greatest friend I have here," he tells me with a small smile.

"I can handle douche. Slut will take a while, but I think I'll manage." I laugh, and he does too and pushes the door open when we hear an "open," though it's muffled.

When he pushes open the wooden door, I come face to face with the large room. Incredibly spacious, it holds two double beds and study desks. The walls are a light blue, and there's an industrial ceiling fan, but it looks brand new. There's a small shaggy blue rug on the floor and blue camouflage bean bag chairs. To my immediate left is an empty bed and area, but to my right is a guy standing on the half-made bed. He's taping up a poster of Cristiano Ronaldo, alongside other athletic legends like LeBron James, Eli Manning, and Babe Ruth.

"Hey," I say, and he looks over his shoulder, a

small roll of tape in his mouth.

He mumbles something and, as Mike plops into one of the beanbag chairs, finishes taping up the poster. "There we go, legend." He pats the soccer ball on the poster before jumping down and landing in front of me, hand out for me to shake. "And *you* get to meet another legend. Tyler Carter, but—"

"Ty! Where the hell are you?" a feminine voice yells, followed by loud heels stomping. And it's coming this way.

Tyler's eyes widen, and he turns to Mike, who's trying to hide his face behind his hands. "One last time. I promise! You saw how she almost *ate* my freaking head off last time!"

Last time?

I hold back a laugh as I listen to them talk while plunking my suitcases on my bed. I pop open one of them and pull out my mini-security safe. I slip my watch and passport and important documents inside before locking it and sitting on the bed to watch the events unfold. I feel bad for wanting a bucket of buttery popcorn and 3D glasses.

"And you want *me* to deal with her?" Mike gasps.

"Come on, man! Just one more—" Tyler begins to plead.

"I. Am. Going. To. *Murder*. You!" the girl threatens, her heels sounding closer by the second.

With frantic eyes, Tyler scrambles into the closet, leaving a very pissed off and groaning Mike, who now has to deal with a girl raging with a blood lust. The door kicks in, and she walks in, all five feet, eight inches of her. She threatens to skin Ty alive for texting a girl named Brenda. Her colorful vocabulary precedes her tight shirt and short skirt. Lofty, platinum curls fly around as she curses him out via Mike—poor, poor Mike—and promises to get him when he least expects it. When her long-winded rant is over and she's left blushing like two apples dropped in snow, she finally notices me, gives me her name and number, via her *mouth*, before sashaying away.

"Well," I say, turning to Mike when the door slams shut after her, "Lyndsey is a radiant ball of sunshine," I say sarcastically.

"Tell me about it," he says as Ty walks out of the closet, wiping away invisible sweat off his forehead. "I've saved this prick's ass more times than I can count."

"Sure you can count that high?" Ty laughs.

Mike stands up, facial expression deadpanned.

Ty swallows and walks over to me. "So! I was saying." He stretches out his hand. "I'm Tyler, but you can call me Ty—I prefer it. And you are…"

"Noah." I take his hand, give it a shake. "Noah Wells."

"Well, Noah Wells, are you ready for the most wicked parties this here fraternity has to offer?" He stretches his arms out in a "look around" gesture. By his smug expression, I'm gonna reckon their parties are notorious.

"Depends." I shrug.

"On?" Mike raises his brows.

I smile. "What kind of tea you're serving, of course. And can I bring my Sunday bonnets? Or are you guys more of a church-hate kind of establishment?" I joke, and thank God they have senses of humor and laugh.

"We're more of a booze and drugs and girls kind of establishment," Ty says, then looks to Mike and nods with a smirk. "I like this kid."

"'This Kid' is right in the room. Hello." I wave my hand a little, grinning. But on the inside, I'm wondering if I'm maybe invisible today.

"Right. *Kid*. We're gonna go set up. Come down and help after you get settled in." Mike pats my shoulder.

"I'll be there soon," I promise, then watch them slip out of the room, Ty conspiring about hiring a bouncer for the night to keep Lyndsey out fading as they reach downstairs, and I turn to my suitcases. As I unpack, I think: my parents may have thrown me in this place, but that doesn't mean I have to do anything they want me to. I'm in college, fine. I'll experience everything it has to me, minus letting it bog me down like I've feared. I'm going to live the American freaking dream.

Chapter Three

Hours fly by with a certain buzz around the house. Everyone is excited for the party, it seems. Guys are dousing themselves in cologne to mask their musky scent after doing push-ups in preparation for the party. Something about getting themselves pumped up.

College guys are weird, I decide as I watch one guy run up and down the stairs, claiming he is going to get so much pussy tonight. As I pass him, I think to myself, *I hope I never become him.* It must get tiring getting so amped up for what may be the very thing they came to college for—the party.

Which, when it hits ten o'clock and people begin pouring in, starts out with a whopping *bang*. Girls wearing short skirts and dresses, faces covered in too much makeup, flood the living room area, claiming it as their dance floor. And like an exhibit unlocked in a zoo, the guys snake behind them and claim their victims.

Grinding and bumping becomes the necessity to pass through the area, so I stay away, nearly holding up the cross-chain around my neck like they are possessed by demons who want to shake their asses just one last time before being sent back to their crevices.

By the time it hits twelve, the party grows to a massive scale. I'm pretty sure the front door is struggling to contain the amount of people scrambling inside of the house. Ty wasn't exaggerating when he said the party would be, in his words, *wicked*. The floor is the Red Sea, in the sense that Solo cups, primarily red, litter the ground, more than the few bodies passed out from over-exertion.

The smell is overwhelming: sweaty, musky, and tainted with smoke, from either cigarettes, or weed, or *crack*. I don't know what people are smoking nowadays. But it must be crack, because there is a guy swinging on the crystalline chandelier above the area next to the stairs. And when he hits the ground, someone has jumped into the large pool out back while—get this—riding a dirt bike...how insane! Am I right? Or am I not drunk enough to understand either of the insane guys doped up on some kind of drugs?

Twenty minutes past one, I am leaning against a wall on the main floor, witnessing my fellow classmates party like the world's going to end tomorrow. I should get something to drink—strong. I did say I would party like a college student, that I wouldn't just lay down and take whatever my parents threw at me. But a sort of precaution is holding me back. Sorry if I'm not jumping at the same liquor Chandelier Boy and Pool Boy gulped moments before almost taking their lives unintentionally.

I remain against the wall for maybe five more minutes before the memory of my father strolling in and destroying my carefully crafted life, and I suddenly need a drink. Or two. Or three. Fuck it— let's get a whole gallon. He didn't have the right to do what he did. I would have flown the coop, discreetly bought a flight for Egypt or something, but something tells me they would have found me the moment I stepped foot outside the plane. My parents may be underhanded and traditionally brainwashed, but they are also very persistent.

Ugh. I want to stop thinking about them. I want to drink, get drunk, and find my tongue down some girl's throat. I just want to forget.

In the kitchen, Mike and Ty are laughing at a lanky boy three inches shorter than them knocking back shots. He looks like a freshman in high school, rather than a college student. When I walk over to them, I tower over him, but really, I tower over everyone.

"Oh, hey, freshie! You finally joined the party, huh?" Ty says jokingly, nudging me and grinning.

"Thought I'd give it a shot." I shrug.

"Did someone say shot?" he shouts like a battle-cry through cupped hands around his mouth.

People cheer and do fists pumps, though I doubt they even know the context. I don't even know the context until Mike leans over and tells me to get ready for a wild night, then nods to another small boy who sets out small shot glasses, his hands shaking and his eyes looking like he's *seen* things.

"Who is he? And *him*?" I ask Mike, pointing to the two boys.

"High school seniors," he says loudly over the dubstep music. "They go to a school nearby and wanted college experience. So—"

"So we made them our bitches. Gotta learn how the big dogs roll before you sprout your canines," Ty interrupts with a smile too big to be sane. He motions us over to the line of shot glasses and begins filling them haphazardly.

"That and they really know how to fold." Mike shrugs.

"That's kind of messed up," I say, laughing.

"Ah, don't worry about them. They can handle it. Aren't I right, boys?" He flashes the lanky boys an award-winning smile, and they give weak smiles back. *Oh, bless their poor souls.* "Now, forget about them and let's have one helluva night!" I'm handed two shots.

"On three," Mike says. "One…two…*three*!"

I throw back the shots, and my nose scrunches as the lava-like substance stings my throat. Trust me when I say I will never get used to the taste. And I've been taking shots and drinking since I've been traveling. One of my biggest mistakes in doing so was drinking the strongest Russian Vodka when I was staying in Moscow. I was blacked out for two days, and when I finally woke up, my right palm was slashed open, there was a monkey in the bed with me, and a Russian girl named Anya was wearing a Scottish kilt. It's safe to say I spent my weekend there like the men in *The Hangover* movies, trying to figure out what the hell had happened.

"Woo—my *God*, that is a *bitch*." Ty wipes his mouth with the back of his hand, then holds up another glass. "But we are *not* bitches. Drink up, fellas. We have a long night ahead of us."

And a long night we had.

After flinging back one more shot, I feel loose all over and sedated. Dazed. We talk and laugh and watch the high school students do pushups with one hand, failing over and over. I slowly but surely melt away from them and find myself on the dance floor. Despite the code of the gyrating attendees, I don't grab a girl and force myself onto her.

I just dance by myself, which means jumping around to the loud R&B song that everyone knows the lyrics to and shouts. One large voice sweeps across the house, drawing people from the backyard and every other crevice of the mini-mansion, making the floor even more packed. It is like standing in a pack of sardines, not including the smell.

I've danced and belted out the catchy pop song that girls shake their asses to for what feels like an hour before one of them backs up onto me. A petite girl with raven waist-length hair and a heavily made-up face, wearing a short red dress that covers almost nothing at all, spins around and throws her small arms around my neck. She howls the lyrics like I am, and I laugh as she tosses her head back and shakes her body against mine.

I cautiously wind my hands around her waist, drawing her into my sweaty chest. But she doesn't mind the sweatiness. In fact, she purrs and brings my head down so her lips are near my ears.

"Wanna go somewhere quieter?" she whispers.

"Show me the way." I hold out my hand, smirking.

Giggling, she takes it and pulls me toward the stairs that's cluttered with couples making out against the railing, and Solo cups. I'm guessing they were too horny and couldn't make it up the stairs. *I don't blame them,* I think as we walk upstairs. She's wearing these really lengthy glittery high heel shoes and keeps wobbling. I'm no better myself, as the liquor I knocked back maybe an hour or two ago seeps into my bones and makes me half-crippled. But I manage to grapple a hand around her waist and help us up the stairs that must lead to Heaven or Emerald City—because *gosh.*

When we finally reach the top of the stairs, I look over the banister. From above, the party looks kind of like a Jay Gatsby party. Part poppers are popped into the air. Dance moves are busted out. And the music is so loud, the walls vibrate. I stand here for maybe two seconds, admiring and smiling from ear to ear, when I feel like there are eyes on me, on every inch of my body. I'm about to let this girl whose name I don't even know drag me into an empty room when the feeling intensifies and my stomach clenches. Tightly.

I look closer and closer, and just when the scene looks like a page from *Find Waldo*, I see her.

Red.

She's staring at me, head cocked to the side, smirking just slightly, but enough to make my heart go crazy. My breathing hitches in my throat as I look at her outfit from earlier, but this time she's wearing a band t-shirt. I think. It's too crowded to be sure. But what is clear as day is the smirk on her lips. Her very red lips. Red like the vivid painting of a meadow of roses. I begin to wave at her, but the petite girl holding my hand pulls me away so I can't see her anymore or a guy in all black sidling up to her and leads me to a bedroom. My bedroom.

"You are so hot," she murmurs in my ear.

"So are you." I smile. I try to wave the thought of Red away from my mind, but she sticks on like she's covered in Gorilla Glue.

The girl pushes me onto my bed and smiles down at me. She drops to her knees, and her small hands work at my jeans zipper and button. With determination to focus on this pretty girl on her knees in front of me, I help her pull my pants and boxers down. The minute her lips find my cock and she moans lightly, the blonde girl with face piercings leaves my brain for a few minutes. Thank God. That would have been awkward if I thought about her while I was getting head from another girl.

Like, could you imagine me fantasizing about her plump red lips? Or the feeling of her cold metal ring jutting into my bottom lip? How her golden hair would feel clutched around my fist as I fucked her mouth…

Shit.

I come hard after a few minutes of imagining Red's cold piercing and vivacious painted red lips surrounding me. What the actual hell? Why am I thinking about her? I don't even know the girl, yet one look at her prior to getting head and I'm coming like a damn hurricane.

"Damn. That was a strong one." The girl chuckles, gulping thickly. I should come again at the sight of her swallowing my release, but all I can do is wonder if she can sense there's some on her cheek.

"Sure was." I feel stiff and stupid, so I pull her onto my lap and kiss her. And I kiss her fully. I'm not one of those timid guys who doesn't kiss the girl after they get head. That's just stupid and unfair and makes them feel like shit. Used. No matter how close or not I am with a girl, they don't deserve to be treated like that.

"I have to pee. Like, really badly," she whines in my ear and pulls back, out of breath and eyes wide and frenzied. "But you stay," she pauses to swallow what I think is vomit, then chuckles, "right *here*." She pushes to her high heels and stumbles. I reach out to steady her, but she laughs loudly and points a finger at me. "I'll be right back. Don't move!"

When the door shuts behind her, I sigh into my palms. "What the hell, Noah?" I mumble to myself. Not cool, dude. Not cool at all. "You've got this. You've got this. You've got…" I pause when I hear her mumble something and see light from the bathroom spread across the floor.

"Shirt off," she commands in a low tone, wearing nothing but…well, *nothing*.

"Yes, ma'am." I take off my shirt, and she giggles and walks over to me. She trips, but I grab her before she can fall on the floor and put her on the bed. As I take off my clothes and fuck this pretty girl, one thing just won't stop nagging at my mind: the girl with a color for a name and that damned smirk of hers.

Chapter Four

Gunshots wake me up the very next day. I jolt up out of bed faster than a bullet en route. But I move too fast and my body is strangely heavier than normal, and I'm hurled off my bed. My face snaps on the floor, and I cry out and groan, but it's all masked by the insistent shooting coming from downstairs. I figure maybe the guys are playing *Call of Duty* or *Modern Warfare* or some other stupid video game.

As I sit up and gingerly rub my aching face, I wonder, *Do they really have to have the volume up so high?* And then as I stand and stretch out my limbs that are tight and lazy, I add bitterly, *And why the hell are they even playing it now?* They are so inconsiderate. I want to stomp down there and shoot them with a real gun. But nothing too serious.

Ugh. Great. I'm grumpy. I guess downing shots like water and dancing in a sweaty, gross, mob pit of people has that effect. Through the tunnel of visions in my head, I remember someone swinging on a chandelier. Someone maybe jumped into a pool via helicopter? I don't know, and they don't make sense. Either I have really bad memory, I have slight alcohol poisoning, or I'm too hungover to think correctly. Or college kids really do party as hard as shown on TV. If so, the party in the movie *Party X* had nothing on the one here last night.

I rub my eyes and moan at the muffled spike of pain behind my eyes. I need a bucket of aspirin and water. I look down at my morning wood and groan. And a nice, ice cold shower. A loud snore erupting the otherwise silent air makes me freeze, and I scramble to remember how I got in bed, naked, last night. I slowly turn on the heels of my feet and breathe out in relief. It's just a girl; I remember us stumbling up the stairs and her giving me head and…*other* things. A smirk can't help but melt onto my face like butter. So I got some last night. Self-high-five doesn't sound too nerdy right about now.

But as I give myself a high-five like the absolute dork I am, I see a flash of red. And I mean the color, not the girl. Well, now that I'm thinking about her too…yeah, definitely a cold shower, I decide as the memory of her smirking up at me from downstairs pops into my head like a firework. Something about the way she was looking at me makes the hair on my forearms rise for some reason. I don't know the girl, yet I have goosebumps thinking about her and *not* the girl lying in my bed. She's naked, for goodness sake!

Frustrated and a little horny, I grab clothes from my dresser and my phone from the floor. I walk into the ensuite, lock the door, and sit on the toilet after twisting on the shower faucet. I call an Uber for the girl, whose name I am ashamed to say I don't know, then hop into the shower. The hot water slides down my back and works out the kinks in my shoulders. I stay under the running water for maybe fifteen minutes.

When I get out, I get dressed in a white V-neck and sweatpants, leaving my hair wet. I do run a hand towel over the forming curls for a few seconds before deciding munching on pain killers sounds more appealing. So I throw the towel in the hamper and grab the aspirin bottle and take two tablets.

The girl is still sleeping when I walk back into the bedroom. I shake two pills out of the aspirin bottle and snag one of Ty's bottled waters he has in his mini fridge by his bed. I leave them on my nightstand, then leave her to snore for a while and check on the Uber. The app says a guy named Craig with four stars will arrive in ten minutes. I drop my phone in my sweatpants pocket when I finally look up and around at the colossal mess the party created.

There are more passed-out bodies and red Solo cups than wooden floor. I bypass a few puddles of what can either be piss, water-vomit, or liquor, or all of the above. A few guys are weaving around the bodies and wiping up the substances and tossing a majority of paper towels flung around aimlessly in huge garbage bags. They look almost immune to the mess. I want to help out, so I tip-toe through cans of beer and enter the kitchen.

Mike is in the kitchen dumping half-empty plastic cups in the sink. Red is beside him, but she's on her phone. A bolt of energy spikes my spine, and

I stand up straighter, smile a little. But it drops when flashes of her lips and eyes cross my mind, while I am in bed with that girl upstairs. *Oh crap.* I completely forgot about that. I'm extra appreciative humans can't read each other's minds.

"Hey, guys." I wave at them to get their attention, drawing them from their barely audible conversation. They look at me as I walk over to the fridge and grab a bottle of orange juice and shut it using my hip. Mike smiles at me friendly-like, but Red just stares at me with an unreadable expression. I wish I can see what she's thinking; she can kill me with those eyes of hers.

"Hey! You're up early. Mind helping to speed up the process?" Mike asks, nodding to the pile of bottles and cans beside him.

"Sure. No problem." I walk over to them but halt because Red's long legs are stretched out in the short distance from the kitchen island, her body slanted with the counter behind her as leverage. "Mind if I get by?"

"Walk around," she mumbles, pulling out her phone. She scrolls through her phone and acts as if I'm not one foot from her. Does she act like this all the time?

Mike snorts out a laugh that says, "Been there, buddy. Good luck." I want him to give me a guidebook on how to handle her, but I guess I'll just have to figure it out on my own. Should be fun, I decide as I smirk and walk over her legs, raising my knees high.

She watches with narrowed eyes, and I laugh as I sidle up next to Mike and begin dumping out unfinished drinks people were too lazy to dump out themselves. People become so self-involved when they get a few drinks in them.

"How was the party last night? Have fun?" Mike makes conversation after a while of uncapping and dumping.

"I actually had fun, more than I thought I would." I toss an emptied can of cheap beer in the recycle bag. "You?"

He shrugs. "It was the usual. They all blur together when you've lived here for two years."

"Lucky. You've almost got two years left."

"And you don't?"

I shake my head. "Nope. Started this year."

"Oh, you had a gap year?" he inquires.

"I tried to have a gap *life,* but yeah." I laugh pathetically. It hurts to remember that I could be in Italy right now, waking up next to a beautiful girl and exploring Rome, maybe. I haven't been there in a while. I would be getting gelato just because I could and visiting the Colosseum and snapping pictures as I rolled down the canals.

Just imagining seeing the sky there gives me chest pains. I feel like a mother ripped from her child. Art is a part of me and always will be, and I'm being limited from it. Painting a girl passed out on the lawn, hair stuck to her drool, is not exactly the same as painting a beautiful girl outside of the Leaning Tower of Pisa.

"Big whoop. Now you're back in reality," Red scoffs and pushes off the counter, glaring at her phone, then at me. "At least you got to have a gap anything. Most people don't get that opportunity."

Oh Lord, I've pissed her off. That guidebook would be really great right about now.

"I know. I just got so used to it. I never had the intention of even coming here," I say honestly.

"Well, then get used to it, prep. 'Cause you're stuck here." She slips her phone in her back pocket, still eyeing me with a fiery gaze. I can sense a hidden undertone in her anger toward me, but I don't comment on it. I don't want to piss her off even more than I already have, which I'm beginning to learn is easy.

A piercing scream sounds, and we all look over to the entry way. Majesty stops in front of it, her hazel eyes blown wide, makeup smudged. "We've gotta go before Ty wakes up."

"What'd you draw this time?" Red actually smiles as she walks over to her friend.

"You don't wanna know." Majesty chuckles, and Red throws an arm around her friend. They begin to walk away when she stops and tells me, "Hey. There's a naked girl in the tub of your bathroom. I would get her dressed before my pervy brother sniffs her out and tries to sleazy talk her."

"I hope whatever you drew is despicable." Red twists her face up in disgust.

"Trust me—it is." Majesty howls in laughter before dragging her friend out of the house. I walk over to the window in the kitchen dining area, pushing the thin curtain back. I watch as they slide into an impressive Chevy Impala, maybe '67, '69, Red behind the wheel. My heart does this weird thing in my chest, and I shortly wonder if I'm going crazy.

"Draw?" I ask Mike, walking back over to the sink.

He smiles and opens his mouth, but before he can answer, Ty comes clambering down the stairs and rushes in the kitchen, looking around frantically. And then it hits me and I burst out into laughter. He has a bunch of dicks wearing tiaras all over his face. And the Hitler mustache above his lips isn't helping anything.

"Where is she?" he sneers, eyes twitching with pure rage.

"Just left," Mike informs him, pointing toward the front door. Ty runs outside, and I can hear him screaming bloody murder after his adopted sister. I laugh even harder, hunching over, imagining what else they do to prank each other. And I wonder what he has in store to get back at her.

"Hey. I think your girl's coming down." Mike nudges me, nodding to the entryway, and sure enough, the girl from last night stumbles inside the kitchen, holding her shoes and wearing her dress backwards.

"Heyyyy, I know you," she slurs and points at me.

Mike smirks, and I nudge him in his side, which only causes him to break into laughter.

"Noah. I'm sorry I never got your name last night..." I put a hand on her lower back, guiding her out the door. Ty whizzes past us on his rampage.

She smiles at me. "Beth. My name's Beth." As we're slowly going down the porch steps as the Uber pulls up, she murmurs, "So hoooooot."

Chapter Five

The rest of the weekend flies by faster than I want it to. On Monday, classes begin, and I almost don't get up. What can my parents do if I don't? Give me electroshock therapy? I think it over and decide to spring out of bed. My parents aren't *that* diabolical, but they have less medieval ways of getting what they want. May as well save the torture and get this over with.

Thankfully, Mike and Ty have a class together that isn't too far from the route to my first class. I would have toured the place if I were given more of a notice rather than being shipped here without even a heads up a few hours before my father came knocking on my hotel room door. Everyone around us is walking sluggishly, like zombies who are too lazy to chase after their next meal. In no time I will become them, I realize as we pass zombie after zombie.

"So, you into football?" Mike asks me.

"I played in high school, made co-captain," I tell him. And I was pretty damn good at it. Loads of scouts came just because they'd heard my name being floated around, but it was never that serious to me.

"Thinking of trying for our team? Ty and I and a few of the guys back at the house have been on it for two years now. We could use extra hands on the field," he suggests. I turn his words over. I promised myself I was just going to get through this semester, then I'm out. I'll take up ten jobs if I have to, but I can't stay here while my passion burns in my chest.

But then again, I could always use something to distract me from this bullshit.

"Sure," I say with a smile.

"You better not have a stronger arm than me, or I'm gonna whoop your ass," Ty jokes and points a finger at me.

"Then prepare to have a major ass whooping." I bump into him playfully and wink at him. He chuckles, and he and I and Mike shit around as we stroll to our classes. He informs we're about a minute or two away when he stops, spots a guy in all black walking toward us, and raises a hand in acknowledgment.

"Yo. Ian, what's up!" Ty calls out, stopping us and our group.

I eye the short girl beside him, who seems to be making a point to avoid us.

"We missed you at the party," Mike says, beaming at the guy with the brooding face. A single strand of gelled black hair curls above his right eyebrow, and his thick biceps flex as he crosses his arms. He grunts a mumbled reply and shrugs.

"Who's this?" I whisper to Mike.

"Ian Jones: captain of the football team." Then he waves at the shy girl, who blushes and looks to the ground. "And Rachel. His step-sister."

"Nice to meet you both. I'm Noah Wells." I hold out my hand to Ian, but he just glares at me like I'm an alien. So, chuckling, I hold it out for Rachel. "Nice to meet you, Rachel."

Peeking at me with quarter-sized brown eyes through her long brown hair, she smiles softly and takes my hand with her small one. "Pleasure is all mine, Noah." She seems cute. I wink at her, and her chubby cheeks blossom like a ripening rose.

"We were just telling Noah here how he should try out for the team," Mike says.

Ian lifts a brow, looking me up and down. "Is that so?"

"Yeah." I manage a smile even though something flares deeply in me because of the condescending smile sliding across his face. His dim blue eyes light up in amusement, and my smile drops just a little. "Why? Thinking I may outshine you?" I keep a light tone in my voice, lifting my lips a little.

His lips tighten and his jaw ticks, gauging me again. "Don't think I'll have a problem there, newbie."

I don't know what it is, but I'm getting a bad feeling about this guy. I don't like the way he's smirking at me or the way he's cocking his head like he's some tough shit.

"Ladies, ladies—hold your catfight for the field," Ty jokes, holding up his palms.

"We've gotta go," Ian says, hooking an arm

around his step-sister. She looks away when I wave at her.

"Bye, Rachel. *Ian*." I watch them walk away, thinking, *Well, my time here should be fun.*

***

Classes aren't as brutal as I expected them to be. To be fair, they were only the first classes for the semester. There is plenty of time for it to progress…for it to crush my soul with loads of class assignments and homework and research and studying and—ugh. I think my brain just died a little. I just need to constantly remind myself that I won't be caged here long. No matter how much it kills me, it won't trap me forever. I have an entire life and a whole world to discover outside of these brick walls.

Plus, if I can manage being snowed-in in Antarctica for a week, I'm sure I can manage a few months at college. I just pray it doesn't kill me first.

Looking over my schedule, I am glad my parents didn't force five classes on me instead of the four I have: freshman history, psych 101, marketing, and English—all in that order. According to the one, seemingly ultra-important text from my mother, I'm thinking of declaring business as my major, which I guess is Father's doing. He's always wanted me to take over his monopoly of businesses. And forcing me into marketing is one push toward his chair behind one of his many big desks. Even though it is *not* what I want to be stuck doing—wielding and planning and bossing people around—or the rest of my life like him.

I can enlighten my parents and express to them my love and desire for making art and traveling until I'm blue in the face, and they still wouldn't understand nor care. I actually have. I wonder if they ever had any dreams when they were younger. Did they dream about becoming poets, or rock stars, or even the greatest surfer on the planet? Did they feel the hurt and frustration I often do when their parents argued with them and preached practicality?

If so, how can they do the same to me instead of just supporting me and my decisions? It pains me to know my parents will never back me up like I wish they would.

One day. I just want them to get inside my brain for one day and experience the euphoric feeling I get from just looking at a painting. I want them to understand the feeling of awe that swirls in my chest when staring up at the Eiffel Tower, the pyramids in Egypt—just somewhere breathtaking and rich with history and culture, you can feel it run through you, and appreciation and respect follows closely behind, burrowing deep inside of you.

But I guess studying until you break out into stress hives is more important, right?

Sighing, I decide to distract my mind from my parents. I pull out my phone from my khaki pants and scroll through it aimlessly. I see a text from Grey. He's the boyfriend of a girl I befriended from childhood and then started to sort of date…it's a long story. To put it shortly, she and I tried to spark something, but it went out, and a firework explosion blew up between her and Grey.

Speaking of which, he sends sporadic texts to close friends of Liv to inform them about her status. Last month, she was tragically caught in the crossfire of a shoot-out, which is a whole other story by itself. Seriously. They deserve an entire novel just to span out their insane love story.

His text says one simple word:

alive.

I smile and pull up Liv's number. I want to call her for more than just the word *fine*, but she could be resting. She has been ever since she underwent surgery due to an accident in August. I was reluctant to just continue traveling when she was so hurt, but Grey made it near impossible to even look at her, he was so jealous and protective. I think he blames himself for her getting hurt. And he's doing everything to make up for being an asshole prior to the incident. But what he doesn't seem to really understand is, she loves him more than the moon loved the sun, for it agrees to sleep and let their sun rise and shine each day.

Anyway, enough about them. I send her a text.

Noah: Hey. How are you doing?

I put my phone away, not expecting a response. But a minute later, my pocket buzzes, and I fetch my phone.

Liv: Hanging in there.

I frown and, wanting to brighten her up a bit, type back.

Noah: *My parents are worse than yours.*

A minute passes.

Liv: *Doubt it.*

Smiling, I text her.

Noah: *My father popped up while I was in Italy and shipped me off to a college in Maryland.*

Liv: *My mother put me in a psych ward.*

Noah: *My father put me in a fraternity.*

I can imagine her laughing as I read her reply.

Liv: *You win.*

A smile works its way onto my face, and we text back and forth for the duration of my walk to my next and final class of the day—English Literature. I wish I could have taken an elective—art. But my parents have connections with the school board and the damn chancellor, and they barred that option from me. As if dragging me here wasn't bad enough, they want to separate me from what actually makes me happy. Doesn't mean I didn't bring my own supplies, though. And I don't need a *class* to do what I love. All I need is a piece of paper and a pencil.

When Liv's replies are more typos than actual words, I ask her,

You okay there?

Her reply is:

Sleepy from the medicine, though.

Go to sleep. Talk to you later.

I promise her in a text, and she replies with a hand-waving emoji.

I slip my phone in my pocket as I near the building where English Literature is located. I let a group of girls leave the brick building before slipping past them. There are lots of hallways and signs, so it takes me a while to find myself in front of the room. *More like auditorium,* I think as I enter the classroom. The lecture hall is similar to my other classes and intimidating like the others. I will never get used to how many students can be packed in here.

"Yes, yes—I fucking heard you! If I knew you would be this annoying, I would have told your ass to stay behind!" I hear a voice snap behind me. And it's incredibly close, like right behind me.

I begin to turn around and step out of the way, but it's too late. Red bumps into me, too busy screaming at a guy behind her to see me.

"Sorry. I didn't see you there," I apologize, and she steps back. She's looking at me in a way I can't decipher as analytically or disgustedly.

"It's whatever, prep," she says and sighs before looking at the guy. I look at him too and find him staring at me. My brows jump in surprise as his dark, hooded eyes look me up and down. I do the same. He's wearing a leather vest over a ripped white t-shirt, jeans, and huge combat boots. "Hello? Tanner? Are you even listening to me?" She snaps her fingers in front of his face, which has a long scar on his right cheek. I'm guessing from a knife fight gone wrong.

"Who's this?" he asks her, pointing at me.

Red looks over her shoulder. "Some preppy guy from a fraternity."

"Rude," I joke, and she rolls her eyes. "Noah. Noah Wells," I introduce myself, and he clucks his tongue in his mouth.

"Yeah. No thank you." He looks at Red like I'm boring the life out of him and smirks. "And I'll see *you* later. Remember to—"

"I know! I'm not stupid! Jesus fucking—" she starts to scream.

He crashes his lips on hers, pulling her into his chest and effectively shutting her up. The kiss is long and wet and ever-lasting as students and even the teacher begin to pour through the door. My stomach rumbles and I feel queasy, so I look away and eventually walk over to the seats. I pick one in the back and pull out my MacBook and begin typing nonsense to distract myself. I tell myself it's to provide distraction from my hatred of even being in this class, but a part of me knows it's to distract me from the disgusting scene down front.

I don't even know why it's bothering me, which bothers me even more. My fingers trace the keys repeatedly, and I type my name over and over in Microsoft Word. I don't like the way I'm fidgeting because of a disgusting make-out session. I don't know the girl, and I don't know Tanner, who seems like a dick, by the way. But it's not like I'm paying attention or anything. Because I do not care.

When they finally pull away and *Tanner* sends me a smirk, I focus my eyes on the professor, who introduces himself as Mr. Harris. He tells us some stuff about himself and then rattles off into the syllabus of the course. I jot it all down and pull up a game on a random site. It's where I am a mouse-thing on skates and jumping in space. Sounds crazy because it is. But it helps pass the time while the professor talks. There's nothing that important to listen to, so why waste my time, you know?

"Move your bag," someone says and kicks my leg.

I look up at Red, who has her eyebrows raised in expectation. "Why?"

"Because I was sitting down there and that *bitch* wouldn't take off her fucking big ass hat," she spits, and a girl wearing a large beanie throws a nasty glare over her shoulder. Red curls her fists and opens her mouth, about to curse her out, but I quickly move my bag to sit in between my legs and gesture to the seat. "Thanks," she mumbles.

I close my laptop and look at her. "You know there are a million other seats in here, right?"

"I prefer the middle," she mutters behind her hand. "For fuck's sake. It's hotter than balls in here," she curses, and I chuckle. Smirking at me, she shrugs off her leather jacket, and my eyes are blessed with her right arm. She has a whole sleeve of colorful and dark tattoos. I spot several things: a mermaid, a patch of flowers, and a ruby on her wrist. I'm staring at the ruby when she pulls her arm away.

"Stare much?" she scoffs. She looks offended and annoyed.

"Sorry," I whisper with beet-red cheeks, then add, "your tattoos are just gorgeous." *Like you*, I add in my head. But I may as well have said it out loud, because she smiles at me. But it's an undercover smile. Barely there but enough to make me feel warm.

"Shut the fuck up," she says and pushes my shoulder. I laugh loudly but quiet down when I finally listen to what the professor is saying. He's assigning us a short assignment that, according to him, will barely affect us. He just wants to see our writing style, in the form of a short story. We can pair up, but before I can turn and ask Red to be my partner—

"No."

"Oh, come on. I'm a very creative person," I plead with a genuine smile as she guffaws. And loudly, but everyone's too busy chatting and pairing up to care or hear.

"No way, prep. I fly solo on stupid shit like this," she claims.

"Really?"

"Yes." She gives me a look that warns me to shut up, but I don't listen to that look.

"Even when I can do this?" I flip open my spiral notebook and pick up my pencil. I put the pencil to paper and quickly sketch a cartoon version of myself holding up a billboard with the words "*Be my partner*" in light bulbs. I even draw a cartoon version of herself, scowl, leather jacket, and all.

I show her, and she bursts into laughter. I think she's going to fall for my ability to pull a drawing like this basically out of my ass like a magician, but she just shakes her head and draws a bubble above her head that says, "*NO.*"

She's going to be a bit of a challenge, isn't she?
I kind of like it.

Chapter Six

The minute Professor Harris announces the class is over, the lecture hall buzzes with conversation and people are packing up to leave. Half of them are groaning because they have another class, while the other half, like me, are relieved to be free for the rest of the day. I can't imagine having a class right after this one. I'd be pretty upset if I had classes all the way up to five o'clock.

However, I can't complain about this one. I actually have an admiration for classical literature and have quite a few books in my room on a shelf. Ty teased me, calling me a book nerd, but I believe in escaping reality and jumping into another world. How does that not sound enticing? Especially with all the tragic and heartbreaking incidents going on in the world, starting with our shitty president, and the rest is never-ending, with terrorism and hatred and cruelty. It's a real wonder how everyone *doesn't* read to get away from it all, even if it's just for a second.

I pack up my things and sling my backpack over

my shoulder. Red passes by me in such a rush, she's mostly a blur. She melts into the growing crowd dispersing out of the room. Watching her shove through the throng of people makes me smile for some reason. Her rudeness should be a warning, a sign to back up and let her fire away. But it only draws me closer. I watch her leave the room and follow closely behind.

"So, I was thinking eight," I say, walking next to her.

She looks at me, shocked, then angry. "What are you talking about, prep?"

I gasp as if offended. "The time you should come over to start our short story. I was thinking it should be about a ballerina and a bad boy. You know, mix things up a bit."

"Are you on something? LSD? Molly? Crack?" she accuses.

"Clean as a whistle." I whistle low, and her mouth tilts upward for a split second. But that glorious second is enough to make my heart go nuts. "And besides, I think we'd work very well together."

"I think otherwise," she says and stops walking. She's looking ahead, jaw tense and locked. Whatever it is, it's pissing her off.

Tanner, her boyfriend I'm assuming, appears from behind a column, smoking a cigarette. Am I going crazy, or is he glaring at me, but also smirking? Does he have a problem with me, or is he naturally this weird? What I'm really wondering is why is she with him?

He creeps me out, so I put my attention back on

Red, who's already staring up at me.

"I really mean no on the project. I'm sure one of the many bimbos in there would love the help, though." She pats my shoulder like I'm a pathetic puppy that tripped over its paws and fell on its face. Then she spins around on her batty combat boots and struts over to her asshole, creepy boyfriend who has this sinister smirk on his face before he pulls her away from my sight.

When I get to the fraternity house, most of the guys are already here. There's a group in the living room playing video games. It's like they're addicted to the PlayStation. I wonder if their parents know they piss away their time here on video games rather than the coursework. But I get it. They need time away from this place, and the controllers are their getaway cars. It's the same with me, except instead of PlayStation, an empty canvas is my way out of this horrible world. And, for the time being, terrible place.

I walk over to the entryway and notice Mike on one of the leather couches, trash talking a guy with dark hair as they shoot at each other on the 50-inch flat TV screen. "I got next game," I say and flop onto the spot next to Mike. He and the guy are playing *Call of Duty*. I'm not the best at the game, but I'm not entirely hopeless.

"All right. Just gimme a few to finish whooping his ass," he says and veers left with the remote. He shoots the suited-up soldier in the face and fist pumps the air. "Fuck yeah!" he shouts. I laugh and accept the remote from the pissed-off guy, who glares at Mike before sauntering out of the living room. "Sore loser." He shakes his head and flashes a grin at me. "Ready to die, fool?"

"Excuse me?" I cue up the next game. "You're the one that should start planning your funeral. Do you want a rose thrown on your casket or…?"

He bumps his shoulder into mine, chuckling. "Shut up and pick out your guns."

"Fine, fine." I choose three random guns, and Mike whistles next to me. "What?"

"Nothing," he says, watching the three-second countdown on the screen. "I just wouldn't have picked your last gun choice."

"And why is that?" I ask as the game initiates. We're on either side of a large yacht. I begin moving my character on the left side, watching out for him all around. I saw a glimpse of him playing the other guy, and he's pretty good. He must clock in some good hours to be able to scope out the guy fifty meters away.

"Because of *this*," he says. It all happens so fast, I don't even see it coming. He rounds the corner, sliding on the floor, shooting me before I can pull out my heavy shotgun.

"Damn," I mutter, and he chuckles. "Don't be like that. I'll just switch out the gun."

"Too late." He veers to the right, and he appears behind me after I re-spawn. I try to whip around and defend myself, but he shoots me in the back, and I watch the last three seconds before re-spawning again. "I'm already whooping your ass."

And whoop my ass he does for the next ten minutes. The rounds seem never-ending. I'm guessing it's his doing. He really seems to enjoy watching me die as I try to defend myself each time I find him a little too late. When I ask him how come he's so good at it, he tells me he played constantly with his little brothers, Nicky and James, and that his parents fought so much it was a routine, so they played to tune it out. My heartstrings are tugged at when he tells me. And when he asks why I suck so much, I tell him I'm an only child and that my parents wanted me to play tennis and learn the piano instead.

"So," I say after the game ends and another pair of guys take the remotes to continue playing, "what do you know about Red?"

He looks at me suspiciously, lips tugged up in a smirk. "Why? You falling in love already?"

"Is it that noticeable?" I joke, and he laughs. I run a hand over my hair. "Nah, it's just...I don't know. She's just a bit *complicated*. And I'm kind of not used to that. Not that I'm into her or anything. I don't know how to talk to her without pissing her off somehow."

His brows concave, and he nods. "Trust me, it took me a while to get the hang of her too. But I sort of had to, since Majesty loves to hang around here and mess with her brother. Once you get used to her intensity, it gets easier." He pauses. "But for real, you thinking of getting with her?"

I shake my head, gripping my hair. "Of course not. We just have a class together and, like you said, she'll probably be around. I want to know how to talk to her. That's all."

"Okay. I believe you," he says but winks with a knowing smile.

Why does he look like that?

"Shut up." I bump shoulders with him, and he laughs. I stand up. "Thanks for the game. See you around." He nods at me before one of the guys begins talking to him. I leave him and the rest in the living room, jogging up the long stairs.

On the second floor, I decide I'm going to take a long nap. When I wake up, I'll work on the English assignment. Red pops up in my brain and how she turned me down comically by doodling a big fat *no* above her head. Even though she harshly turned me down, I can't get over her laughter when she did. It was as if bruising my ego was a fun hobby she'd discovered and loved. I weirdly don't mind, I realize, as I recall how her eyes lit up and she looked so amused.

I wonder how much of my ego she plans on crumbling. And I wonder how much will be destroyed before I'm not solely focused on that damned smile.

When I open my bedroom door, I feel my energy drop. It isn't fully open before I spot a lean guy with dark hair, wearing all black, leaning against a study desk, his eyes trained on the floor, head tilted to the side. I try to recall all the faces of the people living in this house, but even so, he looks a few years older. So he doesn't go to this school. And by the looks of it, he doesn't belong on this campus. I spot a neck tattoo creeping up under the collar of his leather jacket, when he turns his head and looks me up and down. He doesn't say anything, which just makes this even weirder.

"Um, hi." I nod at him unsurely. Maybe Ty

knows him...

He grins, but it doesn't reach his light blue eyes. "Hey." There's something about his smile that doesn't sit right with me.

I should say something. I don't want to be rude. But I have no idea who he is, and he gives me the creeps. What is it with guys dressing like the Grim Reaper today? First Timmy, or whatever Red's boyfriend's name is, and now this guy.

"Yo, Noah!" Ty enters the room and stops short. His face falls a little when he sees the man, almost like he's...scared. "'Sup." He nods at him, and the guy smiles wider. Something crosses his shining blue eyes, and Ty nods to himself. "Mind if I talk to you outside?" he asks me.

He pulls me out of the room, leaving the door cracked with a tiny gap.

"What's wrong? You look like you just saw a ghost," I joke lightly, but the look of slight fear and anxiety doesn't fade away. "Seriously. Are you okay? Is there something wrong with that guy in there?"

"You should not be worrying about that guy."

"Why not?"

"Noah, seriously. Just..." He takes a long, thoughtful breath. "Do you mind lending me a fifty? I promise, I *swear*, I will pay you back. I just don't have it on me right now and he—"

I place a hand on his tense shoulder. "Calm down, okay? It's totally fine. I've got you." I give him an assuring smile. I dig into my pocket and pull out my wallet. He thanks me repeatedly and tries giving me a smile back, but it merely bleeds through the sheer look of terror on his face. Whoever the guy is, he's dangerous. And Ty obviously owes him money—for what, God knows, but I hope it isn't for what I think it is.

I give him the crisp bill, and he asks me to stay out of the room for a moment, so I do. When the guy finally leaves, he leaves deftly, and when I enter the room, his dark presence lingers. I want to ask him about the guy, but the way he sighs into a hand on his bed and claps large headphones over his ears tells me he isn't feeling too chatty. My head floods with theories before I can help it. None of them are good.

Worry fills me, and I glance over at him as I jot down ideas for my short story for a few minutes. Before I can toss a shoe at him and ask if he's in any trouble, my phone buzzes in my pocket. It must be Liv. I pull it out and put my spiral notebook aside. There's a new text message.

Unknown: okay.

I rack my brain for someone I gave my number to recently but come up empty. Ty, Mike, and a few other guys are already programmed into my phone, so this has to be a stranger.

I unlock my phone.

Noah: Okay what? And who is this?

Unknown: Red, idiot.

My eyes widen, and a million thoughts infiltrate

my mind. One: how did she get my number? Two: what does she mean, okay? And three: when did I start to program her in my phone?

And okay means???

I text her and nearly snort when I read her response.

Red: It means OK I WILL WORK ON THE FUCKING PROJECT WITH YOU NOW SHUT UP ABOUT IT OK?!

Noah: All right, I got it, Rossa.

I smirk because I know for a fact she doesn't know what that means.

Red: The name's Red, stupid.

I can perfectly see her sneering at me with a nasty eye roll.

Noah: It means Red in Italian.

I await her response. I bite my thumb nervously, but I stop when I realize I must look like a shy schoolgirl texting her crush. And Red is *not* my crush. And I'm also not a teenage schoolgirl. Duh. But I can't even seem to help it; she has this energy about her that pulls me in when I should be running away. Sort of like an unknowing moth drawn to a flame. In this case, I'm the moth and she's the fire:

hot, enthralling, and painful to touch. Yet I keep getting closer and closer, ignoring the surrounding waves of heat.

Red: Shut up.

I burst into laughter. Ty glances over at me, and I blush, supporting the theory that I'm secretly a schoolgirl, but looks away when something on his phone interests him more. I look at my screen and type back a reply, smiling as I do, but she interrupts.

Red: I've gotta go. But we're only doing this on one condition.

Noah: Which is???

Red: You delete my number when it's done.

I pause.

Noah: Sure you don't wanna keep my number? I'm a great listener. I'd text you good morning every day.

She fires back the way I expected her to.

Red: It's either that or nothing Picasso. I don't need you for that extra gooey shit. K?

Noah: Got it. Talk to you later, Rossa.

I attach a peace sign behind the words.

Her response is almost immediate.

Red: And no emojis.

I'm cracking up at myself when I text her back.

Noah: Byee Red.

I add the kiss emoji and fire emoji.
She doesn't respond.
I burst out into laughter and stare at the lack of text on her side. She's just as unenthusiastic with me in text, and it tickles my funny bone. It's strange because she's reacting the opposite of all the girls I've interacted with. It's refreshing in a way. She's definitely different—a challenge. I haven't experienced much, so it's like a breath of fresh air. Not that girls are supposed to be taken as tests and used for excitement. With Red, it's like a siren whispering in my ear, *Do you have what it takes?* And instead of looking for a hidden message, I'm replying, *Let me find out.*

Chapter Seven

Red isn't in English class the next day. For some reason, theories—insane, *crazy* theories—fill my head the entire class as I repeatedly look toward the door. All involve that strange guy that was in Ty's and my bedroom yesterday. One of them speculates if he sought her out and whisked her away to some island to do God knows what with her…but the idea sounds too crazy and too ridiculous to remain in my head, so I expel it and try my best to focus on what the professor is saying.

When the professor announces the end of class, I realize I drew her lips on the corner of my spiral notebook. I don't know how to feel about it. I chalk it up to the lack of time I've had to really paint anything. Sure, I drew that cartoon and a few other things mindlessly, but it isn't physically picking up a brush and creating a sunset out of a few colors. It isn't smelling the scent of beds of flowers beneath a terrace. It just *isn't*.

The second I step outside, I spot her.

Red.

She's casually leaning against the wall, staring at her chipped black fingernails with a bored expression sketched on her face. A small smile gravitates on my face, and I walk over to her and lean against the wall. Her gaze flies up, and she stares at me for a moment as if struck by a flash of light before clearing her throat and taking a step back for good distance.

"Were you waiting for me?" I ask in a teasing manner.

"Yes, but just because I want to get started on this damned project," she explains and pushes off the wall completely. "And we gotta go now. I have something else to do." She begins to walk away before I can even register her words. I catch up next to her as we walk onto the campus lawn. The quad is buzzing with activity and laughter and lots of groups wearing the school's hoodie.

"Can I ask where we're going?" I ask her.

"No," she says, clipped.

I smile. "Oh, come on. That isn't so far, now is it?"

We walk for a while, her face blank and refusing to give me at least a hint at her mind, before she glances at me and mumbles, "You'll see." Her fingers dig into her jeans that I now notice hug her body very well, and she pops a cigarette between her full lips.

I frown. "You shouldn't smoke." I speak my mind before thinking. I expect her to glare at me and maybe shiv me with the black lighter she's using to spark up her cigarette, but she surprisingly bursts into a pretty-sounding laughter. It makes me smile, and her nose crinkles. God, she is absolutely gorgeous. What I wouldn't kill to paint her lips, her nose—hell, everything about her.

"Don't worry about me, prep." Blowing out smoke up in the air, showing off her long, smooth-looking neck, she says, "This world is too fucked up for anyone to be worried about *me*."

"But that's just it," I say, and she looks over at me, skeptically. "Someone should worry about you *because* of this world. It's already wrecked beyond repair. So why shouldn't anyone worry about preserving one of the precious things left?"

"Do you use that line on every girl to make them swoon?" she mumbles, the cigarette clenched between her teeth. Her eyes are squinting up at me, beneath the glare of the sun, observing me in a way that takes my breath away and breathes a whirlwind inside my chest.

"Just the ones with face piercings."

"Better not say that too loud or your past bimbo flings'll hear you," she jokes, and I laugh. I think I see the corner of her lips curl up a bit, but I can't tell under the sun shining down on her, making her glow.

We continue walking even though I don't even realize we've stopped. Entering the parking lot, I expect to find her Chevy Impala, but instead am bestowed a glorious red motorcycle. From the looks of it, it has a beast of an engine and a sleek body. It burns brightly under the sun, and Red doesn't hesitate in swinging her amazon legs onto the bike and sitting on the seat.

I do a double take as she jams a key in the

ignition and starts it up. It rumbles, and she slightly vibrates but gets acclimated and pulls on a pair of fingerless leather gloves. I have never seen a girl look so badass before. I want to snap a picture, but I also have this instinct in me to run away. Instead, I stare in awe.

"Gonna stand there staring at me all day, or are you gonna get on? Make up your mind quickly before I leave your ass and give myself all the credit on the story," she says and flicks her cigarette to the ground. Her heavy combat boots stomp on it, and she glances up at me underneath her lashes before tugging on a vibrant red helmet. She flips the visor down, shielding her brilliant blue eyes from me.

"Make room." I smile before getting on the back of it, looping my arms around her. Immediately, I am enveloped in vanilla and Marlboro cigarettes.

She says, "Hold on, prep," before we zoom out of the parking lot.

***

I've never ridden shotgun on a motorcycle, which is a lot faster than I expect, but then again, I've never met anyone like Red before. The ride is filled with sharp twists, hard turns, and deafening loud purrs of the engine. I feel queasy for a good few minutes before I tighten my grip and smell her a little deeper, as creepy as it is. I don't know why, but her scent calms me more than gripping her tighter. Plus, she smells like a goddamn angel who rolled around in a field of vanilla and cigarettes.

One thing I notice is how easy riding comes to

her. How her body is never tense but constantly relaxed. How at ease she breathes with each crazy, wide turn. She has a relationship with the vehicle, that much I can tell. I bet she has a name for it, but I'll never tease her about it because she'll probably stab me in the eye with a spork and promptly tell me to fuck off.

We slow down in front of a row of stores. The sun has dipped a little, and people are out walking with friends to the nearest bar or enjoying a night stroll in the park across the street. "All right, we're here," she announces, hitting the kick stand with her heel. We jerk a little, and she whips around with a smirk. "You can stop praying for your mommy now," she teases.

"I was not praying for my mommy." I stick my tongue out at her.

"Sorry! I meant your silver spoon." She deftly stands up and perches her pierced eyebrow, igniting a staring challenge, and boy do I stare. I stare at her pursed lips that are naturally reddish. I stare at her eyes and how they're glowing slightly under the colors in the sky. And I stare at her tongue peeking out of her lips.

Scared I might do something insane, I break and blink rapidly as I get off, but not as gracefully as her. She laughs that pretty laugh again, and I blush as I stumble a bit onto the curb. "Sorry I'm not an expert at dismounting a *motorcycle* like you."

"You'll get used to it," she says ominously before hopping onto the sidewalk and swinging open the door to a store and sauntering in without any second glance toward me, hips swaying and all.

Clucking my tongue against my cheek at her confidence, I hop onto the sidewalk and follow after her. I catch sight of the neon sign that states the place is Jim's Arcade.

The second I walk inside, I am bombarded by strobe lights that nearly blind me and zaps and pings coming from the arcade machines. A bunch of kids, fresh from school, scream at their friends on the games or scrape up earned tickets from the floor. Or steal them. To my immediate left is a ginger-headed teenaged boy in a black uniform who looks like he's two seconds away from slitting his own throat in boredom. I think he's going to stop me and ask to pay to enter the arcade, but he looks away like he doesn't want to bother and sighs. I feel bad for him. But at least he doesn't have a difficult task.

I step inside further on the lookout for Red but come up empty. I'm about to go to the back of the arcade when I spot a sign above a set of stairs going down: Pool Hall (18+).

On the lower level of the arcade is one massive area of pool tables, poker tables, and smoke, which Red is most likely contributing to. Most of the pool tables are in use by burly guys with belly guts and a few younger ones, maybe from the college. I spot her in the back of the room, hunched over with a cue stick aimed at a purple ball. My heart thumps as I get closer to her, bypassing a few big guys cheering over their own game.

"Never took you for a pool player," I say, leaning against the table.

"We can't all get our thrills from riding around

on yachts," she jokes in that husky voice of hers, taking her shot. The ball sinks into the pocket, and she smirks to herself, proud.

"I don't do that," I say, and she glances at me. I smirk. "I also pay people to golf for me while I sit in a gold cart and scratch my pet lion, Robert under the chin."

She actually breaks out in a bashful smile. "Robert, huh?" Her pierced brow sinks low, and her pink tongue plays with her silver lip ring. I dig my right hand in my khaki pants pocket.

"Yeah. I could let you babysit him while I get a portrait done for one of my many mansions. Treat him right and I'll pass your name around the golf club," I continue to joke, and she's laughing now.

"Don't spoil me too much, Richie Rich," she says, eyes gleaming.

"Oh, why not, Old Sport? I have all the riches in the world. Why not relinquish them to you?" I wink at her, and she surprisingly gets my *Great Gatsby* reference as she scoffs after taking a shot and raising that pierced brow at me.

"So you're Jay Gatsby now? No longer a frat boy?" she muses.

I lean with my hands against the pool table, looking her straight in the eyes. "I can be whatever you want me to be." My voice is low, and I cock my head to the side. I watch as her lips tip upward and her brows stitch together in a little knot. Her expression is puzzled, and the other half is unreadable. I can't tell if she's falling for my charm or is gearing up to laugh in my face.

Finally, she draws back—I hadn't noticed she'd

leaned in too—and bends down. "How 'bout we pause being cheesy and get started on the story of us, hmm?" She takes her shot and makes it effortlessly. She is really good…at pool and looking so sexy while playing it.

"I can do that too, I guess." I swing my backpack onto the table. One of the balls shifts down, and she shoots me an icy glare. "Sorry," I apologize, but she just rolls her eyes in annoyance and moves along the illuminated pool table. I fish out my spiral notebook and a black ballpoint pen. I drop the bag onto the ground, resting against a leg of the table. "Okay. First things first: what's the story about?"

She shrugs. "I have no idea. I don't write stories, prep."

"Neither do I," I defend.

"What if the girl can, like, travel or something?" she suggests in a low voice like she's embarrassed.

"That's a good idea," I tell her and watch a smile tug at her lips for a quarter of a second before it plunges into a thin line. I smile and let it rest on my face as I make a thought bubble. "What if she can travel to another world through…a portal, maybe?"

She shakes her head, twisting her cue stick. "That's lame. Through a cigarette."

I don't see the logistics of that, but world-traveling isn't exactly existential in our current times, so it doesn't matter. And she gives me this "duh" look that makes me chuckle and her smile, but it lasts a little longer this time.

"Got it." I jot the idea down. "What are our characters' names?"

"Dunno." She stops walking and pushes her hand

through her mass of golden curls. The neon lights down here promoting beer and half-naked girls make her glow in red and pink and yellow. The colors against her creamy, fair skin make her look like a bad-ass fallen angel, in her tight black pants and leather jacket. Her eyes shift over to me, and I abruptly look at the colors lighting the rim of the pool table.

I dare a look at her, and thankfully, she's lining up for another shot. "Magenta and..." She shrugs, hitting and striking a shot. "You pick the dude's name."

"Okay..." I write down *Magenta* as she takes a shot. She curses—I guess she missed it—and I look at her. She's standing, running her fingers through her messy blonde hair. The neon lights plays tricks with my eyes again, giving her a bent halo in the dim lighting. And then she's bent over again. Levi jeans loose around her slim waist; ripped black shirt rising enough to show a sliver of her creamy, neon skin. My jaw rocks back and forth as I imagine dirty, dirty things.

Chapter Eight

She pops a cigarette in her mouth, then lights it.

"Come up with a name yet?" she asks around the cigarette in the corner of her full mouth. When she doesn't get an immediate answer, as my head is too busy thinking of the colors on her exposed skin, she looks over her shoulder.

I snap my attention to the notebook. "Um, yeah. I was thinking Ethan, maybe?"

Please don't tell me she caught me staring, please, please—

"Whatever." She squints and takes the shot. It sinks in the pocket, of course, and she takes a large puff with a smile. I stare. For some reason, watching her smoke and smile and play pool is satisfyingly...beautiful. She's in her element, and I'm the lucky guy who gets to be in her vicinity, watching her. I sound like such a creep, but I can't even control it. "Now, the story should start off with Magenta doing something incredibly badass."

"Maybe saving puppies for a charity?" I suggest with a teasing smile. I look over my shoulder and find her scowling at me, but it's adorable with her lips pursed and pierced eyebrow raised.

"*Or* she's just finished knocking some guy out for trying to grope her or something, because guys suck, no offense—"

"None taken, I think—" I begin unsurely.

"And she steps out for a smoke," she continues, unbothered by the interruption. "And she teleports to this awesome world where beer is free and Trump isn't alive. 'Cause of the cigs, remember?" She points at me, and I nod, hiding my smile the best I can. She waves a hand around as she speaks. "Anyway, she's auto racing and walking around, tits out because she, you know, *can*, when she sees him—"

"And it's love at first sight?" I ask, smirking.

"No. Shit no." She looks wildly offended and takes a large puff. She blows out skillfully. "She saves *his* ass after he almost gets raped by douches—"

"Thought it was a perfect world. Why would there be douche rapists?" I question her idea.

She rolls her eyes at her continuity error and my pointing it out. "They got there by being dick-weebs. Jumped on my—*her*—ride there or some shit." She grabs a can of beer that was resting on the ledge of the table, pops it open, and takes a long swig. Then she looks at me expectantly. Flushed in the face, I jot her ideas down and nod.

"And then…?" I ask, looking to her.

Setting the empty can down—wow, I am very impressed—she shrugs, wiping her mouth with the back of her leather fingerless glove. "What?"

I chuckle. "What moves the story along?" I ask. She just looks at me blankly, and I laugh some more. "Red, what happens to them?"

"Something has to happen to 'em?" She looks confused and pissed off.

"It wouldn't be a story without *some* sort of conflict."

She pauses, and her face twists. "Dude's almost got raped. That isn't enough conflict?"

"*No*," I say, "it got them to meet. But what draws him to her and vice versa?"

"She's fucking awesome, and he's cute-ish and smells good, so she sticks around him." She stops from sinking a red ball. "Plus he has good quality hair, and she kind of digs hair over everything." She moves to shoot the red ball when she pauses and cracks a wicked smirk. "And jawlines. They're in now, right? Yeah. Throw that in there."

My stomach twists as I think, *Is she talking about us in real life?*

I consciously run a hand over my jaw. "I'm not a computer, you know. I jotted everything down, but I'm not the greatest writer. In fact, I suck. I'm gonna need your help with the writing."

"Thought you were so creative *I* should have been the one jumping to be your partner," she says, recalling what I told her in English. But I wasn't telling the whole truth. I was just trying to get us to pair up. I may be skilled when it comes to art like painting and making little cartoon drawings, but it stops there, right in front of a computer and an empty Word document.

"I thought we were supposed to do this

together." I turn this around on her. She pinches her cigarette between her fingers, as if to keep them from pinching my neck. Instead of *murdering* me, however, she takes a few deep breaths before squashing it in an ashtray embedded in the table. Then she looks at me intensely. Hard.

"I'll do most of the writing—" she says.

"Thank—"

"*If* you make this shot," she finishes with a smirk that makes it hard to breathe.

"What?" I raise my brows, and she raises hers to mock me. My lips fall into a thin line as she chuckles, head tilted back ever so slightly. Her neck looks amorous under the soft glow of purple on the wall behind her. I want to kiss it.

"Make this shot and I'll do most of the writing." She pushes the cue stick in my chest. "I once got a chance to be published in some magazine when I was sixteen for a shit story I wrote."

"Really?" The shock I feel seeps into my words before I can stop it. I just never expected to hear that from her. I wonder what the story was about. How did they find out about it? I want to know so much more and a lot more about her in general. She's such an interesting person. I swear, it's the siren in her. I get closer to her, smiling from ear to ear.

"*Ah, ah.*" She wags a finger, thrusting the stick at me again. "Make the shot and I help you out big time. Go on now." She drops the pool stick, and I instinctively drop the notebook and catch it. She grabs the notebook and pen before they hit the ground, and as I gawk at her killer reflexes, she throws her head back in laughter and stands at the head of the table. She nods to the scattered balls with a knowing smirk.

Devious little thing.

"Come on, preppy." She's wielding a devilish smile. "Take your shot."

"Fine." I walk over to the edge of the table and chew my bottom lip. I may be athletic, but that doesn't mean I'm good at this sport in particular.

Funny story: My father had a pool table in the basement of our house. One day a girl I was crushing on came over, along with a few of my friends. I lost a bet that would make her take off her top because I lost a game of pool. *Twice.* Safe to say I had no friends for a week after that.

"Let's see what you got, pretty boy," Red goads with a teasing smile. She tugs at her lips, lowers her head, and watches me as I bend to the table. I feel hot under her intense, fixated gaze and flash a wink and a smile at her as I line the stick up with a blue ball behind the white one. She makes a grunting noise, making me rethink my position, choice of ball—everything.

"Stop it," I whine, straightening with a pout.

"Oh, hush! Do whatever. Just don't puss out," she says.

"I wasn't gonna puss out," I mumble under my breath, but she must have heard it, because she chuckles and tells me to hurry up. After telling her to hold her horses, I take a few deep breaths.

Make it, make it, make it…

I draw the stick back and take my shot…

It bounces off the lining, completely missing any

and all holes.

"Damn it!" I let my head fall against the table. It's soft under my forehead and gives me safe coverage from her mocking laughter. But when I peek a glance at her, it's worth it.

"Who saw that coming?" She chuckles as she sidles up next to me.

"You're evil," I tell her, narrowing my eyes.

She just grins. "Tell me something I haven't heard before."

"Okay." I turn to her, dropping my voice a notch. "You're extremely beautiful."

...Whoa.

She looks confused too, brows stitched together, lips pursed, and eyes a glossy blue. A few moments of silence passes, each worse than the last. How will she respond? I totally did not just say that. God knows she's testy already, and I just tested her. Big time. "Are you always this flirty?" she finally says after a moment, moving away from me, almost like she's angry.

But I block her, push her hair behind her ear—I just couldn't resist any longer—and say, "You should be reminded every second of every day." My voice is raspy.

Her face softens but looks conflicted. For a brief moment, her mouth pushes open, and her cheeks light with a dusty-rose color. "Shut up and get to outlining while I play," she mutters with annoyance, pushing past me forcibly. I smile in spite of her hostility, because, for however long I've known her, she did it. I freaking made her do it.

Blush.

***

Later on, when she drops me off at the house, the second I step off the bike she speeds away into the darkness. Maybe she's in a rush to get home before it gets too unsafe to be out by herself, though I doubt she wouldn't be able to take care of herself, or she just couldn't get away from me soon enough. I become over-analytical as I watch her speed down the corner, her flaring engine rippling in the air.

"'You're extremely beautiful'?" I murmur to myself, wondering how stupid I can be as I walk to the porch. There are some Solo cups hidden in the grass from the party a few days ago. I focus on them rather than the fact that I am such a dork. I have to or I'll kill myself wondering when the hell I started chasing girls. It's usually the other way around. And if I am chasing, it doesn't take this long or this much effort.

But a voice in me tells me she's worth the chase. I hope the voice is right, because my ego is taking a helluva beating.

I'm so caught up in my thoughts, I almost don't notice the box. It's relatively small and wrapped in white paper, with a red bow tied neatly at the top. I bend and pick it up thinking it must be for one of the guys. But I pick up the tag attached to the bow and find my name written in the most neat and pretty cursive handwriting.

As I use my key to get inside and head straight to my room, I wonder who it could be from. It doesn't say, just my name with a little heart beside it.

"Christmas come early this year?" Ty asks,

briskly walking into the room as I plop onto my bed. He rummages through his study desk, in the pursuit of who knows what, and I think on his question.

"Not that I know of," I murmur, playing with the bow. I pick it up and shake it gently. Something rocks in there.

"Who from?" he questions, glancing over at it and me.

I shrug. "Doesn't say." I pause and pull up a very small list of friends and family...family. "Probably my parents sending me a gift to say sorry for forcing me to be here."

"Wish my parents would get that. I could use a Lambo for them forcing me to do ballet when I was ten," he says, and I furrow my brows. He holds up his hands, shakes his head. "Don't even ask." He snatches up something and nods at me. "See you around."

"Yeah..." I raise my hand and listen to him leave the room in haste. After thinking so hard of who this could be from for a full five minutes, I tug at the ribbon. I slowly reach a hand out and pop off the top.

The smell hits me hard. It's sharp and pungent and, when I peek inside, I let out a shriek I am not proud of and throw the box on the ground.

The small, bloody heart inside rolls out.

Chapter Nine

Written on a single strip of paper in the box with the bloody heart was:

Be careful.

Whatever the hell that's supposed to mean.

I can't sleep, so I drew the moon. Whenever I'm upset or frustrated or anything that doesn't sit well with me, I draw something. Anything. Some guys work out; others react violently. I sketch the moon from the roof. I just have to get my mind off of the weird present, to stop seeing that bloody heart on the ground. Each time I think of it rolling onto the floor, I draw harder. Draw the houses. Draw the couch on the lawn. I draw the entire damn town.

Literally.

I take a stumbling step back, eyes on the wall on my side of the room. I drew so damn much, thought of her even more, that I drew the entire span of the city. From memory when I canvased the city. To Google images. They're all individual and together make up the town, the city, everything. I fall onto Ty's bed and catch my breath and admire my own work. That art contest pops into my head for a brief second before Red does, and I stop the train of thought. That is nowhere as important as someone leaving a bloody heart on the porch for me with a creepy, ominous note attached.

After that, I still can't sleep.

I stay awake in constant paranoia and confusion. I keep imagining a hitman bursting through the window and taking me out with an AK-47. And then I sink into a whole of who would order me dead. I haven't offended anyone in the past year I've been traveling, have I? All I've done is paint and observe and take pictures. I didn't start a blood war with a native in Finland or something.

But that doesn't stop me from recalling every encounter I've had while traveling.

Could it be one of the girls I painted? Did they not like how their portrait came out?

Was it the waiter who caught me when I spit out a piece of the dish he served me because it was too spicy for me to register when I visited Mexico? I got used to it after the first few bites. It turned out to be incredible! I told him that. But that makes zero sense.

I can't even say it could have been a mistake because it had my name clearly written on the tag. Which, believe it or not, is the silver lining. I don't know that many people. I've only been here for a few days. The only people who know me are the guys in this house and a handful of other people. None of them really stand out as psychopaths to me.

Maybe it was Tanner or that Ian guy. But other than them, I can't think of a single person that would do something as insane and weird as that. But then, I don't know them well enough to have pissed them off in some way, to have created some kind of grudge. Or they're just really vicious people. But like I said, I don't know them that well, so I can't make assumptions like *this*. Whoever sent me that heart, which I found out was a *pig's* heart, was a cold, malicious person. Someone who wanted to scare me. They were pretty freaking successful.

I would call the police to report it, but there is no address. Probably no fingerprints. And God knows no one was paying attention to anyone outside of the house, too busy playing their video games to notice someone dropping off a pig's heart on the porch. I wish the house had a security camera because then I'd be able to identify who exactly the culprit is.

I sigh loudly. The entire situation is frightening, weird, and confusing. So much so, I don't see the girl I bump into until I hear her yelp and watch a blur of her drop to the ground. I snap out of the weird daze I've been in for the past five minutes on my way to the fraternity house. I just left my last class. I was so wrapped up in my head I barely paid attention to Red beside me. I actually zoned in on the professor, but not his words really. I was too busy worrying if someone's going to jump out and slash me across the jugular.

"I am so sorry," I apologize rapidly, squatting in front of the girl. When she looks up, I recognize her instantly. "Hey, you're...Rachel, right? I'm Noah.

We met yesterday." I pause when she just stares at me like I'm a Martian reciting the Pledge of Allegiance. "Again, very sorry. I was just…thinking." *About someone wanting my head on a pike.* "But let me help you up." I scoop up some papers sprawled on the floor next to her, then reach for her hand, offering a small smile.

She reluctantly takes my hand, and I pull her up to her feet. "I wasn't paying attention either. I was just looking over these stupid drawings and…" She stops as I hand her the papers, her cheeks and the tips of her small ears burning bright red. "You don't need to hear me ramble. I'm sorry." She tries to step away, but I block her. Her eyebrows scrunch together in confusion, and I gesture to the papers in her hands.

"Drawings? You draw?" I ask.

She begins to nod but stops. "I *try* to draw, but I'm not very good at it."

I wave a hand. "Don't say that. Can I look? I mean—" I run my hand over my hair, thinking of ways not to sound like an arrogant dickhead. Like I know the entire ins and outs of the art world. "I paint here and there."

"Can I see some?" she asks timidly.

"Sure." I pull out my phone and pull up photos I took of some of my paintings. I hold my phone up to her, and her mouth drops, eyes glittering with awe. "You like?" I ask, chuckling a bit at her slack expression. She looks like she just hit the jackpot during the Gold Rush. Almost like I confirmed that I'm the reincarnation of Picasso.

I think you're tooting your horn a little too *much,*

don't you think?

"This is absolutely breathtaking," she exclaims, breaking the little shell of shyness and expressing pinched cheeks and bright eyes. She pushes her pin-straight hair behind her elf-like ears and looks up at me with her huge brown eyes. I laugh, blushing at her overwhelming admiration of my work. And they aren't even my best pieces.

"Thank you," I say. "I've been doing it for years. One day I picked up a brush and just couldn't stop..." I pause in reminiscence. I can still feel the worn brush given to me by my grandfather who passed away a year after my eleventh birthday. A memory of me painting a crappy stick-figure person in a sea of dandelions fades as she speaks.

"You have to check out the art club."

"I don't know about that..." I would love to, trust me. But I'm already trying out for football and don't want to attach too much of myself to college. I promised myself that I was just here for the semester, which my parents forced on me, and then I'm leaving without looking back.

"Please!" She reaches for my wrist, rethinks it, and blushes as she yanks her arms behind her back. "I'm trying to learn, and the teacher is great and all, but she can't paint like you." I'm trying not to let her words pet my ego. Her cheeks burn bright red. "And I don't know anyone there, and you being in the club would help lots."

I seriously don't want to actually *like* this place. If I get acclimated and genuinely want to stay, I will never hear the end of it. My parents would be gloating, *floating* on a cloud that rains "I Told You

So" everywhere I went. I want to turn her down, to just keep to myself and paint and draw on my own. But something in her round eyes and hopeful smile wears my plan down, and I end up nodding and smiling small.

"Oh, what the hell? Sure," I tell her, and she grins.

"Awesome! I can show you where it's being held." She holds her drawings to her chest, smile teetering just slightly. "I was heading there just now before…" She pauses and glances away, probably embarrassed by how we crashed into each other and she fell on her butt. Not before yelping like a bruised Chihuahua, of course.

I laugh and nod. "Show me. And if you want, I can pay for a doctor check up to make sure your butt's all right."

She guffaws and nervously pushes my shoulder; I act like she pained me greatly, and she chuckles. "Shut up. You were the one who ran into me. You're like a big brick wall."

"Thanks." I flex my arms, and she looks away. "I've been working out."

She laughs, and I make small talk as we walk around a bend, then walk down a short way into another hallway. On our very short walk, I find out that she comes from a very small family—just her and her mother, after her father died on his job as a carpenter. I tell her I am sorry and she waves it off, but I can sense the lump forming in her throat. To lighten up the mood, I express how I've been basically all around the world. Not just taking a vacation and having the time of my life; I joined plenty of missions and donated to multiple charities—did everything I could to give back to the places I visited.

"You are something short of an angel, Noah," she claims as we enter a room.

"I'm nothing much." I wave at her absently, shrugging. "Just gave back where I could."

The room we're in is spacious, where there are clutters of stools and white bedsheets. At the back of the room is a wide span of windows that let in the sunlight that dances across the linoleum flooring. There are people talking in groups, mingling around, all wearing some form of worn clothes they don't mind getting dirty with paint. Rachel lets me walk around while she heads off to talk to a few people.

I look around at the hung-up art decor and paintings done by students. They're all so colorful and vibrant and unique. I gasp a few times, taking in a few sketches, and spot a few statues set in one corner of the room.

"Noah, this is a friend of mine," Rachel says, and I turn from an abstract painting of a woman to face her and her friend. I instantly recognize her before Rachel introduces us. "Beth, this is Noah. Noah, this is Beth."

Beth giggles as I anxiously run a hand over my hair.

"Hey, Noah." She waves her fingers at me, grinning.

"Nice to see you again...*Beth*," I say politely. God. This is so embarrassing. She and I made it clear that what went down between us was a one-time thing. I did *not* expect to see her here.

Rachel looks between us both, frowning. "You two know each other?"

"Something like that," I say, voice low.

"Yo, Beth!" some guy in a group of people behind her calls out.

"Be right there," she tells him, then turns to me. Her head cocks to the side, and she purrs while winking at me, "And I'll see *you* around." To Rachel, she chirps, "See you later!" Then she saunters over to the group, leaving me blushing and Rachel confused as ever.

"Don't ask," I say, chuckling. I feel my phone buzzing in my khaki pants, so I hold up a finger to excuse myself and fish it out. I know what it is before even reading the text from Mike. "Shit. I totally forgot, but I have football tryouts. Do you mind if I slip out? But I would like to join…" I pause and look around, my eyes lingering on the easels in a corner, then look back at her with a soft smile. "If that's still a possibility?"

"Yeah, of course it's a possibility! I'll sign your name on the sheet later." She beams up at me and shakes her head, as if a thought occurs to her. "You're new, so you don't know where the stadium is. I can take you there if you'd like."

"I'd appreciate that so much, thank you." I'm grateful for her kindness. Most people are assholes in this world, overrun with greed and malicious intent. It's hard to weed out the nice people, the pure ones. She's a rare, refreshing find. I hope I can make a better acquaintance with her; I could use a few more friends in this place. And the ones I have currently—Mike and Ty—are better than I hoped for.

I actually planned to become mute. Well, thought about it more than committed to it. I thought I could just sit through classes and in the corner of my room, not saying a single word. I'd show my parents that they can't control my life. But of course, the world doesn't work itself around me and my stupid ideas. It dragged me in and college threw people and football and art clubs at me. Art! My greatest weakness. Damned world. It can screw off, that's for sure.

***

A few minutes later, we arrive at a brick building with the word ***STADIUM*** written on top of the blue-painted steel doors. A group of guys are walking up to the door the same time we arrive, and I immediately recognize one of the guys.

"You actually showed up," Ian says with a shit-eating smirk.

"Don't be rude," Rachel hisses in a low tone, glaring at her step-brother.

"It's fine, Rachel." I laugh and look at Ian. "And, yes, I'm here to show you I've got what it takes to make the team."

His eyes light with amusement. "We'll see; just don't get too cocky on me, newbie." Turning to catch up with the group he came with, he tells me over his shoulder, "I hope you're ready for a grueling tryout. It's nothing like your little league team in high school."

"Trust me." I smile, ignoring his insult. "I'm more than ready. You just better hope you are too."

He stays silent, his hard, intense gaze speaking for him: *I'll beat your ass on the field.*

I smirk and let my eyes reply: *I wouldn't underestimate me.*

And underestimate me he does. I push myself through the hazardous exercises. I crank out my old throwing arm. I am a bit rusty there, but besides that, I do exceptionally great. The rust wears off bit by bit, revealing my knowledge and skill from my time on my high school football team. And I actually have fun. I forgot how much fun it is, running plays and cracking jokes with friends. It was one of the few things I looked forward to in college when I was in junior high. Until I discovered my passion of painting and photography and everything art.

The moment I entered high school and talked about my passion, I lost my parents.

I shake the saddening thought away as I stroll up my block, nearing the house. I'm exhausted and sweating in places I didn't even know could sweat. The minute I'm in the house, I plan on taking a long, hot shower, then taking an even longer nap. I forgot how tiring football is.

My plans vanish when I find Red leaning against her bike, smoking a cigarette. I rack my brain, trying to remember if we agreed to continue working on the story today or not. Either way, I am stunned and don't say anything. She's wearing a rock band t-shirt—ripped, of course—and a leather jacket, her combat boots crossed as she blows out a puff of gray smoke.

"Red?" I say, snapping out of my trance. I take a step toward her.

Her gaze falls on mine, and my heart stutters. She throws the cigarette on the ground, crushes it, and holds out a black helmet toward me. "Hop on," she orders.

Chapter Ten

Any other guy would have told her to fuck off and leave her out here, right? I mean, the girl's an absolute asshole to me ninety percent of the time. But for some unknown reason, I like that she busts my balls so much. Turns me down and every flirty, teasing comment I make. And it's not because she's as badass and tough as she appears. She's friendly enough with Mike. I'm pretty sure she dislikes me. Why? I have no idea. But I fully intend on finding out the reason. Even if I have to put up with her sour attitude toward me.

"Can I ask where we're going?"

"No, get on." Her tone is clipped, which pulls on the humor cords in my head.

I stuff my hands in my pockets. "What if you're trying to kidnap me?"

She makes a guttural, choking sound and jabs the helmet into my chest. "Why would I want to *kidnap* you, prep?"

"Why wouldn't you?" I take the helmet, and our fingers brush against each other, and a spark makes her fling her hand to her hair. She glares at me, trying to play off obvious electricity. I wink as I continue. "I am sort of an irresistible guy, if you haven't noticed."

"Trust me, you are ridiculously easy to resist." She scoffs like the mere idea of me makes her laugh. I frown and try to figure her out, but her stone exterior makes it easier said than done. She lets out a tired breath. "Look, can you just get on? I've been doing good with my grades since last year, and I don't need some random frat guy messing with it."

"Random frat guy?" I gasp. "I'm offended in every sense of the word." When she scowls at me like she's imagining stabbing me, I chuckle and tug on the helmet. "Turn that frown upside down, Rossa." I watch her eye me skeptically. To blow her mind even further, I get on the bike and look at her expectantly. She stands there on the curb, staring at me with an unreadable expression. I don't drop my smile as her head tilts, eyes roaming my face.

Finally, she gets on in front of me, and I wrap my arms around her slender waist. I think I hear a small gasp from her, but it drowns out when she curls the engine alive. "The name's Red," she murmurs before swiftly putting on her red helmet and taking off.

An hour later, we're holed up in the back of the library computer room. The last of the people working in here leaves in a hushed conversation, shutting the door behind them. We've been working on our story. Or at least trying to. All we've gotten done is two chapters, and then we sort of hit a wall.

Googling how to strike inspiration, I cued up some music to jog my creative flow while she stares at the Word document like it will write the words for her.

Sighing as another song ends, I turn to her in my rolling chair. She hasn't moved an inch since the last time I glanced at her, face staring down the blinking cursor. I want to pull her away from the screen and make her smile somehow. Relax her a little. But a noise in my ear clearly screams that doing so would most likely end with me sporting a nasty black eye.

So, instead of getting punched, I decide to cue up another song. A random rock-and-roll band I've never heard of. She seems to know who they are, though, because she turns to me, thumb under her top teeth. Her nail clips her teeth as she squints her eyes.

"Didn't know you listened to rock," she accuses.

"What? How can you not? I have a tattoo of this lead singer's face."

Her eyes narrow even further.

"Seriously?"

"Yeah, seriously."

Of course I don't, but she doesn't have to know that.

"Okay." She crosses her arms. She doesn't believe me. Hell, I don't believe me. "Then show me," she demands in a monotone voice. Geez, is she always this serious? Where's the girl that called me slow when she first met me? Sure, she was insulting me, but she seemed genuinely lighter then. It bugs me to wonder what happened since then.

"Fine." I stand up and unbutton my khaki pants.

She lifts her pierced eyebrow, then scrunches it when I slowly undo the zipper. I begin to tug my pants down, praying she's going to stop me.

"You can stop now. I don't need to see your pale ass," she says and gets up and sits on the table. I sit next to her and, to my surprise, she doesn't move.

I chuckle. "My ass is *not* pale." She looks up at me, and I playfully bump my shoulder into hers. I elicit a small smile on her lips. And I want to do anything to make it stay there. "Hey. Why don't we take a break? Recuperate for a bit, then come back with a fresh perspective?"

She doesn't respond, seemingly deep in thought. "Why not? I swear, if I think about this freaking story for another second, my head might explode."

I hop down and hold out my hand, smiling. "I wouldn't want that."

She ignores my hand and hops down herself. I just laugh and follow her out of the building. We end up strolling mindlessly in town. It's a bit chilly but not so cold it bites my skin. It ruffles her golden hair and makes the tip of her ears red. The sun is beginning to set, and the soft orange and vibrant pink against her creamy skin is close to illegal. So beautiful. And seemingly, so unaware. She stares straight ahead, unknowing of my admiration of her beauty that's kind of heart-stopping.

Suddenly, she stops walking. Her face is scrunched up, and she's staring at the ground. I look down, expecting to find a dead rodent or something, but come up empty. When she doesn't say anything for a while, I walk over to her.

"What's wrong?" I ask.

She snaps her head up and smiles like a light bulb went off in her head. I focus on the brightness of her cheeks and her lip ring pinching her full pink lip. "I just figured it out."

"What?" I'm smiling from ear to ear, enjoying the new look on her, her full-fledged smile. My heart stutters and stammers and becomes incoherent. The wind picks up, and it takes every fiber in my bones to not push her flying hairs behind her ears.

"We're writing a story about a badass girl, but you're more of an ass than bad," she says.

"Um, offended, much?" I chuckle, but I'm really fine with it, as long as she's all lit up like a Christmas tree wearing a leather jacket.

She waves a hand and steps forward. "How can we write a story where you don't understand one of the MCs like that?" I can see the wheels of her writer brain churning. It must be the reason for her sudden perkiness.

"I understand, Magenta," I joke.

She pauses. "Shut up." Then she's turning on her combat boots and briskly walking back to the library. I'm stunned and grinning, then chasing after her. My long strides make it kind of hard to keep up, but with a side-eye, she does and picks up her pace, her hair flowing behind her, cheeks flushed from the wind.

"So how am I supposed to 'understand' her better?"

"By doing shit she would do," she says.

"And what would she do?"

"Dunno." She shrugs. "I'll figure it out."

"How would *you* know?"

"Because we're connected."

"How does that work—"

"Shut up, she's my muse," she argues. When we're at the library, we hop onto our bike, then we're off into the night. I quickly wrap my arms around her, and I swear I hear a sound from her. But a few minutes later, we're slowing to a stop before I can decipher if that sound was real or my imagination.

"She brought you here?" I look up at the YMCA building. It looks closed.

"Yup. Either that or she meant UCLA, but we don't exactly have time for a trip to Cali, so…" She trails off, swinging her legs off the bike. She unclips my helmet, staring into my awaiting green eyes…then places the helmet on one of the handles. I smirk as she quickly turns away from me, clearing her throat, and jogs up to the definitely closed building.

"But why would she come here?" I follow behind her, looking around aimlessly. My phone tells me it's eleven.

"Dunno," she says, her voice kind of strained. Like she's really focused on something…I don't understand until I finally look at her again. She's on one knee in front of one of the double doors, picking equipment in the keyhole.

"Whoa! What are you doing?"

"Holding a tea party," she says sarcastically.

"Funny."

"Thanks."

"Seriously, what the hell, Red?"

"Don't bitch and…" She twists the handle, a low creak emitting. She looks over her shoulder with a smile mixed with excitement and self-accomplishment. "Step inside my muse's desire."

I really shouldn't be doing this. I should be in my bed, getting sleep for tomorrow's classes. I've already missed today, and I feel guilty enough. Yet here I am, breaking into a YMCA at eleven at night. Well, to be fair, *I* didn't break into it, per se—

"Come on, princess," she says, standing up, stashing the equipment in her leather jacket pocket. Widening her eyes and grabbing my arm, she hisses, nudging me toward the opened door. "Before someone sees and calls the *cops*."

Huffing out, I give in and enter the cold, desolate building. I look around at the handmade banners, the pamphlets, and the lit-up vending machine.

"This way." She tugs at my shirt, toward the right. I follow behind her but run into her when she suddenly stops. "No…" She turns to the left of the branched-out hallway, pointing. "Down here."

"This is weird and illegal and—"

Red cups her small hand on my mouth as we walk, looking around like she's waiting for something to jump out at us. "Shut up," is all she says.

A smile melts onto my face. "Fine…Magenta, you're insane," I whisper.

"She says shut the fuck up too." Red laughs. Properly laughs. Seriously.

I smile even more. Following her, Magenta—who*ever*—to a glass door that reads: ***Pool Room***. "What the—" Red's hand stops me while the other clamps around the door handle. Slowly, she pushes it open and drags me inside.

The pool lights are left on, illuminating her half-grin, half-smirk, one hundred percent beautiful face. I look around the spacious room, at the glowing pool without the plastic dividers for training swimmers.

"What now?" I ask, nearing the pool.

"This," I hear behind me.

I spin on my heels, and my eyes widen. She's undressing in front of me. "Red!" I'm flustered as she shuffles around, laughing at me. "W-what are you doing?" I sputter.

"What does it look like?" Her voice is close.

I peek between my long fingers.

She's full-fledged smiling at me, teeth and all. *Mocking* and all. I fully remove my hands after she huffs, impatient. I swallow thickly. She's all skin and hips and sexy red underwear and loose blonde hair...I shift and let my eyes seamlessly roam her slim, curvy body.

"Never seen a half-naked girl before?" Her voice is soft, husky...gorgeous.

"I..." I try to speak, but I can't stop staring, soaking in her beauty and shape.

Her lips curl up before she brushes past me, slowly and sinfully. I watch her, damning her and lusting after her at the same time. Once at the pool's edge, she casts a dangerous look over her shoulder.

"See you on the flip side," she croons, voice like silk.

And then, in one swift move, she's gliding through the water. I take a step forward, and she pops up, turns around, swims over to the edge. She pushes up, resting her head on her crossed arms. Eyes strong, lips curvy, and ass raised.

"Join me...?" Her voice leaks something strong and steamy: sex pops up along my tongue, which I use to wet my lips.

Fuck...

And then, in one swift move, I'm taking off my shirt.

Chapter Eleven

The water is lukewarm, but her intense gaze trained on me makes it feel like it's boiling. Her eyes are bluer and clearer than the water. Oceans of another world that I want so desperately to swim in. She passes by me, taking long, soulful strokes. Her skin is soft and hot to the touch as she brushes against me, foot colliding with my thigh. I quirk a smile and turn around to her teasing smile and batting eyelashes as she flings a seductive look over her shoulder.

"Sorry, didn't see you there," she says in that lazy, raspy voice of hers. Too sexy for me to not smile like an idiot.

"Sure you didn't." I sarcastically nod, swimming backward. I hold eye contact with her as I paddle back, until my back meets the cold hard tiles. She smirks just the slightest, and I smile wider. There's a silent connection, an energy passing through us. Each second that neither of us acts on it is slowly driving me insane. I want to swim over to her and just take her lips in mine and—

I'm splashed by her foot.

Gaping at her, I exclaim, "What was that for?"

She's laughing a snort-filled laughter as she says, "You looked constipated. We can't leave any evidence behind, unless you don't mind spending two nights in jail for B&E."

"B&E?" I ask, and she descends into mocking laughter. "Didn't know I made a joke." I splash at her, using my hands like a normal human being.

She groans and pushes off the wall, swimming toward me. "Right. My fault, I forgot you're such an innocent little lamb…" She treads in front of me, and my heart slows as she exudes a breath. "You haven't committed any crimes in your…how old are you?"

"And help you make fun of me? I don't think so."

She squints her eyes. "I'm going with nineteen. You've got a real baby face." She moves her hand to pinch my cheek. I bite at her finger, and she snaps her hand back, squealing in the cutest way that makes my heart stop and a smile take up my entire face. "Shut up," she snaps, pinching my bicep.

"Ouch! That wasn't very nice." I squeeze her hip, and she gasps.

"Oh, you're going down, prep!" she declares.

"Bring it." I pinch her again, and a wonderful snort/laugh bursts out of her mouth. She lunges for me, and we go under. I spin us around, and her stomach vibrates with soundless laughter. I smile widely, gliding my hands up to her lower back as we emerge. We both gasp for air, and she smacks my shoulder. I let her and whip my head around, splashing her with water from my hair.

"Gross! Don't do that, you idiot!"

"Too late."

"Noah," she whines.

"Red," I mock her.

She just rolls her eyes and tries to appear all big and bad, but I see the tiniest hint of a smile curving her full lips. "You're annoying. You know that, don't you?"

I shrug, not letting my grin fall. "Actually, I don't. I was an only child, so I didn't have anyone to annoy really." I pause and clear my throat. "How about you?" This is my subtle way of learning more about her. Right now is the perfect time to do that before we get out and she's more closed off.

She tugs on her lip ring, cheeks flushed. "I...have a sister."

"Must have a hard life."

She gives me a confused look. But also kind of...*sad*?

"I mean, not having a name and all." I run my hand over my hair.

She cracks a sort of relieved smile. "She does have a name." She pauses, and I raise an expectant brow. She punches me in the shoulder. Lightly. "Harley."

"Cute name," I comment honestly.

She punches me again, but a lot harder. "Wipe that grin off your face; she's fifteen years old."

"Okay, I wasn't...I didn't mean to smile like *that*. Geez." I groan playfully as I rub my shoulder. In reality, I like that she's so protective over her little sister. Just knowing she has one makes her seem a little more human. A little more fragile, in a way. She's just always been so hard and badass that it warms my heart to know she really cares about her little sister.

"Oh…" she says and spins in a slow circle.

I watch her for a little bit. "Yeah. I've got my eyes on another Sylvetti anyway."

Did I just say that…for real?

She stops spinning and looks at me with wide eyes. Her mouth opens, then it falls, and she rolls her eyes. "Shut up," she huffs out with a scoff.

"No." I move toward her. Stalking ever so slightly, one step after the other… "In fact, she's a few feet away from me. Wearing sexy-as-fuck underwear. And her cheeks are just the right amount of pink."

"Better watch it, prep." She wags a warning finger my way, but a smile rests on her pink lips. Her chest's rising and falling faster, her heart most likely accelerating with each quickening step. "I said to watch it—Noah!"

She takes a leap backward, but I hook an arm around her waist.

"Not so fast!" I shout before swirling her around.

"Noah!" She laughs and giggles—I think I faint for a second—and wraps her arms around my neck. I hug her tighter, revel in the light sound falling from her full lips. My chest swells, and I find myself laughing as well. I love the way she laughs, how her eyes crinkle, and the feeling of her black-painted nails pinching my skin as she holds on tightly.

Why isn't she like this all the time? She looks so beautiful in this moment. Not that she isn't drop dead gorgeous 24/7...but she isn't this open and bubbly and so utterly *cute*. From the time I've known her, I never thought *Red* and *cute* would be in the same sentence. But they feel meant to be as I stare at her gleaming blue eyes and wandering fingertips.

Her laughter softly fades away, the only sound being our breathing. She looks into my eyes, and I stare right back. I don't notice it, but her legs are on my thighs, her hips touching mine. She's standing so close. My hands are cupping her curvy hips. Her chest rises and falls in a pattern that matches mine, and I swear I hear her suck in a breath when my thumb finds its way to her cheek. I push back hair behind her small ears, and she rests her chin on the inside curve of my thumb and pointer finger. Warm. So warm. And her eyes close just slightly...

But they pop open at the last second, lips snarling, eyes glistening with mischief I don't understand until I'm plunged underwater. We spin as she twists, and I grapple onto her waist. She's laughing under the water and kicks away from me. I swim after her as she takes big strokes toward the other end of the massive pool. When I swim to the surface, I gasp for air and finally hear her maniacal laughter.

"Hey! Get back here!" I shout, and my voice ricochets off the tile walls. Our frantic kicking and splashing and her shrieking and laughing and spinning around like a flawless swan slicing through the water is all too much. I dive underwater, stare at her perfectly shaped butt and long legs curving through the water.

When I pop back up, she's still rotating, showing off her impressive swimming, and says, "Never in a million years." The way she sing-songs it and faces me with a smirk makes my heart leap, and my eyes squint with a mission. Her own widens as I lurch forward, grazing her hip. But she twists and continues splashing around and swimming like a maniac.

"Come here, Rossa." I lurch forward again, but with more effort.

"No way—hey!"

I grab her hand, spin her around. We're spinning by the sheer, quick movement and laughing, and she's pressing her nose into my cheek. I hold my hand out to brace for impact as we near the tile wall. We're out in the eight feet section. I lean on the wall, one arm propped up on top of the floor, while the other is latched around her slim waist. She's pressed against me. Nearly bare chest against my naked one.

It hits me all at once how immensely close she is to me, practically naked. Her breathing is shallow, and I swallow and lick my lips. I watch closely, gawking really, as she licks hers, then slowly tugs on her lip ring. She reaches up and places her hands against my chest. I focus my eyes onto hers, letting my brows fall into a frown. Is she going to push me away? Is she going to revert back to the cold Red, or is she going to remain Red: the girl with the beautiful laugh and even better smile?

"What are you doing, prep?" she asks softly and

gently runs her fingertips up the back of my neck. I shiver and hold her closer. Skin to skin. She is so incredibly warm and soft and…

"I don't…" I pause and catch my breath, eyes falling onto her open mouth. "Do you want me to let go?" It hurts to even ask because I do not want to lose the feeling of her body flush against mine. To not have her scream at me because I *am* touching her. The realization that she's quiet and accepting and, if I dare say, comfortable, makes my heart swell that my heart skips a beat. Literally.

Her eyes light with an unknown emotion. They seemingly take a mental image of my face. Of the water dripping off my jaw, to my hair falling over my forehead. I reach up and push it back. She watches with fascinated eyes as I let it slowly fall, landing on her cheek swelling with red. Her eyes flutter closed just the slightest, like butterflies flapping gracefully.

I lean forward, my forehead resting on hers. I feel like we're in a bubble in our own world…like in the story.

I want to capture this moment. Paint it. Hang it in a museum…no. I want this moment to ourselves.

I'm greedy for her. She makes me so greedy. I'm starving for her. I want her.

But she jerks away, treading water. She pauses, mouth frozen apart, looks regretful, then says in a low voice, "We should go before a security guard catches us or something…"

The words sting, and I want to shove the words back in her mouth. Press my own lips against hers. Feel her warmth again. I feel instantly cold, submerged in a lake of ice. But instead of doing what every fiber of me desires, I give her a curt nod.

Her eyes hold all the words I want her to say: "Don't go. I changed my mind. *Kiss me*." But she stays silent and ends up looking away.

"Sure. Yeah. Let's go." I climb out of the pool, feeling extremely hurt. I shouldn't be this hurt, shocked. I mean, we are total complete opposites. How I could think she'd actually feel something for me? I'm not even sure if she likes me, let alone is attracted to me. She barely gives me the time of day, after all. So why the hell would she let me kiss her? I should probably just lay off her, not catch any feelings for her more than I already have.

But as we're riding back to campus, I think, *That's much easier said than done.* Because damn it, she smells good. Like vanilla, but also something else…*danger*.

Chapter Twelve

A week has passed since Red and I broke into that YMCA. One full week since she's cut all communications with me. I haven't heard any word from her. I've tried countless times calling and texting her but I've gotten no reply, so I've stopped trying and have given her her space. I try my best to not make assumptions or anything, which is easier said than done. I just mean, it sucks a little that she would ditch me like that. Especially after our little...*moment* in the pool.

Despite how hard she tries to appear all the time, I saw a different side to her. A lighter side that knew how to smile and laugh and play around. She was teasing but not mocking or in an underhanded sardonic manner like usual. She can admit it or not, but she's different when she's around me. It's like whatever rests on her shoulders constantly, dragging her down, lifts and I give her a chance to breathe. I want to relieve her of whatever's weighing her down again. If only she didn't fall off the face of the freaking earth.

"Hey, you okay?" Rachel asks, nudging me gently. The worried expression splayed on her petite face tugs at my heart strings.

"Yeah. I'm sorry. I was zoned out for a bit," I apologize and run a hand over my hair.

I feel like a prick. I've been so wrapped up in my own head, I focused on myself and the confusing situation with Red and me, effectively blocking her out. She's been kind enough to accompany me to art club every day, introducing me to her friends and getting me back in my groove painting-wise. So far this week, I've created several art pieces that caught the eye of the instructor, Mrs. Turner. Rachel's been a great friend, and I've been a self-centered bastard who hasn't been that grateful.

"Really. I am very sorry. Maybe we can grab a bite to eat after this?" I suggest, giving her my utmost attention. But she laughs and holds up her hands, telling me to back off a bit, but in a nice way. Blushing, I pull away and think to myself, *How horrible am I really with girls? And why haven't I noticed before?*

"I have a study group with a few friends after this," she says, "but you can join if you want…"

I begin to deny, but then I stop myself and think what the hell else do I have to do? The list of guys that made the team goes up today, but that could be a total bust. Once I'm out of the art room, I'm a sack deprived of inspiration and creativity. I've been painting so long on my own that, once pulled from my comfort zone, I've shriveled up and lost my touch. Either that or I'm more acclimated to painting girls after I've fooled around with them.

So I let out a breath and shrug. "Sure, why the hell not?"

A few minutes later, I'm sitting on a stool in front of an empty canvas. Since it's Friday, we have free range to use what we've learned through the week to make whatever the hell we want. But I have no clue as to what I want to paint. I have creator's block, and it sucks. It blocks my mind from thinking of the cool things that usually bounce around my head so much, it's the reason I keep a sketchpad on me at all times. Maybe if I walk around I'll be hit with some sort of nugget of inspiration.

Setting my brush down, I stroll over to the wall of students' works.

I can't tell if the painting I'm looking at is portraying a man sitting on the toilet or a man contemplating suicide. Either way, there's a man...I think. That's the problem with abstract art: it's half-illusion, half-imagination. You choose what the painting represents. Let your heart decide if a man is shitting or choosing between a gun and pills. Art leaves everything on the canvas and lets you decide. It's one of the many things I adore about it.

A painting of a boy holding a girl with red lips catches my attention as I'm looking at the student's art on one wall. I take three long strides backward. But the painting isn't what I thought. It's a man biting into an apple. My mind is playing tricks on me, yet...I feel a jolt of inspiration run through my veins.

I rush over to my easel, eager to erase every inch of white on the canvas. As I dip my brush in the black paint, I wonder, *When did I pick up the brush?* Stroke after stroke, I quickly sketch the bodies, faces, go into graver detail. My eyes jot back and forth quickly as I mix colors, creating a colorful background. I stand and gently paint her lips, create his playful smile. His eyes are lush forest green, hers blue like the wings of an exotic butterfly.

Minutes pass, or seconds, or an eternity—I can never really tell when I'm painting.

"Noah?" a soft voice says.

They may as well have been from Mars, because I could barely hear them as I focused on her golden hair.

"Noah?" the voice calls again. This time it's followed by my arm being squeezed gently.

"Huh?" I snap out of my little bubble and turn around. Rachel is beaming at me, and the instructor is staring at my quick painting. It could have been five minutes, but I feel like I've been painting for hours.

"You just made this?" the instructor asks, stepping closer with curious eyes. "*Just* now?" She's staring at me behind her winged eyeglasses.

My cheeks burn. "Um, yes?"

Her jaw slacks, and she turns back to the painting. "Interesting…"

"This is so…beautiful. Haunting, really. You can see how much he cares for her from the way he's looking at her."

"Thanks." I blush.

"Have you thought of entering the contest?" Ms. Turner asks me.

"What contest?"

Rachel answers. "It's a contest where, if you win, you get the chance to be a prodigy of Luc Van Wilkson."

My eyes bug out of my head as I gape. "Luc Van Wilkson? The son of the guy who followed in Picasso's footsteps?" I've looked up to that man and followed his works for *years*. Getting to be his prodigy would be mind-blowing. Crazy. Freaking scratch-that-off-my-bucket-list crazy.

"Yes." She pauses. "You'd be perfect for it because *this*," she gestures to the painting and chuckles, "this is freaking incredible. It'd be stupid of you to not even try. So…wanna give it a shot?"

"I don't know." I rub the back of my neck. I want to jump at the chance to be taught under that man's influence. To be by his side and learn so much from him, from basically Picasso himself…it'd be a dream come true. But what if I'm not good enough? Art is a hobby, a passionate hobby of mine, but what if he sees what I can do and laughs in my face?

"Think about it, okay?" Mrs. Turner sighs and looks at the painting with a forlorn expression. "Your talent would be a helluva waste otherwise." Then she walks over to a guy next to me and begins chatting with him about his work.

Rachel places a small hand on my wrist, eyes and smile warm. "Just give it a shot. You'll hate yourself if you don't."

My phone buzzes in my pocket. Holding up a finger to excuse myself, I slide it out onto my palm and look at the screen. My eyes double in size. It's a text from Ty, saying he needs the room to "entertain" a lady friend and that the list for those who made the team is up outside the stadium.

I jump to my feet, shrugging on my jean jacket. "I've gotta go. The list for the team is up."

"I'll come with," she says.

"You don't have to." I don't want to drag her away from this.

"I want to, dummy." She smiles softly, and we leave promptly, excitement admittedly fizzing under my skin, eliciting goosebumps even though I told myself to not get attached. But I think my plan of ducking my head for the semester is shot to shit, don't you think? From Red, to the art club, to football, to the short story I've worked on myself, I'm a full-on college student. I don't know how to feel about it.

There's a large, buzzing crowd in front of the cork board in front of the stadium. Leaving Rachel to the side away from the bustle of guys, I push through the crowd, bypassing more pissed-off guys than victorious ones. As I get closer and the paper comes into view, my heart is out of control. My palms begin to sweat, so I tell myself that this doesn't matter. That I am only here because I was forced to be here. That they didn't say I had to join the football team. But it's all lies. I want to be on the team. I want to be a part of something, I realize as I am smack dab in front of the paper.

"Noah Wells, Noah Wells..." I mutter under my breath as my eyes scroll up and down the list, frantically. Desperately. I'm bouncing on my heels, biting into my palm lightly, when I see it.

Noah Wells**, it reads, **jersey number: 14.

Relief, shock, accomplishment, and elation push through me in waves. I can't believe I actually made it. I'll admit, I was good in high school. But college football is more prestigious and important somehow. Scouts from the actual NFL often sit in. It's broadcast on television. And I made it through the difficult tryouts. I'm still surprised I didn't flunk my way through it. But I guess when you want something enough, you're almost guaranteed to get it.

"The newbie got in. Guess there is no budget on Daddy's card, huh?" a familiar voice slurs behind me.

I turn around to face Ian, who's sporting a shit-eating grin. "Wasn't money that bought me that spot; pure talent and determination. Both things I'm sure you're lacking in."

A few guys overhearing whistle, and he chuckles, eyes low and dark.

"How do you think I got the captain position?" he says.

I shrug. "Maybe you took a different version of suck up, used it on Coach."

His face melts into rage as guys chuckle. "You'd be a fucking expert at that. I mean, you haven't banged Red yet? Which is utterly fucking shocking since once you get some liquor in her, promise she's a pretty girl, she's a real easy piece of ass…" He pushes his black hair behind his studded ear.

Heat overtakes my cheeks as I say, "What the *fuck* did you just say?" He would never know Red in *that* way, right? I barely know her, but something tells me she wouldn't go for pricks like *him*. That weird guy she brought to class, yeah, definitely. But rock bottom is Ian.

"You heard me—" he begins to sneer.

I grab his shirt and push him into the bulletin board. "I will fucking kill you..." I promise in a tone that scares even me. By the looks of it, he's surprised as well, because his dark eyes widen just the slightest tad...then he bursts into mocking laughter.

He raises his hands. "Oh, please don't hurt me," he whines, popping out his bottom lip. A few guys chuckle.

"Definitely not worth it, Noah." Rachel pulls me from the group and pats my arm as she pulls us around the bend, into the bustling activity of students who have five classes rather than four.

"I'm sorry, I'm sorry. I have no idea what just came over me. He was just talking about Red and I..." I run my hands over my hair. I need to stop pulling at it or I'll go bald in the near future, so I pull out a red beanie I keep in my pocket and tug it on. She watches me and seems to be fighting an internal fight within herself. "What?"

"You mean Red? Red Sylvetti?" she asks, and I nod, and that fight turns into an outright battle of the century. "She's utter bad news, Noah. You should stay away from her."

I laugh. "I think I can handle a little bad."

"No, I'm being serious. She's someone you run away from, not toward," she says in a serious, low tone that sends shivers across my skin.

I should be listening to her, taking her words to

heart. The look in her eyes screams knowledge. Like she knows just how bad Red is. I want her to tell me more, to explain why I should stay away because, so far, it's been a hell of a lot easier said than done. I feel this sort of pull toward her. Like the positive end of a magnet seeking the connection of a negative end. If what Rachel is implying is true, Red is a damn inferno of bad news, dangerous. And I'm that stupid moth that doesn't know danger when he sees it. I just keep flying closer and closer, hoping for a sweet heaven, only to be fried to death.

I begin to follow her to her study group, but a nagging feeling telling me to turn around stops me. I wheel around and my breath catches. Up ahead is Red being man-handled by a huge security guard. My hands curl into fists, and I take a step toward them as Red begins shouting and spitting curses in and out of Spanish. Funny, I didn't know she knew Spanish.

"Wait." Rachel grabs my hand, halting me. She gives me a concerned look. "Where are you going? I thought we were going to the study group."

I open my mouth, but Red threatening to kick the guard where the sun doesn't shine cuts me off.

I give Rachel an apologetic glance. "I'm sorry, but I'll catch up with you."

Her face falls slightly. "But—"

"Later, Rach. I'll be there soon, promise." I squeeze her hand, sporting a grin. She smiles a little, but the frown in her eyes doesn't diminish in the slightest. Letting her hand go, I jog over to the arguing duo.

"Hey, Red. What's going on here?" I ask,

making sure to maintain my easy breezy smile. I haven't seen her in a week and this is how I find her? Threatening to kick a security guard?

The guard scowls at me, like I'm adding onto a mountain pile of issues. "*This* one was caught smoking weed on campus, which she knows is punishable by suspension or *worse*." He spits his words directly at her, tugging at her arm. She growls at him in response, which he responds with an eye roll. "And suspected to mess with the fire alarm, which is punishable by time in *jail*."

"She wouldn't do that," I quickly say.

But one glance at Red's hidden smirk tells me something different.

Oh geez, Red.

My smile doesn't falter. "Why don't you just book her for the smoking? But the fire alarm, anyone could have done that."

"She was caught red-handed," the guard says.

"Says who?" I ask.

"Says her hand with the red paint; the alarm was painted over earlier." He holds up her right hand that is indeed smothered in red paint.

Her smile is wicked and adorable at the same time. "Whoops," she says with a shoulder shrug, eyes glinting with trouble. *She* is trouble. And the bad kind…and I'm kind of turned on right now.

"Now, will you move out of the way? She's gotta see the chancellor, let him decide which jail her little ass should be thrown in." He jostles her violently, and I step forward. He looks me up and down like I've lost my mind. "You must've lost your damn mind. Boy, if you don't move out of the way—"

A piercing wailing alarm punching the air cuts him off.

"What the—" He looks around, letting Red's hand go.

Big mistake.

"Come on, pretty boy." Red grabs my hand and begins running onto the campus. I follow after her, heart thundering in my chest, blood rushing up to my cheeks. We run so fast, too fast, our feet barely touching the ground. The guard screams for us to stop, but he's drowned out by her laughter and my "oh, shit!"

Cutting through a group of students, we take a sharp left. I grip her hand, making sure she doesn't fall, but she doesn't seem to need my help. She moves so deftly, turns so sharply, I know for a fact this isn't her first time running from authority.

One of the many tattoos on her right arm peeking from her leather jacket and us running toward her Chevy Impala sets off a thousand warning bells. All telling me the same thing: *Run the other way. She is dangerous, dude!*

I tell them to fuck off and laugh along with her.

The minute we slide into her car, which smells strongly of lemon and beer and stale cigarettes, she jams the key in the ignition and peels out of the parking lot. Our breaths are uneven, my smile physically hurts me, and I feel like I'm floating over Emerald City.

"That...was *insane*," I finally say after a while of silence.

"That was nothing compared to..." She trails off

119

and smirks at me. "I've said too much already."

My heart jumps unsteadily, and I look sideways at her, enraptured by her raccoon eyes and ripped band t-shirt and leather jacket and combat boots, and listen to the Nirvana song blaring through the radio. Mesmerized by the way her black-painted fingers, chipped and all, bounce along the wide steering wheel.

"You are something bad, Red. Something...*bad*," I say around an air of fascination.

She meets my eyes for one fleeting, smoldering second before the car accelerates, and my heart too, and she says, "You just now noticing, babe?"

Chapter Thirteen

I let the questions rumbling around in my head go unspoken for forty-five minutes. Despite the fact that I have no idea where we are going, I am not a spontaneous being. Like, at all. I like plans, organization. Call me a nerd, but there is nothing more satisfying than a day going exactly according to plan. Even when I was traveling, I planned everything: my hotel bookings, flights, where and what I was going to eat, etcetera.

Hanging around Red has put a major halt in everything related to routine. She makes days exciting, spontaneous. Freaking *exciting*. I should be fretting over how much she's changed me in the little time I've known her, but all I can seem to do is smile at her like the creep I'm slowly but surely becoming.

"Where have you been?" The question slips out before I can stop it.

Her eyes stay on the road. "I had to take care of some things. My sister, uh, she got into trouble. You understand, right?"

"Not really. I was an only child."

"Must've sucked."

"Oh, it did. But luckily, I had my army of butlers to keep me company," I joke and sneak a peek at her. She's stifling a smile, but it's enough to make me grin and look back onto the road.

It's silent for the next few minutes. All spent with me throwing long gazes at her. Watching the way she grips the leather steering wheel with one hand, using the other to mindlessly play with a gold curl of her hair. Her nails are slathered with dark blue paint, and there are holes in her jeans, showing off her creamy skin.

"Am I gonna have to pull over and ditch your creepy ass, or are you gonna stop staring at me like my uncle Amos?" she says, shooting me a sideward glance. "He gets handsy and redneck-ish after his third glass of red wine at Thanksgiving dinner. Me and Harley slipped him a roofie last year." She chuckles behind her knuckles, shaking her head. "Good times. How about you? Slipped any of your relatives date rape drugs?" She's looking at me freely now since we're driving down an isolated road, trees on either side.

"No." I chuckle and end up laughing, straightening up. "I have not, unfortunately." I lay my head slack against the seat, facing her with a barely there smile. "What'd you guys do to him while he was unconscious?" She opens her mouth, but I hold up a finger and add, "Though you can keep it between you and your sister if it's illegal."

Her lips puff into a disappointed pout. "Oh, damn. Then nothing. I guess..." She sighs so dramatically, I would have believed she did something totally illegal if she hadn't. Her teeth glisten like shined pearls as she turns to me and says, "We took off all his clothes and had Chad, Harley's gay friend who came cause his family's a homophobic piece of shit, pose on his lap. Dude was wearing full-on makeup. When he woke up, the photoshoot was passed to each gen of the family." The radiant grin on her face should unnerve me, but it just pulls out a similar one out of me.

"Wait, why, though? I thought you'd, like, cut his hand off or something? Why strip him then have a guy pose on him?"

"Because he's a homophobic piece of trash too," she spits venomously, clutching the wheel. Her eyes return to the desolate road. "It was either that or tie him up and leave him in the park stream."

"Well, just for the record, I'm not staring at you because I'm your homophobic, asshole uncle," I say, and my eyes rove her side profile.

"Then why are you staring? Thinking of killing me out here?" she jokes.

"Hey. You're the one driving," I defend and pause. "I'm staring because you're beautiful."

Her lips fall apart, and I watch her swallow gently. Fingers dancing lightly on the wheel, she forces a smirk and looks at me. "Are you always this cheesy?" she asks.

"Only for you."

She chuckles to herself and says, "It's going to take more than pretty words and sticking around me for you to get anywhere *near* my pants."

I frown and shake my head. She thinks the only

reason I'm calling her beautiful and hanging around her is to get into her pants? If so, she is sorely mistaken. I really like her company and I like her, yes, but not for the sole reason of having *sex* with her.

"I'm not trying to have sex with you, Red," I say, gauging her furrowed brows and parted lips. I wait for her to say something, but when she doesn't comment, I lower my voice and confess, "I genuinely like hanging with you. Or whatever we're doing…you just intrigue me."

"Intrigue you?" she questions, flickering her eyes at me. "What? Am I some sort of art exhibit to you?" I sense the rise of anger and hostility in her voice. That and she's glaring at me like I've lost my mind.

"No. I know you're a person," I say with a playful eye roll. "You're just you. And I like it. You, I mean," I stammer, and she smiles at my inability to speak. "You are horrible. I take back what I said."

"Oh, no." She frowns and pokes my stomach, making me laugh and swat her hand away. "Don't stop confessing your love for me." Her crooked smirk is insatiable yet inviting.

"I'll stop whenever I very well feel like it." I reach over and twist up the volume. A rock song that's all drums and strong bass blasts through the speakers. Clearly she was rocking out to it before I got in here. "Nirvana, really?"

"Only the greatest band to bless this planet. RIP, Kurt." She does a salute.

"I think you mean Coldplay." I change the

station, and she smacks my hand away, then turns fully to glare at me like I told her Nickelback was the greatest band to ever exist. Even that's a bit of a stretch, and I didn't even say it.

"Get out," she commands.

"Great movie," I say sarcastically.

Her eyes laugh, but her mouth doesn't move from the straight line it's set in. "You know what I mean."

"I know." I smile a shit-eating grin. "I just like messing with you."

"I can see that." She turns the volume up, singing at the top of her lungs along to the grunge music. She looks so carefree and in her element, with her golden hair flying in the air. The car eats the road faster and faster, the music seemingly louder. "Sing along. I know you want to." Her eyes peer into mine, and my heart skips several beats. Like a pebble thrown across a great lake.

"Not until I hear Chris Martin."

Scoffing loudly, she reaches over and taps her nails along my knee. Her hand is warm and small, and I imagine them reaching up, but it stays put and she smirks at me. "Stop being a weirdo and sing along to an actual good band."

"Fine," I mutter, and when the chorus comes up, we both sing. Very, *very* loudly.

"Woo! There you go, prep. I knew you had it in you." She squeezes my thigh before running her hand through her hair. Her smile is contagious as she bobs her head as the next song comes on that I find myself grinning and staring more than before. Soaking in every curve, her eyes, and her tongue playing with her lip ring.

I have no idea how we ended up here or where we're even going, but I sit back and let her humming and drumming fingers unfold in front of me. In my mind, I am painting a mosaic of this moment.

Before my mind can catch up, I'm brushing my fingers along her wrist of the hand that's wrapped tightly around the joystick. Her words stutter, but she doesn't look over. Keeps her eyes on the road. I take this as invitation and run my fingers along her arm, her leather jacket rippling under my touch. Her tongue tugs at her lip ring harder, then caresses her upper lip, eyes darting over to me in her peripheral vision.

"What are you doing, prep?" she asks, voice quivering.

"Shhh." My fingertip brushes her unruly hair behind her ear. Her teeth sink onto her bottom lip and her eyes flutter for a brief second as I let my thumb linger over her warm cheek. I want so badly to just reach over and kiss her lips. To feel her skin against mine. But before I can do anything, the car jostles, and I reluctantly wrench myself back.

"Fuck," she curses sharply and pulls the car to the side of the road.

"What happened?" I ask.

"Let's see." She pops the door open after opening the hood.

I sit and think about what would have happened if I had done what I desired, if the car hadn't broken down. None of my thoughts are innocent. I get out and join her at the front of the car when she curses loudly. Smoke is spilling out of a part of the engine. I have no idea what's wrong with the car because I'm not a car guy in anyway, but she seems to know and groans, reaching in with a wrench I have no idea where she got from.

"Do you know what's wrong?"

"Yeah," she says shortly, putting her hands on her hips.

"And?"

"*And* I have to go to a body shop to fix it, can't do it here. Don't have the equipment." She leans over and her body jerks as she begins bashing the iron wrench in frustration. I keep my eyes focused on the smoke spilling out and *not* her ass in those black jeans that fit her too well. "Fuck it!" She pulls back quickly, slamming the hood close, then murmurs an apology. I smile at her affection toward the car she clearly loves but hates at the moment.

"Can we drive it to an auto shop? Maybe one's nearby?" I pull out my phone to Google any nearby shops.

"There aren't." She sighs and leans against the hood, biting her thumb. A few moments pass with her face scrunched up in thought. "Maybe I can fix it. Catch the nearest bus to a shop owned by a buddy of mine. But for now, we're staying at a motel," she says then rounds the car without another word.

"Motel?" I question in a fluster, slipping inside the car beside her.

"Yup." She presses on the key in the ignition. It sputters and groans, and she mutters, "Come on, baby. Come on," and the car roars to life. "Fuck, yes." Switching the gear to drive, she slams on the gas pedal and leaves a dust cloud behind us as she peels onto the long stretch of road.

"Motel?" I ask again. Something short of anticipation snakes across my lips, and I lick them quickly.

She sighs, lip ring taut between her teeth. "Yes, *motel*." She glances over at me, eyes roving around my confused expression. "Don't get any ideas. It's just to hold us over until I get my baby fixed. And I'm sure as hell not sleeping on the side of the road in this car."

"Where were we headed anyway?" I have to ask.

"A bar I was going to tend tonight in Penn. I'm good friends with the manager, and he pays me well. And I thought you could keep me company." She pauses and grasps for words, clearing her throat. "Plus I had a few ideas for the story." She looks at me hesitantly, brows caved in. "Sorry if I put you out of your way. Missing any exams?" I'm kind of surprised by her caring when she just whisked me away, but it's not like I was hesitant in jumping in the car behind her.

"No," I answer, and she exhales, looking back onto the road. "But even if there were any exams, I'd still rather be here with you." A risky thing to say, but I have to. Have to let her know how much she's getting under my skin. Thunder cracks in the sky, and she looks over at me, mouth hung slightly ajar. I hear the whisper of words she wants to say, basically feel it swim down my spine. But as lightning paints the gloomy sky, she faces the road, letting the thunder and purr of the jittering engine fill the silence.

Chapter Fourteen

Twenty minutes later, we pull up to a motel with their **'*VACANCY*'** sign glitching. There are a few cars scattered across the small parking lot. I wonder if these people got washed up here because of the sudden rain turned into a storm. The car simmers down to a croak as it shuts off. The sound makes Red close her eyes and sigh as if it pains her just to listen to it. Before I can say or do anything to soothe her, she murmurs, "Let's go," before swinging out of the car.

A bell above the creaky entrance door rings as we enter. A large man in plaid walks off, and we take his spot in front of the clerk. An old lady with snow white hair and crooked glasses looks at us.

"How may I help you tonight?" she asks, adjusting her falling glasses. But she ends up tucking them in her floral blouse, then smiles at us softly.

"What'dya got?" Red asks around a tired sigh.

"Hold on one moment, dear." The lady whose name is Ruby, based on the name tag on her blouse, turns to an aging computer and taps a few keys. "Hmmm...how do ya feel about a king?"

King. One bed.

Red lifts an eyebrow but doesn't comment.

"Do you have a double?" I ask on her behalf, my cheeks heating under her gaze.

"No." Ruby shakes her head solemnly, squints at us. "But that shouldn't be a problem for you lovely couple."

My cheeks double in heat. "We're not a couple—"

"We'll take it," Red cuts me off and nudges me. "Don't be so modest. You'll take the floor. I hear it's comfier than the beds in this place," she murmurs as she pulls out a few bills from her back pocket. "I'm basically doing you a favor."

"How will you be paying?" Ruby asks, clearly ignorant to Red's insult.

"Card." I slide out my MasterCard and hand it to her trembling, frail hand before Red can speak. She side eyes me so hard, I shiver but maintain a grin as Ruby processes it.

"Room 108," she informs, dropping a single key in my palm. "Enjoy."

On the way to the room, Red throws her elbow into my side.

"Ow! What the heck was that for?" I rub my aching ribs.

"I could have paid," she seethes, moving to stomp on my foot. I move out of the way, nearly bumping into a girl wearing a short dress being escorted into a room by a man in a suit. Guess not everyone is washed up here by accident...

"I didn't want you to. You already have the car to worry about getting fixed tomorrow," I explain, but she doesn't look less pissed. Which, by the way, I plan on helping with, even if it's just half of whatever the cost comes out to be. It'd just be rude if I didn't at least chip in.

Room 108 is relatively small in size. The king looks as Red guessed, unpleasant, and creaks as I test it out by sitting on the edge. But it will do. I slip off my shoes and set them by the door. By the time I turn around, Red's disappeared. I frown and take a step forward when I hear the groaning sound and water hitting tiles. Then I notice the bathroom door is cracked, golden light stretching across the stained carpet.

"Okay then." Blushing, I tug at my t-shirt. I pull off my jean jacket and place it on the hook on the back of the door. I look around, not knowing what to do. I end up checking my phone. I don't know what I'm searching for, but I have to keep my mind busy. I kept thinking about Red and me sharing the bed, even if she relegated me to the floor. The thought of us sleeping in the same room is still unnerving, even if we're five feet apart.

I have a few worried messages from Mike and Ty, even more and a few missed calls from Rachel, and one single call from my mother. She left a voicemail, but I don't plan on listening to it. She probably just called to make sure I haven't gotten dragged into a fighting ring. I return the messages from my friends, have a relieved conversation with Rachel, and text my mother that I'm headed to bed and to not look out for a call from me anytime soon.

132

By the time I've calmed Rachel, I feel a presence in the room. I stiffen, send the message, and click off my phone. I turn to find Red staring at me. My breath stutters. She has a small towel wrapped around her slim body.

"You wanna go next?"

"Um…" I look down at my soaked clothes. Even though we parked kind of close to the entrance, we got struck by the rain. Heavily. And I'll smell if I don't change or get sick if I don't at least shower. I stand and nod. "Yeah. I'll see about some candles." I gesture to the flickering fluorescent lights above. "You know, before we're in complete darkness."

She doesn't say anything for a while. "Okay." She nods.

"Yup." I nod back.

We don't say anything before she raises a brow. "Well? Aren't you going to shower?" She holds up a palm in question.

"Right. Sorry." Blushing like a stupid school girl, I walk over to her. She steps to the side, but I brush past her, getting my arm wet. I hold in my groan and close the door behind me. I can practically feel her teasing smirk as I lean against the door.

This night should go by easy-peasy, I think sarcastically.

Twisting the stuttering faucet to the hottest level, I peel off my wet t-shirt and jeans. Don't even get me started on my socks. I grimace as I throw them on the wet pile of clothes. There is nothing worse than wearing soaking wet socks. I pause before entering the shower. Red left her shirt in here. I make a mental note to bring it out when I'm leaving.

I step into the shower and, as I massage my scalp with the cheap scented shampoo, I think of Red.

I reminisce on our moment in the car before it broke down. How gorgeously rock and roll she looked singing to that Nirvana song and how at peace I felt by her side, watching her. Laughing with her. Singing with her. In the short time I've known her, I haven't seen her glow as bright and beautiful. I want her to remain as glowing and breathtaking because she looked happy. And as weird as it sounds, she made me happy just being *near* her, seeing her content.

She isn't what she appears to others. To me, *with* me, she seems different. Like herself. Not rough or hardcore. She is both, but when I'm near her, she smiles a little more. Glances at me some more. Especially when I touched her arm. I saw the flutter of her eyes. Her pulling on that lip ring of hers. I ignite something in her, and I want to do it again and again.

I climb out of the shower ten minutes later with a smile. I swipe my hand against the fogged-up mirror. Plush forest green eyes stare back at me above blushed cheeks and a smile. All because of her. I laugh to myself before splashing water on my face and curling hair. I run a small towel over my face and hair before turning to get dressed.

But the sight of my seeping clothes makes me grimace and pull on my boxers. That's it. The room will be dark anyway, so there's nothing to worry about. I hang up the clothes on the clothes rack, hoping they'll dry by morning, then swipe up Red's jacket and leave the room. The bedroom is pitch black, and I have no idea where to step without accidentally bumping into her.

"Red?" I call out.

Rumbling thunder is my response.

"Red?" I say again.

"Over here," she says, her voice barely a whisper.

"Okay." She must be on the bed, I think, as I remember the layout of the room. "You left your jacket in the bathroom. I'm gonna leave it on the nightstand. Which one do you want it on?"

"Here," she says, and before I can respond, she's standing in front of me, taking the wet, heavy jacket from me. Her body heat is massive and hits me in soft waves. I want to step forward, do something, but I'm frozen as I hear the jacket thud to the ground.

"What are you...?" My voice is rough, low.

"Shut. *Up*. Prep." Her words are harsh, but her palms cradling my face are soft.

My body stiffens as she pushes to her toes, barely meeting my eyes on a level playing field. I wrap my arms loosely around her and gasp under my breath. She isn't wearing any clothes. I look down to her and bite my lip at her black bra and red panties.

"Can I confess something?" I ask, and thunder cracks outside the window beside us. The moonlight pours in and bashfully dances across her open lips, her lip ring, and her heated gaze.

"Mhmm..." is her reply.

Her breath is warm, lips barely tracing mine. My heart hammers like a hummingbird under my skin, and I can feel hers doing the same thing against my chest. Her skin is warm like the sun, smooth like silk. My hands drop lower, lower. Her breath catches, gaze shading darker.

"I want to kiss you right now," I say.

She leans forward, lips sliding, brushing my skin against my ear. "Then do it," she whispers, kissing my earlobe gently.

The second she pulls back...I do.

Chapter Fifteen

My heart can barely contain itself. She intakes air sharply the same time I groan slightly. Our mouths drop open simultaneously, and I taste her all at once. My heart swoons and crashes at the same time. Her mouth tastes so good, so intoxicating. Cigarettes, and strawberries, and a cool, crisp mint rests between her full lips and tongue. Her metal tongue is cold as I slide my tongue against it, tugging gently with my teeth.

Lust and excitement and a foreign feeling buzzes through my veins. Electricity sparks as she tugs at my hair, then slowly glides her nails down my spine. I grunt in her mouth and push forward. I turn quickly, and we hit the bed sideways. She straddles me. I deepen the kiss. Fisting her hair, I tug back until our mouths glide against each other. She makes a groaning sound of frustration at the loss of contact, but it's quickly replaced by a moan as I suck on her long neck gently. Then harshly. Then softly, and repeat until she's grinding against me.

"Fuck, *Red*," I say in a low voice, clutching her

hips as she rolls them against mine.

"Keep…mmm, Noah," is her throaty, soft reply.

I feel so energized and aware of the little gasp she does when I *react* to this present situation…but she doesn't make fun of me or tease me. She moans and kisses my chin, then under my chin, silently telling me to kiss her on the mouth again. I don't hesitate to smash my lips on hers. To hold her face and deepen the kiss. Our tongues graze, and we both moan at the same time, and it's the best thing I've ever heard. I want to hear it again and again and—

She rubs herself against me, long and hard and slow. Every cell in my body explodes and constricts and bursts into flames. I flip her onto her back, pinning her to the bed. I stare down at her as we take deep breaths. Her dark blue eyes tell me what I'm thinking: if we go any further, neither of us will be able to hold back. Not one damn bit.

"Do you…do you want this, Red? Do you want me?" I ask her. I have to. I can't just force myself on her, no matter how willing she seems. I wouldn't ever do anything to her without her consent. That isn't who I am.

Cheeks flushed and eyes dilated, she nods and pulls me on top of her. "Yes, now shut up and come here." She slides a hand around the back of my neck and brings me down. Her lips are soft and her tongue is warm against mine.

Pulling away shortly, I brush my fingertips against her cheek and ask, "What is this, Red?"

"I don't…can we *not* totally fuck up the moment?" is her husky, lustful reply. She brings me back to her mouth, and I groan deeply. She moans lightly, her knee brushing my hip. I grab the back of her knee and wrap it around my waist; she kisses me harder. Her lips taste like cherry lip-balm, her tongue of addicting Marlboro cigarettes.

We roll around, hands wandering, body heat mingling together. I can hardly breathe at one point. Then I'm breathing roughly against her warm neck. Her tattoos glow under the moonlight, and I sit back and just admire every curve and line and blemish like an art piece.

"Stop with the staring. Jeesh," she groans before pulling me onto her.

When I lean down, she chuckles as my hands grope her stomach, fingers tickling gently. I want a laugh out of her. I want to feel her rumble in glee.

She giggles, and it is the most beautiful sound. I grin as she covers my neck with her mouth. Each lick and nibble elicits a moan from me. More tickling and more groans suppressing laughter.

"Noah!" she cries, feet kicking near my thighs.

"*Rossa*." My voice is deep as I lather her skin with my kisses, calling out her name in Italian. My tongue rolls, and she purrs a moan.

"Mmm, Noah." She drags her fingers up my back.

I can feel goosebumps form at her fingertips. My mind is telling me that we should discuss what this is, what we are…but I push that voice to the back of my mind, lock it up, and throw away the key. There's nothing more important than tasting my Red. Kissing my Red. Savoring *my Red*.

Sometime later, I'm holding her to my chest,

eyes half-open. I don't even know when it happened, but we tired each other out just by kissing and teasing and laughing. And I go to sleep safe and sound, all because of the girl named Red purring in content in my arms.

Chapter Sixteen

A flash of warmth and whispered giggles and moans wake me up the next morning. My brain is foggy, and I try to push past the thick foliage in search of something. I can't remember, not even as I push and push. So I focus on the flood of heat running through my skin. Opening my heavy eyes, they land on dirty windows and the sun blaring through them.

Weird. My bedroom doesn't have windows like that, I think with unease.

Sitting up in the creaky king bed, I look around carefully. It takes a few seconds of me assessing my surroundings to understand and remember where I am. The motel we washed up in because of the storm.

We.

Red and I.

Memories of her warm lips on mine, feeling her soft skin, and hearing her heavenly moans fill my head. My neck aches, and as I rub it, I remember her clutching it. Nails digging gently, rubbing my shoulders, my chest. Her hands were greedy as we rolled around in this bed. I clutch the sheets and can't even help the lazy smile that washes over me. I didn't see that coming. At all. But I want to relive it until it gets creepy. I want to feel her again.

I feel giddy. A wire of warmth spreads through my cheeks, traveling under my skin. Each thought of her smiling, looking blissful, whispering my name, kissing my lips, her cold lip ring—they make me feel different than I've ever felt with any other girl I've been with. They make me—*she* makes me—feel alive.

The bathroom door creaks open, and she walks out. She's topless and wearing jeans. It's suddenly hard to breathe. Just one look at her creamy skin exposed in front of me keeps my breath hostage. It's going to take some time getting used to this. That is, if we continue doing what we did last night. Which I am still confused over.

I want to ask her what the hell it was, but I also don't want to shatter the moment in my head, letting reality sink in and ruin everything. So I keep my mouth shut and just stare at her. And she stares back. The air is suddenly incredibly thick. She begins to play with her lip ring. Remembering the coolness as it pressed into me, as I tugged at it with my teeth…I fidget uncomfortably and run a hand over my hair.

"Morning," I say, breaking the thick silence.

Her mouth opens but then quickly snaps shut, concealing what she really wants to say. "We should go. I hiked to the auto shop—wasn't far—and fixed the car," she explains in a monotone voice.

"You should have woken me up. I would have went with you," I tell her, and she bites her lip. My gaze lingers on her mouth, and I fidget some more.

"Wasn't necessary," she says, then pauses. The air is tickling with a buzz of unsaid words, unmoved feet, unsparked wandering hands. "We should go," she repeats in a firm tone and moves to her shirt and socks on the dresser. She hurriedly pulls on her thin shirt, then shrugs on her jacket. All the while, I stare at her, trying to figure out what she's thinking. How she's feeling. But her face is expressionless—angry, if anything.

Noticing me standing still, she spins around and spits, "Will you move your fucking feet? I have to be somewhere and—"

"What happened last night?" I ask her, slicing through her harsh words. Her mouth quivers slightly, and her eyes widen. Something flashes across them. Her face grows soft for a split second before something in her mind clicks, and she turns back to the dresser.

"Nothing," she says in a low voice.

"Liar," I say and slowly walk over to her. She stiffens, noticing my presence, but doesn't run or push away or hit me. She just stays still, her breathing hard, my hand sliding down her arm. My fingertips create a spark when they dance on hers, and I hear a sharp intake of breath from her. "Last night wasn't nothing. And you know that, so why are you trying to act like it didn't even happen?"

"Because it meant nothing," she claims.

"Bullshit."

"It didn't mean anyt—" she begins to scream.

"Stop lying, Red!" I shadow her voice, and she pushes at me. I stumble back, and we both try to catch our breaths, chests heaving and cheeks blotchy and red. I rack my brain, doing a play-by-play of last night's events, and I grow even more angry as it's so freaking clear she wanted me. "You were the one who came on to me, not the other way around. You were the one who told me to kiss. I asked if you wanted me, and you said yes. So why are you acting like it didn't happen?" I rant and gasp for air.

She's clutching her hair and keeping silent. It's frustrating me with each silent second that whizzes by, stealing my breath more and more.

"Answer me, Red! What the hell happened in the past few hours that you don't want me?" I shout, my voice rattles as I try to get her to react. Look at me. Speak. Explain herself. But she doesn't do anything but stare at the ground. Why isn't she reacting to me? Am I that invisible to her now? For whatever freaking reason? Did I imagine last night? Have a wet dream or something? Questions flood my mind, but none are being answered, and it makes me want to rip my hair out.

"Red, please." My voice drops as I plead. I sound so pathetic, and I hate it. I've never been this way before. I'm usually confident, especially around girls. I have never pleaded to a girl before; I never had to. But here I am, begging a girl to say something, anything to me. This is insane, and I don't know what to do. Especially since she isn't giving me anything to go on.

I take a step to her, to reach out for her hands, but she holds them up to her chest and stares me in the eyes. There's something in there, reaching for me, and I want to grab on and pull it out. Translate it on her parted lips and fill the air with an explanation. But the moment I read her eyes, they glaze over with a barrier, and she steps away from me. My heart cracks a little with each step.

"Stay here if you want...but I'm leaving," she says, then grabs her keys off the dresser and storms out of the room, slamming the door after her.

I stand here trying to figure out what the hell just happened when frustration builds up, and I kick the dresser. I grip the edge of it and try to catch my breath. She doesn't get to just take off without talking to me. This isn't fair. I push away from the dresser and chase after her.

The air outside is chilly and makes my teeth chatter. Stopping at the parking space I vaguely remember Red pulling into last night, I strangely find it...empty. I begin to panic, but then I think of last night and assure myself that she wouldn't just *leave* me. Even if she's convinced it meant nothing. That'd be insane since I wouldn't have a ride back or even know where the hell I am. She wouldn't do that, I tell myself. I snag a seat on the bench in front of the spot and call her again. This time, I leave a voicemail. She's just driving off her anger, I tell myself. *She has to be.*

As the minutes pass by, each with more stomach-crunching worry, the thought of her not coming back from wherever she is crosses my mind like a whirlwind of worry. The more and more I think of her not coming, the sicker to my stomach I become. I put it off and ignore Rachel's call ringing my phone, my stomach growing tighter and the irony clouding my thoughts. As more time goes on, an hour to be exact, I end up answering, wondering what the hell I was thinking last night.

"Hey…" I say, rubbing my eyes. "Can you do me a favor?"

***

The ride back to campus is silent, with the exception of Rachel asking if I'm okay every ten seconds that go by. I keep telling her that I'm fine, that maybe she was just at the auto body shop, but she would have left me a note or text or something. Not just vanish in thin air.

Rachel slows in front of the frat house but surprisingly doesn't ask if I'm fine or say anything at all. I appreciate it because, as we were driving back, my heart was peeling away with each thought of her. It isn't even that she left me without any notice; it's the fact that she did it after we had our…*moment* the night before.

Did I break some frail bond or understanding between us? If so, she was the one who pursued *me*.

"Hey." Rachel squeezes my shoulder, holstering a gentle smile. "It's good that you saw her true colors before you fell in too deep."

"Right…" I give her an equally soft smile, but inside my head I think, *Too bad I already did fall.*

A few hours later, I'm at the fraternity house, still dazed and confused and so freaking frustrated.

And angry. All the emotions collide and form one large lump in my throat. I swallow thickly to get it away a few times, but each time I try, it hurts, and *her* voice lying to me fills me. So I stop trying to get rid of the lump and focus on whatever it is I'm painting. It could be a sunrise or a couple dancing or nothing at all, and I've just lost my mind at the hands of Red Sylvetti. Even thinking her name gives me sharp pains in my stomach.

I just don't understand. No matter how many times I roll the events of the past twenty-four hours in my head, I will never understand. Last night, we shared something incredible and mind-blowing and *right*. Nothing felt forced or wrong. If anything, I've never felt more myself, more secure…more alive. I don't know if it makes me weak to say, but being with her in that moment made things fall into one perfect mirage. It was like she breathed life— actual life—into me, and I never wanted it to end.

And I know she felt the same way. I saw it in the way she looked at me through her eyelashes. Felt it under her fingernails. Heard it through her moans and hushed whispers of my name.

So why is she acting like it didn't mean anything?

Why do I feel so heartbroken, when Rachel and even Mike spouted warnings?

Why can't I breathe right now?

Why, why, *why*?

Unable to hold the brush with shaky hands, I let it fall on the easel. I move my hands around my face, pinching and rubbing, then migrate them to my hair. I tug and lean against the wall. I'm in my room, and Ty's across the room, working on an assignment, loud music pouring out of his headphones. He's seen my frustration through my grunts and long sighs and asked me to speak about it, but I turned his offer down. Told him I just needed to distract myself before I go crazy. But the distraction's just making me go even more mad.

"Hey, Noah," a voice says. Shifting my hands to my knees, I look at the door and find Mike peeking his head in, then pushing the door open.

"What's up?" I sound tired. I am, but not physically—emotionally.

His expression is empathetic as he says, "Me and some of the guys are going bowling. I was wondering if you wanted to tag along?"

"I'm coming." Ty yanks his headphones out of his ears and jogs over to Mike. "I've had my head dug into that calculus textbook way too long. I need a damn *break*."

"I don't know…" I say even though I have absolutely nothing else to do. Truth is, I'm waiting for Red to call or text with some explanation. For her to tell me that she just freaked out and last night actually meant something, more than she wants to admit. A massive part of me knows the chances of that happening is slim to nothing. But the minuscule side…I can't help but cling to that little part that has an infinity of hope.

My phone buzzes, and I snatch it up a little too quickly to reclaim my dignity. But it has to be her, and I can't waste any time. I am losing myself with each minute that passes by.

"I told you Red is a complex girl. If you just give

148

her some time…she'll come around," Mike assures me, but I'm too busy staring at the picture sent via text. "Noah?" he calls when I don't blink for maybe hours, seconds, days? I don't know. I can't tell because of how much I am losing my mind on the inside.

Sent by an unknown person is a picture of Red kissing Tanner…and it was taken just an hour ago.

"Yo, you okay? You look unhealthily pale…" Ty says.

"I'm fine." I click off my phone and hop up. "You said bowling, right? I haven't bowled in so long. Hope you guys are prepared to have your asses whooped." I keep a cheer in my voice to mask the raw pain hidden in my throat—it's that damn lump, and it's growing and growing until it even hurts to breathe.

And the entire time we're bowling and laughing and flirting with groups of girls, I'm thinking about Red. Thinking about how much I wish she were here. And my heart breaks a little more at the pathetic thought. Damn, I think to myself, I really let this girl affect me when I told myself to not get attached. How the *hell* did that happen? And how can I reverse it?

Chapter Seventeen

An entire fucking week passes since our night in the motel, and I've done my best to not think about it. To not think about *her*. We made out, she pushed me away, broke my heart. That's it. I've moved past it, past her. If I don't matter to her, then she doesn't matter to me. I have never acted this way before, and I won't let her change that. I'm *that* guy— charming, laid back, and passionate about art and things bigger than myself. I don't get glued to one girl because she showed me her back instead of falling for my smile. Just because she's different doesn't make her better or so desirable I lose myself. That's stupid and unethical.

So I paid more attention to Beth and football and my art. I've painted more than I have since I first got here. Flirted with Beth without a nagging voice in the back of my head saying I shouldn't. And I've practiced my ass off for tonight's game—my first game on the team. I've prepared myself and formed myself into who I am supposed to be in college. *That* guy.

"Might not want to stand out here," Mike says before dragging me into the lockers. A rush of guys wearing the football uniform and helmets storm down the aisle. They woot and cheer about the first game of the year. The energy is high and crackles in the air; I can practically taste it. All the guys are super amped for the first game, and they're definitely showing it.

"Right. Sorry," I mumble, tying on my black cleats. My hands fumble a little because of the tiny nerves chewing under my skin. Something about playing in front of that huge crowd makes me shake—anxiety, no matter how ready I appear on the outside. She appears and grabs me by my jersey and jostles me, making me think about puking on the field or making a wrong call. I've dealt with her constantly in high school but prevailed each time. Pretty sure I can do the same in college.

"Dude, try not to be a wet wipe." Ty nudges me harshly, his easy smile broadening. "This is your first game in the big leagues."

"Thought the NFL was the big leagues," Mike muses.

"Shut the fuck up," Ty snaps. "I'm trying to cheer him up." He does a horrible job of whispering. Seriously. We're a microscopic foot away from each other.

"I'm fine, guys." I slip out of Ty's hold, and they both look at me with raised eyebrows, as if saying, *You sure about that*? "I really am." A lie, but they don't need to know that. I don't know if they're referring to the *Red* situation or my nerves for playing the first time in college. Either way, they need to stop treating me like a nervous baby about to take his first steps.

"Listen, what that Red chick did was messed up," Ty begins. "But now you have to focus on the game. I mean, at least you got her out your system, right?" He gives me a helpless shrug. So it is about Red, I think bitterly. But at least they care about me. All week, they've tried their best to cheer me up: playing video games with me, studying with me, working out together. They're such great friends. I'm lucky to have them support me.

No. I didn't. I just got her into *my system, then she ejected herself and scrambled away like I meant nothing to her,* I want to say, but I don't because of one thing he said: I have to focus on the game, more than ever. It's my first college football game, and I want to do good, great even. A lot of people crave these games. It's their lives…and it should be mine too.

So I eat the words I want to say, flash him a small but bright smile, and tell him, "You're right. Now, let's get out there and win this thing."

Mike claps and woots, sounding just like our teammates. "There we go, Blue Jay!" he screams at the mascot, and I feel my heart do a somersault. Blue Jay…I like the sound of that. In fact, I love it.

A few minutes later, we're headed out to the field. My heart rumbles and shakes under the vibrating floors. I'm confused and think it's an earthquake, until we breach the tunnel and bright white lights flood my senses. I stop short in the cluster of my energized teammates, in shock and awe. The entire stadium is packed, with black and blue attendees who cheer and scream at us with overjoyed smiles and clapping hands.

"Dude, come on." Mike drags me out to our side of the field. The other side is home to the team we're playing against: Morgan State University, dressed in their orange and navy blue.

The constant screaming of school cheer and bright lights frighten me for a split second before I join my team on the sidelines and go over the game plan. As I stand in the huddled circle and look around at my teammates and their game faces and glance over at the cheerleaders flipping in the air, I feel at home. I feel like I am a part of something.

It is like a whirlwind of flashing lights and cheering all wrapped with an anxiety-filled bow, because before I can even blink, I am on the field in our practiced positions. A hot wire of energy flashes through me, anticipation coursing through my veins as the commotion between team players erupt. Numbers are called, plays are murmured…and the game begins.

As the hour rolls by, I get dirtier and more exhausted. But we're doing great so far; we're up by twenty. Halftime is coming up, and I expect to take a seat on the bench for the next string, but Coach gives me an excited look I've never seen on his usually stone-cold face. He wants me to play the entire game. And so I do, throwing with more vigor and running faster than ever.

During halftime, I'm out of breath but so pumped, I can't even sit down and rest on the bench.

"Got something live in your pants, Wells?" Mike

jokes as he fills a cup of Gatorade.

"Nope. Just pumped. We're winning. Did anyone expect that?" I say.

"Uh, me. And it's *because* of me," Tyler gloats and shows off his biceps as a group of cheerleaders walk by. They giggle and wink at him, and he growls at them. Literally.

Mike and I share a laugh.

"You mean it's because of *Noah*." Mike pats my chest and says, "Newbie here is fucking *owning* the field. Did you see that last throw?" Shaking his head, he sucks down the Gatorade before pointing a finger at me. "Coach did a good job of making you quarterback."

"Thanks." I smile genuinely. It's been so long since I played a game; I forgot how exhilarating it is.

"Yo!" someone says behind me. I turn around and find Ian sauntering over to me with a hard-ass expression.

"Yeah?" I say apprehensively. I hope he doesn't plan on saying some shit, messing up my energy boost.

He holds up his hands and stops a foot away from me. "Calm down, tiger. I wasn't gonna tackle you or anything."

"Okay?"

"I just wanted to say…you're doing okay so far, for a newbie, I mean." He clears his throat, and I raise a questioning brow. Did he really just say something nice…about me? Am I dreaming, or has hell frozen over entirely?

"Thanks, man—" I begin with a smirk.

"Only wish Red was around to see her puppy playing with the big boys," he says with a shit-eating grin. Of course, how could I possibly think he'd have something nice to say without a back-handed comment?

Wait.

"Do you know where Red is?" I ask him slowly, watching for the truth in his smug expression. I can't help it. I've put her out of my mind for a week, but the moment he brought her up...*fuckkkk.*

"Have no clue." He finally shrugs, and my heart plummets.

"Great." I turn and begin to walk away, running a hand over my hair, frustrated, when he says something that makes my blood run cold.

"She didn't tell me where she went after we fucked. She was in such a rush to come over to see me after dumping your ass in a shitty motel. Tell me, did it feel nice having her suck you off while she was thinking of me?"

I try to hold it in, but I let the convulsing anger take over and storm over to him, getting in his face. "What the fuck did you just say?" I demand through gritted teeth, ignoring my friends urging me to calm down. But I can't *calm down.* I can only boil up inside like a god damn furnace.

"You mean: who did I fuck a few hours ago?" His voice is deep and mocking. Teasing. I want to shove it up his ass so far that, when he's shitting, all that comes out are his fucking screams.

I don't hesitate to throw my fist in his face after yanking off his helmet. He deflects, pushes my helmet off, and punches me in the jaw. I topple over, dragging him down with me. A crowd gathers around as we go tumbling around, punches thrown sporadically. I get on top of him and throw my fist across his cheek. Blood spurts out of his mouth, and "ooohs" are shouted.

"Hey, get off of him!" I hear Ty scream, but I can't stop punching him. His eye is swelling; his mouth is split. I keep punching. My hand is bloody, or his face is. I can't tell. There's so much, and so much rage. I. Just. Can't. *Stop*. It's like a blood-thirsty parasite I've been sedating forever is finally getting a taste and is greedy for more.

"That's enough, Noah!" Mike screams in my ear, tugging at my raised, bloody fist.

"Wells! Walker!" Coach storms over and pulls me off him like nothing. He shoves at me, then at Ian, who's chuckling even though blood drips onto his uniform. "Locker rooms! Now! You're both done for the night."

Picking my helmet off the floor, I shift my glare to the ground and storm into the locker room. I throw my helmet at my locker, denting it, and scream in frustration. As I drop onto the bench in front of the lockers, I let the tears fall and think, *What the hell was I thinking with her?*

Chapter Eighteen

Hours have passed since the fight between Ian and me broke out. The anger I felt then has not tamped down in the slightest. In fact, it's grown to an unreachable high. I've left angry voicemails directed toward Red, painted like hell, and locked myself in my room. I've snapped whatever boundary in my head that barred me from thinking of her and what happened and *lost* it.

Subjected to the dark, staring at the ceiling, I think, *How could she do that to me?* I ignored all the warnings about Red Sylvetti because I thought she was better than the caution sign people slapped on her name. But seeing how she did *this*, I understand the warnings.

A small part of me begs to not trust Ian. He's an asshole who doesn't seem to refrain from spewing pure bullshit. But I just keep picturing her waking up in the middle of the night and realizing the mistake she made, hooking up with a frat boy. Like she doesn't at least know me as more than some stupid, nonsensical title.

She probably thought about losing her "badass" title and hightailed it to the asshole's crevice to erase me from her memory.

A small knock at the door followed by a "Noah?" brings me out of my thoughts. I take a deep breath, ready to curse out whoever the drunk person is. A party is currently being thrown downstairs to celebrate us winning the game. Every time I think about it, I get even angrier at myself because I let my anger get the best of me and got benched. It makes me want to punch something.

But I end up pulling out my sketchpad and sketch my bruised hand that hasn't been attended to. None of my injuries have been looked after, actually. Rachel tried to help me despite the fact that I got in a serious fight with her step-brother. The girl is ultra-sweet; her brother and I are undeserving of her. I bet it's her on the other side of the door, which makes me try to tune out her small, worried voice and light knocking. I don't deserve to have her by my side. I ignored her warnings about Red. I deserve to sit here in the dark and sulk like the idiot person I am.

Hearing her sigh and her head fall against the door, she whispers, "Please open the door; I want to help you."

"Go away, Rachel." It hurts me to say it, but she needs to stop. I didn't listen to her because I thought Red was different. I got into this mess my damn self.

A sharp click and some jiggling makes me freeze. The door opens, and Ty, holding the key to our room, laughs nervously before running away.

"Thanks, Ty!" Rachel waves after the boy.

"Fucking Ty," I mutter, leaning my head against the wall, returning my gaze and attention to my sketchpad. Maybe if I ignore her, she'll go away. But of course, being the sweet, innocuous girl she is, she sits beside my feet and taps my knee. "Please don't say *I told you so*."

"I would never," she says, slightly offended. When I slowly look up at her, she's frowning with pouty lips, big eyes flapping softly. "Just let me help you, then I'll leave." She takes a deep breath and says, "My brother can be an…"

"Ass," I assist with a smile.

She chuckles and nods to herself, as if committing it to memory. Then she sears me with those big brown eyes and continues, "He was probably lying…or not. Either way, Red isn't that trustworthy of a person. She left you in Greendale when you barely know this *state*." Taking another breath, she takes my less injured hand. "But you trusted her and put your faith in her; you can't be upset about that. It's honorable and, honestly, really cute."

I assess her words, flipping them in my head. She's kind of right. I can't give Ian all the credit; Red left me without a note, text—anything. But she just…left. The waiting wasn't as bad as thinking she was going to pull up with a box of donuts or something. God. I sound like such a pussy. *She* turned me into a god damn pussy. I just thought she was different. I saw something different. Then again, the Devil can easily deceive anyone with an angelic smile.

"So will you let me help you?" Rachel squeezes my hand, taking my silence for an agreement.

A part of me is nagging me, telling me to just wait…and that's it.

Wait for what? I think with a short laugh. *There's no use in waiting if she's already made up her mind.*

"Yes," I answer Rachel, squeezing her hand back.

With a gleeful smile and shining eyes like I gave her the moon, she rushes into the bathroom. My stomach tightens, and that voice screams at me to wait. I push it away and lock it in the corner of my mind. A few seconds later, Rachel returns with a first aid kit. She pops it open and gets to work. Each rub of alcohol feels like a bee sting, but her sweet words soothe it a little bit. After some time, my hands are bandaged, the cut on my left cheek has a Band-Aid, and I'm in the kitchen with a pack of peas wrapped in a dish cloth on my bruised cheek.

"How long do I have to hold it here?" I ask Rachel gingerly, pressing the pack a little tighter. It feels like someone ran a tractor over my face, then backed up and stayed extra-long on my cheek.

"For twenty minutes," she tells me, biting her lip as she eyes me. She looks in pain just from watching me grimace. I try to give her an assuring smile, but the pain elicits a groan instead, worsening her worry. "You should get some rest. Sleep it off."

"No, no—I'm fine," I tell her. I won't be able to sleep, anyway. The party's getting bigger and *louder.* "Just—tell me Ian looks worse."

Her smile is contagious, but I keep mine on the

inside to avoid pain. "He looks like he fell off Mount Everest...*twice*. You really got him good. Sure you're not a fighter in your spare time?"

I laugh, shaking my head gently. "I don't have the best stomach for blood. But I feel even better knowing that prick's in pain...that's not nice, and he's your brother. Sorry."

She squeezes my forearm. "Trust me, he deserved it. I can't believe he would say something like that, *do* something like that." She pauses and leans against me. "Just shows that people can be cruel for no reason but to hurt others."

"How did you grow up with him?"

"Didn't—not really, at least. His dad married my mom when I was twelve. You think this is bad? You should have been there when he 'accidentally' locked me out of the house for *two hours*."

"Oh, you poor thing," I tease, pinching her arm.

"Ouch! Wanna injure me too?" She laughs and pinches me in the stomach.

I throw my head back in laughter. But I slow down when I feel eyes burning through me. Looking around the room for the source of the glare, my heart thumps a thousand extra beats. Finally, I find the source and do a triple take.

Red.

"What's wrong?" Rachel asks me, squeezing my bicep.

"Nothing." I turn to her and put all my focus on her. I have to focus on something other than the girl whose presence beckons me like a siren. Every drop of me—directed to her. To hold her, hear her laugh, kiss her lips... "Nothing is wrong."

Rachel's lips twitch slightly, and she leans forward a bit. "Really? Because you seem different than a few seconds ago—"

"*Prep.*" I feel her before I hear her. I stiffen, and Rachel frowns, then turns to the girl I am trying my absolute best to ignore. "What? You're not gonna disappoint your mommy and daddy's rules about manners and ignore me, are you?" I hear the smirk in her voice, and my blood boils.

"You wanna go outside, Rachel?" I grab her hand and guide her out without a response. When we're among chatty people smoking who knows what, I sigh and tell her, "I'm sorry about that. About her."

"It's fine. I just didn't think she'd have the guts to come here." I sense annoyance and anger laced in her soft tone.

"Oh, she has the guts to do whatever she pleases." I throw a glare over my shoulder. I freeze, meeting her glaring at me. At us. If I didn't know any better, I would think she's...jealous. But what does that make me upon hearing she left me to be with a douchebag like Ian? Rolling my eyes, I face the pool and a string of memories of her and me... "Fuck," I groan, rubbing my eyes.

"Noah..." Rachel says, reaching for my hand. But I pull away before she can and watch her face melt.

The sound of boots hitting the ground helps me say what I need to.

"I'm sorry, but you're too good for this shit. I— I'll see you around, Rachel." I squeeze her shoulder before my eyes land on a fiery blue. Red's on her way over, but I walk toward her, dragging her from Rachel, brushing past her. Sparks sizzle under my skin at the brief contact and our mouths part, eyes lingering. That voice surfaces, pleads…but I push it away, lock it up, and look away.

Inside, I find Mike and Ian and a few other guys doing shots.

"Got room for one?" I sidle up to them, and they give me strange looks.

"You okay there, Rocky?" Mike teases, flashing me his pearly white teeth.

"Perfect." I smile through a pained bruise. Feeling silly that I'm still holding it and the coldness that feels like a glacier sitting on my skin, I set the pack of peas down. "Why?"

I nervously flick my eyes over to the open patio, where Red is watching me with a smirk and crossed arms. Ignoring the skip of my heartbeat, I train my eyes on the line of shots.

"Apart from the girl who broke your heart staring at you from across the room…" Ty begins, nodding ahead, but I keep my eyes on the prize. Liquor. It's supposed to whisk me away to a world of oblivion, right? To help me forget?

"I'm fine," I tell them, and they raise their brows. "Seriously. But thank you for the shot. Means a lot." I grab one of the shot glasses filled with vodka and, ignoring their calls, I move to one of the busiest rooms in the entire house—the living room. The air is thick with smoke and sweat, and people are gyrating against each other. I dodge a few football players wearing the school colors on their faces and jerseys on their backs, disappointed

163

with myself for making the team look bad.

I down the shot in hopes of it washing away all of my problems, but it only highlights the tightness in my chest when I catch Red's eyes somewhere in the crowd. Watching me like a predator stalking her prey—and I'm that stupid, naïve prey. Rolling my eyes, I walk farther into the crowd. I get offered a drink in a cup and, despite my better judgment, I drink it all in one go and throw it away. I need to forget Red. She got inside my veins and poisoned me when I least expected it.

"Hey, you're that guy that fought at the football game," a dark-haired girl says to me. She pushes her thin arms against her cleavage that's held tightly in a purple bondage dress, her brown eyes popping behind a large swipe of sparkling purple eyeshadow.

"Yeah?" I say unsurely.

A giggle pops out of her too-red lips. She grabs my bicep kind of harshly, fluttering her eyes in a flirty way. I think. "That was sooooo hot," she leans in to whisper.

Ignoring the cerulean eyes focused on me, I lean down. "Would you like to dance?"

"Would I?" She giggles, and I inwardly cringe at the nauseating sound. But she is a distraction, and if Red's looking, I want to hurt her like she hurt me. She guides me to the middle of the pit of drunk idiots and begins grinding on me. I wrap an arm loosely around her and let my head rest in the crook of her neck. Again, I cringe at the over-saturated perfume, but I don't move. Not even as I feel a tap on my shoulder.

Red growls at the girl moving against me vigorously. Her blue eyes are fire pits, arms crossed her chest. "Really? *This* is your type? She looks like a Jersey Shore reject."

"Why should you get to judge me when brooding assholes like Ian seem to be *your* type?" I slur and grip the girl's hips. This is so petty. So unlike me...but damn it! Red makes me this way. She makes me feel something so bad for her, I would resort to using this girl who admittedly isn't the kind I'd blink at twice.

Red's face hardens, and she blinks like I caught her, but she sinks back into her natural state of annoyance and rudeness and snaps, "I never took you for this kind of guy, Noah."

What?

"And I never took you for a girl who leaves a guy in a motel to go *fuck* someone else!" I scream louder than I intended.

She opens her mouth, eyes ablaze more than ever, but the girl I nearly forgot I am dancing with turns and whines.

"Stop arguing with her and focus on me. Ya cutie!" She giggles, sounding like nails on a chalkboard, before wrapping her clammy hands around my neck and bringing me down to her short height. Her lips are on mine before I can even say anything. I try to pull away, but her hands are too strong.

But that doesn't even matter because Red yanks her back, turns her around, and drives her fist in the girl's makeup-caked face.

Chapter Nineteen

"What the hell?" the girl screeches like a banshee, blood pouring out of her nose like Niagara Falls. She stumbles back and there is commotion, and I can hardly think as she lurches after Red. Long nails as sharp as a blade, eyes wide like a dog on crack, she screams and goes for Red's eyes. But Red punches her again without much effort.

"Red! Stop!" I shake her shoulders and yank on her hand frantically. We have to get out of here before this girl's friends come after her. And as much as she can handle herself with one, I doubt she can take on five, maybe even eight. Just like I predicted, a herd of girls dressed like the one with the bleeding nose rushes over to her and scopes the crowd.

"I can handle some bitches, trust me," Red sneers and tugs me around, making me bump into her. We bump into a couple making out and, apologizing, she shouts, "I am not walking away when I'm not fucking done with her. That bitch fucking kissed—"

I smack my hand over her furious mouth. "We need to get *out* of here before it's bitchy hell in here." I am not messing around. I may be pissed at her, but I'm not leaving her to fend off hyena-like girls in glitter. Well. There's a sentence I never thought I'd say. Ever. "Now, stop arguing and come *on*." I pull at her hand, making my voice firm.

Her eyes flash with something, and she opens her mouth, but she's interrupted by a hyena battle call behind her. Not having enough time for her simmering thirst for blood, I turn back around and begin running. We squeeze between grinding bodies that reek of body odor and alcohol until we reach the stairs. The floor is clearer up here. I pull her into my room and lock it behind me. Thankfully, it's empty.

"Come on." Grabbing the first aid kit on my bed from when Rachel patched me up, I lead us into the ensuite, locking the door behind me. I also lock the door that leads to the hallway, in case they go searching for us. Hopefully they'll assume a couple is using the room and move on. The door jiggles for a moment, causing me to hold my breath and Red to roll her eyes, but it stops after a second, and I hear whining and stomping heels.

"Pack of wild bitches," Red murmurs as I get close to her. She's gripping the sink, head hung in front of the mirror. "I should have skinned her alive!" She whips around, eyes wide and blue and lips snarling. She looks insane...so why am I smiling?

I take her hands and look into her eyes. "Take a breath," I instruct.

She looks away, ignoring me. "I'll take a knife and—"

I press my lips against her forehead, bringing her head back. Her eyes snap open like she's just realizing I'm in the room with her. I pull away when her gaze becomes too much and grip her wrists lightly. "Breathe, Red. Now."

Clicking her tongue in her mouth, as if telling herself to not kill *me*, she does as told. Her eyes flutter closed, hands tightening around mine, before she mutters, "I didn't fuck him."

My heart stammers and my fingers loosen, but seemingly fearing me letting go, she tightens her hold and flashes her eyes open, face softer than before. "Who?" I feign ignorance because if I acknowledge what she's talking about, it'll be my turn to turn blood-thirsty. For his blood. On my knuckles. I wiggle my fingers just to loosen the vein thumping under the bandages, but not knowing that, she tightens her hold and tugs me closer to her.

"You know who," she says, her voice low like she's afraid to acknowledge it too. Is she...nervous? She doesn't get to be nervous, though. *She* left *me*.

So, as much as it physically pains me to, I take my hands away from hers. She jerks forward and her eyes close. I swear I think she's going to cry, but when they open, she looks forcibly hard and I shake my head at her, incredulous.

"You don't get to be ominous," I snap, and she bites her lip, tongue playing with her lip ring.

"Noah," she says in a breathless way.

"No. Don't *Noah* me." I sound breathless too in a way, but it's because I'm hurt. Even after bashing

168

Ian's face in and sulking in the dark, I'm faced with her and the pain. Dropping into the edge of the bath/shower, I plunk my head in my hands. "Just tell me…is it true? What he said? At least—you going to him?"

Silence greets me. It wraps around me like a banshee in mourning. Screaming against my eardrums but sad and—and I just want her to tell me. To make me kick myself for jumping to conclusions. But her silence just confirms what I truly didn't want to believe.

"Jesus, Red!" I finally snap, lifting my head. I find her gripping her hair, rolling her beautiful blue eyes.

"I didn't fuck him!" she seethes and takes a single step forward…then rocks back one step, stumbling into the counter. Then why does she look so hesitant? So guilty? I don't understand, but I want to.

"Then what *did* you do with him?"

Her tongue sweeps against her top lip. "Nothing," she lies.

I push to my feet and storm over to her. "Why are you lying to me?"

"Why do you care?" she screams, walking backward to escape my approach, but she ends up hitting the wall. I trap her with my arms, think about pushing the wild curl by her eyes back, and end up pushing my hands over my hair, tugging at the ends. But the urge to cage her before she can be a coward and flee, leaving me unanswered and pained, surges, and I let my hands rest on either side of her head.

"Because I fucking like you!" I let out before I can think it over.

Her eyes blink rapidly, and she looks to the ground. Fuck. Now she's going to twist this around and make it seem like I'm some stupid kid that shouldn't have gotten involved with her. She's going to brand me some more, like hearing what they supposedly did wasn't enough to scar my heart.

"Well, that's your fault now, isn't it?" she says, plunging those blue knives she calls eyes into my soul. She pushes against me, and I go stumbling back. I catch myself before I can trip and storm over to her because she's seemingly desperate to flee.

"Stop running away and tell me what you did!" I am desperate myself, I realize, as my voice comes out strangled, the liquor I ingested earlier pushing out the frustration into a burst of frustration and sizzling need. I need to know. I need her to tell me. "And while you're at it, tell me what you were doing with Tanner after you left me."

She pauses. "How...how?" she sputters, either too guilty or stunned to talk in a complete sentence.

"Don't worry about how, and tell me why," I tell her. I'm finding it hard to not scream my lungs out, to tell her how much she's gutted me.

Silence ensues before she whispers, "It was just one kiss. I tried to do more...but I thought of...of you and us and I *stopped* it. Completely. Left him. Tried again with Ian. Failed a-fucking-gain, because of you."

What? "Are you seriously trying to blame me for you going around screwing with other guys?"

"I didn't screw either of them! Okay?" She still isn't facing me, and it's pissing me off. "Before you, I didn't have to think about a fucking moral compass, okay? But now it's instilled in me, and I can't stop thinking—" She stops. Why did she stop? Why doesn't she ever speak her mind? I mean, really, *truly*, speak her mind?

"Don't stop talking, Red! Red!" I shout her name, my patience growing scary thin.

Spinning on her boots, she hits me and screams, "I left you, okay? I left you and I went to him because I wanted to get you out of my system. I was so close to screwing him, but I—I left before I could. *Okay*? You enter my mind every time I don't want you to. You and your stupid face, and your stupid smile and laugh, and your stupid, stupid ability to look past the warnings people tried to throw at you. You trusted me. And you still do because you're not letting me go. You're trapping me with your stupid—your stupid arms. And I need you to let go before I kiss you—" Her eyes are glued to my lips.

I shouldn't do this, I battle myself as I glance at her lips. I really, really shouldn't do this. She hurt me.

And yet, I find myself leaning forward, connecting my lips to hers in a bone-chilling kiss.

Chapter Twenty

I press forward, head ducked, and our lips collide. Short circuits seem to explode between our mouths. Opening and closing around each other. I taste the cigarettes, the beer, the dangerous toxins lingering on her tongue. But I don't care. She tastes so sweetly poisonous; I want to drink her up in one go. As her arms wrap around my neck, I pick her up by her hips and slam her on the counter. She kisses me passionately like she's been craving me for years, and I kiss her with a ferocity I've longed to bestow upon her since the second I knew what these beautiful, tasty lips felt like on mine.

Between quick breaths and teasing bites, she whispers, "I didn't like when that skank put her lips on you. I have..." Nibble. "Half a..." Lick. "Mind to..." Suck. "*Murder* her."

"To say that means you have feelings for me," I explain, slowly drawing a breath before smashing my lips on hers. She moans lightly, back arching, breasts pressed against me. *Oh, fuck.* "So, what—" Her fingers glide underneath my shirt, nails digging.

Goddamn it. "Are we? What is this?"

She groans and tugs at my bottom lip, lifting my shirt and groaning again at the sight underneath. I can't even hold back my smirk. She seemingly giggles, making my ears perk and a smile to grab hold of my cheeks, but she stops and pulls me in for one long kiss. "Nothing," she answers.

"Nothing?" I pull back, and she stares at my lips.

"This doesn't need to be anything serious. Just—*come here.*" She takes hold of the hem of my shirt and drags me back into her embrace. Lips of hers, sweet and toxic and so utterly intoxicating, drown me in the red. I almost get lost in them, in her, when her words resonate in my head until I literally can't swim between her lips anymore.

I pull back again, and she half groans, half whines, eyes rolling into the back of her head. "No, don't be like that. What you're doing, *suggesting,* is cowardly. And I like you too much to just *not* be anything."

She blinks rapidly, shaking her head and rubbing her eyes. "Cowardly? How am I being cowardly?"

"By not giving us a chance—"

"That doesn't make me a coward!" Her voice rises.

"Yes, it does!"

"I'm not being a coward!" She sounds strained, on the verge of crying. I close my opinionated mouth and step closer. I begin to push her reckless hair behind her ear to soothe her when she snaps up, lifting her sagging shoulders, but avoids my worried gaze.

"Red, look at me," I say around a sigh, trying to

find her brilliant blue eyes under their shadows.

My heart shrinks as she shakes her head to herself.

"Red." I nudge my finger under her chin. Her eyes, dimmer than usual, look into my green ones, and I lean my forehead against hers. "Talk to me," I plead softly.

Her warm breath fans against my nose as she sighs. I smell mint and nicotine. "I just—" she begins slowly. "I'm not...I'm not *good* for you, Noah. And you need someone good."

"Like the glittery hyena from downstairs?" I tease, and she chuckles. I look at her smile from underneath my eyelashes and nudge her head up by her chin again. Her eyes meet mine, fierce and fiery like the soul behind them. "You gotta have faith in me. Or this—*whatever* we are—will. Not. *Work*...okay?"

Her eyes dart down to my lips, and she leans forward, biting her own. I watch with intense hope that she'll say, "Yes, I do trust you, Noah." I want her to put her trust in me—in us—and I want to feel all of that under the pressure of her fine, sweet lips.

"*Okay, Noah*," she says softly, lips brushing mine. Teasing me. But hell will freeze over before I let her get away with it.

"*Ho bisogno di più rossa,*" I whisper back, licking her bottom lip slowly. *Teasingly*. She moans, and I smirk. *Payback*, I think in my head. (I want more, Red.)

"Wait, what does that mean?" she begins, but my lips crush hers into silence. Silences me. Silences the entire freaking world.

Chapter Twenty-One

A light buzzing sensation under my skin on my forehead wakes me groggily. The groan that ripples from my mouth into the warm air massages me out of the sleep I desperately cling to, but it slips through my long fingers. I fall in my dream, once in a cloud where red butterflies and blue oceans swam between my bones, and onto cold concrete pavement. Slowly, I lift my head and prop myself onto my elbows, rubbing my buzzing head.

What happened last night? I begin to wonder, then am hit with memories by the boatload: Rachel wrapping my hands, Red showing up, her punching a hyena wearing glitter...? Anyway, there's more. Better things. Like, kissing her in the bathroom. So caught up in her strangely addicting lips. I rub my own lips, feeling the shit-eating grin before realizing I'm even doing it. I rub and rub as if it's a genie bottle and Red will appear out of thin air.

Red.

Where is she? Did she go home or wherever that ball of fire lives?

Sitting up fully against the wall, I run a hand through my hair. Eyes foggy, I focus them on the empty, wrinkled sheets of Ty's bed. She isn't there. My head hurts with a soft pang as I try to remember what happened after we left the bathroom. I recall us going downstairs, after I did a thorough search for the pack of glittery hyenas. They were nowhere in sight, most likely opting to head to a sorority party where there weren't fiery punching girls.

Anyway, after it was all safe downstairs, we took a few shots, danced in the pit, and kissed some more. We were like lovers separated after a century spent apart. I don't know how to feel about that…happy. I feel happy, I decide, feeling the smile before really knowing.

But I don't remember much after that.

Could she have just left…*again*?

I'm searching through my puffy white bedsheets like a zombie looking for a brain when I hear metal grinding gently and the constant beating of water stop instantly…all coming from the bathroom. I didn't even hear the water until now. I sit up the second the door swings open and Red emerges wearing a towel…and *nothing else*.

I try my best to not let my jaw drop, but I just woke up and have very limited energy to actually think. I must look like a rabid teenage boy as I drag my eyes up her long, long legs dripping with water, all the way up to her busty chest being held up with one of her arms, the one with the sleeve of tattoos. Beyond the normal *yowza* factor muddled by my teenage boy genes, she looks very cute and freshly gorgeous. Like a gently plucked sunflower.

"Lion got your tongue?" she says.

After centuries of ogling and admiring, I focus on what she said and chuckle a little. "*Lion*? I think you're still a little drunk, because the phrase is 'cat got your tongue.'"

"If it were a cat, I'd flick the fucker away with a flick of my *wrist*," she claims around an air of arrogance. "A lion, now…then I'd be a goner." She walks over to me, eyes squinting lightly at the ceiling as she continues, "That and I wouldn't be able to tell you that you were blushing like a little schoolgirl when I walked in."

"Oh." I blush some more, and she chuckles. "I was not blushing…" She narrows her eyes, and I end up running a hand over my hand before muttering, "*Much*."

She laughs broader, and I indirectly focus my attention on the dusty pink of her cheeks and the glow of her eyes the color of cerulean fire. Ablaze and quick to scorch me until I'm nothing but ashes, a victim of Red Sylvetti. A willing victim, I correct, as she gets closer.

"You're too innocent, Noah Wells," she says and walks over to me.

Each stride is sure and sexy, with her legs wet and slender; and I swear they appeared in my dreams sometime before. My breath hitches when her knees meet the bed, a few inches away from me. So far, yet so terribly, teasingly close. I could just reach out and pull her in and—

"You are absolutely insatiable, aren't ya, boy?" She pokes a teasing finger at my chest. She just loves to tease, doesn't she? I bet it's a favored hobby of hers. The fire in her eyes confirms my thoughts.

I quickly clasp my fingers around her wrist and tug her closer. Her breathing visibly gets stuck in her throat as she gulps at the sudden action. She looks deliciously cute when I catch her off guard. It doesn't happen often, but when it does, she has me under a spell that watches every nervous tongue flick and holds her sparkling gaze.

"How could I not be? You incite a hunger in me I never knew to be possible, Red." My voice is low and lazy like molasses, smooth like velvet. Nervous tongue flip there. Glimmering gaze there. I hold her intense, soft eyes and watch her tongue run across the pink valley of her bottom lip.

"Is that so?" she says, taking enough control of her staggering breathing to make her voice firm.

Her hands squeeze my shoulders, then gently work their way up to my neck, then around it as she plops onto her butt. Her slender legs wind around me, and I literally melt, shoulders sagging and mouth jarring open and everything. Laughing and obviously liking the power switch, she pushes at my chest, straddling me.

"Are you hungry for me now?" she asks softly, lashes fluttering.

For fuck's sake...

"Ravenous," is my shaky reply.

Smirking at my shy response, she leans down and licks my lips. "How about now?" she asks even softer, raspier. She is a siren at heart. Swaying her hips against me. Wet to the touch. Hair wild and lips smelling like pure honey.

I groan, and my hands fly to her barely covered ass. She moans and closes her eyes as I roam her round ass, squeezing and pushing the towel up slightly. Inching. Teasing. *Payback.* I am going to pay for this. But like I said, she makes me hungry. Creates this hole that needs to be filled with her kisses, her *touch.*

"*Starved,*" I say, nearly growling in hunger. Hunger for Red. Hunger for *my Red.*

Licking her lips, so close that her tongue grazes my own lips, she clutches my wrinkled t-shirt and whispers ever so softly, "Then have me."

Don't have to ask me twice.

Gripping her ass, I swivel us around, flipping her onto her back. She squeals, but it's very short lived as I spread her legs using my knees. Her chest falls and fills with emotion as it sprawls onto her neck and cheek with redness. I stare into her eyes, she stares back with frazzled anticipation before slowly pulling down the small towel. I grow hungrier and hungrier, the pain becoming more apparent as my eyes meet her chest. I bite my lip and suppress the groan as I stare at her beauty.

"So beautiful," I murmur, voice heavy with lust. I lean down and cover the top of her right breast with kisses. Licking. Nipping. I tease the pink hard nipple and gently cup and fondle the other. She moans and writhes gently under me, pressing into me.

"Noah," she whispers and gets a hold of my wild, untamed hair. Her fingernails drag down my scalp and grip gently, then hard. I moan at the feeling of her tugging and massaging me and nearly come in my pants as she grinds against me.

"Red…" I trail off as I lift my mouth, planting small kisses across her chest to her other breast. She begins to say something, but the moment I flick my tongue against her, hardening it, her words melt into a soft moan.

"Noah, please touch—" she begins.

"Heyo, motherfucker! I brought donuts!" A sudden shout followed by the door cracking open interrupts Red's moaning plea.

"Ty!" I scream and throw a pillow at his head. Luckily for him, he ducks, and it goes flying down the stairs. I hear a little giggle from Red. I blush and sit up quickly, helping her wrap the towel around her chest. Marked by me. So pink and perky and…I am going to fucking *murder* this boy.

I would have checked to make sure the door was locked, but I was too caught up in tasting Red, and boy did she taste beautifully delicious…like a sucker I didn't ever want to fade from my taste buds.

"Sorry, sorry!" he yelps, throwing his free arm across his eyes. "I uh…" He slowly inches over to his bed, trips over a shoe, and falls onto his bed. But to his credit, he doesn't look up or even peek, though he's a total creep half of the time. "Didn't mean to…*interrupt*. I can leave."

Yes, please!

"No, it's okay. I was feeling like breakfast at the diner," Red says, and my heart shatters into a million pieces. She stands up and bends over to whisper in my ear, "We can continue where we left off later."

180

"Promise?" I almost reach out and drag her onto my lap to finish what I was so close to starting. But Tyler mumbling apologies and suggestions to join stops me. I throw a pillow at his head at his stupid suggestion and roll my eyes in frustration. *Asshole.*

"You're not the only hungry one here, prep," she assures me, her voice heavy and dreamy.

"Get dressed in there and..." Grabbing hold her hands, I smile lightly. "Make sure to lock the door."

"Duh. I have to keep that idiot out." She begins to pull away, but I tighten my hold and brush an unruly lock of hair behind her ear, holding her gaze.

"I wasn't talking about him," I whisper, and she gulps.

Chapter Twenty-Two

"Fuck pancakes...we'll have some chocolate cheesecake," Red orders with a big, hungry swipe of her tongue.

I capture the action with a long, assessing gaze, then chuckle at her words and frenzied big eyes. She looks like someone's pinched the life into her cheeks, leaving them splotchy red, hair thrown up into a messy bun, tendrils curly and wild. It takes everything in me to not reach over and tuck them safely behind her small, blush-tipped ears.

"Sweet tooth much?" I tease her as the older waitress walks away with our menus.

I didn't take Red for the kind of girl who ate dessert for breakfast, but I don't want her to retract her order, however slim the chance of that happening. The girl would think twice before accepting water from me if she were on fire. Obviously she has trust issues stemming from something that happened in her past. I want to know what it was, to assure her that she can trust me, but I don't want to push.

She flips me off and rests her feet on my lap underneath the table. "What's wrong with something sweet in the morning? You got your fill this morning." I choke on my ice water, and she claps her hands, drawing her legs into a cross under her side of the booth. "Was it something I said?" her sweet, but teasing voice echoes as she brings her cup to her lips.

"You're just lucky Ty walked in when he did; otherwise I would have tasted something else..." I blush at my own words and instantly regret speaking my dirty mind, but by the raise of her pierced brow, I can tell she doesn't mind one bit. Actually, she looks kind of...flushed, if the red color swelling on her cheeks is any indication.

"We are on a roll of being lusty teens," Red teases, rolling her straw paper into a tiny ball.

"You started it," I point out, ripping my own straw paper into small pieces.

I have to keep my hands busy to avoid taking hers. Or pushing those frisky hairs behind her ears. As she bad mouths a guy with wide eyes staring at her a few tables away, I push away the urge to give him something else to stare at and give in to my urge. I lean across the table and push a wispy lock behind her ear. Her mouth parts gently, and she clicks her tongue in her cheek, ducking her head slightly.

"Why are you so sweet, Noah?" she asks, sounding genuinely confused.

My eyebrows crease, and I shrug. "Why wouldn't I be?"

Stuffing the paper ball she made, she says

quietly, "Most guys either want to get in my pants and just be dicks because, well, most guys *are* dicks. Except you, of course." She pauses and seems to struggle as she bites her lip, tongue poking her lip ring. "You're...different. Why?"

"Because you deserve sweetness. Speaking of which..." I point to the incoming slices of cake behind her, but she doesn't even perk up as the plates are served.

"Enjoy, and call me if you need anything," the nice woman says.

"Of course. Thanks so much." I offer her a kind smile, which makes Red grow an inch toward me, eyes searching for some sign of deceit. But when she finds none, I dig my fork into the cheesecake and take a bite. Instantly, I groan at the delicious creaminess.

"You have to try it—"

"I don't deserve sweetness," she interrupts. There's a hint of something behind her words that leaves me shuddering. Literally. Sureness? Absoluteness? Like, she committed a heinous crime and is positive she deserves nothing but bitterness. I sure as hell won't let that happen, I decide as I dig into the cake.

"Yes, you do, Red. Open your mouth." I guide the forkful of cheesecake to her lips. But she just stares at me like I'm some sort of puzzle with a cash prize on the other side of me. "Please, Red." I can't help the pleading in my voice.

Her brows curve downward, and I think she's going to deny my offer of the sweetness—the kindness, the *best*—that should come with expectation, not hesitation, but she opens her mouth. Smiling of relief, I gently guide the fork in. Her lips clamp around the utensil, and I slide it out, leaving the cake on her tongue.

I think and roll her words around in my head as she chews and I cut another small piece.

"What happened to you that makes you believe you don't deserve anything good? Me included," I ask her before I can stop myself, but I don't think I would have stopped myself. Maybe asked slower for her to process it. Either way, I have a desire to know to reassure her otherwise.

She stiffens and quickly finishes chewing. "Nothing," she lies.

But instead of jumping on her for the answer, I let it go. "Okay," I say with a small, apologetic smile.

"Okay?" she mumbles around a bite of cheesecake.

I chuckle at her puffy cheeks and nod. "Yes, *okay*." I take a sip of my water and tap my fingers along my hairline. *Maybe I should start off slower.* "Can I ask about your childhood?"

"Why?" she snaps, offended.

"I just want to know some more about you." I hold up my hands with a smile. "You don't have to answer if you don't want to, but I'll say mine was quite...lonely. I was an only child. I had friends. I actually had a *best* friend..." I trail off as I think about her. "But we grew apart. *But* luckily, we reconnected over the summer. What about you?"

She bites her lip ring, a crease between her brows. I don't think she's going to answer when she

185

says, "It was fine…I guess. I mean, my dad was dead before I came outta my mom." She slowly sinks her fork into her cake, *forlorn*. "My, uh, grandparents raised me. Basically, after she was murdered—" She swallows thickly, and her eyes grow empty.

"I'm so sorry." I place my hand over hers that's resting on the table. She flicks her eyes up to meet mine, and they light up with a bursting color before something washes over them like a rough wave, and she rips her hand from mine. I try not to look hurt as she continues, pushing a lock behind her ear.

"Doesn't matter. She's gone…" She shrugs again. I can practically see her pushing the solemn thought behind a familiar, rusty cage in those brilliant blue eyes of hers. Taking a rejuvenating breath, she sits up and meets my eyes with a small smile. "I just had one annoying-ass sister to keep me company as we grew up in lame-old Washington."

"You're from Washington?" I ask curiously.

"Yup." Her eyes squint, and I notice the hesitance when she asks, "Where you from?" like this is the first time she's ever talked about more than just quick hookups and motorcycles or whatever she talks about.

"New York."

"Upper East Side?" she teases.

I blush and shrug. "Upper East…*Queens?*"

She chuckles and digs into her pie. "Always wanted to visit New York. The place looks amazing, especially at night."

"Oh. You mean Times Square. Maybe we can

visit together one day." I want to push the words back in my mouth because I made it sound like we'd be...together? We'd be *something* long enough to visit New-freaking-York.

But she doesn't seem to mind because her smile widens a tad. "That'd be great, prep." Her cheeks brighten to a rosy color, and I smile, watching it dim as she coughs and changes the subject. "So. That mural of the city, state? The one on your wall...what the hell is up with that?"

"Oh." I rub my neck. "I had a bit of insomnia one night and ended up drawing...*that*."

Her brows rise like she's never heard of such a thing. "So you're like some sort of artistic genius or something?"

"Just a li'l bit." I shrug, hiding my smile. But it comes out anyway when she narrows her eyes at me skeptically. "Okay, I can paint the *Mona Lisa* while blindfolded. It's one of my many amazing talents. Give me a bottle of ketchup, and I can recreate *Starry Night*."

"Shut up." She throws her head back in throaty laughter. Her eyes shut, and she hugs her knees. I almost take a picture of her in her most gleeful state yet...okay, I do. What! Don't judge me. She's beautiful...

When she opens her eyes, she says, "Prep, sometimes you're just too much for me."

"Why do you call me prep?" I ask.

"I mean, besides the khakis and the fact that you reek of trust funds?" She scrunches up her nose, shoving a fork of cheesecake in her mouth.

"Shut up." I throw one of the torn-up papers at

her. It merely floats right back to me, and it's back to that adorable laughter of hers. My heart freezes in awe of her.

Her phone buzzing across the white bistro table yanks her back to reality too quick, too damn soon. She loses the luster in her eyes as she cranes her neck, flips the phone over, and stares at whatever's on the screen. I want to crane my neck too, to know who exactly just ruined this perfect moment of this perfect girl, but I refrain myself and casually bite into one of the last pieces of my cake.

"Something wrong?" I ask her before sipping on my melting cup of water.

"No," she lies, voice clipped.

But I don't push.

I just nod and offer her a smile. "Mind giving me a ride back to the house?" I lightly tease the idea of her ditching me here like she did at the motel. My heart screams at me, curses me to the moon and back, for giving her the idea. But it doesn't see the gleam in her eyes, doesn't hear the laugh in her voice.

"Only if you rain-check *your* dessert this morning." She slides out of the booth.

I follow her, throwing down a twenty. "As long as it'll always be open for me."

Stepping up to me, chest to chest, her body heatwave crashing into my cool blue hue, she whispers, "Oh. I wouldn't leave these, *prep.*" She reaches up and glides a finger down my lips.

I connect my eyes with her teasing ones and sink my teeth onto her finger.

She doesn't even flinch.

Just smirks.

Fucking dangerous, I tell you...so why am I smiling?

***

I'm practically bouncing on the balls of my feet as I jog up the frat house's stairs. I bypass a couple of guys bringing in a boatload of cases of Corona. Doped up with Red's presence, I slap them on the back and give them friendly smiles.

"Good day, boys." I bid them a wave as they branch off into the kitchen.

They raise their brows but continue crab-walking with the heavy cases.

"What's got you so giddy?" Mike asks as he walks by, texting on his phone. He stops to give me a once-over, searching for the answer. But he can't see my Red-shaped heart pounding to the beat of her laugh.

"Oh. Nothing in particular," I tell him in an upbeat voice, starting up the stairs.

"He's lying! He almost got some pussy this morning!" Ty yells from his spot on the couch inside the living room.

"Fuck off, Ty!" I yell back over my shoulder, middle finger poised. Red doing the same thing flashes through my mind, and I laugh to myself. I bask in Mike's chuckle downstairs. I'm so high on cloud nine, I doubt anything can knock me off. Not without a fight from me, at least.

Opening my bedroom door, I'm shot off that cloud and served up as Noah-stew, because sitting on my bed are my parents. My very, very, *very* angry-looking parents, if I'm honest. I feel my heart drop to my ass.

Chapter Twenty-Three

In life there are moments when I wish I could hit a pause button and get the hell away before shit hits the fan. One of the first moments I can remember is the time I bit the tongue of the first girl I kissed, Molly Wendell. She spread the incident around middle school, and I experienced my first facepalm moment. The next was when I broke my leg from painting a mural on a building in my hometown, the night before the homecoming football game.

But none of those moments compare to this one because of two things: 1. My mother is tapping her foot, lips screwed in her mouth—which is a tell-tale sign that this is going to end painfully with a lecture I should get popcorn for, to be honest. And 2. My father is standing very, very far from her—which just highlights how much I am in for it with Mother. She's always been the disciplinary one. The one that lectures and scowls and flicks you on the head when your posture is like a sloth's.

"Are you going to just stand there like a statue?" My mother is wearing a white pantsuit with a red blouse underneath the jacket, her makeup light, lips a bloody red.

My brain whirls at warp speed to formulate a sophisticated response.

"Uh…*hey*?" I say unsurely.

My father's jaw tightens in the background.

Mother rolls her honey brown eyes. "Noah, we sent you here so you would learn how to be a responsible adult with a clear head on your shoulders and a diploma in your hand. Not some delinquent who gets into fights like he doesn't know how to talk *first* and *not* use his fists like some…some…"

"Barbarian?" Father assists, and I glare at him. He holds up his hands, palms up in defense, an annoying smirk on his face. I see he hasn't changed since he hauled me out of Italy.

"Yes, Robert." She nods to Father in thanks, then swivels those fiery eyes back to me. "A barbarian is the right word I'm looking for. Noah, what are you doing? What could have possibly gone through your head that would make you raise your fist to some innocent boy?"

"Innocent?" I laugh before thinking, and she raises a brow. "Ian is anything but innocent. He…" I trail off, holding back why we got into a fight in the first place. Something tells me she won't appreciate my involvement with Red.

"He what, Noah? Did he bully you, sweetie?" she asks softly.

I'm not some little kid. God, I hate it when she treats me like I'm some little boy who needs her protection and sweet tone. A boy who doesn't understand that without his mother's guidance, he will turn into a caveman delinquent who only knows a few slobbering words without a college diploma. I am so much more than that. I am artistic through and through. I just wanted to travel the world. See some things. Do *more*.

But she will never understand.

"No, *Mother*," I say with a bite in my voice. "I am nineteen, meaning I can handle it if someone bullies me. I'm not a little kid on the playground. He didn't bully me. He was just a dick."

"Language!" she barks.

Father hides a smile. "Yeah, language," he adds. Walking over to Mother, he puts a hand on her shoulder. She shakes it off, glaring at me with laser beams. "Maybe you should listen to your mother—"

"She's calling me a child!" I interrupt.

"I did not call you a child," Mother spits.

"You implied it!" I shout.

"Hey, now—enough with the arguing." Father's voice has deepened, and he looks at me with intense, dark green eyes behind his square black glasses. My father rarely raises his voice or takes a stand between my mother and me, so when he levels his eyes at the *both* of us, I make sure to listen. He is the saner of the two. "Noah, we sent you here to get an education. You're passionate about art, I get it." His eyes flick over to the mural of the city I've yet to take down. "But you have to give this college thing a chance—"

"*College thing*?" Mother gasps, wide-eyed.

"Gemma, please," Dad pleads softly. She merely rolls her eyes before settling them on me. "Thank you." He kisses the side of her head, and I swear I see a hint of a smile on her crimson lips. "Noah…you have to give this a real chance. I know it isn't your passion or anything, but it will get you farther in life. Your art is incredible…but you need to have a college diploma. After that, you can paint the eight wonders of the world and resurrect Picasso with your art." He laughs and I chuckle; Mother remains stoic. "But for now, college needs to be your priority. No *fighting*. Please. For me?"

Normally, I would rebel and argue with my mother despite all he's just said. But the calmness and understanding in his voice and soft green eyes compel me to be a good boy for just this once and do as they say.

Sighing heavily, I nod. "Yes. You're right. But even so, you have to accept that not everyone here has good intentions. Some people can act like dicks…" I stop myself as Mother narrows her eyes. "I didn't start these fights to get back at you or anything. He's just a *very* frustrating person and, well, he brings out the worst in me." And I'm not lying. I'm normally a chill, low-key guy, but he's yanked me into two fights without much effort. He's just an asshole.

"You *started* the fights?" Mother shrieks.

Uh…whoops?

Luckily, Father gently squeezes her shoulder, quieting her to the point where she diffuses her anger and instead mutters under her breath. He's so skilled at calming her down in record time, he should be on the Bomb Squad.

"We'll check up every once in a while. Enjoy

yourself, but no more fighting," Father says as he leads Mother out of the room.

"Got it," I assure him.

I listen to Mother's quiet rambling about how I should be looked after and Father's quiet attempt to hush her. A few high heel clicks later, I hear the front door shut. I jog over to the window that looks out over the front lawn and watch as they get in their porcelain white Porsche and drive away. I slump against the window, letting out a breath I hadn't realized I'd been holding. At least now we got that surprise visit out of the way and I can relax. I just can't get into any more trouble or they'll hire a bodyguard to watch me or something insane like that.

"Your parents are insane," a voice whispers in my ear.

I whip around and face Ty, who's staring at my parents' Porsche turning down the street. "*You're* the insane one, sneaking up on me like a weirdo."

I push at him playfully and walk over to my bed. Grabbing my backpack, I dump it on my bed and let out a grumble. I promised my father to focus on college, and he's actually a lot better at being persuasive than my mother, so I will do as promised and do better. Actually try my best. And the first sure way of trying is studying.

"Hey, you coming to the fair tonight?" he asks, dropping onto his bed.

"Fair?" I prop open a chemistry textbook. Rachel crosses my mind and a quiz we have on Tuesday, and I reach for my phone to see if she wants to study together. I need to pass this quiz since I nearly bombed the last one. The girl's a chemical wizard. She could be a mad scientist if she chose to be one.

"Just this bullshit fair the school puts together to 'support' the football team." He puts up air quotes.

"What's up with the air quotes around support?" I furrow my brows, take one glance at a review question on a random page, my brain explodes, and I close the book. I'll study later.

"Nothing except the fact that they put *us,* the *team*, into stupid games, like that dunking shit, so people will donate money for equipment or whatever. This school's fucking loaded, probably. Coach just loves to see us suffer," he exclaims with such vigor, a vein thumps on his forehead. I'm a laughing mess. "Laugh now. Coach is still pissed about that fighting stunt between you and Ian. And he's got something *extra* special for you two."

My laughter dissipates. "Wait. What?"

"No, keep laughing. It's so freaking hilarious." He jumps to his feet and winks at me before slinking out of the room.

"Wait! What's that supposed to mean?" I call after him, but he closes the door.

Ugh.

I guess I'll find out what he means later tonight. It bothers me that I didn't know about the fair until now. I'm on the team, but I didn't find out about the *team* event until Ty asked if I was going...I guess I've been so focused on Red and whatever the hell we are that I've been blurring other important things out. I really need to focus on everything in whole. Not just her. Easier said than done, I think as I find my thumbs sending a text to her.

Noah: Feel like spending time with a frat guy who could definitely win you a collection of bears from carnival games tonight?

When the response isn't immediate, I flip open the textbook. Stare at the formulas and...end up texting Rachel. I ask her about the fair and if she wants to attend, though she may have already gotten the message since her brother's the team captain. But it doesn't hurt to ask, right? Her response is almost immediate, but to be fair, it's just a thumbs-up emoji followed by a smiley emoji.

As I type back a response to get a conversation going about the chemistry quiz, my phone buzzes. On top of the screen is a text back from Red. My heart drops incredibly low as I read it and tap on the banner.

Red: Busy.

My thumbs hover over the necessary keys to ask if she's okay. Her tone is clipped and distant, even if it's over text. I think I know her well enough to know when something's off with her. I skim through our previous texts, smiling at the silly emojis and her sass and my corny jokes she seemingly doesn't find funny, but I knew when I sent them she was dying of laughter. I could just sense it over the phone. Just like I can sense she isn't okay now.

But when I finish and hover my thumb over the *SEND* key, she replies.

Red: OK, Prep. Dont worry.

A slight smile melts onto my face because I think, like me, she can sense what I'm feeling. So, instead of getting her upset, which happens a lot, I send her an *Okay* and study over the phone with Rachel with a smile.

***

I've quickly come to learn that Coach is a vindictive man. What Ty hinted at earlier in regards to my "punishment" at the fair is wearing nothing but the school's basketball shorts while holding up a sign that says:

I am an idiot who can't stop fighting like a wild animal. Kiss me to soothe my animalistic ways. A dollar.

At first, I think I was let off easy compared to other guys getting dunked in freezing water and having fruits thrown at their faces through cut-out holes, and then I stand for an hour. In that hour, I get kissed by twenty women, all purring after me and mocking me. Some write their numbers on my chest, which I immediately wipe off when they stumble off with their friends, drunk out of their minds.

I've been here for almost two hours now, and my nipples are frozen solid, there's too much lipstick to get off, and I really have to pee. I would have someone cover for me, but Coach hasn't stopped glaring at me since Ian claimed he was sick and got left off. *Damn lying asshole.* He just didn't want to do this stupid job.

"Anyone gotta dollar on 'em?" Mike teases as he and a group walk over to me. He and most of the other guys on the team played their roles in this freaking fair and are now enjoying what it has to offer. I want to get cotton candy, but I have more fear for my balls Coach threatened to kick after the incident than desire for sugar on a stick.

"Shut the fuck up and move on or he'll kill us all," I warn through chattering teeth.

"Oh, you can stop now," Ty says with a secretive smirk.

"What? No. Coach's still watching." I nod to the angry man ten feet away.

They all laugh like there's some inside joke I don't know about.

"Why're you laughing?" I ask.

"That isn't Coach," Mike says, laughing. "Ty paid some guy to stand there for a while just so you'd stand here looking like a fool. Completely his idea, of course."

"What?" I roar, and the group bursts into laughter.

"Yeah, Coach left, like, an hour ago," he adds.

"Got you gooooood." Ty shoots finger guns at me.

Picking up the cardboard sign, I run after him. He made me stand there forever when I could have been free this entire time? Girls purr after me as I run around the fair. For a receiver, he runs like a little chubby baby who just learned how to walk.

Does he only know how to run on the field or something? He even goes as far as pushing people in my way, trying to dodge the certainty of death by my hands. I didn't get quarterback for no reason. I tackle him between a rifle shooting game and a basketball free-throw game.

"You. Are. *A dead man!*" I scream as I begin beating him with the cardboard. The group and Mike have caught up with us. Some people record using their cell phones while Ty screams like a bitch. He deflects horribly, and after a while it just gets sad, so I end up punching him in the shoulder and telling him, "Don't do that shit again. I'm not entirely sure my nipples haven't fallen off."

Laughing his head off, he stands up. "Want me to check?" He makes grabby hands at my chest, and I push him off. He can be such a dick.

"Get off of me." I laugh as he comes at me again. I'm looking around for booths that interest me since I am finally off the clock, no thanks to *this* dick, when I see her. I almost think I'm going crazy and a little obsessed with her, but then she screams and that's a distinguishable factor if there were ever any.

"Red?" I say breathlessly.

Chapter Twenty-Four

I'm being tugged physically, urged to join the group conversation. They're talking about seeing a movie some day during the week. I'd love to interact with them, have fun. But I can't stop staring at Red. She said she was busy, so what is she doing here? And with a guy, nonetheless? My hands curl into fists as I eye the man as best I can so far away.

I'm about to storm over and confront her when I hear a very cheery, "What did I miss?" It's Rachel. I begin to smile at her as she bounces over to us, but then my eyes land on the tall, brooding asshole of a step-brother.

"I thought you were sick," I say to him when they walk over.

"Yeah. Of doing that dumb shit." He smiles sarcastically, an arm around his sister. She pushes his arm off, much to my pleasure, and scampers over to give me a quick side-hug.

"Don't mind him; someone pissed in his Cheerios this morning," she says, earning an eye roll from Mr. Scrooge behind her.

"That person must hate the cereal to do it every morning," I joke, and she laughs, though her brother scowls at me. Now I'm really wondering if someone *does* piss in his cereal. It would explain *a lot.*

"Anyway, I was thinking we could get on the Ferris wheel and…" Rachel begins with a huge grin. I try to focus on her words, on her warm smile and excited eyes, but I can't erase the presence of Red, even if she's so far away. I can feel her and her obvious lie weighing on my shoulders. It becomes hard to ignore when I can't stop imagining punching the guy she's with. But then I think of it and I hate myself for it. Jealousy. She evokes so many emotions in me, but jealousy is one I despise because it's toxic and sometimes all-consuming.

"I need to go do something," I interrupt Rachel and hate myself a little more as her smile drops into a small frown.

"What? But the Ferris wheel…" She trails off, and I mentally stab myself in the eye with a fork. Sweet Rachel doesn't deserve being ditched because of Red, who blatantly lied to me.

"It'll be quick, I promise," I assure her, squeezing her shoulder lightly.

"Okay," she says with a smile, eyes swimming in gloom.

"Way to break my li'l sis's heart." Ian wraps his arms around her, and they get into this bickering fight, and I slowly slip away, kind of grateful for him getting those big sad eyes away from torturing me. Each time hurts more I pull away from her kindness to embark toward someone so complicated, it makes my head hurt sometimes.

As I grow closer to the…two, I pull on my jersey and run a hand through my hair. I end up pulling on my dark blue beanie that matches the jersey. Ignoring the shudder of fire under my skin as I approach her, I paint on a smile.

"Hey, Red," I say in an easy tone.

She stops screaming at the man and looks over at me. Her eyes do a double take, and she quickly glares at the man before sighing, eyes settling on me again. "'Sup."

What?

"That's all you have to say to me?" I thought she'd be shy about being caught then explain why she lied to me. I like the girl, I really do. So I would have forgiven her easily and gotten her a cotton candy. But if she's going to act this way…

"We'll continue this later," the man says, and I finally notice him. And I mean *really* notice him. He's tall, maybe six-foot-two, so a little shorter than me. He has sharp features, hooded. And he's dressed in all black, from his biker boots to the huge hoodie.

"Whatever." Red rolls her eyes.

He grips her arm, and I widen my eyes. "Answer when I call," he murmurs before roughly letting go and brushing past me. I stumble back and register what just happened but come up empty handed.

"Who the hell was that?" I turn to Red, who tries to walk away, but I instinctively grab her hand. She pulls away and looks at me with wide eyes. I apologize immediately. "I'm sorry. I didn't…" But then I think of what we've been doing—kissing and…other things, wisely—and I trail off. "Actually, no. What were you doing here with *him*?"

"Don't get all jealous, *prep*." She pauses and glares off into the distance where the mystery man wandered off to. Something pierces her tough, cool exterior, but it's gone the second I notice it, as she sets her fixed gaze on me. "He was nobody."

"He didn't *seem* like a nobody." I keep up with her as she storms off aimlessly. She pushes past a laughing couple, and I apologize on her behalf. "Red, slow down. Please. I need to talk to you."

She scoffs and picks up speed. "No, what you *need* to do is fuck off and leave me alone."

"Why are you acting like this?" I ask and get no response, just more speeding. "Red! Did I do something to make you act this way?" We were fine this morning. Great, even. We got deep enough for me to get to know her better, we were playful. And now…now she's acting as if she doesn't even know me.

"Last call for the last cab," a lanky boy calls out, standing in front of the Ferris wheel Rachel was talking about. An idea pops into my head, and I hold up a hand to catch his attention.

"I'm making you talk to me whether you like it or not." I grab her hand and drag her to the Ferris wheel. My fear of heights kicks up, and I pause for a second in front of the boy holding open the door. But the screaming, violent girl slapping my arm pushes the fear to the side, and I pull us into the cart.

Slapping the ride, the boy says, "Enjoy the

riiiiiide."

"What the hell is *wrong* with you?" Red snaps as the cart jingles and the ride starts. She scoots over to the side and peers over the side, then snaps a furious look over her shoulder.

"I'm just trying to understand," I tell her, frustrated myself.

A heavy sigh leaves her lips as she shakes her head. "There's nothing to understand. I didn't feel like spending the night with you being dunked in tanks and winning bears and shit. I just had some business to take care of. I was going to leave right after." Her words are packed with a sting I never experienced.

"Why come here to conduct 'business?'" I question, and she reddens with anger, fisting her untamed hair.

"Because he's an asshole." I sense irony hidden behind her words, but she covers it when she turns to me and spits, "Trust me, I wouldn't come here if he didn't drag me here."

I grasp for words. "Why are you acting like this?"

"Like what?" she snaps through grinding teeth.

I pause and scoot closer to her; her eyes flash wider, and she looks down. "Like you don't know me. You're acting cold to me for no reason, and I want to know if I did something wrong."

"You didn't do anything *wrong*," she says, and I frown.

"What? Then why are you being like this?"

"Because…" She swivels to meet my eyes, visibly gasps for breath, and groans, "Because

I…*like* you, or whatever."

I am so confused.

"And how is that a bad thing?" I ask, unable to control my smile.

The corners of her mouth seem to fight a smile of her own. Grunting and groaning as if the fight of the century is occurring within her, she bursts into a rant of words. "It's a bad thing because I don't *want* to like you. I shouldn't. I'm seriously bad for you. If you knew that…" She pauses, and I want her to continue that train of thought, as my curiosity is piqued. But she brushes the words away using her frazzled, waving hands and goes on.

"You're just really different than any other guy I know, and sometimes it…" Another pause, and, growing too stressed over her words, she grabs me by the collar of my jersey and tugs herself over to my side. "Sometimes I get crazy thinking about you, and I want to kiss you. Like, badly. But then I think about…about how you should have more, and—"

My lips crush hers into silence. I wrap my hands around her slim waist, pulling her into my chest. Her small hands cup my face, and I melt at her soft, warm touch. Fire floods my veins and sizzles beneath my teeth; they vibrate as my tongue meets hers, and a moan escapes her open mouth. Her toxic taste buds make mine go crazy, and I press her against the side, desperate for more. I don't think I will ever get tired of kissing her lips. Feeling her hands slowly find their way into my hair. Hearing her heart if the buzzing of fire is low enough.

I gently pull away, smiling against her needy lips

pecking mine. "I don't want anything that isn't you, Red. You make me wild for your kiss, and just...*you*."

"So I don't need to burn down your shrine?" she jokes in a whisper against my lips.

I laugh against her warm, full lips and feel her chuckle into my mouth. I groan at the strangely familiar sentiment, like we were doing this in another world, and pull her to me. "I won't melt down yours if you don't melt down mine."

She laughs, and it's free and snort-full, and I love it. "Deal." She holds out her pinky. I take it feverishly, kiss the tip, gauge the air catching in her throat, the flutter of her beautiful blue eyes.

I whisper against her nose, "Deal," before pecking her forehead. As she sighs against me, a crease in her forehead like the entirety of her can't accept that the rest of her is content, we're jerked slightly.

"Ride's over, lovebirds," the boy who let us on jokes. I think. I can't tell by his blank expression.

We get off the ride much happier than when I dragged her into it.

"What now?" she asks as we stroll aimlessly. I eye her hand that's next to me with the inexplicable urge to take it in mine. To feel her small hand in my large one, watch her fight a blush. But I don't know what we are, and it'll just ruin the content peace between us. So I push my hands in my pockets to avoid looking like an idiot and answer her.

"We do what friends do at a fair."

"And what's that?"

"This." I grab her hand, but it's short-lived as we

stop at the cotton candy stand. "One pink, please," I tell the young girl behind the register. She accepts the five dollar bill and hands me the cotton candy and tries to give me my change, but I let her keep it.

"I don't like this," Red says as we walk away.

"What?" I sling an arm around her, lean down, and pick a piece off. "How can you not like cotton candy? It's like saying you don't like puppies." I push the sweet fluffy treat in my mouth and notice her silence. I gasp, nearly choking as I exclaim, "You don't like puppies!"

She reddens and nudges me in the ribs. Hard. But I just laugh. "I didn't say *that*. I just don't like sugar on a stick." She makes a face of disgust.

"Come on. Just give it a try." I pick another piece off and push it near her mouth.

"No way! No! Noah!" She laughs as I tug her mouth open and plop the candy on her tongue. I watch it dissolve and smile widely as she twists her lips, punching me in the shoulder. "Not cool, prep!" I catch her incoming hand, kiss the knuckles, and then her forehead. And then again. And again. "Stop with the kissing! Ah! Stop!"

I throw her over my shoulder and wheel her around. "Tell me I'm the cutest ever and then I'll let you down!"

"No fucking way that's happening!" she screams.

"Okay, then I'll wear you like an accessory," I sing-song, ignoring her pleads to put her down, spinning in slow circles. She laughs more than she pleads. My heart expands more and more as I listen to her hearty laugh.

"Okay, okay!" She kicks her legs.

I set her down but keep my hands locked around her waist. Her soft glare into my eyes only makes me shine brighter. "I'm sorry, I didn't hear that." I lean down to her mouth, hand cupped around my ear.

She groans against my chest, "You're cute or whatever."

"What? Oh! You want me to spin around but upside down this time?" I move to hook my hands around her knees, bent over so we're kind of eye level.

"No! No!" She pushes then grips my shoulders. "You, Noah Wells...are the cutest, and I'd *appreciate* it if you didn't pick me up again."

"I can't promise anything." I let out a breath and push some hair tendrils behind her small ear. She gasps lightly and lets the blush melt onto her cheeks. I'm gutted and moved by how simply beautiful this girl is, even though she doesn't seem to try at all. I just want to draw her face and blend our lips like paint. I want to hold her and kiss her, and so I do.

The kiss is slow and soft and incredibly warm. There's no explosion underneath my skin. Just an inkling of familiarity and a bubbly feeling in my chest. Her fingertips gently hold my cheeks, like she's afraid I'll slip away from her. And when I slowly pull back, her eyes frantically search mine.

"What was that for?" she asks softly.

I break into a smile. "Just 'cause."

A smile breaks out onto her face, but before she can completely turn soft, she laughs and pushes me back. "Don't get too soft on me, prep. I want to see what you can do with a gun." She nods toward the booth with the fake rifles and the bottles no one seems to be able to break. But isn't that the point of these booths? Being impossible to win so you spend more money for more chances that won't matter?

"Oh, you don't wanna see what I can do with a gun." Spinning her a bit because I love to hear her laugh, I grab her hand and walk us over to a pissed-off couple. "When I was ten, I shot and killed a deer. We had it for dinner."

"Really?" Her eyes search mine, and I shake my head.

"Nah, but wouldn't that have been cool?" I say.

"Shut up." She chuckles and slaps my chest.

I listen to her laugh and almost don't hear the man behind the booth asking if we're going to play. I give him a ten dollar bill, which pays for five games, and am handed a large rifle. As we shoot and mostly miss the green bottles—Red hits two of them, pissing the guy off—I can't help but feel like I'm being…watched. But when I try to look around, the man threatens to take the gun away, so I just brush the feeling off and continue shooting beside my girl who teases me for not making *one*.

Chapter Twenty-Five

A few hours later, Red and I are laughing over an incident at the carnival. After winning a booth game where we have to win a race by shooting water in a clown's mouth, the guy attending the booth refused to give us the teddy bear we won fair and square. I tried to talk him out of being a douche, but Red had other plans. She socked him in the mouth, snatched the huge bear holding a honey pot, and we booked it out of the fair altogether.

I still can't believe we did that. She didn't punch the guy so hard he gushed blood, but I didn't apologize nor get him to the nursing tent. I just let Red grab my hand and ran as someone threatened to call the police. My heart never pounded so hard in my chest before; it's a miracle I'm not passed out right now. I don't ever do things like this, at least until I met Red. And now I feel like a criminal on the run most of the time. Which should make me worried...but all I can do is look at her with a smile on my face.

"That was unexpected," I say and look over at

her. "Do you normally clock guys and steal their teddy bears?"

"If a guy has a collection of teddy bears, then he *deserves* to be clocked."

I laugh, and she smiles at me. "A little harsh, don't you think? I mean, once I take my half of our little stash back there, are you gonna punch me too?"

She scoffs and pulls to a stop in front of the fraternity house. "If you dress them up in princess dresses and have tea parties with them—*yes*."

"Then you can just beat me up right now," I joke as I turn to her. She narrows her eyes and moves her small hand to punch me in the shoulder. But I have too fast of a reflex. That and I knew she'd try to hit me. Grabbing her wrist, I tug at her, pulling her onto my lap.

"See that coming?" she asks, crooning in that slow, raspy voice of hers. Her hands loop around my neck and rest in my hair. Her fingers tug lightly, and her chest is pressed against mine. She molds to me so perfectly it makes me giddy on the inside. But don't tell her or I'll be hospitalized.

"Maybe. You become predictable after a while." I tighten my arms around her waist, erasing whatever space bubbled between us. Those bubbles explode, and my smile widens when her eyes lighten.

"Oh. Then I'll just have to change that then, huh?" Her tone is dark, and her hands are sliding down my chest.

"Please do, but I'll still know what you're going to do," I tease. Bullshit. I could know this girl for a thousand days and still be in the dark about what she's going to do next. She's a firecracker without a warning.

"Then I guess you just know that I'm going to do this…" she says, fingers gliding down my stomach.

"What do you—oh. *Oh.*" I bounce my eyebrows as her fingers tighten around the waistband of my jeans.

She giggles, and I kiss her mouth. "Don't act surprised, Mr. Know-It-All."

"I'm not surprised, just taken aback."

"Basically means the same thing." She squints an eye at me. She's making fun of me, and I laugh at myself because I actually didn't see that coming. Doesn't mean I'm opposed to it, though. Jesus Christ. Why am I actually talking to myself right now? I may have traveled the world in a year opposed to normal nineteen year olds, but I know when to shut up when a girl has her hands digging into my pants.

"Sorry, my brain shuts off when you tease me." I push open the passenger door.

She pulls back and looks outside, then at me, confused. "What are you doing?"

"Getting out of the public view before cops roll by and give us a ticket for indecent exposure." I grab her hand.

"They still do that? I thought that was made up because cops catching teens doing it in a car reminds them of their depressing lack of a sex life," she jokes as I unlock the front door.

Admittedly, her talk about sex makes me clam up a bit. I'm not a virgin or anything. I'm far from it, actually. Ask a few girls in Italy, Moscow, India—I've gotten around, okay? But with Red, it'll be different because I have feelings for her. Actual feelings that run deeper than my brief visit before I haul ass to another continent. She'd linger and it'd lead to something bigger, make us more intimate. I want that. I really do, but to her, it sounds like it wouldn't be a big deal.

"You okay? You seem a little…off." She walks over to me and palms my face. I stopped walking on the way to the stairs, and she looks genuinely concerned. My heart tugs at the frown on her mouth and forehead.

I smile and wrap an arm around her. "I'm fine. Perfect…if we can get to my room in less than ten seconds."

"Guess we better run, huh?" Her face brightens like a blossoming sunflower, and I shake my head. If I look any longer, I'll be serenading about how much I really, really like this girl.

"I have a better idea."

"What are you—Noah!" She squeals as I hook my hands around the backs of her knees. I bring her to my chest and accept as she hits my shoulder. "You are insane," she claims but snorts in laughter, eyes pinched closed as I walk to the stairs.

"I prefer tenacious," I say, and she merely rolls her eyes.

In my bedroom, I gently set her down. I become very aware of what will happen. Or what I think will happen. My heart's pounding. I take subtle, slow breaths to calm myself.

"Noah? Why do you look like you're either

about to kidnap me or pass out?" She laughs, and it's a light, glorious sound I want to listen to forever.

"Sorry." I blush, and she waves it away, eyes growing…sharper. Watching me as I close the gap between us. "You just make me a little insane and a little bit alive. But right now, I want to feel your lips on mine. Is that okay?" I push my hand into her hair while the other gently cups her lower back.

Her lips part, and she gazes at my lips, then smiles as she looks into my eyes. "Noah, it's more than okay. And just to be clear…" Her fingertips, black and chipped, dance their way up to my hair. Literally. I laugh, and she chuckles before sighing deeply. "You make me a little insane too, not that I wasn't before."

I shake my head and duck to be near her height. "You aren't insane. *You're perfect*," I whisper and watch her eyes drop silently closed. I smile and erase the distance between us.

The minute our lips press together, we sigh into each other's mouths. The fire that usually sparks when we kissed in the past is less intense. More intimate and slow-burning. But then her hands fly to my pants and hellfire burns. I nudge her until the backs of her knees hit the mattress, and she tilts toward the mattress. I turn last second and we land sideways, but she straddles me. She breaks the kiss to sit up and take off her jacket and tank top, leaving her in a black bra.

My breathing becomes difficult, and she smirks as if she knows it. After taking off my own shirt and kicking off my shoes and socks, I reach up and tug her back down using a bra strap. She smiles into the kiss as I cup her breast. But that teasing smile fades into a moan as I dip my hand inside and tweak her nipple. She rubs herself against me, eliciting a groan from me. I push her hair out of the way and begin nipping at her skin, gliding my tongue on the smooth surface.

"Noah," she moans, and her hands disappear behind her back. A few seconds later, she flings the bra across the room.

I push her to her back on the bed and stare down at her. I thumb my bottom lip, trying to not lose my shit like I am on the inside. She is the most beautiful creature on this planet. I want to paint her body. I want to paint *on* her body. I kiss her lips, then her chin, then her neck. She moans my name when my lips softly press into her stomach. Her back arches, and I smile against her right hipbone…then the left.

"I've wondered what you taste like on your lips…" I pop open the button on her jeans, and she gasps. "*Down here.*"

"Please do," she murmurs, getting lost in the sensation of me slowly dragging her panties and jeans down her long, slender legs. Pushing her shoes, socks, and other clothing onto the floor, I bend down.

"Such soft skin." My voice sounds different, deeper, as I kiss the inside of her right leg. I listen to my delight as she moans and tries to catch her breath. Each kiss on each leg pushes her more and more, but I keep her legs open as she squirms.

Reaching her pussy, I kiss her center, gauge her sharp, "Noah," and smile.

"Absolutely *beautiful*." I kiss her again and slowly drop my mouth open, tasting her. *All of her.*

"Noah—oh, *God*." She fists the sheets.

"You're so wet, all for me…it's insane," I murmur mostly to myself, but she shudders having heard me, and I smile against her.

I gently suck her, making small strokes, and she grips the bedsheets. Harder. I harden as she moans and fists my hair. I love this. Love the *taste* of her. How she's getting so riled up, each time I flick my tongue and call her sweet names, "beautiful," "gorgeous," "perfect," that fall out of my mouth and onto her soaking center. I grip the backs of her knees and fling her legs onto my back. I can't get enough of how fucking delicious she tastes. I need *more*.

She giggles loudly. "Fuck, Noah. Get a little caveman on me, why don't ya?"

"Sorry." I come up for air, and she stares at me with glossy eyes, and messy blonde hair. "I can't get enough of you. You just taste so fucking *good*." I dip my head and continue making random patterns.

"For fuck's—ah!" She throws her head back and holds mine. She's gripping me for dear life, it seems. But I don't mind. In fact, I love it. So much I have a boner the more she tugs.

I imagine I'm painting our bodies joined together. Starting with her long legs tangled with mine, ending with her pouty red lips. I envision her eyes stretched closed, my mouth tracing her soft neck. In real life, she's moaning and writhing.

"Oh, Noah," she moans as my tongue gently lays

against her, swirling.

"Let go, *Rossa*," I instruct, my voice low and vibrating against her. It sends her over the edge because she screams my name, and I taste every inch of her arousal. I harden so much, I'm pretty sure I came in my pants. Her hips buck in the air, and I press her down, my hands flat on her abdomen. I smile like an idiot as she whines my name as she comes down from her high. Her sounds, the way she's reaching for me, is so fucking sexy. I want to make her scream that way again.

"Did you like that, Rossa?" I ask teasingly as I kiss my way up to her. She's rolling her eyes and pushing at my chest when I sidle up next to her. I hold her to me, and she stares into my eyes with a dazed smile, a wild blonde curl resting on her cheek.

"I loved it…whatever your name is in Italian." Her voice takes on a sexy, raspy tone.

"It's just Noah; yours is different because it's a color."

"Fuck you." She laughs.

"Will you?" I bounce my brows.

Hers raise and she pushes my shoulder, straddling me. "Gladly."

"Wait." I grab her hips, stopping her from moving. "I already…you know…"

She looks utterly puzzled, and then it dawns on her and she's all smirking. "I'm that hot you busted a—"

"Please. Save me from the embarrassment." I cover my face with my hands, but she pulls them away and chuckles, hovering over me like a breathtaking angel.

"No way. If I made you come in your pants just by getting head from you, just imagine how I'd be in bed. With you. And your excited fella down there," she says with a huge, shit-eating grin.

"Stop, you're killing me," I groan and roll around, clutching my groin.

"Me in a bikini. No. Naked. Honey dripping down my—" I put a hand over her mouth, and she laughs against it as I straddle her, putting a pillow between us...down there.

"I'm all tapped out from tonight. And another word out of you..." I say between my own laughter as her cheeks turn bright pink, eyes scrunched closed. "I might explode. So, if you will. *Please*." I remove my hand enough to lean my forehead against hers, prolonging her heavenly laughter by tickling her sides.

"Ah! No! I hate tickles. Stop, stop, stop—STOP!" she roars, but I don't listen. I throw the pillow away and wrap her in the thin bedsheet. I continue my assault, gauging her red face and that damn dimple on the left corner of her mouth. I kiss it, her lips, her neck—everywhere my hungry lips can get.

The ringing of a phone interrupts. I plan to ignore it, enjoying making her laugh too much, but she pats my arms. Sighing dramatically, I sit back on the heels of my feet. "Whoever that is better be damn important," I say playfully, and she chuckles, but it dies down to nothing as she fishes her phone out and stares at the screen.

"Everything okay?" I ask after a while of silence

and her staring at the phone.

I hear her breath intake.

"Red?" I walk over to her and move to put a hand on her shoulder. But she flinches away and stands up. Her eyes are wide, and I swear I see fear in them before she turns from me. She begins to get dressed and throws the sheet at me. I catch it and stand up, trying to catch her eyes.

"Hey, Red. Red. What's wrong? Where are you going?"

"I'm...I have to go. I'm sorry." She buttons her jeans and moves for her shirt, jacket, and shoes. I move to grab her hand, but she sidesteps it and runs out of the room like she's on fire.

"Red, wait!" I follow after her, tripping on my shoes. The front door slams shut, or open, I can't tell. My heart stumbles as I push to my feet and rush down the stairs. Damn, she moves fast! By the time I fling the front door open, she's already peeling onto the road. My heart squeezes, and I blink rapidly as I try to make sense of what just happened. "Fuck!" I kick the front door.

Chapter Twenty-Six

Red has been distant for quite some time. Since the last we were in my room, I haven't heard from her much. She's ignored me: every call, text, voicemail. I hate to say that I'm beginning to get used to it. The last time she left me on silent put me in a daze. I barely knew how to operate.

I've never cared about anyone before like I care about her, so when she drops off the face of the planet, it's safe to say a part of me that's linked to her in some way dies a little. And it'll resurrect the moment I see her in the flesh, safe and sound.

Until then, I constantly feel like I'm on the edge of some seat. Waiting for the shoe to drop. Sitting by and expecting her to pop up and break things off with us. A sadist part of me is bouncing on his feet, wishing for her to end this brighter side of me she's created. Hoping for her to come around with Tanner and screw him in front of me. Why not throw Ian in there as well? As long as she ruins whatever kind of chance we have. Just get it over with before my feelings for her blow up until it's uncontrollable and

I'm unable to recuperate.

Nonetheless, I'm worried about her. The look on her face before she up and left was haunted. Pained. And it looked like she'd been gutted from the inside out. I wanted to reach out, fix whatever broke her. But she slipped from my fingertips before I could even get a grasp on her. And she took my heart with her, my sanity. Leaving me with a cloudy, muggy mind that revolves around her.

I drew her in sketches and portraits in and out of the art club to keep myself occupied, to keep my sanity intact. But it doesn't work. It never does. Not like touching her warm, soft skin. Knowing that she's alive and well.

"Thinking about who you're taking to the bonfire tonight?" a voice croons in my ear.

I look to my right and smile half-heartedly. "Hey, Beth." Upon me saying her name, she twirls her chunky brown hair and bats her extended eyelashes.

Her glossy lips pull into a smile. "Hey, Noah," she muses, then her touched-up eyebrows raise as if she's expecting something to happen from me. I don't understand until she sighs and giggles, touching my arm as if I'm being silly. "Didn't you just hear me? The bonfire. You know, the one the school's throwing for the football team? To celebrate them being *gods* and winning all of the games so far."

"I'm far from any *god*," I tell her, and she cackles. Across from me, painting, Rachel looks to be stifling laughter after her friend. I suck my lips into my mouth to keep from laughing myself. Her laugh sure is…something else.

"But have you thought of bringing someone?" she asks, purrs more really, and touches my arm that's resting on my thigh. Then her hand's on my knee, sliding up my thigh…I stand up quickly. Red may be MIA, but that doesn't mean she doesn't mean anything to me, that I don't respect her and what we have…whatever that may be.

"I have to get more paint, but I'm going. It'd be great if you came too, I guess," I say as politely as possible. Her face falls like I just told her her eyebrows are uneven. I give her a small smile before turning around and walking over to the art supply shelf. I don't really need any paint, but I make it clear I just wanted to get away from her.

Now that she brought up the bonfire, I begin to think. The moment I heard about it, I was stoked and jumped to call and ask Red to accompany me but then remembered she apparently doesn't answer her phone nowadays. My mood sank instantly, and I kept my mind busy, tried not to fall in a glum state that previously kept me hostage. I just wish she'd answer me, just once, to let me know she's okay so I don't have to wonder if she's in a ditch somewhere. My stomach churns at the idea, and I inwardly hit myself. I can't think that way or I'll go nuts.

"You okay there, Noah?" a smaller voice asks, one that doesn't drip with forced seduction.

I look over and find Rachel flashing me a tiny, worried smile. "I'm fine. Not the greatest…" I sigh and run a hand over my hair. "But I'm fine, I guess. I just keep thinking about her, you know?" I know she doesn't approve of Red and me, but I like to confide in her. She's been a great friend to me; I shouldn't keep this from her. She's an excellent listener and knows how to stop thinking so cynically.

"I thought we talked about this," she says. "Give her some time and space. She'll come around eventually."

"Easier said than done," I mutter, referring to the cluster of text messages sitting on Red's phone, sitting unread or read and she just doesn't care enough to reply. Fuck, she's great at making me feel like utter shit.

"Maybe she's going through something personal, like a family matter or something," Rachel defends, which throws me off for a second. She isn't exactly Red's greatest advocate. She's warned me about her time and time again, but I never listened, and now that she's proving to be "*bad for me*," I expected Rachel to be all *I told you so* and continue telling me why Red's horrible, but she hasn't done any of it. She's by my side and helping me through it all, and I can't thank her enough.

"You're right, as usual." I roll my eyes jokingly, and she pinches me. I howl in pain, and she just laughs, clapping her hands for emphasis. "No need to laugh at my pain," I say, and she sticks her tongue out at me. "Anyway, about the bonfire…are you going? Of course you are. Your brother's on the team. But you can always wait for me after the game ends."

Before the bonfire, we're playing another school. Whether we win or lose, I hope the energy at the party is high and mighty. I need a positive vibe to get me through this Red funk. Just a glance of her around campus isn't enough to keep me satisfied. It drove me even wilder because it was like I got a taste of her presence but wasn't allowed to touch her, not really. She's like a ghost, and I am the only one who understands and sees her.

"Sounds like a plan." Her eyes dart behind me, and she laughs in her hand before looking back at me. "I think Beth's waiting to draw you. Either that and she's just outright painting your butt."

"What?" I turn around, and sure enough, Beth's eyes are focused on my butt, but now that I'm turned around, she's staring at the front of my pants. Even though I wave at her to get her attention and she blatantly waves back, her eyes zone in again, and she paints even more ferociously.

Rachel is hunched over in laughter.

***

"Noah, watch out!" Rachel screams, her eyes wide as she stares at something behind me.

I turn around quickly but am too late. I drop my cup of vodka soda as Mike and Ty run up to me. I hold out my hands as if that can guard me from water or whatever the hell they're tossing on me. The substance is full in volume and doesn't sting my eyes, which luckily means it isn't alcohol. A scream and a string of incoherent curses leave my lips as I hear an empty thud by my feet. When I take a step forward, my shoes squeak, completely drenched with water against now-soggy grass. I don't take any more steps, terrified of feeling my wet socks. And everyone knows how truly disgusting wet socks are—just *ugh*.

It takes a while of me digging my fingertips in my ears, but when the water finally pops out, the muffled laughter and chanting is clear, and my anger zeroes in on the two idiots hunched over in laughter. I am going to kill them, I decide as an extreme gust of wind brushes against my drenched clothes attached to my skin like a second one.

They're so busy laughing that they don't see me rushing over to them. But one of my teammates calls out like the asshole he is, drawing their attention. They finally look up at me, and their expressions transform into fear as I begin chasing them.

"I'm gonna kill your asses!" I scream on the top of my lungs. It's only drowned out by joyous laughter from people enjoying the show. Winding through couples and groups and around the bonfire itself—twice—I catch up with Mike. I tackle him to the ground and flip him over. I begin punching his stomach, but not seriously. He flips us over, and we tumble around in the grass. We're trapped in a bubble of laughter and shrieking and people recording that it all becomes ridiculous, and we end up bursting into laughter ourselves.

Everyone is buzzing with such positive energy because we won the game today. And staff members and professors are blatantly turning their heads as we openly drink around the fire, which just sounds so stupid, but we won, so who cares? I try not to wonder if they'd be this giddy if we'd lost.

Most likely, I think, because by the looks of it, everyone's having a great time dancing to the ear-shattering music and the concession stand migrated to the large, grassy area outside of the stadium.

"Help me up, you fucker!" I groan and hold out my hand. He grabs it and tugs me up. I jump on the balls of my feet, groaning again as I wring out the water out of my jersey. "Jesus, Mike! I'm soaked and it's colder than Elsa's *balls* out here," I complain, grimacing as the wind decides to punish me some more with a gust. I could get pneumonia, for Christ's sake!

"Calm down, Ms. Prissy. They're handing out blankets by the hot dog stand," he tells me and points in the direction of the concession. "Apparently it's chilly and players are getting splashed with water," he muses and chuckles as he looks me up and down. My clothes are pressed to my skin and my hair is stuck to my forehead, which I hastily brush back behind my ears, the curls tickling the tip of them.

"Why, thank you," I jokingly hiss, and he laughs. I begin to walk over to get a blanket when I see Ty tip-toeing behind him. I smile from ear to ear and step back, ready to watch justice be made. "And thank *you*, Ty."

"What?" His face scrunches up in confusion until Ty and a few other guys help raise a bucket filled with water over his head and tip it forward. Gallons of water splash onto his head, and he skyrockets into a fit of rage before the entire thing can soak him.

"Traitor!" he screams before running after his

227

friend.

All around, players are either drenched or on the lookout. They're such dicks—Mike and Ty especially—but they're just pumped about our win. And I'm one of those pumped dicks...God, that sounds so wrong. Good thing no one can read minds.

Wrapping a fleece blanket around my shoulders, I watch as Rachel comes up to me, laughing. Without saying a word, she guides me over to the raging bonfire.

"Really? You're laughing at me? And here I thought we were friends," I tease lightly, teeth chattering like those model teeth in dentist offices. I rub the blanket against my body, hoping I won't take long to dry. And thank God my phone died and is back at the house charging. I would have really killed them if they destroyed my phone.

Don't call me insane or creepy, but I stole a snap-picture of Red when we were at the fair. We were tossing rings on bottles, and I had just won her a giant fluffy pink teddy bear. She was holding it up like Simba from *The Lion King*. And she had this— this *smile* on her face. It was so consuming, it took up every inch of her face, and she had this light in her eyes. I took out my phone, snapped a shot, then basked in the moment before her stomach rumbled and she made me buy her a churro, one of her absolute favorite treats ever.

I wrote that down in my memos. I had planned to buy her a whole case of them, tie them to the bear and surprise her with them the next time I saw her. But that hasn't happened. So, that leaves me, a fool, reaching out to somebody who obviously doesn't like me as much as I like her.

"Hey, I'm sorry I laughed." Rachel touches my wrist. Her eyes glow against the flames, a shadow spreading over her frown. "I just found your face kind of hilarious. And getting splashed unexpectedly is generally funny—"

I hold up a hand. "It's fine, really. I wasn't all silent because of that." I pause and look away from her, ashamed to say, "I was just thinking about...*her*."

"Oh," she says.

"Yeah. I'm horrible. I know. But I just can't stop. It's like walking in on your parents wrapping Christmas presents. You've faithfully believed Santa was real, and with one mistake, the truth is revealed and you're left heartbroken." I shake my head. I'm probably not even making any sense. "I don't know. I just thought she could confide in me. Thought we had something more concrete. But I guess not. I mean, she hasn't even answered even *one* of my texts. Just an 'alive' would have sufficed, you know?"

"I get it. She just up and left you. And now you're hurting," she says. "But, Noah, you should really just put her out of your mind." Her hand reaches up to touch my cheek in a comforting gesture, and I smile and lean down to accommodate her sweet action when my skin tingles and my breathing stops for a dying second. I pull back and watch her face scrunch up slightly, panic flashing across her brown eyes. "Noah? Are you okay?" She reaches for me, but I take a step back.

"I'm sorry, it's just..." I trail off, my attention pulled elsewhere. I feel like something or someone is watching me. I look around, but no one catches my eye. Then I look past Rachel, tuning out her worried words, and squint through the crackling flames. They burn brighter as I step toward them, craning my neck around it, then really looking through it. I'm about to step away and apologize for being so weird and paranoid, when the flames dim for a few seconds. It's enough time to find what my body discovered before my brain could catch up.

Red...and Tanner has an arm around her.

Chapter Twenty-Seven

Three things hit me square in the chest at the sight of them. One being relief. She isn't in a ditch somewhere like I had hoped wasn't the case. I can now breathe and call off the idea of calling the police and reporting her missing or *worse*. I don't have to worry that she's going through some horrible breakdown, whatever the cause may be, and release the breath I've been holding desperately for an entire week.

The next thing is confusion. A million—nay, a *trillion*—questions form and swirl inside of my head like parasites digging into my spine; it's so hard to stand upright. Among the questions, one stands out in this very moment: why the hell is she with *him*?

I latch onto the last one in particular: anger. How could she just leave like that and reappear with this asshat after what we've been through, after what we've *done*? And then relief swells in my throat as I swallow the rage and emphasize how she is alive and well. Alive and sort of an asshole, but alive

231

nonetheless. But then the anger pops back up.

"Noah?" Rachel touches my arm. "Are you okay? What are you staring at?"

I don't answer. I just stare at them. She gasps, and I'm guessing she sees them as well. Well, there goes my theory that I've completely lost my mind and am seeing things. Seeing her. God. I have turned into such a pussy, and all because of her. She made me think that maybe I could have something serious with a girl. She made me feel like I could be myself around her. She just…she fucking played me.

And I'm pissed.

"Don't waste anymore of your time on her," Rachel says. "Look, I see Beth over there. God knows she isn't a saint…but she's gotta be better than *her*. Or literally *anyone* else—" She begins to laugh almost nervously, but she's just sympathetic for me. Maybe even pities me. And I hate that she may feel that way about me. She's been by my side while Red was off doing God knows what with God knows *who*, so it pains me to think she feels sorry for me, that I'm such a pussy-whipped frat boy who got his heart sucked out by a damn succubus.

But I am more. I am so much more.

And I'm really, *really* pissed.

"I've just gotta talk to her," I tell her, never once looking away from her and *him*. I watch as they look around, chins raised, as if they're the shit. And then I see more people behind them, drenched in black and tattoos, and I feel sick to my stomach. She's torturing me or mocking me, or both. She knows I'm on the team, knew I'd be here, so she brings a posse along with her boy toy to watch me realize what an idiot I'd been for trusting her, trusting us?

Real dick move, Red.

I move to give her a piece of my mind, but Rachel's small fingers grab my wrist and yank me back. Her eyes are wider than ever with fear and her puffy lips are parted, moving slightly, searching for words. "Don't let her get to you like this. You'd only be proving her right."

"I only want to talk to her, that's it. I'll be back," I promise her, but she doesn't look convinced. I reach down and rub her shoulder comfortingly. "Promise, Rach. If I'm not back in a few seconds, you can call the SWAT team after me, okay?" I joke half-heartedly, mostly for my sake. To cool myself so I don't blow up like a lit fuse the second I reach her and her *boyfriend.*

"Noah," she croaks.

"Rachel," I say, then sigh. "Be back," I promise her again and begin my trek over to the crowd. I feel her eyes zoned on my back as I approach them. My heart pounds inside of my throat. I decide to speak from the heart and let her know whatever she's done on her little trip fucked with me more than she could ever truly understand. And then I'm going to scream and question her coming with him and her friends like this.

I'm not even a foot away before Tanner notices me. A nasty smirk takes up residence on his face, and he taps her arm, getting her attention. "Look what we have here—"

I hold up a hand, eyes zeroed in on Red. "Fuck

off, leather pants." I make fun of his appearance and Red's friends or his friends—I don't give a crap—make hissing sounds and chuckle.

"You better watch your fucking mouth, preppy!" he growls. Literally.

"Or what? Are you gonna write a super emo song about me dissing your horrendously tight pants?" I mock.

His friends are hunched over in laughter, and he glares at me. A promise flickers across his dark eyes, but he bites his tongue, which I'm sure has a tongue piercing. I smirk at him, angering him even more.

She still hasn't even glanced at me, finding the guy at the cotton candy stand much more interesting than me, boiling with simmered rage. Seriously? She isn't even going to look at me after what she's done. She's left me worried sick for days, after just taking off into the night like she'd been informed the FBI was looking for her, and she won't even have the common courtesy of looking at me? I become even more pissed than before, if that's even possible.

"Red?" I call out. "Aren't you even going to say hi?"

Nothing.

"Tell me where you've been? Or what made you leave so suddenly?" I ask, ducking my head and trying to break her focal view, but it's glued to the depressed expression stamped on cotton candy guy. "Can't you at least explain why you're here with this prick?"

"Who the hell do you think you're talking to—"

Tanner spits.

"Red!" I shout at the top of my lungs. I just lost my temper, and I have no patience left. It's gone thin, and this prick isn't helping much.

Her tongue plays with her lip ring, but besides that, she's quiet.

"Red! Answer me!" I scream again.

"I don't have to!" she finally shouts and looks at me. Her face is flushed, eyebrows crunched, and upper lip snarling upward. "I don't have to because we aren't fucking anything! I'm not your girlfriend, you're not my boyfriend. And—fuck. I left because I had shit to do. Just because you had your face between my thighs and we kissed a few times doesn't mean I owe you an explanation for every little thing that I do! Jesus. Fucking. *Christ!* We don't mean anything!" she snaps. She's panting for breath and tearing up at the end.

Every single word that left her now-trembling lips pierces through my heart, leaving gaping holes and causes me to pant for air too. I'm tearing up as well, but I bite my tongue and nod. I seriously thought we had something, but if she says we're nothing...then that settles it. I mean nothing to her, and she means nothing to me. The kisses, the glances, the laughter, the motel, my room...nothing mattered to either of us, and I should just let her go. Let her be with Tanner or Ian or both. Hell, she can fuck everyone here and I shouldn't give a shit because *she* doesn't give a shit about me.

"Okay," I say and, even though I want to appear tough, my voice wavers slightly. Just for a second. I almost don't hear it, but I do and hate it and myself because she just crucified me in one freaking blow of air. Her friends are whispering and her face is hardening like a crystal, and Tanner's a smirking asshole, and my heart is crushed in the grass.

"Okay," I repeat. "Then how about you don't come to me, and I don't come to you, and we stay the fuck away from each other. Yeah? How does that sound?" I pause again and watch as she gulps thickly. "Nice knowing you, Red."

She looks like she's about to say something, maybe take everything back and let us kiss and make up, but when I give her just a fraction of a second to do just that, she steps back and turns to Tanner. He grins down at her, and my stomach tightens and curls and does freaking cartwheels as puke rises up my throat. She just threw freaking acid on my heart after ripping it straight out of my chest.

And I let her. Because I fucking *fell* for her. How pathetic am I, right?

Turning on my heels, I storm over to Rachel. She runs up to me, meeting me halfway, and her expression tells me she heard some of what was said. I mean, we weren't exactly quiet.

"I'm gonna murder her," she promises. Then she bites her lip and her face softens into a marshmallow-like expression. "I'm sorry, Noah."

"It's all right," I lie.

She frowns even deeper. "Noah..."

"Where did you last see Beth?" I ask her, cutting off her sympathetic tone, nature, look—everything. I can't take this shit with Red and her feeling sorry for me like this. And I need to get over her, right?

We meant nothing, right? So she won't have any problems with me being with another girl, *right*? This is so petty and so very, very unlike me, but Red...Red brings out the very freaking worst in me, and I have a difficult time remembering how I was before I met her.

"She was by the cooler. Why?" she says, frowning.

"I'll see you around," I tell her and move in the direction of the cooler, but she grabs my hand, pulling me back to her and her confused expression.

"Noah, what are you doing?"

"What you suggested," I say. "Anyone's gotta be better than Red, right?"

"Yeah, but not when you're like *this*—"

"Beth!" I call out, and she whirls around from giggling at a team player named Jack. Her eyes seem to sparkle in the dim light as I say, "Wanna get outta here?"

"Noah!" Rachel hisses in a warning tone.

I turn back to her and duck my head, smirking. "I'll be fine, Rach. I'm just gonna have fun like a normal college student."

"You called me?" Beth purrs beside me.

We both look at her, and I take her hand.

"Come on." I nod to the parking lot, and her eyes are definitely lighting up.

"Noah..." I hear Rachel say before I pull the hand she's holding away and fling it around Beth's shoulder.

"See you later, Rach. You're the best." I wink at her and ignore the sinking feeling that what I'm doing is very fucked up, as Beth and I slink away to the parking lot. A nagging voice in the back of my head cries and wails that I should stop, that this is very wrong. But what does he know? I followed his advice with Red, and look how that ended up. So I reach inside my head, turn his voice off, and press Beth against a random car and kiss her.

Her lips are cold and taste like oversaturated strawberry Chapstick. I gently press her into the cherry-red Nissan, listening to her moan against our closed mouths. She opens her mouth, trying to deepen the kiss, but I keep it close-mouthed. A part of me, that annoying voice, creeps up and begs for this to be as conservative as possible. As if to save Red from my kissing another girl deeply like I kissed her, but with ten times more passion and desire and…and affection.

"Mmm…Noah," she says, and a flash of imagery of the motel and rain pouring and her whispering that exact phrase crosses my mind. I press into her more, deepening the kiss like she wants so desperately. She smiles giddily and sways her hips slightly, clutching my face, seemingly satisfied with my giving in. "Noah—" she begins, but I look to my left and spot a particular car that grabs my attention.

"Shut…" I begin, rethink how mean that would have been, smile, and drop my voice as I pull back slightly. "Wrap your legs around me," I command her, then run a thumb over her bottom lip. She licks the tip as a yes and hops up. I grab her quickly and walk over to the car, allowing her to kiss my neck.

Dropping her ass on the car, she howls in laughter as it makes a little beeping sound.

"Oooh, you're so bad," she croons and pecks my lips, hands traveling under my shirt.

I just smirk and kiss her again. The kiss is open and closed and filled with her moaning and swaying her hips, which I find very annoying and un-intimate, for some strange reason. When I kiss Red, it's passionate as hell, sure. But it's also closed off and sweet and filled with unspoken words of...*admiration* between our lips. There's no purring or "ooh-la-la's" or bouts of high-pitched screams.

How I ever had sex with her and not double over in cringe-attacks and laughter is a real wonder. That makes me chuckle a little, and realization hits me square in the chest like a freight train: I don't like this, don't like her, and I definitely don't like that we're doing this on Red's car.

As I pull back and try to unlatch her arms from my neck, she groans and desperately tries to pull me back into the kiss.

"What are you doing? Kiss me," she says, dramatically breathlessly, probably trying to imitate the girls in romance novels or movies, but all she achieves is looking hilarious, and I feel horrible for thinking it, but I can't do this. The more I try to hurt someone who isn't even looking, the more I feel dumb and silly.

"Beth, I—" I begin to gently let her down easy when I'm interrupted.

"On my car? Are you *fucking* kidding me?" Red screams, clutching her keys so hard, I'm pretty sure blood is dripping onto the pavement.

Oh, crap.

Chapter Twenty-Eight

Time freezes on my behalf. I need time to think for some reason, even though my conscience reminds me that, technically, I'm not doing anything wrong. Nothing except for the fact that we're on her car. But besides that, I have free range to do whatever the hell I please without her having the right to be pissed. Like she just screamed in my face a while ago, we mean absolutely *nothing* to each other. So why should she be bothered by what I'm doing with Beth?

"Noah," Beth whines, gripping the collar of my jersey. "Let's take this back to my place." She lets out what I assume is supposed to sound like a flirtatious giggle but ends up sounding eerily similar to a rooster crowing in the morning.

I open my mouth to reply but am abruptly interrupted.

"Like hell you will," Red snaps. Her eyes are wide, and a promise of violence flashes against them like a flashlight. She wouldn't dare hit her, I think, but then I notice her taking a small step forward, glaring at Beth. "Now get the hell off my car, get off of *him*, and fucking *leave*," she demands loudly, keeping her hands at her sides, balled into fists.

I look at the ground. "You're bleeding," I say when there's other matters to be discussed. Like why she even cares what I do with Beth or any other girls, but there's blood in a small puddle on the ground. And she doesn't seem to be in the least bit of pain. Worry floods me instantly.

"Did you not just hear me?" she screams and shifts her scowl to me, but I keep my gaze down at the puddle, at the fresh blood dripping into it.

"Exactly who do you think you are?" Beth shakes her head, eyes batting.

Red scoffs. "I'm the one who should be asking that."

"You're bleeding," I repeat.

"I'm the girl who was making out with the lovely Noah here." Gripping my shirt and tugging my body to her, Beth says, "Isn't that right, sweetie?"

"Get. Your. *Fucking* hand…off of him, or I swear to fucking God—"

"You're bleeding!" I say a little louder.

The girls stop having their stupid girl fight; Red's gaze is intense, while Beth's is annoyed.

"Who gives a shit? I saw her blowing up at you," Beth says. "She doesn't deserve you. Never has. Never *will*."

"Like a whore like you will last two seconds with him." Red laughs.

Whore? She doesn't even know her. The wind

gushes suddenly, sending Beth's short pink skirt flying upward. She pushes it down and Red chuckles, as if proving her point right. And I hate it.

"Don't talk to her like that," I warn her.

Her jaw drops like I just said something completely outrageous.

"See how much of a good guy he is? How could you have possibly thought he would like you? All you do is hop from bad guy to bad guy and fuck a few people over. He deserves better, hon, and I'm that."

Now wait a minute—

"You better take that fucking back or I will stab you in the fucking eye with your skanky heel!" Red howls and storms over to us. I give her a pointed look, and she stops. Surprisingly, she looks obedient and stares into my eyes.

"The only thing I'll be taking back is him—to my apartment," Beth croons and runs a hand down my chest. I grab her wrist and give her a look as well, one that shouts, "Shut up, please, before she kills us both."

"Touch him again! Do it! I fucking dare you!" Red shouts.

"Okay." She cups my face, sending a shit-eating smirk Red's way.

"I am going to *murder* you!" Red cries, launching forward.

"Stop. Please." I grab her, wrapping my arms around her waist. Pulling her back to the driver side door, I gently push her against it. "Stop this now, Red," I command. She thrashes, and that violent lust flashes in her eyes, and I look down to her bloody hand. "You don't get to do this." My voice cracks, and she stares at me with this wide-eyed expression that tugs at my heart.

"Murder?" Beth giggles, nails dragging down several chalkboards. "Don't you favor another crime? Or are you just sticking with what you know *best*?"

What? "What are you talking about?" I look back at her, but Red makes a pained noise, and I look back at her, then her hand. She gulps and presses her forehead into my chest.

"Get her to leave before I slit her throat," she growls, and I stiffen.

Murder?

"Red?" I say in a low tone, drawing back slightly. She looks into my eyes and pleads. Tears well up in her eyes, and I say, despite my gut telling me to shut up, "I'll see you around, Beth." Red looks taken aback but doesn't comment.

"Seriously, Noah? But she—" Beth exclaims.

"Beth." My tone is firm, and so is my glance. Her overly glossed lips pout, and she looks between Red and me before grunting loudly and stomping away on her high heels. I listen to her cursing louder and shouting like a madwoman before the sounds of the party drown her out, and I step away from Red.

"Thank God." She lets out a heavy breath. "Thought she'd never leave. This is why girls shouldn't wear clothes that tight, shuts off the blood flow to their *heads*."

"Don't do that." I shake my head.

"Don't do what?"

243

"Make fun of her."

She chuckles. "The girl's a joke! Which makes me wonder about your taste in girls. If the bar's really set that low, then man, did I do you a *favor*—"

"You don't *get* to speak about her or anyone I decide to spend my time with!" I snap unintentionally, and she clamps her mouth shut, staring up at me, shocked. "You don't get to be upset that we were kissing, either. You made sure of that the second you fled and didn't respond to me any of the times I reached out to you. I was worried about you, and you just left me on the back burner like I was a used piece of trash. And according to you, I meant nothing, nor will I ever mean anything to you."

"That doesn't mean you can make out with some skank on my fucking car!" She waves her hands around wildly. Her eyes are wild, bluer than ever, and wide like the moon hanging above our heads.

"But it does, though! I don't mean anything to you, Red. Would you have had me take her on another car?"

She's shaking with anger and words she won't speak into the world, her teeth bared, hands dripping with more and more blood. I move to take her hand, get her some help, when she moves back and looks away from me. Seriously?

"Why do you even care?" I ask.

"I…I don't…" She turns away from me, eyes downcast.

Why does she keep turning away from me? Why can't she meet my eyes?

244

"Huh, Red? Why do you care so much about me and another girl? Do you like me now? Or are you just gonna pack your bags and leave at the first signs of feelings?" I duck my head, trying to get her to look at me. But she's persistent and leans over the hood, hands splayed on it. When they shift to grip her hair, a bloody handprint is left behind.

"Why are you so silent now, Red? Why are you even remotely pissed? After what you just said, I'm entitled to a good lay. Am I not?" I think I hear her mumble something, but I keep going. "In fact, I'm just gonna go get her back. Do this right—on my *bed*." I move to the party, bluffing like hell. A part of me knows she'll just hurt me again and wishes she'll let me go, but the other part...the other part's praying like hell.

"No!" she shouts and grabs at my jersey. Her once-hard expression has melted completely, like sugar on lava. Tears spill out of her large blue eyes, and I finally see her true self seeping through her leather jacket and piercings. I see Red Sylvetti. And although she cut me into a million pieces with what she said, it's enough for me.

"Stay here," I tell her calmly.

Her trembling lips move slowly as she asks, "Why?"

I cup her face, tilt it back, and repeat, "Stay here." Then I add quietly, "Trust me."

Those two words spark a flourish of emotion in her bright blue eyes. They sink into her brain, and she bites her lip, tongue jutting out to play with her lip ring. "Okay," she murmurs.

I leave her with a concerned look. I ask the nurse

245

on-call at her little station for a first aid kit. She questions me with a long, suspicious sweep of her eyes, but I lie and tell her my friend got drunk and smashed a beer bottle and is now bleeding like crazy. She sighs like it's the fourth time it's happened tonight and hands it to me. I feel bad for lying to her, but I don't confess. I take it and rush back to the car. I know she isn't bleeding out or anything, but a surge of protection fills me greatly. I need to make sure she's okay, the voice whispers. I agree.

"Hold out your hand," I command Red when I slide into the car. The door hasn't even closed yet. When I turn back around after locking it, she's staring at me. But the minute I look into her eyes, she blushes slightly, tucks hair behind her ear, and sheepishly holds out her hand. The blood makes my stomach rumble. Not because the sight of blood makes me nauseous, but because she's bleeding in the first place.

Sucking in a much-needed deep breath, I begin to work. First, I gently wipe her hand with several alcohol wipes. She doesn't react much, which scares me. There's something in her dead eyes that makes me uncomfortable for her, makes me want to curl her up in a ball and just comfort her. But I work past it and keep my focus on her hand as I examine it.

"Luckily, you won't need stitches," I tell her.

She just nods slightly. She's staring at the center console, or my lap, or nothing at all.

What is going on in that head of hers?

"So...murder?" I ask, my voice rough. Her

fingers tense around mine.

"Rumor," she says, and I look up to find her already staring at me. Black eyeliner is on her cheeks. "I'm not a good person. Done some bad shit, but not murder." She takes a shaky breath. "People love to assume the very worst about me."

Wonder why, my mean-ass conscience sneers. I push him away, lock him in the farthest place in my head, and throw away the key.

A few minutes pass by as I slowly wrap a bandage around her palm. We're quiet, and the energy between us has shifted to something more...calm. More manageable. I revel in it as I take my time wrapping the bandage. The seemingly temporary peace between us is sweet, and I don't want to warp it with us yelling at each other. But I can't just pretend to be a fool, either.

"You have blood on your jersey," she says, the same time I ask, "Did you mean anything before?"

She pauses, frowning. "No. No, of course not."

"Then why say it?" I drop her hand, and she looks hurt, but she looks out the windshield and leans over to her side. When she doesn't immediately respond, I take off my jersey, leaving me in the plain white t-shirt beneath it. I stare at the blood smearing the blue numbers. She looks over at me tentatively, and I ask, "Why push me away just to get upset when you find me making out with a girl?"

"Why make out with a girl?" Her tone is harsh.

"Red," I reply just as harshly.

She sighs and nods. "Sorry..."

Silence wraps around my throat with its sharp

claws and squeezes. I stare out the window like she is, let the lack of words surround my sanity and poke, each more infuriating than the last.

"I hate you a little more each time you leave me…" my voice croaks, and I hear her gasp.

"No…no you don't." Her voice is small, hopeful.

"You're right. I *don't*." Tears bleed through my eyes, and as one drops, I continue behind a pathetic little laugh. "But I should, because you hurt me, Red. More than any girl ever has before. And trust me, I know one that I thought ruined me, but you…you're doing a god damn good job of out-doing her."

She stares at me with a horrified expression, like I just backhanded her. "I don't *intend* to hurt you. I've tried my best *not* to hurt you, but…" She stops briefly, bats her eyes, and looks away, reconsidering what she was just about to tell me.

"But what?" I demand.

Why does she always do that? It's becoming so frustrating. I just want one straight, truthful sentence out of her. I want a lot of things, I realize, as the things I foolishly want grow. I want her to stop leaving me out of the blue. I want her to like me the way I stupidly, whole-heartedly, like her. I want her to not be bleeding, crying. I want to wrap her in my arms. And I want to kiss away our problems. Let them blow in the wind like black smoke. Never to poison us ever again.

But this is reality, and in reality there is pain and the truth.

She looks at me and her resolve fades, and she's left with a strong emotion unknown to me as she says, "But I can't stop myself from doing it. I'm bad for you, Noah. So, *so* bad. You should just stay away." She moves to the door, fingers on the handle, but I grab her wrist and stop her. Her brows are furrowed, lips pursed—puzzled. There is no way I'm letting her go without some sort of explanation. She's hurt me enough that I deserve the right to know everything.

"You aren't going anywhere," I tell her, and she sighs.

"Noah—"

"Where did you go?"

"I..." She pauses, as usual.

"You have to tell me. Please. You owe me that, at least." My voice breaks like glass, and I wipe away my tears. Fuck. She has me crying after she just humiliated me in front of so many people. How much more can she turn me into putty in her bloody hands?

She closes her mouth and looks me in the eyes deeply before saying, "I had some business to take care of," in the vaguest way possible, and I let out a frustrated groan and stare up at the ceiling. "I don't need to tell you everything I do, Noah. Couple or not. What I do is my business alone."

"Even when it can be dangerous?" I look at her.

Her eyes are hooded. "Especially if it's dangerous."

I cover my face with my palms. This is killing me slowly. "Why do you have to be so damn mysterious all the time, Red?"

"Why do you have to be so fragile all the time, Noah?" she shoots back. How is *she* getting upset with me when I'm just frustrated? I have a right to be when she keeps jerking me back and forth constantly!

I remove my hands and glare at her. "Don't I get to be? I mean, am I just supposed to take what you said back there with a grain of salt and be at the ready for when you change your mind and want to screw around or something when you get tired of the guys you have already?"

"Fuck you," she spits.

"Wonder what took you so long!" I snap before I could think.

Her eyes glaze over, and she sits back, stunned. "Wow, Noah. I may be a lot of things, but a *slut* is not one of them."

"Of course you aren't. I didn't mean that," I defend, but she ignores me and gets out of the car, slamming the door behind her. "Oh, come on!" I get out swiftly, slamming the door behind me. She's walking briskly down the lot, headed toward campus. "Red! Come back, I didn't mean it like that!"

"Then why'd you say it?" she shouts over her shoulder.

I chase after her; my long legs easily place me beside her. I swivel around, blocking her, and she halts in my chest. "Because you make me fucking crazy, Red! That's why! Completely mad! And it just came out." I pause, glancing over at the raging bonfire. "But can you blame me? For why I'm mad, at least?" She stiffens and crosses her arms, looking away. "You came here with Tanner. But before that, you left me after our moment in the hotel to be with

Ian. And Tanner. And—fuck. How else am I supposed to act? *Feel*?"

She doesn't say anything.

"Don't just stand there. At least tell me why you would say those horrible things to me," I plead.

"Because I don't want to be around you!" she shouts, and I take a step back. "Because I *like* you too much to understand how in the world someone as sweet and kind as you could possibly want anything to do with me. Because I want you. Because you're so good and I'd only ruin you. Because I tend to self-destruct every time something feels too right. I make shit wrong. And I'm fucked up. Way, *way* too fucked up for you. And because..." She covers her face. "Because liking you scares me more than anything in this shitty world," she mumbles.

My heart sings and my veins spark with euphoria. She just said everything I've wanted to hear for so long. I don't know how to react, but I watch her slowly shake her head. And then I frown and am confused. Why is she upset when she just told me the truth, what she is feeling? Why, especially when it's melded me back together after she broke me earlier?

In her own way, she really does like me. It's a fucked-up way, believe me...but it's her way, and she doesn't mean me any harm. I guess it'll just take some time getting used to.

I wrap my hands around her wrists and pull them down.

"What are you doing? Why aren't you running away from me?"

I duck my head and blow out a breath. "Because running away from you scares me more than not giving us a shot. I will run toward you if you just give it...give *me* a shot." I look into her eyes, bracing for her to push me away and leave me for another week, or a month, or even a year.

But she surprises me.

She nods. "If you promise you won't sue me if I break your heart again. I don't have much. Just my bike and my car. And you can't drive both. You'd look too much like a pussy driving either."

I crack a smile at her insult. "Too bad you're only mentioning suing you now. I could have added a few more million to my billion-dollar trust fund."

She playfully wrinkles her nose. "You're a horrible man, Richie Rich."

"And you're a terrible liar, *Rossa,*" I say and stare at her lips. "Can I kiss you?"

"You don't have to ask, stupid," she grumbles before pressing her lips on mine. Her kiss is soft and commands my hands to wrap around her, walk us back to her car, and sit her on the hood. It grows more intense with need, and she cradles my face with her small, soft hands, and I melt a little on the inside. Under her leather jacket and face piercings, she is vulnerable and soft and warm and easy to make giggle when I touch her above her waist or make hum when my tongue hits a certain spot inside her mouth.

And as I kiss her under the blanket of shining stars and judging moon, I think to myself, *How the hell did I end up here, and how do I stay forever?*

Chapter Twenty-Nine

"I have to pee," Red announces.

I pull away, wrinkling my nose. "I was glad you said something. I thought for a second the blood on your pants was something else," I joke, and she blushes. She pushes at me playfully, and I laugh.

"It's from my hand, weirdo." She pushes her foot against my thigh, causing me to stumble back. Hopping down from the hood, she tells me, "Stay here and try not to make out with anymore girls on my baby." Her hip sways into the side of her car, near the trunk.

I lean against the hood, smirking. "Can't promise anything. I look too good to keep the ladies away." I give her a smirk that makes me want to throw up.

"You're gross, Noah Wells. Absolutely deplorable." She pops the trunk and rustles in it for a moment before it closes and she's holding up a pair of sweatpants. She keeps clothes in her trunk? That's weird. "Try not to sell yourself as an escort." With a wink, she stalks away to the party.

The minute I am left alone in the eerie parking lot, I laugh to myself. I'm not crazy or anything. It's just…like, half an hour ago we were yelling at each other, and she said the nastiest thing to me. She actually crushed my heart and spat on it. Foolish enough, I made out with a girl on the hood of her car. Later, we fought some more, cried a little bit. And then a few moments later, we're making out on the hood of her car. To say this girl drives me insane would be a gross understatement.

I don't know. When I'm around her, it's like she fries the wires in my body. Whenever I think of her. Just whenever. Just a mention of her name could send my body into shock, and I think about her smile and the way her eyes light up when I look into them. Little moments and glances and kisses and everything about her rolls into one big ball of infatuation that's practically sewn into my veins. No matter how hard I try, I don't think I can shake her.

I hear footsteps and begin to jokingly say, "You're too late; two girls just tried to jump my bones," when I look up and find Rachel a foot away. She looks sort of distraught, with her arms crossed over her chest and a frown stitched on her face. "What's wrong?" I walk over to her, worried and thinking the worst: drunk assholes that get grabby when they have one too many beers.

She must read my mind because she shakes her head frantically and says, "No, no—God no." I release a heavy breath and uncurl my fists. "I just saw Red and…" She trails off, her eyes squinting. I can clearly see her trying to put this all together in her large hazel eyes. "Did you guys work things out? Are you actually forgiving her for what she said to you?"

"How do you know what she said to me?" I ask suspiciously.

"I may have snuck a little closer," she says, cheeks flaring. "But I only did that because I care about you, Noah. I care a lot."

"And?"

"*And* I don't think it'd be smart to just accept what she says and kiss and make up without even thinking it over," she says.

"I get that you care, but what happens between Red and me should stay between her and me," I tell her earnestly. I appreciate her to no end, but Red is complicated beyond words. She will definitely take some time to get used to, but I can handle her without Rachel advising me against her every time she fucks up. Which, so far, may be more often than I would want, but something in me tells me she's worth it. And I agree.

"And I get that, but the girl's got a terrible temper. Not to mention she literally *just* broke your heart." She pauses. "Maybe her blowing up like that was a sign for you to just leave her be. She's a horrible person; I don't even know why she took an interest in you."

"What's *that* supposed to mean?" I ask defensively. "And she isn't a horrible person. She can be...*difficult* at times, and so freaking confusing." I press my fingers to my temples, rubbing. "But she isn't a *bad* person."

"I meant that you're the kindest, goodest person I know." She smiles. "And I don't want her to ruin you."

"She won't ruin me—" I begin to defend.

"And if doing bad things makes a person bad, then she's downright villainous," she snaps, her eyes widening.

"What has she done that makes you hate her so much?" I ask. She seems to really despise Red for some reason, and a part of me doesn't think it's just because of a few arrests for small misdemeanors or something. She hates her for a larger crime that doesn't involve jail cells. And I want to know what exactly.

She seems lost for words, and I frown. "I just don't trust her is all. She's done awful, terrible things."

"Like?" I inquire. "I think I deserve to know why to stay away from her, don't you? Otherwise you have a vendetta against her I can't help or encourage. It's not fair to Red or me. The girl may put me through hell and back and may be stubborn, but she's made being here in college actually worth it."

When she doesn't say anything, I sigh in disappointment. "I'll be careful, okay? I can promise you that. But *you* have to promise to let up about her." She huffs incredulously and shoots me a wide-eyed look. "Come on, Rach. You're my best friend. I'd hate for you to hate the girl I really, *really* like."

"How can you like someone like her?" she snaps.

I open my mouth to snap back and tell her her hatred for Red is crazy when I see her walking toward us. She's not doing anything that makes her stand out. Her hair is untamed, as usual. The sweatpants she's wearing hides all of her soft curves, and blood is seeping through the bandage on her hand. But still, there's the way the moonlight hits her golden hair that makes her shine, makes her skin glow, and I find myself falling a little deeper as I watch her brilliant blue eyes shine at the sight of me. That damned little dimple pops next to her mouth.

And I breathlessly answer Rachel, "How can I not...?"

***

On the following Wednesday, Red and I are working on our short story for English. The deadline's creeping closer and closer, and because she was distant for a whole week, I worked on it by myself. But it turns out my writing skills are even shittier than I thought they were. So she and I are working out the kinks and making the story actually legible.

We're currently jotting down important points for a chapter, but I can't seem to focus on anything but her. She isn't dressed how she normally is. She's wearing lighter toned jeans, a white V-neck that doesn't have tears or pins, white Converse. Her face is glowing with the aid of the direct sunlight beaming through the cracked window. I eye her glossy lips—when she came over they were the first things I noticed—and wonder if they're the flavored kind.

She looks different but beautiful all the same.

"It's rude to stare," she grumbles, peeking a glare beneath her slightly tamed blonde curls.

I reach out and push some behind her pierced ears. She has an entire row of shiny silver and colorful earrings decorating her ear. "More like admiring." My voice comes out rugged. I notice the slight tug of her lips, the emotion crossing her milky blue eyes.

"Well, find another time to do it," she commands, but I just stare at her lips. I like the way she talks—so slow, yet confident—and her lips look very provocative when she does. She's talking, talking, talking—

"Ow!" I yelp and rub my arm that she pinched. "What was that for?"

"You're not listening to me!" she exclaims, then smacks my leg with the spiral notebook we're using to take down notes. All I can do is laugh. She looks ridiculously cute when she's mad. Usually her scowling and plotting someone's death looks menacing, but to me, she looks like a pissed-off bunny. Cheeks puffed and red, provocative lips moving a mile a minute.

She hits me again.

"I am *talking,* prep—" she begins to shout.

I lean forward and press my lips to hers. The usual sparks of electricity run through my veins, hitting snags and striking my heart. I explode under her smooth, glossy lips. Her small hands drop the notebook and grip my shoulder. Nails free of black nail polish dig into my skin, then her fingers gently grip onto the back of my neck. My blood sings under my flesh when she makes this sound. It's not

258

a moan, but it's not a whisper. It's something in between, guttural and raw and heavenly.

I grab the back of her leg that's wrapping around me and put my weight on her, bringing her to her back. I kiss beneath her full lips, sucking gently on her soft skin. "So beautiful," I murmur as I paint her creamy skin on her neck with my mouth, biting gently, creating red marks. She moans my name, and it encourages me to run a hand under her loose white shirt.

"Noah," she groans, arching her back, pressing her chest into me. Slowly, to torture her just a little bit, I glide my hand down to the waistband of her jeans. Her hips buck slightly as I pop open the button.

"Can I touch you?" I ask.

"Please," she pleads softly.

I don't hesitate and push my hand into her black underwear. The second I touch her, all wet and needy, she sucks in a breath and shudders out an exhale. I watch her face as I toy with her while kissing her neck. From beneath my lashes, she has hers shut closed; her glossy pink lips part, eliciting sweet moans that make me hard instantly. So hard my breaths come out in pants as I suck her skin a little harder, rub a little faster. I grind myself against her thigh, and her hands pull me closer.

I press a finger against her, move slowly...and she gasps, fingers scraping against my heated skin under my blue shirt. She yanks it up, and I grind into her a little more, pleasure teasing me and my dick. I want to rip her panties off and my jeans and fuck her so badly, it's killing me just to imagine how amazing she feels on the inside.

"You like that, *Rossa*?" I whisper haughtily in her ear.

She moans. "Yes. Please. More." She's dragging her nails up my back, and a whisper of a tingling sensation runs straight to my dick. I make an unholy sound, and she moans so loudly, so deeply, it motivates me to push a little harder, rub a little slower, then faster, then repeat.

Her breathing is out of whack, her chest rising and falling at a rapid pace. I watch with satisfaction and absolute awe as she gulps and moans, eyelashes fluttering and squeezing tightly. Her fingers are clawing at the base of my neck, her hips pushing upward, greedy for more. So I give it to her.

I add another finger, curl them, and feel her tighten around me.

"Noah. Yes," she pants out, biting her lip.

I lean forward and kiss along her sharp-as-a-razor jawline. I hover my lips over hers and lick her bottom lip. She makes this deep growl-like moan, and I smile softly. My tongue plays with her lip ring, and she's losing it, gripping my biceps, nails puncturing, my name leaving her trembling lips. I grind against her harder, and I can feel myself reaching my own climax, just by basically dry-humping her. This is insane.

"Noah!" she screams my name.

Her hips buck up, legs shake, and her breathing is frantic. I reach my own climax and mumble into her warm skin. I press my lips onto hers and, when our mouths drop open, she lets out the sexiest sound, between a growl and my name. Pure bliss is evident as she pinches her eyes closed and bites her lip.

Her eyelashes flutter, and I kiss her deeply, caressing her tongue with mine. I suck and she seems to come again, moaning my name against our feverish mouths colliding and tasting and biting and teasing.

She breathes heavily, lips red and puffy from our rough, passionate kiss. "No one's *ever* made me come like that," she admits in a fluffy tone, almost sedated, with the way her eyes flutter and she subtly gasps for breath. I decide I love the sight of her after I make her come. I love the flush in her cheeks and the soft stutter of her chest.

"And no other guy ever will," I say playfully and bring my fingers to my mouth. She watches with hooded eyes as I bring the fingers that were just adorned by her body.

"Didn't know you could be so sexy," she murmurs jokingly.

I thread my fingers through my hair, staring at her staring up at me. Cheeks flushed, golden hair cascading on a pillow, pouty pink lips pulled into a genuine grin—she looks like an angel. I can't even help it. I pull out my phone and take a picture of her.

"Stop!" she shrieks, covering her face in such a cute way, I take a few more at different angles.

"Baby, move your hands." *Baby?*

She peeks between her long fingers, nose wrinkled. "Baby?" she questions, and I blush. I have no idea what came over me. I move to take it back, but she sits up and wraps her arms around me.

She perches her chin on my stomach and stares up beneath her long, dark eyelashes. "I like it," she decides and gently presses her soft lips on my skin. She's genuine and not mocking.

An emotion so strong swells in my heart it makes it hard to breathe. I lean down by her head. Neither of us says anything. I'm too busy admiring her features, and by her flitting eyes, I can assume she's doing the same. I glide a fingertip along her collarbone and listen to her breathing pick up as I trace an outline of an exotic flower tattoo.

"Go on a date with me," I say. I look at her, hopeful.

She's staring at my lips, her own tugged up in a soft smile. "What's in it for me?"

A brow shoots up. "Maybe a little of this…" I lean down and kiss her chin. "And this…" Then her nose, which wrinkles, making me smile widely. "Possibly some of this…" I press my lips onto hers, and the world goes silent. My heart crumbles and rebuilds itself. The kiss is gentle and filled with little zaps of electricity.

"I'll think about it," she teases against my mouth. I growl and push her onto her back, bite onto her jaw. She shrieks and laughs. "Okay, okay! Yes, I will go out with you," she promises, but I don't stop nibbling my way down to her neck. Her snorting laughter and body spazzing beneath me in glee makes me glaze over with emotion.

Chapter Thirty

I'm taking Red Sylvetti on a date tonight. Red Sylvetti, notorious badass girl that has dangerous, dark rumors of *murder* swirling over her head. I don't care about the rumor, though. She told me it was fake. Obviously. As much as she loves wearing leather and an expression that could kill, I don't believe she could actually *kill* a person. I may not have known her long, but I know her well enough to know she couldn't be that harmful.

Anyway, she's a lot to handle and complicated and a real fireball, and I'm going on a real date with her tonight.

I have no idea what I was thinking when I asked her out. Not that I didn't want to. I had been yearning to take her out on a proper date and establish whatever the hell we are when I started falling for her. I normally have enough confidence to fill two cargo shipments, but it seemed to deflate like a sad balloon around her. Even more so whenever I thought about asking her out. Actually working up the courage to say the words *will you go out with me?* I imagined her screaming *no* before pistol-whipping me, but with her motorcycle.

Obviously she didn't do any of that. She smiled at me like she had been waiting for me to ask her out. My heart clenches at the image of her giggling beneath me as I covered her skin with my greedy lips. I have never seen her so happy, so at peace. The fact that she only appears that way around me speaks volumes and makes me feel accomplished, in a way. Because it means I can crack that barrier she has built in front of her heart, and with each strike I make, I'm closer to finally knocking it down.

My phone buzzing across my study desk yanks me out of my thoughts. I pick it up and look at the screen. A grin creeps onto my face as I read the text.

Red: I'm outside. Wow me.

Noah: Prepare to create a shrine dedicated to my wow-factor.

I playfully reply before looking in the mirror for the millionth time. I asked her out a few hours ago and, since, have set up something special. I hope she likes it; that's all that matters. I fiddle with my unbuttoned white dress shirt, then look over my black fitted dress pants and slim suit jacket. She replies as I'm fiddling with my short curly brown hair that's slightly moussed.

Red: I'll just add to the one I already have.

A snort leaves my lips as I pat my pocket for my wallet and keys.

I reply as I'm jogging down the stairs:

Ditto.

A few guys woot and pat me on the shoulder as I pass them. As if going on a proper date that isn't snagging a seat at McDonald's or hanging out here isn't valid. I give them all eye rolls at their teasing, flicking them the middle finger.

"Leaving already?" Mike asks, leaving the living room to walk up to me. He doesn't even attempt to hide the broad smirk on his brown skin. "You not gonna let me give you a good luck kiss before you go?" He puckers his lips and leans forward.

"I don't need your crusty lips," I joke, and he chuckles, rolling back onto the heels of his feet. Noticing Ty engaged in a video game, I nod to him and say, "Why don't you give that kiss to Ty? Heard him crying over Lyndsey dropping his ass last night."

"I heard that, and it's not true, you fucker!" he shouts.

"See you around. Have fun, all right?" Mike laughs, giving me a bro hug.

"Yeah, I'll see you guys later. Have fun with your boy-toy." I pull back and push him toward the living room.

"You know I will." He struts into the room filled with guys jamming on game controllers, beer cans clouding their feet. "Oh, *Ty*!" I hear him say in a high-pitched voice and listen to Ty groan and cuss at him in return. I laugh and shake my head at them before stepping outside.

I spot her the second I am out of the house. My heart freezes and so does time as I take a long, admiring sweep of her. She's wearing this short black dress with straps and a black peacoat. Her golden blonde hair is perfectly tamed and lays over her right shoulder. And she has her lips painted this gorgeous, make-me-sin red. She looks absolutely stunning, breathtaking, really. I struggle to breathe as I walk over to her.

"Wow," I say in awe, sweeping my eyes over her again. I can't help but sound surprised; I just never expected...*this*. There aren't enough words in this world to describe how incredible she looks.

"Did you hear that?" She cups a hand over her ear, leaning in as if whispering a secret, and says, "I think I just heard a few candles and photos of my face joining your shrine." The tips of my fingertips buzz at her making fun of me.

I chuckle and stuff my hands in my pockets. "Har-har," I say, and she smirks, then looks me up and down with the same amount of awe I showed her. Her head cocks to the side, tongue playing with her lip ring. I stare at her mouth, then her eyes. Her vibrant blue eyes spark with a heavy emotion as they meet mine, the tip of her mouth upward. "And I'm pretty sure I just saw a cardboard cut-out of me join the bulletin board of chunks of my hair."

She grins. "You're a total stud. Happy now?" she asks sarcastically, and I nod frantically.

"Very," I answer, smiling.

"Great. Now that I've stroked your ego, can we get going?" she asks, pouting. "I didn't spend two hours getting ready to have us chatting outside of your *frat house*."

She's right; I want to get this night started.

"You *are* very right." I take her hand. "But you dressing up wouldn't have been a waste. You look really beautiful." I watch for a reaction. She looks away in an attempt to hide her soft smile and the redness in her cheeks.

"Fuck off." She pushes into me, but I just laugh at her brutishness and wrap an arm around her shoulder. Her hand shoots up and plays with my long fingers. I guide her over to the black town car I rented for the night. I really should get my own car; it'd be nice to have one of my own instead of borrowing Mike's or having Red drive us around whenever she decides to whisk me away.

"What's this?" she asks skeptically, eyeing the sleek black 2016 BMW 2-Series. "Besides being a dope-ass car." She whistles as I prop open the passenger door. I guide her inside, and she openly gawks at the velvet leather seats and high-tech GPS. I laugh under my breath. She is such a car geek. I wonder who she got her love of cars from. I'm guessing her father. The image of a little, sassy Red helping her father fix a car's engine makes me smile.

"Rental for the night," I tell her as I slide into the car. The seats warm at my touch, and I try not to close my eyes in bliss. I jam the key in the ignition and start up the car with a low purr. She cocks an eyebrow, the pierced one, and then looks over at me. "Impressive?" I take off onto the road and admire how smooth it feels.

She leans back in her seat, scoffing. "It's all right, I guess, for a showy car. Really suits you." She looks over at me with a grin.

"Why, thank you...I think." I scrunch my eyebrows. I can't really tell when she's making fun of me or being genuine.

"Compliment, prep." She pats my arm, chuckling at my expense. I blush and look ahead to avoid crashing this beauty of a car.

Since I don't know this town at all, I have the address of the location of our date plugged into the GPS but was able to block out the name of it. Hopefully she doesn't know the town too well to recognize street names and such downtown.

About twenty minutes flows between us without much of a conversation, which is my fault. I'm admittedly nervous about tonight. I haven't really been on a date since the summer. And God knows how *that* relationship turned out. Ever since, I've been screwing around with girls, minus the roses and restaurants.

Who needs all of that when you're not even going to remember the girl's name in the morning after boning her?

I sound like such a tool because, honestly, I was one. I didn't care as much as I should have about the girls I messed around with. I used them for two purposes: pleasure and painting. They were a means to an end, and I hate myself for it.

But that's all changed—I've changed—since I met Red. I haven't managed to screw around with half of the university's female population, and I've kind of committed to one girl. The last time I did, I experienced a heartache like never before. I discreetly vowed to never fall for another girl, yet here I am with the beautiful Red at my side. I stare at her as we're sitting at a red light, and I decide that I will break that vow.

Let her wreck me.

Let her burn me.

I will enjoy every second of torture if I get to feel what I do when I'm with her.

A loud honk behind me snaps me out of my expressive thoughts, and I push on the gas pedal.

"Everything okay?" she asks, and I smile at her, reaching for her hand. Her brows furrow in suspicion, but her lips curl into a slightly there grin.

"Yeah, *yeah*. Just thinking about what I have planned tonight," I lie.

Her pierced brow cocks, and she hums. "Right." She doesn't believe me, but she doesn't push it. "Wanna give me a hint on what it is?"

"Nope." I shake my head affirmatively. "You'll just have to see when we get there."

She frowns and tugs at my hand. "That's no fair."

"Yes, it is." I bring her hand to my mouth, kiss her knuckles; she intakes a large gulp of air, then stares up at me with a more-slightly-there smile. "It may not be what you usually like, but I planned it all out real nice. You'll like it." *I hope she does.*

"Fine." She sighs and stares at the road for a moment. "This song sucks," she murmurs before switching the pop station to an alternative station.

An Arctic Monkeys song about wanting to know something. Her head bops to the beat, and she croons the lyrics under her breath. The sound is rustic yet smooth and makes me look at her a little too long when I should be paying attention to the road.

"I didn't know you could sing," I say.

"There's a lot you don't know about me," she replies.

My gut clenches because she's right. Tonight, I decide, I will know more about her. That's what dates are for, right? Interrogating a person and finding out their life goals and blah, blah, blah. I wonder if she's been on a date. But of course she has. She had to have gone out with somebody. The thought makes me sick to my stomach, but it's my damn fault for thinking. Still, the idea of some prick taking her out on a date makes me want to punch something, maybe even his stupid fucking face. I take deep breaths, calming myself.

About fifteen minutes later, I pull up in front of the location: Wired Expressions—an art gallery.

"Art? Since when are you into *art*?" she asks skeptically as I help her out of the car. She narrows her eyes at me, then glances over at the gallery. Glass spans the front of the store, revealing how many people are observing art. I shut the door behind her and take her hand again.

"Since forever. But I guess there isn't a lot you know about me," I murmur under my breath, hoping to correct the matter by the end of the night.

Inside, the air is warm, and I take off her coat. I shrug mine off and hand them both to the male attendee, and he hangs them both with the other coats behind him.

"Where do we start?" Red asks. She's walked off to one of the paintings in the massive, open area.

"Wherever you want. I'd say here since it's attracted you first," I tell her, sidling up next to her. I watch her eyes roam over the abstract painting of vibrant yellows and strong hues of orange and other sorts of colors, wondering what she's thinking—*how* she's thinking. I've only ever studied art by myself, never with another person. But with her, I decide I like to ponder her thoughts on art pieces such as this one.

"What are you thinking?" I finally ask after a few moments of silence. The small group of young people stalk off to another painting, leaving her and me alone. Thank God. I broaden my stance next to her and glance over to her.

"I don't know what the hell this is," she finally says, and I laugh. Here I thought she was going to say this genius statement that defines art itself, only for her to admit she doesn't even know what she's looking at it. It's such a Red move, I can only laugh before explaining what I see.

"And you're supposed to interpret it in your own words and views," I instruct her, and she scoffs.

"Sounds like a load of crap and stupid." She looks up at me, brows furrowed. "Artists get to concoct whatever bullshit they want and make people construct their own *interpretations*? I just call it lazy." Her tone is stone serious.

I laugh. "Again, whatever you think is up to you. But the point of art is to express yourself, your thoughts, and let others view it and understand you a bit better. It's an outlet to escape the world and jump into colors and the feeling of infinity in just a stroke of a brush." I pause and find myself blushing. I sound like a total art buff, or more like I have a few brushes wedged up my pretentious ass. I turn to her curious gaze. "I'm sorry, just my opinion."

"Your opinion is…" She trails off and squints. "Do you paint for that reason? To get away, or whatever?"

"Yes," I answer and look at the painting. "That and I couldn't get the muse in my head to shut up." She tugs on my hand, dragging me to a photograph of a naked woman, but it's her side profile, and she's sitting in the forest. The shot is warm, and there's a streak of black down her flushed pink cheeks.

"This is better." She reaches out, but I touch her elbow.

"Can't touch it, babe," I warn her.

"Fuck that rule." Her fingertips touch the girl's unruly black hair. Her eyes are glancing at us in her peripheral vision. It sends a shudder of grief through my body. This artist did an excellent job. I study the sunlight hitting her thighs and eyes and the little rustle of leaves in the air, while Red glides her fingertips down her back.

"Excuse me, miss? You can't touch the art," a security guard warns as he rounds the corner. He shoots us an annoyed glare.

"Oh, sorry," Red surprises me by saying, batting her eyelashes submissively. I cock an eyebrow, watching the guard nod satisfactorily before walking away. When I look back at Red, her sweet smile drops, and she's glaring at his back. She pops her index finger in her mouth, then presses it onto the framed photo, then shoves her middle finger in the air, drawing quite a few onlookers' attention. "Asshole!" she shouts, and he whips around, and she pokes at the photo.

"Hey! Hands off the art!" He rushes toward us, gripping what I think is a taser in his belt. Why does he even have a taser? And is touching an art piece enough to get *tased*?

"Oh, Red," I groan. Why didn't I see this coming? I mean, this is Red I'm talking about. Nevertheless, I grab her hand and tug, grabbing her frenzied, excited expression. "Follow me," I instruct firmly.

I pull her out of the photography section of the gallery. Clusters of people standing in our way curse as we brush past them roughly. I drop many apologies over Red's explosive curses. My eyes dart around and my shiny loafers slide on the heated wooden floors. I drag her through a throng of people admiring a newly arrived painting of a couple. We weave through crowds and pass exhibits and colorful judging eyes.

I get a text message buzzing in my pants, but I'm a little too busy at the moment to check. My heartbeat's risen in the past few minutes of running and dodging and hiding. Red laughs maniacally and skips a few times, and all I can do is laugh and dodge the husky security guard. How she finds this entertaining is beyond me. But I have to admit, she seems to be having fun, and it's all I wanted for tonight. Even if she kind of looks like a crazy person in the process.

She's *my* crazy person.

I dare a look over my shoulder and spot the guard standing still, eyes probing around like a hawk on the search for food. I skid us to a stop, and we press against the brick wall. Who would have guessed touching photos in an art gallery would create such a frantic, bloodthirsty security guard to chase after us?

"What now, genius?" she asks, barely out of breath.

I look around, and the crowd is thinning out, as we are at the back of the gallery. An idea forms in my head, and I look around to see if we're clear. "Through there." I nod at a metal door with a sign above it that reads **'EXIT ONLY,'** and she pauses, lifting her pierced brow at me as if I've lost my mind. "Trust me," I whisper, tugging on her hand. I know what's up there, and it isn't just a roof.

She nibbles consciously on her lip ring, then nods. "I trust you." She says the three little words that melt my heart. They sound simple but mean so much to me.

"Then come on." I cast short looks over my shoulder as we jog over to the door. I quickly pull out a set of keys in my pocket and unlock it. She side-eyes me hard, skeptically, as I pull it open and usher her in. Nonetheless, she rushes in, and I shut the door after us.

"Are you gonna, like, murder me now?" she asks from two steps up.

"No." I laugh and jog up, slipping the keys back

in my pocket. "I have something planned up here. It's a little too early, but you can never plan for a security guard to hunt us down," I tease lightly, and she rolls her eyes, but a smile is on her lips. "Now come on. It's just up a flight or two."

She groans but climbs the stairs with me. My heart pounds like crazy when we get closer and closer to the door of the roof exit. I had this set up earlier, and it's now hitting me that it's possibly not even set up altogether. We were supposed to roam around for about an hour before everything would be all good for us to come up here. I sneak a peek at my phone and breathe in relief. The text from the owner of the gallery let me know everything is put together. If it weren't, I was gonna have something short of a heart attack.

After a few minutes of climbing, we finally break through the door, and she gasps in awe. There's a cube-like wall surrounding the small balcony, encasing us from the outside. But that isn't what drew the breath from her; it's what's projected on the walls: images of several, if not all, of the paintings and photographs downstairs on a loop. There's a fire heater in two of the corners, and in front of us is a bistro table filled with food from a famous restaurant in the city. The enticing, heavy aroma of the hot food wafts into my nose, making me groan in appreciation.

When I look over at her, she's staring around, cheeks flushed, mouth agape.

"I thought we would eat first, talk a bit. Admire the paintings on a more visual aspect for a while. Then finally…" I glance at the empty canvas on an easel, a plush white couch in front of it. Her gaze is intense yet warm. "I could create the most enthralling painting in this gallery using you as my ultimate muse." My voice is low, and I stare at the slight tug of her red lips.

She doesn't say anything for a long while, just returns her eyes to the walls, and then the food, then the easel, and then back to me, and then anywhere else that appeases her. I stare at her glowing presence, allowing this to sink in. God. She is so beautiful it physically hurts to look at her. So why am I staring so intently, drinking in her essence? Why am I gently pulling her into my chest? And why am I brushing a lock of her hair behind her small ears, looking into her eyes as if they hold the answers to everything, like, why can't I breathe right now?

"Say something," I urge her, looping an arm around her lower back. I raise my hand and brush my knuckles against her flushed cheek.

She leans on her toes and pulls me to her. Her lips press into mine, and I bring her closer. Our bodies flush against each other. Sparks fly under my tongue as it glides against hers. The kiss is unnaturally slow and so passionate my stomach twists and the world tilts us to the side. I hold her hips and breathe into her mouth. We pull back slightly, quickly catch our breaths, then continue to tease the fire between our skin that seem to be doused in gasoline. I run my hands along her sides, causing her to moan in my mouth, before I cup her face and hold our lips together in a long, sweet position.

I would deliver my heart, body, and soul to this girl if it meant I could kiss these lips, hold her beautiful face, even if it's just for a moment longer than breathing. I want to kiss her everywhere, and still, I won't satisfy the craving for more that cries in the pit of my stomach. This girl will be the absolute death of me. Funny thing is, I don't mind one damn bit.

"This is perfect," she whispers against my mouth.

"No." I shake my head, smiling softly. I kiss her gently, then whisper, "*You* are perfect."

Chapter Thirty-One

The obnoxious sound of Ty snoring wakes me from my slumber. I thought after almost two months of sleeping in the same room as him I would get used to it, but no such luck. I grab the pillow beneath my head and toss it at his thick head. It does nothing but bounce onto the floor, on top of his pile of clothes. On top of his inability to sleep without sounding like a dying walrus. He's a total slob.

"I should get my own place," I murmur and rub my face, a heavy sigh leaving my lips. The green numbers on the clock on my nightstand read *5:03* a.m.

The sheets shuffle and so does the bed slightly. I look over my shoulder and turn around fully. A grin instantly makes its way onto my face. Red's mumbling something softly in her sleep. She looks so much like an angel, with her mouth parted and eyelashes falling gracefully on top of her cheeks. Her facial expression is soft and relaxed, free of her usual scowl.

Unlike what most people would assume, she and I didn't fuck last night. She just drank one too many flutes of expensive champagne to drive back home. Thinking about our date brings a herd of butterflies in my chest, and I don't know how to feel about it. No girl has ever made me feel this way before. Then again, no girl I know skips joyfully while being chased by a security guard.

The memory of us gazing up at the art splayed on the walls fills my head. So does her and I talking about anything and everything over a top-notch dinner. I found out so much about her, I could write a mini essay. She told me about how rough her childhood was after her mother was murdered and how she mostly rebelled through her life because of it. I felt so bad, but she pressed for me not to, and we changed topics. So I told her about my obsession with horror movies, which she revealed that she also adored the genre, thus encouraging me to set up a movie date with just horror movies.

It feels like a dream to know more about the badass girl everyone's either afraid of or wary of. Knowing more shapes her out to be more real than I've ever seen her before, and I appreciate it. And even though I learned little things that supposedly don't matter that much in relationships these days, like how her favorite color is black and how she strongly despises chick flicks, I find myself growing more and more in...in *like* with her. If that makes sense. But with her, it just does.

"Noah," I hear her groan. She shifts around and slings her arm around my mid-section. I smile at her instinct to get closer to me, even in sleep, and watch her snuggle her face in the crook of my neck.

"Red," I reply, toying with a blonde curl of hers.

"Move, I have to pee," she surprises me in saying.

When I look over at her, she's groggily peeling one eye open. The crinkle in her forehead and the scrunching in her face returns, and I nod. "Sorry." I begin to get up so she can go to the bathroom.

"No. It's fine, don't move," she grumbles and pushes to her arms. I watch her climb over me. I look down, then up at the ceiling to be respectful. She isn't wearing her dress, only her black underwear that looks too sexy on her. My eyes are glued to the ceiling when she appears over my face like a pissed-off angel. "I have work soon, but you should come to Lava Springs later."

"Lava Springs?"

"A hot spring or whatever." She pauses. "Some friends and I are having a party there. You in?"

"Yeah, yeah. I'd love that." I nod, and her lips tip upward in a smile.

"Great." She moves to go to the bathroom when she pauses and leans down again to whisper, "And last night was great." Then, with rosy-colored cheeks, she pads to the bathroom, leaving me with an embarrassingly large grin that I try to cover with a pillow.

***

A few hours later, Red and I are in her car driving through back roads, massive trees on either side of the road. Nirvana is blasting through the radio, but it's no louder than the silence between us. I keep expecting her to make fun of my beanie or something in the mean but sexy way she does so often, but she just drives. Worry floods through me, and I move to ask her if something's wrong. Everything was fine between us a few hours ago. What could have changed in such a short time?

"Red, is everything okay?" I reach to take her hand that's resting on the clutch, but she moves it to the steering wheel. I frown, and she glances at me. "Red?"

"Yeah. Yeah. Everything is fine," she says, short and clipped.

Raising my brows, I warn, "Red. You can tell me things, you know. It doesn't matter what it is. I'm not going anywhere anytime soon."

She doesn't say anything, and Kurt Cobain and the engine purring fills the void of silence. I feel myself shrivel up a little because she still isn't letting me in. It is the most frustrating thing I have ever experienced. *She* is the most frustrating thing I have ever experienced. Just when I think we've taken a hundred steps backward, she pipes up.

"My friends are just a bit…fucked up." I sense worry in her voice, and I take her hand she forced onto the wheel and kiss the back of her hand. She looks at me with wide, terrified eyes, then softens and looks back onto the road. Seriously, her friends can't be that bad…unless they're like a pack of mongrel serial killers. Then there will be a problem.

"Who's aren't? Ty screws around with half the campus, and Mike hasn't dated anyone since a bad breakup *years* ago." I pause. "And there's this guy

281

named Noah. He's a real sucker for Red. Though he never thought he'd find..." *Love.* "Someone to call his own after he had his heart stomped on by a girl who has comically tiny feet."

She chuckles, and I pause and relish in it, then continue.

"But when he did, she turned out to be this badass chick that has him so wrapped around her black-painted finger, she didn't even realize. Not when he stared at her like she was his world. Or fantasized kissing her just because." I shrug, and she looks at me, gulps hard, while staring at me.

"He sounds like a pussy," she scoffs and looks back onto the road, but I catch a flash of a smile before she does.

"He is, especially since he doesn't even know what they are..." I let my words fade, and she drives on, jaw set and a look of struggling on her face. I let her drive in silence and sit back, focusing on the vibrant trees we pass. As the car hounds on, my friends in tow in Ty's truck, I wonder how her friends even found this so-called hidden spring. She told me they were hiking one day and stumbled upon it. I call bullshit, but I don't want to create any bad vibes toward them without meeting them.

I'm meeting her friends.

It doesn't sound like a big deal, but it is. Meeting them officially creates a tie between her and me, as will her bonding with Mike and Ty and my other friends. We are walking one step closer to being something. And being something with this girl is more than anything, and I will gladly jump on it. God, I'm a pussy. But she makes me feel different, better...*happier*. And if that makes me a pussy, well, so the hell what? As long as I can sneak a glance and catch her glancing back a few seconds later, I'll take any fucking title.

Thirty minutes later, the sun has set and we're among the trees, driving down a dirt path. Her Chevy Impala cruises up, and I look around in curiosity. I think swimming in November in any kind of outdoor water will result in pneumonia.

"Are you sure this hot spring is...you know, *hot*? Enough, at least?" I ask her as we slow down. It looks like we're in the middle of nowhere, until the car shuts off and I hear distinct splashing and laughter and loud music.

She chuckles, directed at me. "Yes, dummy. We wouldn't come out here if it wasn't."

"No need for name calling." I smile as she rolls her eyes and swings out of the car. I follow behind and wait for my friends to hop out of the truck before following her to her friends. They're surrounded by a raging fire, drinking and laughing and talking loudly over some rap song. So far, so good. They don't look too fucked up.

As she walks over and talks to a girl with pink-tipped black hair wearing shorts and a black bikini, I look around aimlessly. I don't really know what to do. I feel way out of place, more so than my friends, who have already gravitated toward the cooler full of beers and branched out to talk and mingle. Maybe I didn't read *How to Make Friends* when I was younger. Or I'm latching onto what Red called them in the car.

"Joey!" I hear a girl yell before a loud splash

splits into the air.

I turn to the sound and creep up to a group of guys, all staring down. I look over and feel my heart drop. The way down to the hot spring is ridiculous, maybe twenty feet long. I feel my heartbeat rise and clash as the girl pops up and directs her middle finger up at the guys, who I'm guessing pushed her. A few other people are down there, splashing and playing games of chicken. As I'm wondering how deep the spring actually is, hands nudge at my back.

I whip around and face Red, who's laughing like a hyena. "Jesus Christ, Red! You almost gave me a damn heart attack!"

"Oh, calm down, baby." She reaches up and taps my nose. I swat her hand away, and she laughs again. I can't help but smile at her sudden mood change from when she was in the car. There isn't anything for her to worry about anyway; her friends seem pretty chill. Heavily tatted and pierced, but chill nonetheless.

"Can I take you to meet some people, or are you going to scream like a little bitch again?" she asks, cocking her head to the side.

"What is with the name calling? Did I ever hurt you?" I playfully slap my chest, and she rolls her eyes. She grabs my wrist and winds us between grinding bodies and people smoking to a group of people.

"Guys, I want you to meet Noah." She sounds nervous, and it makes me weirdly smiley. "Noah, this is Sarah, Neo, Lola, and Vince."

"Hey." Sarah, wearing an American-flag shirt and jeans, nods at me the same time Lola chirps,

"Hi!" Lola twists her platinum blonde hair and winks at me with hazel brown eyes and moves her hips to manipulate me into checking her out. But I merely examine her outfit—a black leather crop top under a jean jacket and a short red skirt.

Neo raises his hand. "'Sup." He looks like the typical stoner with his long brown hair tucked under a dark beanie, wearing a leather vest and a silver chain.

And Vince just nods at me. He looks like a supreme phantom of the badass, in his Levi jeans and black shirt and cropped black hair. His muscles pop under his crossed arms, and I wonder if he did it to come off as intimidating. He just looks like an asshole, but I'm really trying not to judge, though he's making it hard by the stare-down he's giving me.

"Nice to meet you all," I say honestly, minus Vince.

"Can I ask you a question?" asks Neo.

"Sure," I say as Red spits, "No."

Lola snickers. "Let him ask it, Red."

"Don't you need to pop your tiny ass on some douchebag?" Red sneers, and I momentarily wonder if they're friends or not. But they could be the best of friends and Red just gets harsh when pissed off. I mean, she does it with me and we're...I don't even know, but she's not so different with me, which kind of hurts. But I've learned it's who she is.

"I do, but I was waiting for *him*." Lola bats her long, fake eyelashes and tries to saunter over to me, but Red holds a hand out to my chest and growls. Quite literally. My heart soars like a bald eagle for some reason.

"Hold up, Lola. Do you *want* to get a black eye?" Sarah laughs as she yanks her tiny friend back, who pouts and winks at me. Again, Red growls, and my heart does a flapper dance.

Neo is laughing his skinny ass off, too entertained by the weird moment to finish asking his question.

"I think what Neo was trying to ask was..." His brown eyes swivel to my green ones, and he plays with the lip ring in the middle of his fat lower lip with a vicious smirk. "How are you still with her after—"

"Shut the *fuck* up, Vince," Red snaps, and I move to hold her hand and calm her down, but she yanks it away and side-eyes me. "Can you just go away for a bit? I need to talk to my *friends*." Her tone is sharp and not easy to fight with, so, with a damaged ego, I nod and walk over to the cliff.

What the hell is going on? Things were kind of going well, before Vince, the seemingly a-hole, finished Neo's question, which doesn't even make sense. But in his defense, he didn't get to finish before Red stomped on it and pushed me away. I feel like an idiot somehow, even though I was just trying to know her friends.

Sighing, I look over my shoulder to the group and a fuming Red, who tries her best to keep her tone low and secretive.

"Are you guys stupid? Do you not want your—" she begins to rage, when Mike steps into my line of vision.

"That time of the month?" he asks with a smile,

referring to Red.

"Fuck off." I hit his shoulder. "And no. I don't think so. It's just so *weird*. One minute her friends and I were sort of talking and the next she commands I step away after this guy asked some question that resulted in Red blowing the hell up. And I have no idea how to react," I rant a bit and look over at them again. They're all glancing over at me and smirking, which sets me on edge and makes me feel self-conscious.

"Girlfriend's friends are always assholes. It's just a thing." He shrugs, grabbing my attention. "Sometimes you're lucky and you bond with them. Other times…you just miss bullseye and are caught between making friends with them, or not and coming off as a douche even when *they're* the problem. It's best to just be buddy-buddy, to appease the lady."

"Easier said than done," I mumble.

"Hey, sorry to interrupt." Red sidles up to me, glancing at Mike.

"It's okay. I was gonna get another beer anyway." Mike holds up his empty Corona, then walks away.

"Vince here has something to say." Red nudges her "friend" while giving me a grin.

I look to Vince and find he's smirking at me. But it caves into a sigh when Red nudges him harder.

"About earlier, I interpreted something totally wrong. My bad, honestly." Everything he just said sounds rehearsed and makes me uncomfortable and suspicious. I try not to side-eye Red and hound her with questions and just give him a nod.

"No problem, man," I tell him with a forced smile.

"Now that we have that out of the way…" Red reaches down and pulls off her shirt. I lick my lips and push my hands in my jeans, admiring her lacy red lingerie. And then she unzips her jeans and kicks off her boots. And I'm panting over her in my head, and she winks at me, as if she can read my mind. And I blush. "Let's get to jumping."

Jumping?

"Into the springs, idiot." She pushes Vince out of the way, and I notice him ogling after her as he walks away. I make fists and glare at him, ready to punch that freaking smug expression off his face. "Calm down, Rocky," she teases in my ear, reaching for my clutched hands.

"But…" I begin, then sigh and look at her staring at my lips. I smirk and push my hands through her hair, cupping the back of her neck. She plays with her lip ring with her tongue as I feel multiple eyes on me. "Let's jump, okay?"

"I suggested it first," she says, and I pull away, rolling my eyes.

I reach down and pull off my gray t-shirt. Her eyes not so subtly fall onto my chest and fall down and down as I slowly pull down my jeans. I hear a few whistles and woots from passing girls, but they all run away when Red growls at them. Is this going to be a thing? Because, if so, I can definitely get used to it, to her claiming me. I chuckle as I take off my shoes and socks, leaving them in a pile next to other clothes.

When I stand and face her, she's biting her lip

and her eyes have darkened. My skin tingles with goosebumps that definitely aren't a result of the cool temperature. Her stare is fixed and ravenous. I walk up to her and tip her head back using my index finger. She sucks in a breath as I curve my finger down her neck, then lean down and whisper against her lips, "Are you going to stare at me all night…or are we going to jump?" I mock her from earlier in the car when she was mocking me.

Realizing this, her eyes dim, and she pushes me away. "Fuck you, prep."

"Anytime." I walk over to her, biting my lip. "Anyplace."

She begins to reply when Lola yells out a battle call and winks at me over her shoulder. She murmurs a long list of curses before grabbing my hand and walking us over to the cliff. Pushing people away, we stand at the front, and suddenly I'm very aware that I don't know how deep it is. What if it's shallow in a majority of the water, and only the jumpers know where the deep area is, and I break my neck and die?

"What? Pissing your pants, prep?" Red whispers in my ear. I can feel her smirk without looking at her.

I look at her, and she is indeed smirking, with an unknown emotion crossing her mesmerizing blue eyes. *What did she just say?* I frown at her teasing me and tug on her hand, pulling her and me off the cliff. The wind rushes up, too fast and too hard. My ears pop, and I hear her scream out jubilantly before we smack into the water. Laughter and the loud rap song fades out as we sink and idle in the clear water.

My limbs feel like jelly and my movements slow as I look for her. A few seconds later, I find her swimming toward me with the biggest, most beautiful smile. I have to kiss her, and I have to do it now. I swim over to her, the stars and moon above staring down at me, and I grab her face and kiss her with everything I have. My lungs are squeezing and my body is fizzing with so many emotions.

But all I can do is kiss her and feel her lips part and just *know* she is sighing in contentment. I smile against her lips and she does too, and my heart soars and races and beats…all for her, because of her. I pull her closer, and our bodies turn and turn and trace through the water. We are one and I never want to let go. Ever.

But my lungs being the bitches they are scream at me, and we're forced to swim to the surface. My ears pop, and I gasp for a large grab of air. My lungs fill joyfully, and I ruin their party by kissing her again. Deeply and openly, I kiss my beautiful Red, who I have admittedly fallen so damn deep and hard for. I'm cupping her face under the stars and galaxy and people shouting after us when three words pop up in my head, and I scream it in the form of our shared laughter and her squeals as I spin us around in the water…

I love you.

Chapter Thirty-Two

"Will practice ever ease up?" I huff out as I hobble back into the living room. It's the next day after the cliff, and I just got finished up with football practice. We have a football game in a week, so Coach has been pushing us hard today. He desperately wants us to continue our winning streak, but that'll be difficult to do if we can barely walk.

"Never." Mike grins as we head to our lockers. I roll my eyes but gingerly pull off my soaked gray muscle tank top. "So," he says and glances at me with a knowing smile. "You and Red..."

My throat clenches.

I love you. My thought from yesterday circles in my head at the thought of her.

"What about us?" I ask him in my calmest voice. I still can't believe I had that thought. I don't regret it or anything; it just surprised the hell out of me. I've never loved someone before, and it's scary as shit.

He chuckles. "You guys seemed to have a great time last night. Are you guys, like, serious or anything?"

"Why? Thought you had a chance with her?" I tease, and he tosses his stinky shirt at me. I smirk and throw it back in his face, but he only laughs and dumps it in his gym bag.

"Nah, but you guys look like you're getting pretty heavy," he says.

I pause as I'm pulling off my sweatpants. *I love you*...the words echo, but I find myself shaking my head. "Not anything like that. *But* we have been doing great so far. I don't want to ruin it by saying or doing something stupid, you know?" A buzz floats in the air from somewhere in my gym bag. I fish out my phone as he speaks.

"If she freaks out, then there's no point in a relationship at all," he says earnestly. "Plus, I haven't seen her this happy in a long while. Not after..." He pauses, and I flick my eyes up at him from my phone. He's looking down at the floor, and I wait for him to continue. But he doesn't.

"After what?" I ask him, then look back down at my phone.

There's a text from my mother asking about my studies. I delete it. Neither she nor my father deserves to check up on me after throwing me in this place. I'm still pretty pissed off about it.

When I look back at him, he's smiling forcibly. "Nothing. I didn't mean anything." He pauses and lets out a breath. "We should hit the showers, you especially. You smell like the sewer shit on you."

I punch his arm as he passes me. "Fuck off," I jest and glance at my phone. "And I'll be right behind you. I'm gonna ask what Red's up to later."

After he leaves, I text Red.

Noah: How do you feel about grabbing a bite at the diner?

She doesn't respond after a few seconds, so I leave my phone in the locker and jog to the showers.

After two hours of no reply, I decide to follow up as I'm studying with Rachel for a chemistry test this week.

Noah: Dinner then?

No response after a little over three hours.

My next text is when I'm playing a video game with Ty and Mike and a few other guys.

Noah: Hey, are you okay? You're not responding. Just let me know. Please.

Thirty minutes later when I'm working on a project for the art club, I text her again.

Noah: Red? Are you okay?

And then, a few hours later past midnight when I'm climbing in bed.

Noah: red?

***

A week. Red has been gone for an entire week. Days have passed and no word from her, my resolve has crumbled to nothing, and my concern has grown an unfathomable amount. I call and text and leave voicemail after voicemail, but she ignores them all. I often think of what could have possibly made her act like that, flee without an explanation.

Whatever is going on with her, I hope she is okay. I just wish she'd let me help her. Be there for her. Whatever it is makes me wonder. Why does she always leave me?

The little bell above the door chimes as I walk into Joe's Diner.

"The usual?" Majesty asks from behind the cashier. She wields a look I've been encountering every day Red's been MIA—sympathy.

"Yeah," I answer around an exhausted smile. I'm just coming from a football practice, and I'm sore from head to toe. I'll be joining the guys at a local gym they visit a few times a week, but I promised to meet them there. "Have you...?" I trail off, taking my seat on the red stool at the countertop.

"No, I'm sorry." Her eyes drop to the counter she's wiping with a rag. My heart sinks a little more each time she says that. I've been coming here for a week, asking for updates on Red, but I just get the same answer each time. I thought since they were best friends, Red would have at least told her where she was going or why she left—but no. She left everyone in the dark. It hurts even more because she didn't even leave me one shred of light.

Majesty's kind of my solace, apart from working out and painting, this past week.

"It's all right." I take the mug of black coffee she pushes toward me.

"It isn't, though." Her brown eyes search mine. "You have bags under your eyes. She'll come back around. You shouldn't stress yourself out."

"How do you know?" I run my hands over my hair. I want to rip it out from all the frustration packed under my skin. I end up cupping the mug and staring at a coffee stain on the counter.

When I look into her honey-brown eyes, she lowers her voice and says, "Because I know her. And I know that she...cares for you."

My heart stampedes. "She does?" I pause and blurt out, "Then why the hell would she just *leave* without a text or anything? She has me worrying— *you* worrying. It's unfair and cruel and—and—*fuck*. It's just not right." My throat tightens.

She puts a hand on my wrist. "The girl likes to be closed off sometimes. She used to run off without telling anybody anything back in our hometown in Washington, but she always came back." She laughs a little and draws her hand back. "Always with new tattoo..." She pauses as I laugh too. "But she did come back. This time is no different. Just...just give her some time. Don't give up on her. She likes you...a lot. You're...you're good for her, and you make her happy."

"How would you know?" I scrape at the counter nervously.

She does a little shoulder dance that makes me smile. "What are best friends for other than gossiping about a boy?" Her voice rises, and she bats her long eyelashes. I laugh some more and she

295

does too, her eyes sparkling more than I've noticed since I've been coming here. She didn't say it, but each time Red leaves, she takes a little bit of her friend.

Reaching for her hand, I suggest, "Until then, why don't we hang out? Stay close and keep ourselves from bawling over our lack of Red." She laughs and swats at me with the dirty rag. "I'm being serious. My frat's throwing a Halloween costume party tonight."

"Not into douchebags or costumes." She shudders at the idea.

"Oh, come on. You don't have to dress up or interact with any of the guys. You can bring a friend or two or a hundred with you. I don't care."

She nibbles on her lower lip as the bell rings over the door. Her eyes flick to the new customer before settling them on me with a small smile. "I'll think about it," she promises and walks over to the customer.

"Don't think too hard," I call after her, bringing the coffee mug to my lips. I sip slowly, enjoying the warmth that spreads through my chest. I'm brought out of my coffee trance when Rachel sits on the stool on my left. "Hey, there...what's got you so down?"

"This." She looks around, keeping her voice low, before pulling out a manila file from her velvet brown shoulder bag.

I raise my brows, nodding toward it. "What's in there?"

"Don't freak out at me," she warns. The wideness of her brown eyes and flushness in her cheeks scare me a little, so me freaking out is looking like a guarantee.

"Rachel…" I say, setting my coffee down.

"Just…" She bites her full lower lip, pushing the folder toward me. "Don't say I didn't warn you about her." She moves to leave, but I grab her wrist, not moving my eyes from the file. Written with black Sharpie marker on a little label toward the middle is Red's name. And on top of the file is the stamp of the college: *Johns Hopkins University.*

"Where did you get this?" I ask her, taken aback by the darkness in my voice. I look at her wide eyes and how she gulps. Whatever is in here is bad…*real bad.* She won't even keep her eyes on me; she keeps darting them around. She must have looked inside, and my hold gets a little too tight, but it goes unnoticed before I can loosen it.

"You're hurting me, Noah," she tells me with a whimper.

I let go. "Sorry, but—Rachel, where did you get this from?"

She rubs her frail wrist with scared doe eyes, like she might run away from me. "She really turned you out," she says. Glancing at the folder, she tells me, "I have a friend who works in the main office. I did you a favor. You'll be doing yourself a favor too if you leave her. She's…" She shakes her head and hops off the stool. "Just read for yourself."

Chapter Thirty-Three

I don't read the file. Whatever is in it won't come from Red's mouth. The information in it is pure facts derived from whatever shit source that's no substitute from her word, and hers alone.

I stare at it on my bed before covering it with a pillow. I would burn it and scold Rachel for digging up Red's past, but it's the school's property, and I don't want to get kicked out and disappoint my parents even more.

"Dude, you coming?" a voice asks behind me.

I turn around and find Ty poking his head inside the room, a girl wearing a slutty nun's outfit hanging off his arm. Kind of literally. He's wearing red suspenders clipped to a fireman's pants he bought off eBay, and he has on a hard hat. Oh, and he's shirtless. Obviously.

"Yeah, I'm coming now," I tell him. I take one last glance at the pillow before walking over to him and his nun. The outfit's incredibly offensive to the Catholic religion, but what outfit isn't? On the way down, I spot several vampires, policemen, and

Jokers. All make me glad I dressed up simpler: in a black leather jacket, black jeans, combat boots, a red scarf, and the infamous spiked bat.

"Who are you supposed to be again?" Ty asks the second I walk into the kitchen. Around the counter, girls are getting their bellybuttons filled with vodka sucked at by werewolves and pirates. Halloween truly is a gift to mankind.

"Negan," I tell him with a smile.

He crinkles his forehead.

"Lucille." I hold up the bat, posing like I'm bashing it over someone's head.

His eyes squint, and I sigh.

"I'm guessing you don't watch *The Walking Dead*," I assume, and he shrugs.

"Never seen it. But I'll see you around. Me and Lyndsey are gonna—"

"Don't wanna know. Just...*go*." I wave at him, and he snorts, but they walk off to the back. More like stumble over her cloak. I rub the back of my neck and lean against a wall, watching Hulk make out with Ariel the Little Mermaid on the kitchen table where we eat. I close my eyes and imagine I'm somewhere else.

I rather be anywhere other than *here*. I want to be where Red is. Watching her smile out of the corner of my eye when she thinks I'm not looking. Listening to her laugh or curse me out for not liking her taste in music. Feel her warm, creamy skin as I tickle her. I just miss her presence.

I know I sound whipped, but I don't care. Red...she makes me feel like myself. Like I can climb Mount Everest and not care about the freezing cold because she'd be by my side giving off her potent fiery energy and just because the journey of the climb outweighs anything else. The exhilarating, out-of-body rush of excitement and fulfillment.

"Noah?" I hear a familiar voice call out.

Snapping my eyes open, I look to my right and smile, finding Majesty dressed in a flapper outfit. "Over here, Josephine Baker."

She turns on her sparkly small heels, blushes, and walks over to me. She punches me in the shoulder and chuckles behind her white gloved hands. "Shut up, Negan. You're lucky Party City was open this late."

"You know who I am!" I exclaim and shake her a little, the silver tassels on her short dress shaking.

"Yes! I love *The Walking Dead*. Now, will you stop shaking me? I feel like a traumatized baby." Her tone is light, but her expression is violent. I stop, and she beams up at me. "How's the party so far?" She looks around and grimaces at Jon Snow groping Mary Poppins. "Never mind, I know the answer—traumatizing. Is that the theme for the party?"

"I guess so." I look away from the weird couple, and we shudder together. I laugh out loud, and she looks around. I guess I should get her a drink. "Want a drink?"

As a shirtless Pennywise 2017 edition guy walks by, she laughs out, "Yes. *Please*."

We end up drinking a few vodka sodas and talking for half an hour. In that time, we get to know each other better. I learn about Red's rough time growing up with the tragic loss of her mother, about her own childhood and how she was bullied for being Muslim. I promise her that, if I lived where she grew up as a child, I would have beat up every jackass that teased her about her beautiful golden hijab and she, Red, and I would swing after school every day, me acting as their bodyguard. She laughs at that, calls me sweet, then leaves to get us decorated cupcakes.

Now, she's in the corner of the living room making out with Thor. I'm keeping an eye on her even though she promised she's fine and equipped with pepper spray and a ninja star. I choose to believe she was joking about the star, but that doesn't stop me from watching out for her. I'm on my fourth cupcake when I am tapped on my shoulder.

Rachel is standing beside me, wearing an angel outfit and looking sheepish. "Um…hey, Noah."

I take a while to fold the cupcake paper before answering. "Hey, Rachel." I toss the folded paper into the garbage bag beside me.

She takes a deep breath. "I'm…I'm sorry about earlier. I was just thinking about her hurting you and…and I don't want to see that happen. Is that such a bad thing?"

I shrug, ready to ignore her when I get a good look at her costume. A halo rests on top of her hair, glittering and gold; her face holds a small splash of glitter, and her white tutu and corset makes up the entire outfit. I can't help but tie her actions to her costume, and I shrug again.

"I guess not," I say.

Her eyes light up, and she breathes out heavily in relief. "That's great. I was hoping you'd see it my way. I just wanted to protect you, Noah." She throws herself at me, and I stumble backward, ending up in front of the open front door.

"Prep?" a weak voice says beside me.

My muscles loosen, and I whip my head toward the door. What I see makes my knees buckle and heart race like never before.

"Red?"

Chapter Thirty-Four

I feel like a statue, frozen in place as I take in her presence. She looks okay in the sense that she doesn't have any bruises on her face. Her hair is the same—disheveled and tossed to one side; so is her ripped tee and beat-up combat boots. She even smells the same from where I stand. But she doesn't look the same. Her black eyeliner is smudged and heavy bags are hidden away under her dim blue eyes that are usually brilliant—well, around me, at least.

I want to run over to her and ask her a bunch of questions. Maybe scream at her for just leaving and not answering any of my calls and worried voicemails. Then I want to crush her in a relieved hug. But like I said, I can't move, frozen in shock. A million emotions seem to staple me to the ground, and I look away to catch my breath. Anger courses through me, helping me get through just standing here with her staring at me like I'm an artifact on display.

"Well? Aren't you going to say anything?"

Rachel snaps and turns to Red, who doesn't flinch. Just stares at me. Her eyes have so much impact on me because I feel a shiver run up and down my spine. "You left and he's been worried sick about you. You're even worse than I thought."

Red says nothing, which surprises me so much I pull away from Rachel and walk down the stairs toward her.

"Noah, what are you doing? She isn't worth it," Rachel calls out.

I ignore her and stop in front of Red. She stares up into my eyes, and I curl my fists in my pants. "Where have you been?" My voice comes out stern, no bullshitting allowed. I think I deserve to be a hard-ass for one night, right? After what she did, I deserve so much more from her.

The sound of constant chatter from drunk partygoers on the lawn almost drowns out her silence. Almost. She opens her mouth to speak, but something crosses her eyes and she closes it shut. I wait a few more seconds but receive nothing but earth-splitting silence. Either that or it's my heart crumbling just a little more. I hate that she just left me, and now that she's back, she won't even tell me anything about why she did. She's just staring at me like I should be able to read her mind. Like always. But this isn't one of those times.

"Right," I say around an airy, pathetic laugh. I take a step back and watch her eyes flutter. "You just get up and leave, which Majesty says is normal. Majesty, by the way, is worried sick too. But I guess you don't give a shit, right? You can do whatever the hell you please because you're Red—

the unreliable badass. You can just crush me and I should expect it because I give you my all when you give me *shit*, like you just fucking leaving," I snap and pant for breath.

Tears are forming beneath her fluttered shut eyes, mouth ajar, like she's ready to reveal everything to me. But she shuts her mouth and looks away. Again. She's pushing me away. Not trusting me enough. When will she ever? I hide my frown, spin on my heels, and begin walking back to Rachel, to the party, to where, in Red's mind, I probably belong instead of by her side. When, in reality, I don't give a shit about the party the way I give a shit about *her*.

"Grey," I hear her mumble barely. With the party racket, I could have heard something entirely different. But the name makes me stop in my tracks and turn to her.

"What?" I say.

Eyes clearly avoiding mine, she inhales deeply. "I was on a...a road trip..." She trails off and burns whatever is left of my heart. I hate and am amused that she has that ability to just crush me up with one glance or silence or that freaking name.

"Grey? As in *Wyler*? Grey Wyler?" I don't miss the shock in my voice. I thought I'd heard the last of him a few months ago, when I was sort of dating my childhood best friend, Liv Westerfield.

Just when I started to fall for the girl, Grey Wyler—the most shithead asshole I know, well, he and Ian are neck and neck—swooped in and stole her from me. But to be fair, they had their own thing. I was just in the way of their grand, epic love.

So I gladly took a step back. Though, with his track record of fucking up, I doubt they'll be anything more than a couple. The asshole's basically allergic to commitment; it's actually kind of hilarious.

"Yes." Her eyes shine and then her brows curve together. "You know him?"

I scoff and look around. "Know him? I hate the guy. A real prick...but so far he's been paying his dues to society, helping his girl after the..." The words melt on my tongue as I visualize her and me holding hands as I cry for her in the ICU, a tube in her mouth, chest... "How do *you* know him?"

She licks her lips, shrugs her shoulders. "Been hanging out with him, I guess."

I take a long, deep breath to calm myself. "And you just left town with him?" I ask through grinding teeth. If I gritted them any harder, my teeth will shatter like my resolve.

Her eyes bore through mine, arms crossing her chest, as if bracing herself for my reaction. "Yes," she says, and I keep my calm. I really, really try. But imagining him and her in his car, driving across the freaking globe, in that confined space, ignites a spark that creates an entire forest fire within my chest.

"That it? You're not even gonna *try* to elaborate?" I spit out, and she looks away, looking annoyed. I want to wipe that look off her face because it's pissing me off even more that she doesn't hear the wrong in her confession. "Wanna at least tell me *why* you left to do God knows what, in God knows *where* with a prick like Grey Wyler?"

"I don't *need* to explain anything to you," she

claims, scowling at me.

"Yes! You do!" I storm over to her and shout, "You left the second after we established *something* between us. Just up and left without a notice or anything. You worried Majesty and me, and now you're pissed because I'm questioning your sudden decision to go on a cross-country road trip with an asshole? How is that any fucking fair, Red?"

"We aren't boyfriend and girlfriend! I don't mean shit to you like you don't mean shit to me! I don't need to tell you jack shit. So why don't you hop off my fucking back and go back to your angel-sweetheart bitch who's staring me down?" she screams and gestures wildly behind me. But I don't budge. I keep my eyes on her and pant as the fire fans out in my veins. My anger dissolves like sugar in water, because of the glossy ripple in her eyes and her silently grasping for words.

"I don't want to fight." I run a hand through my hair.

"Neither do I," she says, glancing behind me. "I gotta get to a job. And you gotta get back to her." Jealousy floats between her words. No. They sting with bitterness, and I actually laugh. She runs a finger across her lip before wheeling around on her boots.

No. No freaking way! She doesn't get to just walk away without an explanation.

Following her to her bike, I shout without thinking, "What? You start to get feelings for me and go back to your cowardly ways? So you leave me and go run off with some tough-ass fighter? I'm guessing you have a type and were shaking in your boots when you actually *felt* something with me?" She stops getting on the bike but doesn't face me. And it pisses me off. "Tell me, Red. Are you ever going to stop being a coward and tell me how you feel? Or will you keep hopping to assholes instead of admitting you feel something for me?" I yell at the top of my lungs, drawing attention from partygoers. But I can't help that she makes me insane.

"Shut up!" she screams and turns around. Her fist collides with my eye before I even see it coming. Pain bursts behind my eye, and I stumble back onto the patch of grass. She gasps as I scream out in pain.

"Noah!" Rachel screams, and I hear heels hitting the concrete.

"What the fuck, Red?" I cup my eye and hiss as a stinging sensation comes from it. Has she lost her fucking mind? But then I look up at her with my good eye and she's crying and hugging herself. My anger melts into a puddle as she stumbles back, hitting her bike. In just a few seconds, she's transformed into a girl with a broken heart and so much story behind her glazed over eyes. I want to scoop her up and hold her for however long it takes.

"Wait. Don't go," I plead and stand, wobbly, but Rachel reaches me in time and stabilizes me. "Red, you can't just leave. Please don't leave again." My voice cracks and breaks.

"I'm sorry, but you're better off without me," Red croaks before jumping on her bike and riding off without even putting on her helmet.

Fear of her getting into an accident without a

helmet sparks urgency under my ass, and I move to stop her, but she's already down the street, leaving behind an aching eye and a cloud of dust. Just like that, she's leaving me. Again. Tears bubble in my eyes, and I wipe them away.

"I can't believe her," Rachel says under her breath. Then she reaches up and cups my cheeks, smiling softly. "Let's get you inside and put an ice pack on your eye. You should really forget about her." She moves to take my hand, but I yank it away and shake my head.

"No," I say, voice low, eyes not leaving from down the street.

"What do you mean, no?" she asks around a nervous laugh, reaching for my hand again.

"I mean no. I have somewhere I have to be. I'm sorry." I turn away from her reaching hand and widened eyes. Her heart seems to be breaking as I race toward the house.

"Wait, Noah! Where are you going?" she shouts after me.

"After my Red!" I yell over my shoulder, on the search for Mike. I need to borrow his truck.

I am not letting her get away that easy. I deserve an explanation and—and it's more. It's her crying and looking so broken down. I have never seen her like that before. Ever. And it breaks me down, molecule by molecule. And even though I'm breaking, I need to help her first. Hold her. I need to fucking take care of my girl. No matter how maniacal she's acting lately.

***

I may love the girl, I think as I park in front of the apartment complex. Or at least I really, really like her to chase after her after she punched me in the freaking face. Which, by the way, hurts like a motherfucker. But I can handle the pain as long as she doesn't experience hers any longer.

I stare up at the building, hoping it's the right one. I glance down at the text from Jaimie, one of Liv's friends I kind of got acquainted with over the summer. She was hesitant but thankfully didn't act too suspicious. I sit back and rub my uninjured eye, kind of expecting to leave empty handed. I just came from the bar Red supposedly works at here in Pennsylvania, and she wasn't there. So maybe she's here...?

The thought makes me sick. And then the visions of her and Grey in his car, laughing and enjoying the music they both love, fills my brain, and I punch the steering wheel. A loud honk resonates through the empty streets, well, apart from the drunk partygoers celebrating Halloween.

"Fuck," I murmur and pinch the corners of my eyes.

I hope I don't walk in on them fucking or measuring each other's leather jackets. Even though I know for a fact he's deadly in love with Liv and, according to her, has been on his best behavior. But seeing as how he left her too, I think he broke his good record. But who didn't see that one coming? The guy has a short timer for being a good boy.

Gathering whatever courage I have, I get out of the beat-up pick-up truck, lock it, and walk up to the building. On the way up, I go over sentence starters.

I mean, how do you tell a friend her boyfriend and my girl—if I can even call her that—went on a road trip and, when she got back, she punched me in the eye? I don't think there *is* a correct way to start that conversation.

But I have no time to think of any because the elevator comes to a stop and Liv's ranting stops mid-sentence as she flips on the light. I cower back at the bright light and lean against the elevator wall, sighing.

Pointing to the bruise, I say, "Red."

Chapter Thirty-Five

Her mouth parts in shock, and I can practically see the million questions floating in her brain. Like normal. She's a very inquisitive girl, but she sets them aside and her natural kindness shines through. "Come on, let's sit you down and ice that," she suggests, leading me out of the elevator and into their admittedly nice loft apartment. I moan the entire way to the couch, gauging her pursed mouth and curved eyebrows.

"What are you doing here in Pennsylvania?" she asks as she gets up and walks into the kitchen. I watch her open the freezer and, wincing at my now-swelling eye, I answer her.

"I came looking for her." She still looks confused, so I try to explain a little more clearly. "She works here at some bar a few times a week. Apparently she gets paid good money and is friends with the owner?" I still don't find the appeal to spend three hours driving out here, when there are jobs in Baltimore, but that's Red for you—confusing as hell.

"We are talking about *Red* Red, right?" She walks over to me and hands me a pack of peas before sitting cross-legged. The pack is freezing cold, and I shiver as it meets my skin. "Blonde hair, blue eyes, frightening scowl?" It's kind of scary how well she just described her. I would have added "incredibly drop-dead gorgeous," but that's just me. Thinking about her smile makes me feel like I'm drowning, so I put on a smile and focus on what she said.

I laugh quietly, licking my lips. "Yup. That's my Red." But is she really even *mine*? She's so afraid to be anything related to me, unless I can rack up a high pain tolerance for an arm tattoo and wear leather jackets like it's stitched to my brolic, fighter muscles. I let out a hefty sigh, wishing I could change things so I can just kiss her without her jetting to freaking England or something.

Liv's eyebrows screw together, and I can see her picturing Red and me together and failing. Many, many times. But then she focuses on how we'd be together in the first place, and she gasps. "Are you two dating?"

My cheeks feel extremely hot. "I wouldn't say 'dating.'"

"So what would you say?" she teases, and I narrow my eyes at her. Nice to know she can still poke fun at me. She smiles because she's a cocky shit and knows it.

"It's something...*complicated*." I sigh again and roll my shoulders. Complicated doesn't begin to cover it. Whatever we have, it's something more than I've ever experienced. Even with Liv. With her, I latched onto our previous friendship over the years, and she was a nice girl. Sure, we weren't what the universe planned like her and Grey are, but I did grow feelings for her. But with Red...I feel...I don't know—alive might be the word I'm looking for. But instead of letting whatever needs to happen happen, she pulls back a little each time, and it is the most frustrating thing ever.

"How did you guys meet?" Liv's sweet voice pulls me out of my overworked brain. I swear, if I even think about what two plus two is, my brain will implode.

My cheeks grow even hotter, and I rub my neck. "Um, bumped into her at a party. She was super rude, but I saved her life a few minutes later, so I'm not complaining. Oh, yeah, we go to the same school." Of course there's more to the story, like how each time we interact, even if it is just a glance, I feel my entire being relax and my heart lift just a little. Like, when I am around her, I stop being what my parents want, what my friends expect—I am just...*me*, and it is okay. God, I miss her and the way she makes me feel like myself.

"Sure..." Liv says, lips trying their best not to curl into an annoying smile. She tries to act neutral and cool, but I can just see the questions and doubts circling her pretty head.

Not as pretty as Red, my subconscious sneers like the little bitch he is.

"And the bruise? Does she...hurt you often?" she asks softly, sucking her full lips in her mouth. Oh, God. How pathetic do I look on the outside that she asks if I'm being abused, using her psychologist-in-training voice? She's going to make a kid cry in her office one day.

Laughing at the idea, I wave a free hand. "She doesn't hurt me. If I were in an abusive relationship, I would be dead first. No." I shake my head and clear my throat, shifting uncomfortably as I recall what I said. Sighing, I explain, "I said a really nasty thing to her because, well, she and Grey have become close, and I just thought the worst when I found out they've been...*on the road*. Which—" I look at her incredulously. "How are you fine with that?" Red and I are barely forming a relationship if she allows it, but Liv and Grey have more history than anyone I know. A very dark, tight-knitted, epic history. They've been through hell and back, so I know she must feel gutted about this.

"I'm not. Keep going." She smiles forcibly, and my heart hurts for her. She is one of the most caring people I know to ever walk this fucked-up world. No matter what's going on, she cares about others first before herself.

Brows knitting together, concern swells in my chest. I consider wrapping her up in a blanket and hunting down Grey myself and beating him up for hurting her like this. But she gives me a look of desperation to put the light on me before she bursts into a ball of tears, and I do not want that to happen. I care about her, obviously, but also because I hate seeing others cry. It's my kryptonite. Which is why witnessing a badass girl like Red break into tears slices me open from the inside out.

"Anyway, she swung the meanest right hook and gave me Ed." I tap the pack of peas, a gloomy smile tugging on my lips. "My bruise."

"Ed?" She laughs, blue eyes lighting up like a thunderstorm during a summer day. "Why Ed of all names?"

"Oh, I'm sorry my name-picking abilities aren't superb right after being *punched*." I chuckle and roll my eyes; however, my right eye is swollen, causing her to erupt into this beautiful laugh, head thrown back and everything. She gives me a little push, and I yank at her big toe playfully, wanting to keep her laughing. Light her up. Make her forget asshole-Grey.

"Hey, don't injure me just because you are," she shrieks, attempting to pull her foot away, but I grab the whole thing and tickle her.

"If I'm suffering, so are you," I say with a huge grin. I like having her laughing and *not* looking depressed because her boyfriend's a freaking idiot. But then again, I wasn't exactly having a jolly-great time myself on the way over here after my—whatever the hell she is to me—punched me in the face.

"Tell me more about you and Red." She sits up, pulling her feet under her to protect from my hands.

"You're no fun." I rest my head on the headrest, lips jutted in a pout. Her head follows me, and her smile is too bright for this world, too damn sweet for *Grey*.

"Shut up and tell me about your Red."
Your Red...I like that.

I sigh but, in reality, I'm relieved to talk about her. Despite this nasty bruise on my face, the girl is really sweet and easy to talk to. I tell her that and

316

how she loves Nirvana and how we broke into a YMCA to swim. I rant about Ian being a dickhead ninety-nine percent of the time, the time he and I fought...both times. How utterly breathtaking her smile and laugh is. I go on and on about the way my body buzzes whenever she's near. How she doesn't talk about her feelings that much, but when she does, she rants, and how her nose scrunches when she does. I talk about...everything, and when I finish, I can't stop smiling.

"So do you know why they just up and left?" I ask her, calming down from the thought of Red, cheeks burning, eyes most likely dilated. Wow. Imagine how I look when I kiss her...maybe even more. I clear my throat. Focus on my friend who looks so heartbroken as she brings up her knees and fidgets.

"No. I just came home and he was gone..." Her voice breaks and her eyes glaze over as she dives into deep thought. But before she can drown in them, I gently touch her hand and she looks at me.

Smiling at her softly, I say, "You guys will figure it out. You've been through hell and back, so I'm sure this is nothing."

"It's just...I don't know. Maybe he's hiding something from me, but that wouldn't make sense. We've been on the straight and narrow for a while. A few bumps here and there, but we were solid as far as I knew. I just wish I didn't have to worry about what else will get in our way, waiting for the next heartache. I want more than anything for him to come to me for anything. Not leave me and go God knows where with some girl. Sorry, Red," she adds quickly, blushing.

I wave it off and sigh. "She'll tell me why she left soon enough. I think. But I think you should find out why he did, ASAP, before things get worse." And things tend to get worse for this couple.

"If only I could find him, Noah," she tells me with a sad smile.

I move to hug her when a phone interrupts our moment.

I pull out my phone and shake my head. Nothing. "Not me."

Holding up a finger, she rushes into the hallway. I saw the look of hope and desperation and relief on her face, and I almost grab her hand and hold her down. She doesn't need nor should she put up with his bullshit.

Neither should you with Red, my subconscious croons.

"You bastard. You're not helping, you know," I talk to myself like the insane person I am. I run my hands over my hair, wishing I had Lucille so I could just smash something. I don't know what I can do without any information from Liv, like I hoped I could get. And Red's not answering her phone. Surprise there.

A loud sob makes me freeze. Sitting up quickly, I listen for the sound again. A few seconds pass before a louder sob hits my ears. I burst into the bedroom before I can process it. "Liv, what's wrong?" I scramble onto the bed, wrapping my lengthy arms around her small body.

"I—I—they found him!" she cries and I frown,

not understanding. Until I smell medicine and am staring down at her pale skin in the hospital those months ago. And I understand everything. She sobs into my chest and holds me closer, licking her lips. "They…" She tries to speak, but the words lodge in her throat, and she clutches me like I am her lifeline. Nodding, I rub her back soothingly. Even though I know she wants the love of her life holding her, I don't say anything and let her cry into my shirt.

Chapter Thirty-Six

In my dream, Red and I are on our way to a Nirvana concert. And I don't mean a venue that plays Nirvana songs, their music videos and concert diary videos projected on a huge screen in the middle of nowhere, if they even do that for a band that no longer plays gigs. No. We're genuinely going to a Nirvana concert, sometime in the 1990s. She's decked out in basically what she wears today: black ripped tee of the band, ripped jeans, messy hair, heavy eyeliner, and flannel. I'm matching her, but I'm wearing a snapback and fake piercings she jammed into my face thirty minutes before.

She's laughing at my ridiculous outfit and I'm posing ridiculously for pictures, via Polaroid, duh. The night seems to stretch on and on forever. The music is ear-shatteringly loud. My heart stops with each bass that kicks in. She's dancing like she's electrocuted. And I'm holding her from behind, swaying to a surprisingly sweet song. And then we're reckless, grunge teens jumping to one of her favorites: "Smells Like Teen Spirit." Kurt's screaming, his lengthy blond hair covering his face. I feel infinite and badass and myself, and it's all because of the beautiful girl dancing under my chin.

And then the world reminds me Grey Wyler exists.

"Wake up, bitch!" I hear him roar and kick the bed.

Groaning, I climb up out of the sheets. I want to rip his stupid boots off his feet and beat him with them. He ripped me out of the most peaceful sleep I think I've ever had. I want to go back under the sheets and continue dreaming of Red and me at a Nirvana concert, but I rub my eyes and decide to entertain this raging bull.

"What's going on?" My voice is deep and I sound so confused, mostly because I am.

"I should be the one asking that!" he yells, and I mentally slap him with his boot. "Did something happen here that I should know about, Liv?" He turns to her, and I honestly contemplate burning his stupid face off. Did he really just accuse her of cheating? With *me*? I'd laugh if I weren't so pissed off.

"Answer me!" he screams, and she flinches.

Oh, I'll *answer you all right*, I think as I begin to push myself to stand and give him a piece of my mind. And my fist. I've become good at it lately. Even if going against a professional fighter would most likely put me in the hospital.

Before I can even move a muscle, Liv jumps up and wobbles, the effects of us drinking wine last night in a celebratory gesture for that maniac being put behind bars. And she does the last thing I'd expect. She slaps him. Hard. I gasp and look away, trying my best to tune out their personal conflict. But I don't miss the tears and frustration and pent-up anger in her screaming.

I would pray that this doesn't happen between Red and me, but I think it's a little too late for prayer. She already has me wrapped around her little black-painted finger. I'm slowly but surely falling for the girl, and she makes it seem like I'm burdening her. Like she can't possibly feel the same way about me. When I notice how light she looks and possibly feels when I lay one glance in her direction. Brush my fingers against her cheeks. Say her name.

She likes me. She's just too afraid to admit it, and it hurts me more than she can possibly understand. More than *anyone* could understand.

When Liv's screaming fades away and Grey obviously *lies* about leaving to clear his head, I tune into the conversation.

"There's something called yoga," I recall in a nasty croak.

Being the Grey man he is, he snarls, "Shut the fuck up and get out before I strangle the loafers out of you." I am so offended; I don't even *wear* loafers! I don't think I ever have!

"Don't talk to him like that," Liv snaps and does some weird twist thing with her hands. I try to imitate them, probably looking like a fool. But they're too wrapped up, angrily eye-fucking each other to notice. "I'm sorry he's being a major dick right now. He hasn't taken any of his pills since they're all in the *trash*." She looks over at me. The girl may be small and kinder than Mother Theresa, but she can be a fiery little thing when she chooses. I have my hands tied with Red, enough.

I get up with an exhausted sigh, cracking my neck. "No problem." I smile dazedly as I walk over to her, completely ignoring the raging lunatic glaring at me. "It was nice having your company, Livvy." I really did miss her. Last night was a hoot after the whole crying on the bed thing. Playing drunk charades with only two people is a lot more fun than it sounds.

She smiles warmly at my nickname for her, an oldie but goodie. "It was my pleasure, No-No," she says, and I burst into laughter. Memories of her and me playing hide-and-seek in each other's backyards warms my heart until my cheeks hurt from my smile. I miss those good old days, where the only real problem I had was after I stuffed worms down her dress and got a time-out for a week. Apparently it wasn't gentleman-like…

"Ooooh, No-No on the No-No." I shake my head furiously, and she smiles at me.

"I'll punch you in the nose-nose if you don't leave. Now." He tenses up behind Liv, and she rolls her eyes in annoyance, ready to burst into a ball of flames and attack. A random image of Jack-Jack, the little baby that could turn into fire, from *The Incredibles* pops into my head. And it feels impossible to unsee it.

Anyway…

"Oh, I'm not scared of you, Grey. You get used to assholes with pent-up anger when you deal with Red Sylvetti." Feeling extra brave, I put a hand on his shoulder. "Speaking of which, you better hope you didn't lay a hand on her head. If you did…well, let's just say the color red will be on these walls." My smile drops and I squeeze harder and add, "If you ever go on a 'road trip' with my girl again, I will not hesitate to *kill* you, understand?"

Normally, I wouldn't have said half of what I just said. I would have been intimidated by Grey, but I wouldn't have threatened to *kill* him. He can lock his big, fat arm around my head, give one good squeeze, and I'd be hospitalized for a *week*. But having been around Red and the boost of confidence she seemingly injects into me each time she's in my presence, the words come out easily.

The room is deadly silent, but I don't regret what I said. If he did mess around with her in any way, I will not hesitate to rip his freaking tattoos off his skin and toss him in the Atlantic Ocean.

That isn't too intense, right?

"Get your fucking hand off me before I throw your scrawny ass out of the window, spilling *Red* on the concrete," he warns, promise lingering on his low tone. Beside me, Liv shivers, but I don't remove my hand. In fact, I squeeze a little harder. I can take him on…for two point five seconds, but still!

"Okay, that's enough of that. I'll walk you out." Liv rips my hand from his shoulder and guides me to the elevator, where she presses the button to go down. She's shocked as she keeps glancing over at me to see if I'm still the Noah she mimed popular movies with last night, drunk on red wine. Two bottles to be exact. No wonder I have a head-splitting headache.

"Where did that come from?" she asks around an uneasy laugh.

The elevator doors prop open.

"Told you, from being with Red." I wink at her, then enter the elevator. Grey appearing forlorn behind her back and her tired eyes glazing over are the last thing I see before the doors close.

But one thing I saw makes me feel hopeful about Red and me: the undeniable, colossal, never-ending love swirling beneath the exhaustion in her eyes. The relief washed over her face. However much she puts up this tough, exhausted front, she loves him. Through and through. And she doesn't give up on him. Ever. Even when there were many, many, *many* times she should have...she didn't.

She pushed through whatever obstacle and fought for him and their love that, admittedly, is kind of beautiful in a way. I want Red and me to have that: an unbreakable bond, a love that blossoms into something so strong, nothing can matter more than our love...I mean, our feelings toward each other. I plan to fight for us, not only because of how she makes me feel, but because each second that she isn't in my arms, I go a little more insane.

***

The drive back to campus is uneventful but very thoughtful. I thought of ways to make Red see that she can trust me enough to talk to me. Whatever made her skip town took a toll on her. I saw it in her dull eyes and weak posture. I hate how I reacted, what I said, and I wish I could take it all back and just hold her. Sometimes words can be too much to speak into the world. But nothing can go wrong with a simple hug that lets the other person know that you are there for them no matter what.

I turn the truck onto the frat house's block and plan to take a long, hot shower. Hopefully the tension and slight heartache will swirl down the drain. I park the truck and hop out, locking it behind me. I'm rubbing my groggy eyes, ready to just jump into my planned shower, then bed, when I feel my skin tingle and my chest tighten. I remove my hand and literally stop in my tracks because Red is sitting on the porch, shaking like a broken leaf, tears welled in her bright blue eyes. Shock fills me.

Sensing my stare, she looks up and her eyes seem to glaze over with warmth. But then she blinks rapidly and I walk closer. She gulps harshly before saying in a cracked voice, "My grandma died."

And everything makes sense.

Chapter Thirty-Seven

"Stay here," I tell her, holding out a hand.

"W-what?" she stammers and looks up at me with red, puffy eyes.

"I said to stay here," I repeat and walk over to her, bending down in front of her. She tries to cringe away, probably embarrassed to be openly crying in front of me in public. But I need her to know that she can without any type of judgment. "Don't move a muscle, okay? Can you do that for me?" I keep my voice gentle to keep her calm, not to patronize her.

Instead of fighting me like she normally would, she nods slowly and sniffles. "Yeah, I g-guess," she stammers, her voice chalky and raw. It sounds like it's been dragged through the dirt for hours. Hours that could have been spent with me holding her as she poured her pain out to me. A pang of darkness grips my stomach, and I give her an assuring smile before rushing inside the house.

I jog up the stairs like my ass is on fire and prop open my bedroom door. I almost wrench it closed when I find Ty making out with some girl wearing a tiny devil costume. "Sorry," I apologize and walk over to my bed. There's a girl and a guy sleeping in my bed. Or, rather, the Scream guy and Tinkerbell. Kids all around the world must require therapy sessions after Halloween.

"No promemlbem," Ty promptly grumbles into the blonde's mouth. She giggles, finding it cute or stupid.

I drag the blanket off the weird couple, ignore their groans and reaching hands. I step back and pray they didn't do anything under his cloak on my bed last night. This is the exact reason why I want it locked.

Burrowing my annoyance for a more convenient time, I close the door behind me. I rush down the stairs and bump into Mike. He seems to be the only one not dressed in some ridiculous costume, and sober. Which isn't that surprising. He has more sense than to drink himself into a coma and pass out on the living room floor.

"Hey, did you know Red was sitting outside?" I ask him as I walk to the front door.

"Yeah. I tried to get her inside since it's ass-freezing outside, but she said to fuck off and that she was waiting for you."

"Really?" If she was waiting for me, then why didn't she call me? Answer any of my calls and texts? I don't understand that girl, but I think she's in the mood to let me in on her peculiar mind right now.

"Yes, really." He chuckles, and something short of amazement flashes across his brown eyes before he pads into the kitchen.

With one hand on the door, I smile broadly. Red came back here and just sat on the porch, waiting for me. Though she could have gone inside and waited for me to come back. She just sat here as if her mind was on a one-track mission to see me. The idea is heartwarming and a relief that I've cracked a tiny spot in her bloody hard shield. The crack may be tiny, but it's a starting point.

"Sorry I took so long," I apologize as I close the door behind me and sit beside her. "Scream and Tinkerbell were hogging my sheets...well, there's a sentence I never thought I'd say." I chuckle in an attempt to warm her up a little, but she just stares at the concrete below us. Feeling my heart yearn to just hold her, I gently wrap the blanket around her. I tuck stray tendrils of hair behind her small, red ears.

"We should get you inside," I tell her softly. Her skin is pale, enhancing the dark circles under her dull-blue eyes. "You're freezing."

"No," she says after a moment of silence. She shakes her head slightly. "I'm fine here. I like the cold, actually." I see a hint of a smile on her pale-pink lips. They're cracked, and I want to run my tongue along them, moisture them. I want to kiss her cheek, bring some life to them. But all I can do is stare at her fluttering eyes and the shallow pace of her chest.

"I hate the cold," I tell her, making conversation. "I prefer warm weather. The beach and a piña colada. A beautiful girl by my side."

"IQ short of fifty your type?" she jokes, voice raspy.

"No." I shake my head seriously. "Pure blue eyes and face piercings are more my type. It'd be a huge plus if she can ride the motorcycle."

"You should really change your type, then..." She trails off and sniffles, wiping a shaky hand against her red-tipped nose. "Because I will break you, Noah. I'll chew you up and spit you out and every other fucking cliché line there is."

"Why would I do that, Red?"

"I just told you!"

"But I don't care." My voice is more stable than hers as it floats in the wind. Tears start to flow down her face. The urge to kiss her cheek wins, and I pull her into my chest and press my lips onto her cold, now-warming cheek. "Tell me what you went through. And FYI, I will never not be there for you. You just gotta learn to trust me. Please," I whisper, my voice cracking, losing all stability. I can't maintain control around her it seems.

She turns to look me in the eyes, and I grip her now-flaming hot cheek. I coax my thumb across her soft, red-patched skin, and it seems to yank down her protective walls, because she sighs and nods. "The call I got was from my sister who I told you about—Harley." I nod, remembering how protective she looked when she spoke about her. "She—she told me Grandma was basically lying on her deathbed, and I...I just had to get out of there. I went straight to my job at the bar in Penn, and somehow I agreed to join Grey's pursuit to wherever the hell he needed to go, and I was there when she...when she..." She stops and closes her eyes.

"I could have gone with you. All you had to do was say so." I rub her shoulder, adding my body heat to the thick comforter. I want to give it all to her. I kiss her cheek some more, and she smiles and tickles my neck with her golden hair. "I would have swept you away."

"Using what?" She laughs and looks up at me through her eyelashes. My heart stops beating for just a second, and I lean down to kiss her forehead. She cringes back...pauses, then leans into my lips. I smile at the action, at her trying. I appreciate it, I really do.

"Bus? Skateboard? *Scooter*?" I list off, and she's a laughing mess. I watch her and end up chuckling myself. "Anything as long as I can take you to where you need. Funeral. Mall. Anywhere."

"You shouldn't waste your money on me." She pushes her fingers through her hair, and her tone pisses me off. She thinks she isn't worth it, but to me she's worth every damn breath she steals from me.

"Why not? Would you just take it all and spend it on your millions of cats?"

"I don't have cats," she protests in a squealing tone that cracks me up. "Shut up. I'm serious. I'm not a cat lady!" She pushes at me, but I just sigh and place her head on my chest. I rub her head, ignoring her whining. She's really the cutest non-cat lady I know.

"It's okay, cat lady," I shush her, and she pushes me. I hunch over in laughter, and it hurts my stomach so much. She just sits back, arms crossed, red cheeks puffy, cracked lips trying their best not

331

to break into a smile. I lean back and gently, seriously look into her eyes.

"I'm just kidding with you," I say.

"Right." She looks miserable, but her eyes are gaining their brilliance back.

"You know what I'd do with my insanely large trust fund?" I joke, but not really. It is insane, but I won't tell her that. She'd buy loads of cat food with it.

"What?" Her voice is lower, losing its humor, as I rub the tip of my nose against her cheek, brushing my lips against the corner of hers.

"I'd buy you a chest of blue diamonds just to see which would perfectly match your eyes," I whisper, and she sucks in a breath. "Then I'd buy a bucket of pink pearls to find the shade of your lips." I brush my fingers against her lips, and she gasps, her eyes falling shut. I pause to stare at her beautiful...*everything*. "And then I'd buy a million cans of tuna for your precious kittens."

She laughs breathlessly as if falling back into Earth. "Shut uuuuup," she groans and bangs her small hand on my chest. I grab it, slip mine in, and kiss her knuckles. There are scattered scars and bruises, and I kiss them again, wishing to wipe them clean. And to do what I exaggerated. I would do anything to see her smile...like she is right now.

"No." I cup her face and look into her eyes; she tries to cower away, but I pull her closer, thumb her cheeks gently. "I want to be with you, Red. I don't care in what context. I just want to be by your side, through thick and thin. I want to see you laugh. I want to see you groan. Feel you hit me—which I'm counting—so I can recount them with kisses." A tear slides down her cheek, and I kiss it away but don't pull away. "I. Just. Want. *You*."

Her eyes are glossy and her lips quiver. I have never seen her like this before. It's like she's slowly breaking out of who I've seen her as: this tough biker chick who has warnings said about her. But she is so much more. She's a Nirvana enthusiast. She apparently a cat-hater. She's a damn good person to jump off roofs with. And she's the girl I am madly in...like with.

"You don't have to say anything back," I rush to tell her, pulling back slightly. Maybe I'm overcrowding her, pressuring her. I don't want to do that. "In the meantime, why don't we just...I don't know... *sit here*? If that's cool with you?"

Sniffling loudly, she looks into my eyes. "Yes," she says hesitantly.

"Great. Because I was going to hold you hostage on my chest, even if you said no," I joke, and she punches my chest lightly before resting on me. I wrap the blanket around me, linking our feet together. Leaning back on the railing behind me, I hold her to me, almost cocooning her like an exotic butterfly I'm terrified to expose in the cold.

"But I don't wanna stay here forever. I'm not helpless," she says firmly. And even though I can't see her face totally, I know her mouth is set in a line, a frown virtually creased on her forehead.

"No one ever said you were," I hum and rub her back, listening to her contented purr. "There is something called assistance and *friendship*."

She scoffs. "Friends? That's what we are now?"

I raise a brow and lean over, peeking into her little nest. Bright blue eyes and red cheeks meet my eye, and I grin. "Are you saying you wanna go steady?"

Her small hand reaches out of her shell and pushes my face away while she chuckles. "I never said that, prep. Do *not* put words in my mouth."

"Fine. I'll put other things in there." I wiggle my eyebrows, and she covers her mouth because she's laughing so loudly, so freely, it tugs at my heartstrings.

"Don't be gross. And just—" Her smile turns watery, and she rolls her eyes. "Just be here for me? Maybe? Without the steady thing?" Her voice lowers, and she chews on her lip ring. Fear and worry rustle around in her blue eyes. Like...like she's afraid of her becoming vulnerable in front of me, and I'll run away to the nearest "good girl." But too bad, I'm already falling for this bad girl who's wrapped in a blanket, looking up at me with humongous blue eyes and taut lip ring. There's no going back now, I realize, and my heart skips once or twice...or *thrice*.

"I'm not going anywhere, Red." I lean forward and kiss her forehead. "Promise..."

Chapter Thirty-Eight

Red and I stay outside on the porch for about a century. I freeze my butt off and want to jump in a fire to stay warm, but I never complain. How can I? I have Red in my arms and she finally opens up to me. After a while of delightful silence, she speaks to me about her grandma. She tells me she is a sweet old lady who left a big bowl of candy out on Halloween. And that should tell me enough about how kind and trusting she was of strangers, how she loved her and her sister dearly...at that she bursts into tears and asks me to take her inside.

Now I'm rustling out of a dream that included Red. She was dressed in a loose dress, standing in a field of sunflowers and dandelions. Her eyes were extra blue and her smile extra pink and hair extra gold. I want to stay longer, feel her soft skin press against my bare chest as I hold her to me. I don't ever want to let her go. Ever. I'm sinking back into the sunny dream filled with her airy laughter when I feel another rustle. I thought it was just my imagination. But I guess not. Whatever's waking me up better be damn important.

And she is.

My eyes open to find Red sitting on my legs, shifting a bit. She's staring up at the mural of the town on the wall.

I'm so focused on how the moonlight brightens her eyes, makes a shadow on her cheeks, that I almost don't notice what she's wearing, or lack thereof. She's wearing one of my plain white tees and no pants. She stole the shirt I was wearing when she thought I wasn't looking before slipping under the sheets. I smirked to myself and didn't say anything then, but seeing her now, hair disheveled and smoke billowing into her hair...I can't stand to be silent.

"Enjoying what you see?" I ask her, my voice thick with sleep. I brush a hand over my untamed curls as I sit up against the headboard.

She doesn't jump in shock at my voice, just nods, eyes darting across the wall. "Very much." Her voice is husky yet silky at the same time. I spot a hand she's using to prop herself up. I take it and kiss her palm. She finally looks at me and giggles, yanking at her hand, but I hold it firmly to my smile. "Stop," she whispers.

"Fine." I drop her hand and scoot over to her. I push her hair to the side and gently kiss her shoulder. She sighs but doesn't tell me to stop. Her skin smells like bar soap and strawberries. I bite the base of her neck softly.

She giggles, pushing my face away. "Didn't anyone ever tell you it's not nice to bite people?"

"Nope. My parents gave me free range to bite

people," I joke and kiss her neck. A moan leaves her mouth, and she wraps an arm around my shoulder. I smile against her and whisper, "So beautiful," against her skin.

"Then you should be taught that people bite back," she murmurs before tackling me to the bed. I gasp and stare up at her laughing with her eyes pinched shut. She's straddling me now, mouth colliding with mine. I feel sparks of heat slide under my skin. I will never ever stop loving the way her lips mold to mine and how fire tickles my senses. I hold her hips and hold in a groan, not wanting to wake Ty and his girl, as she teasingly rubs herself against me.

My head rolls back as she nibbles on my lower lip. Kisses, teases. And lets it go. I lick it, where it's no doubt going to turn red and swollen in a few hours. But until then, I'm marking her too.

"C'mere!" I exclaim in a hush before flipping her onto her back in one swift move. I nibble at the soft skin on her neck, and she giggles in my ear. She yelps and writhes against me but doesn't try to break free as I bite her neck. Then kiss it. And liiiiick it—

"Gross! What? Are you a Pomeranian?" she groans.

"Maybe." I chuckle and do it again, and again, and again—

"Noah!" she screeches, her complaining turning into earthy laughter. I stare at her as I plop kisses all over her. Forehead. Nose. Chin. Cheeks. "Noah! Stoo-oop!"

"Yes. Please. Noah. Shut the fuck *up*!" Ty

grumbles from his side of the room.

I blush as it sinks in that he's in the room with us. It makes me want to get my own place for the sole purpose of making her laugh and squeal my name. And maybe other purposes…but this one alone, for the time being.

"Sorry," I say and drop onto the bed beside her.

"Don't stop." She sounds annoyed as she faces me.

I chuckle as I reach down and pull the covers over our bodies. "But you were just begging me to. Sounded something like—" I clear my throat and raise my voice several octaves. "Stooooop! Noah! Oh, stooooop!" I add a little sass and raise my pinky.

"Oh my God, shut up." Her laugh is rumbling and contagious, because I join her, further pissing off my roommate. Seriously, I think I should get my own place…with her.

Whoa there, buddy. You've only known her for a little over two months. Calm down, my realistic subconscious commands.

You're right, I tell myself. I don't know what I was thinking.

"Hey." She brushes hair out of my face, her features cutely scrunched up. "What're you thinking up there?" She taps my forehead, and I lean into her touch, resting my forehead against hers. She smiles against my lips.

"*You,*" I whisper, kissing the inside of her wrist.

"Well, then…" She kisses me softly, gently, then pulls away. "Stop. 'Cause I'm right here."

"Not leaving my side?" I melt into her lips, giving little, slow pecks.

I feel her suck in a breath and slowly shake her head. "Not anytime soon."

Cupping her cheek, I whisper, "Not ever..." My eyes flutter shut, exhaustion creeping into my peripherals. Her body is so warm and flush against mine, feet entangled. I think I smile. I also think I hear her respond, but I'm too far gone to hear her.

***

I wake up a few hours later feeling very hot. Way too hot. And there's something squishing my face, adding pressure. And adding...and adding...And—am I being suffocated with a pillow? Is Ty finally killing me because he found out I ate the last pizza in the box last week? I thought I didn't leave any evidence pointing toward me, but criminals always leave behind a fingerprint.

"Red?" I mumble against the fabric of the pillow. It's yanked back, and I'm met with Red smiling down at me like a serial killer gifted a brand new set of shiny knives. Only her choice of murder is a pillow.

"Should I be worried about you suffocating me? Or the fact that Ty isn't doing anything about it?" I glance wryly at my roommate, who merely waves his fingers at me jubilantly while munching on a cupcake. I shift my attention to Red, who's smiling and lowering the pillow slightly.

"Get ready. I wanna go to IHOP. I'm hungry as fuck," she says, beaming.

"Okay, but only if you agree not to provoke the security guard." I crack a teasing smile, and she scrunches her nose and hits me with the pillow again. She seems lighter, almost like she's on drugs...I don't even want to ask, shatter her energized state. I have to admit, it's concerning, to say the least. But also really cute.

"Shut up. And we should go to the one on..." She stops and shakes her head, smiling. "I forgot, you're a newbie to the town."

"Sorry that I was in Venice, Italy, a few months ago." I laugh, and she watches with fascinating eyes.

"You a traveling boy?" She sits next to me, fingers feather-light against my knuckles.

I smile, while she looks so focused. "Something like that."

"Where have you been?" she asks and rests her head on my shoulder. My heart hammers against my ribcage at her PDA move. Ty left a while ago, but that doesn't matter. She's comfortable enough to hold my hand, lean against me. I feel a sense of victory as I rest my cheek against her soft blonde hair.

"You name it, and I've camped there," I tell her.

She pauses. "Paris." She taps my pinky on my left hand.

Curling the finger answers her, and we continue on with cities all over the world. When we're down to her own, and I tell her there's more, she looks up at me with amazement and wonder and...sadness.

I brush a hand against her cheek. "What's wrong?"

A solemn smile sweeps over her beautiful face. "Nothing," she lies, and I quirk an eyebrow. I think

I know her enough to know that it isn't "nothing." And she seems to read my mind, because she sighs and looks at the door, causing my hand to lose its grip on her face. "I've just never been anywhere exotic or anything like that. I'd love to go to Tokyo or Milan…I've dreamed of traveling since I was a kid. But we never had the funds for even a bus ride to a state outside of Washington. So I gave up the dream and took on countless jobs to help out."

I don't say anything for a while as I reflect on her words. I can imagine a young Red: dressed in pastel dresses and bows, eyes brighter than the future. With a map glowing with multi-colored tacks in cities all across the massive globe. There's a look of adventure and passion driven in those eyes…but then reality hits and she realizes she can't even step foot out of her home. I want to grab her hand and steal her away to Seoul, or Dubai, or even Paris. Where, in this time period, I shower her with tiaras and the most expensive dresses and tell her she can have it *all*.

I fall back into this world, and a sense of protectiveness I already had for her surges to a great amount. Every fiber inside of me reaches out as I reach for her face. Slowly, I tug her to face me. Her eyes are elsewhere, her breathing shallow. I want to take her to places she's dreamed of setting foot in. I want to shower her in silk and diamonds, and I want to make her happy. Her being happy is all that matters to me.

"I've been all around the world, and it's glamorous…" I pause and run a thumb across her bottom lip. "And it'd be damn lucky for you to venture out and discover it all."

She scoffs incredulously. "Maybe someday."

"Whenever that day comes, I want to be by your side." I'm serious, and I watch her intake a sharp breath. She looks like she wants it too, to have me hold her as we overlook the Northern Lights. They are breathtaking in pictures but even better in real life. I was with a group of the natives, the people who lived nearby, but I wanted someone that meant something to me by my side. Smiling and laughing the same way I was.

I close my eyes now and lean my forehead against hers. "I always want to be by your side," I confess in a whisper. I picture her gloved hands intertwined with mine. Her golden hair in the wind, cerulean eyes matching the blue hue flying through the air above us. Weaving and entertaining and so, so…*beautiful*. But I want beautiful next to me, under my arm, smiling in the same cold air as me.

"Noah," she breathes against my lips. I lick mine, and she shudders as it swipes against hers.

"Tell me you want me," I say. I want her. Want her so bad. But not in a sexual way; I do, trust me. But I mainly just want to be near her. I want her to be…*mine*.

"Noah," she says again, as if it's the only thing she can say without spilling what she truly desires to say. "I want you too. I want you more than I should. But I'll just hurt you." Her voice cracks and, when I pull back, her eyes are glossy. There's something behind them that makes me shudder, but I push it away and crack a smile.

"There is no way you can hurt me. Not when

342

I…" *Love.* "Like you so much."

Something in her face breaks, but a smile overtakes her face. "I…I like you a lot too, Noah."

My heart soars.

"You do?"

"Yes." Her eyes laugh, and her mouth does too.

I rush forward and swallow the heavenly sound. I cup her face, and hers rests on my shoulder. Our mouths drop, sighs are heard, and I smile against her full pink lips. The kiss is smooth and gentle. The fire is sizzling under our tongues, against my fingers cradling her face, but it's low and not the great amount it usually is when we kiss. Touch. Glance. I can never get tired of these lips. Ever.

A knock and a small gasp, "Noah," breaks us apart.

Rachel is standing at the door, sheepish and jittery. "Sorry for…" She pauses and clears her throat. "Can I speak to you for a moment? Please?"

Red's hands curl into a fist.

"No. I think he's good here." Red's tone is harsh. It even makes me cringe. I try to figure out why she'd be harsh toward someone as sweet as Rachel when I remember that Rachel wrote her off when she came to the house on Halloween. I remember the pleading look in her eyes when I pulled away and chased after Red. As usual. The girl's so sweet, she doesn't deserve it—*me.*

"It'll be quick," I tell Red, and she frowns at me. I kiss her nose and flash her a smile, admiring her tinted pink cheeks. I let her fingers go and get off the bed. I walk outside and gently pull the door, leaving it open a crack. When I face Rachel, she's staring up at me with a nervous expression. "What's up?" I ask her.

"The art contest," she says.

My throat tightens. "What about it?"

"Entries expire tonight at midnight," she informs me and pauses. "I thought I could help you with yours. I already sent mine in, but I know you'll win or at least come close to it. If you just *try*."

I let out a sigh. "Look, I don't think it's a great idea. I already have my hands full with the football team and studying and—"

"Just give a try. You'll regret it later if you don't," she interrupts me.

I don't say anything because I know she's right. Art is my passion. It always has been and always will be. To be the prodigy of that man would be a huge accomplishment. Just thinking of what he could teach me, to help improve my techniques, makes me shudder in excitement. My parents can lock me in a cage of textbooks, and I'd rip them to shreds and make origami.

But am I good enough?

The door being dragged open and revealing Red holding up brushes she must have stolen from my art supplies interrupts my pessimistic thoughts.

"What are you—?" I begin.

"Shut up and get in here." She grabs my hand and tugs me inside the room. My bed is pushed up against Ty's. As I turn to face her, she's locking the door. I hear a barely audible sigh and squeaking shoes outside the door when Red walks up to me and pinches my arm.

"*Ow!* What was that for?" I yelp and rub my

aching skin.

"I overheard you and Rebecca—"

"Rachel," I correct her, and she pinches me again. "Ow! Red, that *hurts*!"

Rolling her eyes, she continues. "And I want you to enroll in that contest." I blink rapidly and look away. I won't last under her gaze, and she seems to catch on, because she reaches up and forces my eyes to look into hers. "And I want you to win. But you won't be able to do that when you act like a pussy. You have real talent. So take these damn brushes and make something spectacular and *win*. You idiot."

"Thank you." I smile at her words even though she half insulted me and pinched me. Twice. *Hard.* But she has a point, and I can see how much she wants this for me in those dazzling blue eyes of hers. She cares about me, for me. Even though she tries to appear invincible and hard, she's extra-soft and almost...*loving* toward me.

My heart soars because of this beautiful, amazing girl before me. And I cup her face and bend down, forehead against hers. "I'll do this if you help me. By my side."

She stares into both of my eyes, and her chest lifts, a smile overtaking her face. "I'd just fuck it up."

"Passion, my love, is what art represents. You don't need to practice it for years to make it. Just gotta have a passion for it." I pause and thumb her lips, feeling her shallow breathing between them. "What do you have a passion for?"

"Being honest?" she says.

"Always."

"*You.*"

Soaring, crackling, *burst*—my heart is in flames.

"Then, Red Sylvetti, assist in the making of my masterpiece." I step back, holding out my hand, and bow my head.

She hesitates, says, "This is so stupid," but takes my hand nevertheless. I drag her over to my art supplies and pull out my paints. All colors of the rainbow, some unique shades. I find a blue that reminds me of her face, and I take it to the sky of my mural.

"This is gonna be your enrollment piece?" she questions as I finish one piece of paper of the seemingly hundreds as companions.

"Yep. I don't have much time to paint your body naked," I murmur, and her small hand pumps mine.

"Perv," she claims, but I hear a smile in her voice.

"No fair. Jack Dawson did it with Rose, and he was considered a swoon-worthy guy," I joke, and she stands closer to me, watching me. I feel subconscious of my work overall. It really is kind of impressive, but that opinion's kind of biased, don't you think?

"How long did it take you to do make this?" she asks as she dips her brush into a lilac color. She is hesitant to put it on the paper, almost as if she's afraid of messing it up.

"A night and half a morning, I think. Don't really pay attention to time when I'm doing things like this." My voice comes out mumbled as I focus on filling in a boy riding his bike down a market lane.

"It's gorgeous," she murmurs.

When I take a peek at her, she's staring up and looking at every paper that flows onto another. Some overlapping, others perfectly symmetrical. Up close it looks realistic. And with each dab of color, the people come alive and it breathes.

"I know," I whisper.

She looks at me and blushes. "Shut up."

"Okay." I shrug and move to painting a hot-air balloon. Silence fills the room, and she squirms next to me, still holding up that lilac brush. She's frowning and glancing at me, letting it sit just above the paper. She's waiting and glancing, and finally, she sighs and punches me.

"Say something, idiot," she commands.

I laugh and look at her. "You just told me to shut up." She is so confusing.

"Yeah, well, I didn't mean it." She turns to a paper of the park, and she bites her lip, then huffs out and backs up, holding up her hands. "I can't do this." Turmoil and doubt creep onto her face, tug at her lips. I walk over to her and hold the hand that's holding the brush.

"You just gotta have the guts to put the brush to paper," I tell her, pushing her hand forward. It touches the paper, and I feel her suck in a breath, hold it as the brush leaves behind a dob of lilac. "*Like that.*"

Her head turns, and something electric passes between our eyes. My heart thrums like crazy, and I wonder if she can hear it. I brush a tendril of hair behind her small ear, and she smiles slightly. I smile back and lean forward. I wish she could be kept by my side forever. Whenever I am around her, my stomach clamps up and I look at her too long to appear sane. My skin tingles and my fingertips buzz with a fiery need to just touch her.

She turns around, and the tip of her brush hitting my neck makes me reel back. "Sorry." She laughs and covers her mouth.

I narrow my eyes playfully, drawing my brush out to her like it's a sword. "Did you just declare war, Red?"

"I mean, if you're totally up for defeat." Her lips slowly dip into a mischievous grin. The light and childlike being in her dance in her eyes, and I watch in complete and utter awe.

"I think you mean the other way *around*!" I lunge after her and swipe my brush against her chin. She shrieks and makes her move. I dodge and pick her up, spinning her around. And as we dash for ammo and paint each other's faces and clothes and hair and the mural, I realize I am falling for this girl. *Hard.*

"Okay! All right! You're getting paint in my ears!" she shrieks, digging her finger in her ear. Her nose is crinkled, and all I can do is admire how colorful and exploded with red cheeks and a glowing smile she looks.

"Fine." I chuckle and nod to my bed. "Help me move it so we have more room." I walk over to the bed and she nods and, together, we push the heavy double-size bed out of the way. "Get the other side," I suggest when it's well away from the wall. It weighs like steel, but I don't want her to hurt her back. I'll handle it on my own for her.

"Aye aye, Picasso," she teases and rushes to the other side. I jokingly roll my eyes at her nickname for me and pull. I know it's too late since the bed's moved and there's paint all around the room, but I hope Ty isn't planning on using the room today.

"All right, it's out of the way." I brush my hands together, finding her bent down. "Ready to paint this masterpiece?"

She doesn't reply.

"Red?"

She slowly stands up…and she's holding the file.

The file that holds her past.

Fuuuuuuuck.

Chapter Thirty-Nine

I don't know what to say. I've always been loaded with easy-going, charming words clouding my mind. I've heard it a lot, that I always know what to say. But I don't know what the hell to say in this moment. I can't tell her that I just so happened to stumble upon the file in the middle of the street. Even then, I'd have to explain why I kept it. And I definitely can't tell her I sought it out because she doesn't like to elaborate on her past. I'd sound like a dick. So there's only one thing I can say really.

"A friend of mine gave it to me because they care about me. They don't want me to get hurt." The moment the words fall out of my stupid mouth, I hear what I just said.

She looks hurt. "You think I'd hurt you?"

"To be fair, you have before." Stupid, stupid, stupid.

Now she just looks pissed. "So because I leave you to take care of some shit a few times or bruise your ego, you have a friend pull this from the university's record?"

"No, no—of course not." I wave my arms around frantically. "I didn't even ask her to do it. She just did and gave it to me. But I swear, I didn't read it. I didn't even open it. Just shoved it under my bed. I never ever planned to read any of it, I swear."

"Then why not get rid of it? Why keep it, Noah?"

"I was going to, but—"

"But your curiosity got the best of you," she accuses. I swear, if looks could kill, I would be cold dead and on the floor with mutilated limbs. She's slightly shaking with so much anger, I wish I could rewind to the last five minutes when we were playful. This is going to blow up in my face; I can see it on hers.

"No, no. I promise you, I was going to throw it out." I run a hand through my short curls, frustrated and frantic. "But I completely forgot about it."

"But I bet you were tempted to sneak a peek, right?" she seethes through clenched teeth. She takes slow steps toward me, and I back up some, admittedly put off by her glare and burnt-red ears. "Do you want to give it a read? Find out about my fucked-up past, which I have already expressed to you on our *date*?" she barks.

"No, of course not! You're putting words in my mouth!" I accuse. She should believe that I didn't mean to keep it around. Honest to God, I forgot about it. I wouldn't ever read it; I have more respect for her. And it hurts that she doesn't think I do.

"No, I am not! You kept the freaking file, Noah!" she screams and waves the file around, tears welling in her eyes. "There are things in here that

351

would make you hate me. Prove that I'm not right for you. Just holding it is..." She pauses. Her eyes squeeze shut, hand shaking.

"Look, I'm sorry. I'll put it back. No one will know it was taken," I promise and get closer to her, but the second she notices me, she jumps back and her eyes fly open—fiery and free of tears.

"No, it's too late." She moves to leave, but I step in her way.

"You can't just leave because I forgot to put it back. That's insane!" I snap, and her eyes widen slightly. God damn it! I didn't mean it like that. She's just acting a bit...unhinged for no reason. "I'll have my friend put it back. She'll put it back where she got it from."

Damn. I realize what I'm hinting at before I even have time to reel my words back in my mouth. The somewhat extinguished anger comes raging back in a hellfire held in her eyes, and her free hand forms a tight fist.

"She—as in that *bitch* who was just here?" she roars, and I shake my head. "Don't lie to me, Noah!"

"Yes! Fine, it was her. But like I said, she was just doing it to protect me."

"Protect you from what? Me?"

"I don't need protection from you." She sounds incredibly insane right now. Why would I ever need protection from her? I take several steps toward her, but she backs away, making my heart still as I watch her stare at the ground with finality.

"Maybe this is what we needed—what you needed." She flicks her eyes to mine and nods to herself. "Noah, there are things I haven't told you. Seriously *messed*-up shit. And you—you really shouldn't be with me. Rebecca was right to give you this. Here." She holds it out to me with a wobbly hand as her eyes tear up again. "Just take it. Read it. You need to know how much I don't deserve you..." She pauses before her voice cries out, "Please, just fucking take it!"

"No. I will not take it." My voice cracks, and she lets out a shattering breath. I don't know what to say or do to erase the doubt that I truly care for her, past all the wrongs she committed in her past. I've done messed up things, too. And maybe hearing about it will make her not feel alone in what makes humans humans.

"Noah—" she begins.

"I did drugs." I slice through her words, and she furrows her dark brows at me. Tears stream down her face, but she doesn't say anything, so I continue. "Mostly party drugs, and I partied *a lot*. I fucked girls more than I breathed. And after, I treated them like nothing. I was a horrible guy, but that doesn't make me any less worthy of you. Nor does your past make you any less worthy of me."

"Believe me when I tell you I'm doing you a favor," she says breathlessly, turning to the opened door. I dart my eyes to the door and shake my head. I reach for her, but she snaps her hands to her chest and rushes out, grabbing her shoes and jacket. My heart plummets to my feet, planting me to the ground.

"Wait, Red! Don't leave!" I shout and chase after her, clambering down the tall stairs.

She can't just leave because I wasn't going to look at the file. I wouldn't disrespect her like that, go behind her back and find out more. I want to wait for her to tell me everything without the ridiculous fear of me leaving her. I don't have the heart to even think I'd leave her because of something she did in her past. I'm in way too deep, and I have no plans to dig myself out. I thought she'd know that by now.

When I run out of the front door, she's climbing into her car.

"Red! Please, don't go!" The fear of her leaving me for another week makes my voice tremble. I race down the path toward her car, but when I reach out for the handle of the passenger door, she pulls into the road. My heart drops as my hand touches air, and I watch her speed down the road.

Oh God.

I stumble and drop onto the curb, pressing my face into my hands. "No," I murmur, tears welling in my eyes.

Chapter Forty

If there ever were a trait about Red, it'd be the ability to tune me out with ease, it seems. It's been a few days since she found that damned file and split without even giving me a chance to reassure her that I wouldn't leave her, that I wouldn't ever abandon her because she fucked up in the past. And it sucks and hurts how easily she can leave me at the drop of a hat. As if I mean little or nothing to her despite the obvious connection we've built. But maybe I'm the only one that sees it. I possibly am making it up, this relationship we have.

I just wish I could turn a knob in a clock, rewind to that day. Stop her before she could bend down, not push the bed out of the way at all. I would remember that the file that holds her past was under my bed and distract her with a kiss. Kissing her always seemed to pull me from the world a little, throwing us into our own bubble, where we could focus on us and us alone.

If I'm wishing for things, I wish Rachel hadn't given me the file. What she did was sort of insane.

Sneaking into the administration office to steal a file of another student. Her action resulted in this silent battle between Red and me. I'm not saying she created this divide between Red and me completely, but she gave me the bomb, and I wasn't able to disable it. And when Red found that detonator, the explosion was unfathomable and the casualties were even worse.

I don't want to, but I ignore Rachel for the first few days. I know she only meant well, but each day that I barely see Red, the more my forgiveness sheds itself, fading away into black smoke, which promptly hangs over my head like a dark cloud. For days, I draw morbidly depressed paintings: a few broken couples there, a weepy dog there, and some distressed ballerinas there.

Along with painting, that always lets me express my feelings I like to keep bottled inside, I work out. I have been slacking lately, so when I have all the time in the world to brood like a depressed loser, I drag my friends Mike and Ty to the nearest gym.

I'm here now on the treadmill with some alternative rock band crooning in my ear. My heart is beating much louder than the music heavy with bass and drums. I can feel my limbs turn to licorice as I pump my legs and arms, but the numbness feels a helluva lot better than feeling emotionally tortured. I promised to give Red some time to come to her senses, that we belong together. But as the days faded into one another, that promise crumbled into broken pieces and left me in despair.

I quickly became a heart-sick teenage boy. I'd seen them when I was in high school. Moping in the halls after their girlfriends grew sick of their doucheness and staring at other girls' racks or asses or simply cheated because he was on the football team and he thought because of that, he was entitled to more than one girl.

And now I'm that idiotic, pussy-whipped boy. Except I'm not in love with what blooms between her lips; I am in love with her in whole. Her mesmerizing eyes, her pink lips, her cheeks that naturally glow—just everything.

And now I've fucked everything up, and the only time I get to see her is in class. I tried sitting next to her, but whenever I tried, she gave me pleading eyes or just moved to the other end of the massive lecture hall. My heart broke the first few times, but to avoid any more pain, I stopped and kept a steady worried gaze on her even when I saw her eyes well with tears. It only made me want to get up, say screw it, and kiss her. Let her know that whatever she's done isn't enough to deter me.

I stop the treadmill and grip the handles. "Stop thinking about her," I command myself. The ache in my chest is beginning to form, producing a lump in my throat. Red will come around. Right?

"Noah?" a familiar feminine voice says behind me.

I turn around and am shocked to see Beth...and Rachel. My throat closes briefly. "Hey..." I say unsurely, cheeks most likely reddening. The last time I dodged Rachel was outside of the art room after a session. She looks the same: desperate to apologize. I switch my gaze from her pouty mouth and full brown eyes to Beth's green-hazel eyes and grinning, glossed mouth.

"I didn't know you worked out here." Her eyes blatantly look over my gray muscle-tank top that's attached to my sweaty skin and black Adidas trainer pants. I shift on the heels of my Adidas sneakers.

I laugh nervously and pick up my water bottle, focusing on it so I don't look at Rachel, who's staring at me. "I started here recently this week. It seems less pathetic than moping over…" I clear my throat, burning at the memory of her and Red screaming at each other at the bonfire. Even though that night half sucked, I wish I could teleport there. At least I would be able to get close to her without her crying.

She scoffs and rolls her eyes, understanding without my having to finish the sentence. "Don't even get me started on that." She steps closer to the treadmill and bats her eyelashes, which are obviously fake and…why wear makeup to the gym if you'll just sweat it off? She touches my sweaty forearm. "You should totally get over her. Like, *now*. She just isn't good enough for you. I already told you this, but you don't listen. And now look, crying while looking hot; you deserve so much better."

You deserve me, is what she doesn't say but translates in the frantic batting of her lashes. If she bats them any harder, they'll fly off.

"Hey, Noah," Rachel interrupts Beth's odd way of flirting. I look at her, then at the floor. "Mind if we talk for a minute?" she asks.

I can't find it in me to say no. "Of course." I step off the treadmill and follow her over to a corner, near the weight-lifting section of the gym.

"I'll just be over here, running!" Beth calls out, and I glance over to her running dramatically. Her black shorts are ridiculously tight over her tanned skin, her chest bouncing like melons in a loose bag under her small hot pink sports bra. She bats at me, and I'm afraid she's going to get too distracted and fall.

I look back at Rachel, brows tucked in. "How did you know I'd be here?"

She's wearing less flashy and tight clothing than her friend, dressed in a simple white tank top and black leggings, black and white running shoes on her small feet. Her pin-straight brunette hair is placed in a delicate high ponytail, and her face is free of makeup, save from some swipes of Chapstick.

"Ty posted a picture on Instagram of him flexing in the mirror, and you and Mike were in the background," she explains, and I flick my gaze over to Ty at the lifting section, who's currently trying and failing to get a blonde girl's number.

I roll my eyes. "He's hopeless."

"Yeah." She chuckles. "He really is." I smile and laugh a little too at my constantly thirsty friend and roommate. But when I focus on her, her smile dips into a sort of sad frown. "I miss you."

I let out a staggering breath. "I miss you too," I tell her earnestly. She quickly became my best friend, always there for me to listen to my bitching about Red leaving all the time, and this time, I didn't have her to lay my head on her tiny shoulder. I just want her back; I want to study, help her practice drawing, watch her favorite cheesy chick flick movies. I sort of feel even more empty with her gone from my side.

To be fair, it's my fault. I pushed her away, sort of pissed off because of the file and the aftermath it caused. But she was just trying to protect me. In her weird, screwed-up way, she meant well.

"I'm sorry," we both blurt out, then laugh. "You go," we say again, then roll our eyes at our weird sync together.

"Really, you go first." I gesture toward her, and she sucks in a deep breath, shoulders rolling back. Then she breathes out heavily and hangs her head a little.

"I didn't mean for what happened to happen," she says. "I didn't think she'd find the file. If I had any inkling of her actually finding it, I swear to you, I would have never given it to you. I just wanted you to read about the horrible things she's done."

"But I don't care about the things she did in the past," I tell her, exasperated, running my fingers through my damp curls. I want her to see the light in Red's eyes, the smile she gives me under her tough exterior; I want her to experience her hearty laugh when I look at her in a funny way, or the way she gets so passionate when she defends her favorite band of all time, Nirvana.

But she doesn't see anything beyond track records and whatever the hell Red got caught up in the past.

"You should, though, Noah," she presses. "She's a really bad person."

"Maybe back then, but now..." I grip my hair

and look away. Now she's avoiding me because she's insecure about herself, insecure about us.

"But now she is hurting you," she finishes my sentence, but a lot harsher than I would have gone for. I frown and tuck my hands in my pockets, avoiding her probing eyes. Sensing my hesitation to soak in the truth, she sighs and her face is softer when I look at her. "But you care for her, and I guess that's all that matters."

I grin and nod frantically. "I like her a lot. Like, a *lot* a lot." My cheeks heat up like they're in a fiery oven as I put emphasis on my words.

She giggles and chews on her lip, as if fighting the fight against Red, and sighs again, nodding to herself mostly. "You love her, don't you?" she says, and her question makes me freeze like I'm in a box of ice.

The word *love* unlocks a door I locked a while ago. I figured I loved her that day on the cliff, but maybe I knew before, and I just didn't want to admit it to myself. I haven't known her long enough, according to the traditional world, for me to love her, but I do. Whenever I think about her, I get hot flashes and crave to see her smile, even if just for a second. She ignites a craving and feeling of *home*, just by a thought, a glance, a kiss.

She's a flame that promises danger and burns, but I float to her, preparing for the passion and pain that she's bound to give me.

Yet I keep coming back for more, despite everything. Despite her doubt, her insecurity, Rachel's warnings, Mike's caution—everything. They're like road blocks, and she's this ball of light of hope and happiness, and I'm plowing through the blocks to get to her in a state of depression.

"Yes," I finally answer Rachel. "I do."

Her eyes flutter with what I think is subtle happiness, then she exhales deeply. "Then I'm happy for you. I won't interfere anymore, even if I don't mean it. Truly." She pauses and blushes two patches of dainty roses. "Does that mean you forgive me? For the file? Which I've put back safely where it belongs?"

It's my turn to exhale in relief. "Yes, *please*." I bend down and sweep her into my sweaty, stinky body.

"Gross!" she squeals as she wraps her arms around my neck. "You stink! Like, *reeking* bad. Did a skunk roll around in trash then shit on you?"

"Wouldn't you know?" I tease, and she pinches my neck. Cringing, I pull back and rub the spot she abused. "Abusing me after we made up? How distasteful."

She giggles and sticks a tongue out at me. "Get used to it, bestie." She pokes my stomach.

I grin. "I've missed you," I admit.

She smiles wider. "And I've missed you." She walks back into my arms, but this time, it's sincerer and lasts longer. She smells heavily of vanilla and her hair is drenched with sweet-scented shampoo.

A sharp whistle behind me breaks us apart, followed by an obnoxious, "Oh, lover boy!"

"Ty," we say in unison before I turn and find him running over to us.

"What's up?" I ask him.

"There's this drag race tonight, down by the

docks," he says and smiles, like I'm supposed to catch onto something I'm missing.

Rachel gasps behind me. "The one on Carnal Street?"

"Yep." He winks at her, and she flushes, crossing her arms over her chest. He looks her up and down, and I reach out to punch him in the chest. He chuckles and gives her one last shitty wink before looking at me. "So are you in?"

"I don't know. I have a test coming up, and I have to study for it—"

"He'll be there," Rachel cuts through my words and nudges me with a small smile. "The place may be the hub for criminal acts and delinquents...*but* you should have some kind of fun. Distract yourself a bit," she surprises me by saying. She's a sweet girl who would rather stay in and watch Disney movies, so the fact that she's suggesting I go to this supposed magnet for crime is a little more than shocking.

"Really?" I can't hide my surprise, and she laughs.

"Yes, really." Turning to Ty, who is such a hornball he doesn't know how to *not* stare at anything with boobs, I find him staring at her with a creepy smile. "Text me the details so I know when to get ready."

"You got it," he says, but his attention is on something behind us. Shock and lust flash across his blue eyes as a gasp leaves his lips, that he licks ferociously. "Who is *that*?"

I turn to Beth, who's waving at us. She stumbles over her hot pink Nikes but quickly rights herself and winks at me like she didn't almost face plant on the running treadmill. I'm not even facing him fully before he's brushing past us, sauntering over to her like a gangsta with a heavy machine gun in his Nike shorts.

"How you doin'?" I hear him say to Beth, before Rachel rolls her eyes and drags me over to the room for spin-cycling.

Chapter Forty-One

I don't know what the proper attire for a drag race is, so I end up pulling on a black long-sleeve crew top and dark jeans. After tying up black Converse and tugging on a black knit beanie, I feel relieved when neither Mike nor Ty nor any of the other guys tagging along are wearing chains or leather or something.

Of course, I imagine the dress code to a supposed place where criminals hang out would be what a metal band wears on the front of their latest "totally rocking" album. I wonder what rave reviews I can accumulate dressed like this. Probably something along the lines of: *Eh. He tried.*

Rachel's beside me in one of the guys' cars, fidgeting with her thumbs. She has her brunette locks braided over her shoulder, a glittery black headband pushed on her hair. She's wearing jeans and a frilly white shirt with a jean jacket over it. I admit, she looks pretty cute, and when I tell her, she blushes and bites at her thumb. I frown and finally cave into my worried thoughts. She looks like she's on her way to her own execution.

By the way, should I be prepared for a band to be called Execution playing when we arrive, lead singer swinging around on a chain or, like, *not*? I wave the frightening image to the back of my head and lock the door on my way out.

"Regretting agreeing to come?" I tease her, nudging her gently and drawing her attention on her immaculate white Converse to my probing eyes. Hers are wide saucers, and I lose my humor in a matter of nanoseconds.

"Seriously. Is everything okay? I don't have to beat up a guy, do I?" I hold up a tight fist, and her frown cracks into the tiniest smile. It may not be a beaming grin, but it's something, at least.

"No. No boys need to be beat up," she says. "My mother just texted me some sad news earlier. That's all." She tries to show me a bright smile, but her eyes are too dim for me to not notice.

"Can I ask what the news was? Unless you just don't want to talk about it? That's fine too," I frantically add. I don't want to pry into a wound that's barely holding up as it is and make things even worse for her. That'd be a really shitty thing to do, and she's been such a great friend to me; I want to be there for her, like she was for me. It's the least I can do for her.

"My mother used the money I had saved for spring break to help my stepfather with some kind of business transaction. She says that it will help everyone in the end, but it's hurting me now, and I don't think that'll change when *he's* a few thousand dollars richer." She huffs out and goes back to picking her nails.

"That's horrible." I briefly dislike her mother for going behind her back and using her money *she* saved on her own to help her husband. If he's involved in the business world, he should have enough money and more to pay for some sort of fee or whatever. My father taught me how to fit a large amount of money in dress pants without looking like a thief with items stuffed in my pants.

I bite my lip and watch her nod solemnly, her large brown eyes fixated on the deserted area we're passing by. The party's on the abandoned side of town, at some factory that shut down ages ago and is now used for rave parties and the occasional drug business transaction. No parent would allow their child anywhere near the place, which is why the rebellious attraction pulled kids even more to the place. A wicked game of psychology, the factory is.

But back to Rachel. She's obviously heartbroken over what her mother did, and I want to put a smile on her face. Even if it's just for a fleeting moment. "How about you and I do something together for the break?"

Her eyes light up like a moon. "Really?" She sounds more surprised than I am comfortable with. She needs to know that I can be there for her as she is with me. It's only fair for me to invite her on vacation for spring break. I didn't have any plans before, but now I do.

"Yeah." I nod, sporting a grin, hoping it's contagious enough; sure enough, it is, and she's grinning up at me like I'm her savior of the sorts. "We can go anywhere you want, except Miami."

"Why Miami?" she asks with a tilt of her head.

"Weird, bad, and really confusing memories there," I tell her, referring to my summer trip there. Memories I'd blocked out for my sanity and well-being of my heart flood my head like it's The Grand Rapids. And it takes a while to shut the floodgates, but when I do, I offer her a small smile.

"Okay, that literally leaves everything else. Thank you, Noah." She touches my bicep, flushes as if doing so is extremely ridiculous, and curls her hands in her lap. "You are the sweetest person I know."

"Then you must not know a lot of people," I joke, and she laughs and pushes my arm playfully. I like this lightened version of her, and I will myself to keep her around for the rest of the long drive.

When we arrive, I'm stoked to finally get out and stretch my unnaturally long legs. The building is tattered and browned from years of deterioration from the weather. Covering a massive part of the dirt area are flashy cars and plain ones weaving throughout. From where we are, the spotlights illuminate the factory. I hear loud and distinct guitar riffs and screaming and can practically feel the ground shake from the jumping bodies that are gyrating shadows in the broken and grimy windows.

This party isn't my type at all. When I was roaming the world, I experienced many different versions of parties tied to contrasting cultures, but none had a band that could be heard from about fifty feet away. That image I had locked away before, with the lead singer swinging around the stage by a chain, and perhaps now a ball-gag in his lips painted in black lipstick, unlocks itself, and he swings before my eyes. I wave him away, tuck him in his room, lock it, *burn* the key, and wait for everyone else to get out of the car so we can walk up to the party.

The rest of the guys hop out, and I overhear Ty ask Mike quietly as we walk toward the building, "Do you think they'll let me race this time?"

"Noah! Wait up!" I hear a familiar squeal behind me. I have no time to look over my shoulder, because Beth's sidling up next to me, baring more cleavage than the seductive smirk and eye squint she's throwing at me shamelessly, and unsuccessfully so. "Hey there. What do you think of my dress? And my heels are kind of amazing, don't you think?" She reaches out and pulls me closer to her petite body that's one wrong breath away from spilling out of the short, nude dress with rhinestones, her heels matching the design.

I watch her pucker her velvet-red lips for a while, for entertainment purposes, before answering. "You look...are you not cold? It's the middle of November," I remind her, but I'm sure she can feel the slight bristled wind against her bare thighs. At least she's wearing an oversized jean jacket, which has sequins spelling her name on the back. I smile a little more for some reason.

"I'm fine, but I hear body heat works wonders," she whispers and moves to grab my butt, but thankfully, Ty swoops in and whisks her away to a line of cars with neon lights around the wheels and girls dressed like her surrounding them and the muscled men lounging on them.

I hear her curse him out and him counter each colorful phrase with a "Damn, you're a fiery one. I love it, babe," followed by a field kiss to the cheek. I look away laughing when she smacks him and stomps somewhere into the buzzing crowd.

"I'm sorry for her." Rachel chuckles beside me, crinkling her nose after her friend. "She can be a bit...much. I swear she isn't always so horny and shameless. She only seems to know how to flip that switch on and is full-on frisky around you...or any other guy for that matter."

"Except for Ty," I point out.

"Except for Ty," she agrees, chuckling.

"So...do you know what we can do besides gawk at cars?" I ask her, but I don't expect much of an answer. She knew where this place was earlier, but I doubt this would be her usual weekend activity. Then again, you never really know a person. You can know every single detail of their life, but not know what goes on inside their heads or hearts, their true desires or pleasures.

"Nothing you and I would do...*drugs*." She whispers like it's a bad word she can get spanked for uttering.

I smile tightly because I don't know how to tell her that I loved doing drugs at one point in my life. I wasn't a junkie or anything. I didn't need rehab, but I was sort of hooked to an extent. It was shortly after graduation and my parents barely batted their eyes at my disappearance. I fell into a brief hole of depression and took to drugs and alcohol and partying and flying to dark parts of the world. I thought I would never get out of the continuous loop of darkness until I broke free and did what I set out to do in the first place: paint and travel and learn.

But now, I don't do any drugs. It's not like if I got a whiff or puff or *snort* I'd turn into a wild pack animal; I would just rather not get caught up in the harmful side effects they bring.

"You're right. How about we just check out the cars?" I suggest, and she nods, smiling without showing her teeth.

For the next hour or so, we slowly roam around the spacious lot like we're in an art museum and not a drag race/rock and roll type party thing. The cars are similar to those I've witnessed in Tokyo, Japan. Neon lights surround the wheels and impressive engines are showed off like show ponies. I've driven one of these before. I nearly flew off the side of a cliff, but that was mostly my fault for having not driven one in my life. Ever. The important part is that I survived, right?

Cars are speeding around, racing up and down the deserted roads, and spinning around on the lot, creating a storm of golden clouds. I get her and me a few beers from the cooler, and we find ourselves dancing to an R&B song. She's a terrible dancer, with her shaking like she's being electrocuted, but I can't say I'm any better. But it doesn't matter because we're having a great time getting tipsy over the next few drinks and stumbling around to the catchy beat and lyrics.

For a good while, I am carefree and enjoying myself. I'm not moping around the frat house like I got kicked in the ass or had my teddy bear taken away. I'm enjoying myself and not thinking about Red. I've given her enough time to decide if she wants me or not, if she wants to give us an actual chance or not. As much as my machismo wants to reign victorious, I can't let it happen. I can't just sit around and watch her cry and feel like an ass when she made the decision to ditch me for the millionth time since I've met her. I need to chill out and let her come to her final decision, whenever that happens, anyway.

Rachel's moving toward me with an unreadable expression when the racing cars growl for attention. I whip around and raise my beer bottle in the air, letting the last drops fall onto my tongue. I watch the two cars speeding toward us. One is a red Porsche that's pleasant to the eye, and the other is a familiar Chevy Impala or a classic Mustang—I can't see that well. But it becomes more apparent as they get closer and closer.

I don't think they're going to slow down or stop and prepare my funeral, but the Chevy Impala stops before us about ten feet away before the Porsche screeches to a stop.

A wave of gold dust wafts into the air, and there are people cheering and jumping around. There are a few guys grumbling and making hand gestures. It's weird until I realize they're handing off/collecting money—bets placed on the race. There are a lot more disgruntled people than there are victorious people, and I just need to see who mostly everyone betted against.

The door to the Chevy Impala pops open, and I'm shocked to find Red. She's wearing her usual leather jacket, ripped band t-shirt, and combat boots. But she has a red bandana wrapped around her untamed blonde hair. She sports a cocky grin as her opponent hops out of his expensive car, cussing and screaming in a language unknown to me. My heart beats like it's tumbling in a dryer as I watch her.

Popping a cigarette in her mouth, she waltzes over to a tall man with tattoo sleeves, who hands her a massive chunk of bills. She pockets it, stiffens, and looks around. Her eyes are frantic and narrowed as they search the crowd. *Find me, find me, find me...* I find myself chanting in my head, and I hate myself for it. Not even a few minutes ago, I was a confident guy who wasn't going to stick around and wait eagerly for her to decide if she wanted me or not, and here I am, begging for her to find me in a crowd as I imagine hugging the hell out of her.

What?

I've missed her; leave me alone.

"Noah, where are you going?" I hear Rachel say. I don't understand until I look around. I'm a few feet away from her, and I'm headed toward Red. I shake my head in confusion and shock, but I don't stop walking. I don't have any control over my body at this point.

"I'll be right back," I promise her over my shoulder. I turn back around and continue my pursuit of the girl who's flipping through her stack of bills while smoking a cigarette. Something about the sight makes me hard in all the right places, and I find myself admiring how relaxed yet focused she looks up close.

I stand here for what feels like an eternity, just watching her. Hoping she can sense me as I can sense her a million miles away. Praying that she feels even a sliver of what I feel for her, because, if she doesn't, then I get the award for Biggest Sucker on The Planet—ever. I've only had to deal with one girl who didn't feel the same way I did, and I barely made it out unscathed. I promised myself I wouldn't ever get hurt like that again. But here I am, standing in front of a girl, hoping she loves me the same…

I really don't miss watching Rachel's shitty romance movies—gah, I sound like a whiny girly character.

As if hearing my yacking inner turmoil, Red's hypnotizing blue eyes fly up from her wad of cash and strike into my green ones. My nerve cells stand on end, and my breathing becomes uneven and short. I gulp harshly as she stares into my eyes, unmoving, smoke billowing into her hair. She looks even more beautiful up close, so enchanting. The only time I ever got a peek of her face was when she was rushing across the lecture hall or speed-walking away from me outside of classes. But now…now I get to re-memorize every dip and curve and smooth texture.

Neither of us speaks for a considerable, uncomfortably long time. I don't know how she feels. Is she upset I'm here? Angry? Sad? Does she want to punch me in the face? Scream at me? Or kiss me? Or maybe all the above, and she'll explode like a star that's burned for a thousand years.

"Hi." I decide to break the ice.

Chapter Forty-Two

She takes a few puffs before answering. "Hi." She sounds unsure.

Oh, fuck this.

"Can we talk?" I ask her.

"I don't think that's a good idea, Noah." She sighs and looks anywhere but my eyes. I couldn't feel a more intense sharp pain in my chest. She's acting like I don't mean anything to her, and it's pissing me off because I know I do. I didn't imagine our passion-filled kisses or the way she lights up around me; nor did I freaking hallucinate our date.

Fed up with her BS, I flick the cigarette out of her hand.

She gapes at me. "What the hell, Noah?"

I ignore her and pop open the door behind her.

"What the hell are you doing?" she barks at me as I sit in the driver seat.

Wordlessly, I reach out for her hips. I pull her in so she's sitting on my lap like I'm a chair and, ignoring the hardness that I'm struggling to control because of this...position, I close the door, then lock it. She shifts around so she's straddling me and pinning me with not only her hands on my shoulders but her fireballs for eyes.

"Noah! Have you lost your mind?" she begins to shout.

I press my lips to hers, shutting her up. If there is anything I know about girls, it's that kissing them is the best way to get them to listen to you. They can go on and on rambling and ranting at you when you just want to make them slow down enough so you can get a word in, but they keep going and going, and they don't take a pause to just listen. I've suffered multiple days with this girl, so I think I deserve to have her listen to me for once, to hear me out.

That and I've been craving her lips.

The kiss is hungry and nipping and licking and tugging. Her lip ring is ice cold against our heated mouths as they mold to one another with a desperate need. I move my hands to her thighs, then the back of them. I glide them up and up, until I feel her warm skin underneath her tight band t-shirt. I push up until I see the warm sliver of her skin, and I tug at her bottom lip. She moans. Wanting more space, I blindly search the side of the car seat. When I finally find the lever to push the seat back, I yank on it and we're flat down, and she's grinding against me.

I find both of my hands on the hot skin of her lower back. I feel her sexy back dimples above her round ass, and then her actual ass and squeeze. She lifts her head and lets out a sultry moan. I've missed that sound so much, I grow hard instantly.

"We shouldn't be doing this," she mumbles and gulps for air. I look up as I'm laying a fat stripe of my tongue along her gracefully long neck. She is so god damn sexy. Her blonde hair is tousled and framing her flushed and glowing cheeks and neck. Lips bruised and red from our heated kiss are being bit, and her pink tongue is toying with her lip ring. I reach up and brush my tongue against hers before pulling us both into a world-crushing kiss.

"Why not?" I breathe when I pull away briefly. My skin is buzzing with excitement and need for more, but I need to calm down. I got her to listen, or at least *open* to listening. And I can't wreck it just because I'm horny as fuck and am so quick to jump her bones at a drag racing party.

Her eyes have lost a little spark of her lusty fire, and her shoulders slump. "Because...I already told you. I'm not...I'm no good for you, Noah." She uncharacteristically plays with a frayed section on the collar of my shirt. I've rarely seen her this vulnerable, this unguarded—that shocks me.

But then I take into consideration the situation and her puzzlingly strong assertion that she's this big bad creature I should stay away from. But how can I when, in her own freaking insane way...she cares about me? Cares so much she doesn't want to hurt me. However, what she can't seem to understand is, her past nor anything she can do today can push me away from her. Nor can they take away how much I...how much I love her.

"You're wrong, Red." I thread my fingers into her hair and pull her closer. Her warm breath fans against my mouth; it tickles and makes me sigh and hold her even closer until there's only a thin inch between us.

"No, I'm not." She shakes her head, looking away from me. I see tears in her eyes and my heart melts, and I cup her face and force her to look into my eyes. I have seen her tearing up one too many times around me. I hate it; I want to see her smiling, not like she's at a funeral all the time.

"Yes, you are." I pause, and a glimmer of sadness flashes in her eyes. "I like you, Red. I like you a lot. And I would do anything to make you smile. To make you want me…why can't you just want me?" I sound wimpier than I was going for.

She sniffles and looks confused. "What? I do want you. How can you possibly not see that I have never wanted anything more in my entire life? Noah, you are the only light I've ever experienced. The only thing that makes the days worth living…I'm sorry." She brings her leather jacket sleeve against her nose and licks her lips. "I sound like a whiny chick that you're probably used to."

"No, you don't. You sound like you're opening up to me, and I appreciate it." I brush the pads of my thumbs against her cheek. Surprisingly, she doesn't pull away or look away, and I thank the heavens. She's letting me study her without deflecting. "Red, you are by far the best thing that has happened to me. These last few days have been torture…please, don't prolong this pain anymore. I need you in my life. N-need you." My voice breaks, but I hold deep eye contact with her. Peer into her inner conflict of accepting me with open arms and letting us be a thing, and pushing away yet again, which seems to be her comfort move.

"You don't understand the horrible things I've done—the things I *do*," she emphasizes, her own voice cracking under pressure. Her head hangs and her voice is slow and painfully melancholy, devoid of much emotion except despair.

"I don't care, Red." Bringing her head down to meet mine gently, I tell her, "Nothing you can do can make me stop liking you as much as I do. I care for you more than I ever have before. You're permanently on my mind, and I don't wish for that to ever change. But you have to give us a chance. And I mean a real one. No..." I pause and forget about all the "manly codes" and murmur, "No more *leaving* me. I won't be able to function the next time, God forbid, you leave me."

She's silent for a long while, busy thinking, I presume. I give her the time but not the space. I need her closer. I've spent so long without her, it felt as though I were missing a limb. My cells are currently re-familiarizing the feelings she brings to me, how my body used to react. I can see her leaning toward the prospect of us, but there's that thread holding her back.

Oh God.

I have to cut that thread, pull her to me.

I lean forward and brush my lips to hers, looking up at her under my lashes. "I'd never leave you, Red. Say yes to me..." I peck her lips, leaving our lips molded and gentle. Still, fire simmers under my skin and my heart rocks in the nearby atmosphere. "Say yes to us," I plead softly. My voice is raspy and hopefully persuasive.

Her throat bobs slightly as she gulps, and she cups my face. "I don't want to hurt you again."

"And I don't want to live another day without you by my side," I whisper back.

Her brows furrow, lips suck into her mouth, and she looks into my eyes. That conflict battles in her vivid blue eyes, and I nudge her nose with mine. "Noah..." she groans.

"I need you, Red." I kiss the top of her upper lip, her cupid's bow.

She sighs a melting sigh and timidly nods, then melts into the rest of my body, relying on me physically and emotionally. "I need you, Noah. So much."

My heart soars, and I grin against her mouth. "Then have me," I murmur before pulling her on top of me in a mind-blowing kiss that surely splits the planet down the middle. Well, it splits our own planets, but I don't care about the wreckage.

Just her.

Only her.

Only *ever* her.

Chapter Forty-Three

"I do not appreciate this obvious conversion you're forcing on me," I claim with a voice of authority and annoyance, but also loads more humor.

Red spins around. "It's not conversion if it's the better option," she says with utmost sass. I can only smile and watch her from my bed. She's wearing one of my dress shirts I almost never wear unless my mother decides to pay her only child attention and drags me along to charity events or my father wheels me around one of his many offices.

I can't even be modest or chivalrous and look away; she is too damn sexy for this god-awful world. The shirt stops around her mid-thighs and hides her curves, but the many buttons unbuttoned in the front makes up for it. No, we did not have sex. We fooled around earlier, but not full-on sex, which makes me hot to think about and imagine but also hesitant.

Neither of us are virgins. At least, I'm not. And I'm pretty sure she isn't either. I don't want to make any assumptions, but I'd be extremely shocked if she is. I mean, just look at her. She's the most beautiful creature on this planet. The way she carries herself is graceful, but you wouldn't notice if you hadn't been paying attention. She tries to put up a tough front, but I see past it—I see her. I see her vulnerability and beauty and her intelligence and sass and everything in between. I see it all, and I can't get enough.

"Did Kurt's heavenly voice put you in a trance?" she teases as she turns to face me. My heart aches at the genuine smile on her face. Sometimes it's hard to pull her from her tough appearance and get her to warm up to me. Keyword: *sometimes*. Now, she's lighter, and I don't see any inward attempt to pull her back behind her barrier. I want to take advantage of her freedom for a little while longer.

"Nah. It was more like the sexy girl wearing nothing but my dress shirt." I let my lips curl up in a smirk, and she rolls her eyes, but I see the blushing in her cheeks. My heart and arms yearn for her. I reach out for her, and she pads over to me before jumping into my arms.

I laugh as she kisses underneath my chin. I love this side of her so much, it makes my heart hurt. But in a good way. A very, very good way. I lock my hands around her, and she melts into my chest, toying with the collar of my t-shirt. Kurt's raspy voice singing about coming as you are fills the room. Mostly everyone in the house is out doing who knows what, leaving us the chance to turn the volume all the way up. But he can't possibly be any louder than my heart.

It's been days since the drag racing party, and we've been in a peaceful limbo I'm afraid will dissolve, so I am holding onto her for dear life and praying that we don't hit any more icebergs. I don't want us to go down like the *Titanic*. I need our ship to stay alive— my life depends on it. But in a less dramatic way.

"Did you turn in your submission for the art thing?" she asks softly, breaking the comfortable silence.

I rest my chin on her hair. "No."

She looks up, puzzled. "Why not?" she asks. She glances at the mural over my shoulder, then back at me. "You finished it, and it's a freaking masterpiece."

"I dunno." I shrug.

I do know, though. I'm terrified that I'll fail. Who would have guessed years of being judged and criticized by your parents could make you insecure?

She pinches my arm.

"Ouch!" I yelp and look down at her incredulously. "What was that for?"

"Being a douche-wad. A dumb one at that." She hops up onto her knees and straddles my sitting position, arms looped around my neck. She tugs on the bottom of my hair, pulling my head back, and leans over like a dark, intimidatingly gorgeous angel of common sense.

"You can't not put yourself out there because you're a pussy. Man up and press that damned SEND button." Then, in a softer tone, she pecks my lips and says, eyes smiling, "You'll blow away the snobby assholes. So much they'll pick you over the million other artistic assholes out there."

I laugh and hold her hips. "Wow."

"What?" she snaps.

"Nothing. It's just..." I laugh some more. "I never realized how hardcore you are. Cursing at me in an attempt to persuade me to do something."

"Did it work?" She raises her pierced eyebrow.

"Big time." I peck her lips but linger, enjoying the sweet, calming taste. All I can taste is the softness of her lips. Her nimble fingers latch around the back of my neck. We find ourselves falling back on the bed, and I'm on top. She moans, and her slender legs drag up my thighs. I hold the back of her knees and press into her. Her breathing becomes heavy and she's saying something I can't quite make out. I move my lips to her jaw and suck lightly, then kiss tenderly. She moaning more, mumbling too.

What is she saying?

But before it can go any further, she pulls away. Her eyes scream out the want her voice doesn't say. "You should submit your thing now."

Stung, I nod and reluctantly sit back. "You're right. I, uh, already took pictures of it. Just gotta send it in..." I stand up and stare at her, confused by her avoiding my eyes. She gets up and walks over to Ty's radio I'm using for the music, and she doesn't acknowledge my confused stare.

Did I do something wrong?

Sighing, I walk over to my study desk and drop onto the chair. I log into my email and type in the email address I'm supposed to submit it to. As I write the subject and a bit of a description in the text box, I think of what just happened. She and I were just kissing when all of a sudden she interrupted, pushed me away. But why? I didn't force myself on her, right?

My heart drops at the thought.

I don't ever want her to feel that way, or any of the girls I've been with in the past. I never got any complaints, and I always *always* ask if they want me. I've never taken a drunk girl, except for Beth. But even then, I asked repeatedly and she said yes repeatedly. If anyone said no or anything like that, I pushed off immediately, apologized, offered them some sort of consolation or just left altogether, once again apologizing.

Cursor over the SEND button, my heart thumps wildly in my chest. It's now or never. So, with a heavy heart, I click SEND and take a step back.

I turn to Red and catch her eyes in the mirror in the corner. "Did I make you uncomfortable?"

She turns around, frowning. "What?"

Sheepishly, I point to the bed. "Did I...I'm sorry, Red. Truly. If you didn't want *that* or me..."

She looks confused before something clicks in her head and she rushes over frantically. Gripping my biceps, she assures me, "No, no, *no!* You didn't...*no,* Noah." Then her lips fall into a sort of soft, conflicted smile. "I wanted that. You make me insatiable, believe me."

I smile, relieved. "Great. Because trust me, I would never make you feel that way. At least, I hope not. And please tell me if I do make you uncomfortable."

"Noah, you sound insane."

"How?"

Her mouth drops open, then her tongue pokes inside of her cheek. "Because I kinda want to jump your bones ninety percent of the time I'm with you."

My heart leaps, but I keep my expression calm. "Seriously?" I ask, and she hesitantly nods, watching me. "Then why are you so hesitant? Not that I'm rushing you or anything," I quickly add. I don't want her to feel any pressure.

"I don't know." She sighs, flinging her arms around my neck. "Sex is intimate as hell. Something you can't take back. You're just as close as possible with a person and there's feelings and shit attached and..." She draws short. Her eyes are zoned on my chest, her head not in the moment, like she's looking into another world and she's stuck there.

"And you're afraid you'll fall madly in love with me?" I joke, and it seems to bring her back into this plane. She thumps her hand into my shoulder, lips tugged upward, but she doesn't say anything. I sigh and cup her face, brushing flyaways of her hair out of her eyes. "We don't need sex for me to know that I..." I stop, and she sucks in an expectant breath. "That I have feelings for you. And believe me when I say they're deep. *So*, we can wait a week, a month, a year—fuck it. However long you want. I don't care as long as I have you in my life."

Her smile is contagious. "I really have you wrapped around my finger, don't I?"

I lean my forehead against hers. "You have no idea."

She huffs out a deep breath and scrapes her

fingers underneath my chin, causing me to chuckle deeply. Pulling back, she looks up at me with the sort of smile that lights up her eyes and makes my whole world spin. "How about for now, we just dance?" She holds out a small hand, and I take it and spin her into my chest.

"I should warn you, I'm a fantastic dancer," I say in a mock Spanish accent. Her laugh is hearty and makes me smile as I spin her around the room. With her pressed into my body, I twirl us around the room. The ground is our dance floor and the music is my heartbeat, crooning my love for this amazing, beautiful, incredible girl with golden eyes and tattoos that make me spin.

She regards me with amusement as I twirl her around the room to Nirvana: not the most ideal song choice for our technique of dancing, but who cares? I get to hear her squealing laughter as I pick her up and spin and spin until we're both dizzy. But as she shouts facts about the band between screaming the lyrics and dancing like a loose wire as I twirl her around, I find myself in trouble—I find myself even more in love with this girl.

Chapter Forty-Four

I promise to take her out on a date on Friday, and the two days can't crawl any slower. When I'm not nervously tapping my pens in classes and pushing through grueling football practices and painting projects in art club, I am planning our date.

Our last one was extremely classy, fancy, and obviously not her thing. Not that I'm typecasting her or anything. She said she had a great time. But I could tell she felt a little...out of her element. And although she looked drop-dead gorgeous in her little black dress, makeup done, I could tell she was uncomfortable. She tried not to appear that way, but I could see it in her slightly dimmed, wandering eyes. And when people looked at us a beat longer than necessary, even I felt out of place. And *very* pissed off with a rage bigger than Hades.

So, this time, we're slipping into *her* world. No matter how loud her music and movements are, I love her for the way she is. She shouldn't have to change for me, even if it's just for one night. I want her to be totally comfortable and able to put her hair down and run from security guards that are on her heels, or rather, *combat boots*. Where no one looks at us weirdly.

To be fair, I do forget how different in appearance we are. Standing side by side, you would never be able to tell how much of my heart she holds in her fists or that we even know each other. I want to hold her in my arms and make her hold up a sign that declares our whatever-the-hell-we-are relationship. And in parentheses at the bottom: *KINDLY FUCK OFF AND FIND SOMEONE OF YOUR OWN. BITCHES.*

I stare into the mirror and search for a fault in my outfit. I'm wearing a plain black t-shirt, black pants that are tighter than I expected, black Converse, and a dark denim jacket. I slip on a dark gray beanie, play with my curls, and run a thumb against my nose. I cock my head to the side. Something's missing...I spin in a circle, looking for the puzzle piece. When I spot it, I smile and slip the silver chain around my neck. It has a cross on the end, and I thank Ty for wearing shit like this.

I hear a whistle behind me, then Ty appears in the mirror behind me. "Fancy. Going out with Ms. Thang?" He waves his finger and shakes his shoulders at me as he walks up to me. He's holding a Hot Cheetos bag, and his fingers are dusted with the snack. Stopping next to me as I laugh, he looks me over and pops a finger in his mouth like the slob he is.

"Yes. And you'll have the room all night," I say and stop, hearing my phone buzz on my bed. I walk over to it and grab it, barely listening to him tease me. Red texted me she's outside, so I type back that I'm on my way down.

"Oooooh shit, you two finally getting freaky?" He pops his finger, and I roll my eyes, swiping my finger across the screen to unlock it. "Finally. I was beginning to think you were celibate."

I walk over to him and grab my wallet off my study desk. "See you around, Ty." I slip my phone in my back pocket, and I'm out of the door. I jog down the tall stairs, adrenaline pumping my blood. I am so ready for tonight. I feel like I've been waiting centuries when, in reality, it was two days.

"Have fun, ya nasty!" I hear him call after me.

"Remember to use protection," Mike decides to join in as I'm on my way out.

"Yeah, yeah." I wave a dismissive hand at him. I shut the front door after me and quickly step down the stairs. I tuck my hands in my jean jacket, and when I lift my head, I let a grin sweep across my face.

Red is in the same position as me as she's leaned against her car. She looks hot as usual: in her ripped and pinned *Metallica* band t-shirt, ripped black jeans, leather jacket, and combat boots that I swear are too clunky for her small feet. But if she loves to wear them, who am I to say otherwise?

"Are we gonna be that annoying couple who matches?" she says in that husky, low voice of hers I adore.

When I'm close enough, I loop my arms around her waist and pull her flush against me. Her grin is contagious, and I shrug with a sugary smile. "Are we a *couple*? Hmmm?" I rest my chin on her hair, waltz us around a little; and she's a laughing mess. "Have you decided you want all of The Noah?"

She raises a dubious pierced brow. "The Noah?"

"Yes. The Noah: a sexy, cute, e-*bae* worthy boy that is great at being a reliable boyfriend," I tell her in an obnoxiously loud announcer voice like I'm in a boxing ring.

Laughing so much, she bends backward. "Do not *ever* do that again," she demands and stands up straight. Taking my hands, she spins herself over to the front of the car. "And get in the car."

"Nuh-uh uh." I rush over to her and pull her back from the curb. I wheel around and walk her back to the passenger side. "I'm driving tonight, little rocker lady."

"Oh hell no." She turns to me with a seriously deathly expression. "No one—and I mean *no* one—drives my baby."

"I thought I was your baby." I pout playfully, and she shakes her head. "Oh, come on. It's just for one night. Tonight is about letting you relax and be yourself." I lay two handfuls of her untamed golden hair and flop them in my palms, fluffing them out. She just glares at me, but it softens like I knew it would when I play with her hair some more. "Huh? How about trusting me? Be yourself. Laugh for me, *Rossa*. Laugh!"

"Okay." She chuckles and ducks her head in the cutest way, and my heart blossoms into a garden of exotic flowers. Licking her lips, she seems to think it over for a while. I poke her some more, hoping to drive her closer to persuasion town. Just gotta push her over this little pesky edge, but she's getting there; I can tell by the crinkling of her nose. That or I'm annoying her. But in a cute way.

"Okay!" She stomps over to the passenger door. "But if you crash her, I—"

"Will not do anything but forgive me because you're so in love with me and my abs. I know, I know." I smile at her, but she doesn't look amused. "Come on, grumpy pants. We have things to do, places to be." I wave her butt inside of the car. After closing the door after her, I—ignoring her stank face—jog around the hood. I slide into the driver seat and tap my fingers along the large, leather steering wheel.

"You *do* know how to drive, right?" She raises her brows, and I throw her a smile.

"Of course I do. Just…" I look at her and raise my left leg, doing a model pose. "Mind taking a pic for the Gram?" I am totally kidding. God no. God. No.

"There's gonna be a long line of shit you can't do if you keep doing shit like *that*." She laughs and claps her hands. I watch for a few seconds, enamored. Until I glance at the clock on the stereo and realize we gotta leave. Like. *Now*.

I pull out onto the road and focus on driving. I would take my usual peeks to admire her goddess-like beauty, but she cares very much for this car, and I do *not* want to ride home in an ambulance. The car drives surprisingly smoothly and the air smells distinctly like her: cigarettes, fresh bar soap, and scented shampoo. I may sniff a little harder as I'm driving.

I merge onto the freeway, headed to a nearby

small town. According to Google Maps, we'll arrive in an hour and a half, give or take, depending on traffic. Which, thank the Lord, is lighter than I expected. When ten minutes on the freeway passes, I feel uneasy because of the comfortable, yet staggering, silence between us. I need to hear her voice. Hold her hand. But then the image of me hobbling up the frat house with crutches pops behind my eyes, and I firmly grip the wheel.

"So, how did this lovely contraption come into your possession?" I say, and she looks at me, lips parted as if she's shocked.

"Oh." Then she blushes. "My, um, my birth father died. My mom was gonna get rid of it after it sat idle in the garage. I think it reminded her of him every time she saw it too much…so she was gonna sell it. But my grandpa told her to wait till I was old enough and claim it for my own."

"Wow."

"What?"

"I feel like shit for just now finding out," I admit and fidget in the seat. I really should have quizzed her earlier.

"No, don't feel bad. I didn't want you to know."

"Why not?" I take the chance to glance at her. She's frowning and staring out of the windshield. I want to reach over and take her hand, but, like I said: Ambulance. Crutches.

"Because it's shitty." She shrugs, glances at me. "And no one really likes to talk about shitty things."

"Well, I do." I pause, glance at her hand on her lap. *Fuck it!* I reach over and take her hand in mine. She doesn't pull away or scream at me to put both hands on the wheel, so I keep it intertwined with hers and grip with the other one. "Tell me everything shitty, and I promise I will not judge. I swear it." And I mean it.

When I glance at her, she's staring at me with a sort of surprised face.

I chuckle and look back to the road. "Don't look so shocked. Contrary to popular beliefs, I do have a good ear for listening, and I give tons of shit about your shit." I squeeze her hand gently, look at her, and smile. "Spill, babe."

Babe?

Babe, her smile says.

And then, I hear all the shitty shit about her life, well, all that she allows me to hear. I can hear more to some stories, but I don't force her to elaborate. I just listen to everything she has to say. In the span of an hour, I learn that she ran away when she was fifteen, joined a rock band, and got arrested, all in the span of—wanna hear something funny—an hour. She tells me about dropping out of school for one month, then rejoining but at the boarding school her sister attends. Which, in her words "was two bank robberies' worth—piece of shit education system." And she tells me about her mother being murdered, which she gets quiet about, so I attempt to ease her a little by going next.

I relay some of my finest shitty moments: about the time I got so trashed at a party in Tokyo that the next morning I woke up with a sumo wrestler attached to a handcuff. I tell her about jetting off hours after my graduation and getting fucked up in Seoul. And I even admit to my parents forcing me to attend college. I tell her about them arranging meetings with college scouts, even hiding my canvases and paints and basically anything I can use to do the one thing that makes me truly happy.

By the time we are done, we both feel like shit, and I regret we did it.

"I'm sorry," I apologize, rubbing my thumb against hers. "Didn't think it'd ruin the mood like that. Not your best, Noah," I murmur, and her grip on me tightens. I look over at her and her glowing smile. Even in the dark, she is my ultralight.

"You didn't ruin anything. We got to know a little more about each other. That's all," she says, and I feel a little better, but still like shit. Ironically enough. But I will not let this cast a blanket of darkness over us or our night. Yes. This will be Our Night, goddamn it!

Noticing a sign as I pass, I grin and look over at her. "How much can your mouth fit?"

She pauses, looking worried, then says, "Um…what?"

"I didn't mean it like *that*, silly." I reach over and tap her button-nose; she tries to bite my finger. "Stop trying to *bite* me, and wait for your dirty-gutter mind to be blown out of the water."

"What water?"

"There is no water."

"Then why'd you say it?"

When I look at her, she has this shit-eating grin as she mocks me. I can't get over her lit by the warm orange light of street lamps as the car rolls down several streets.

"Stop with the sass and just wait." I reach out to

poke her shoulder, but she bites at my wrist and, wrenching it back, I gasp dramatically and glance over at her with a dropped jaw. "And the biting! This needs to stop right now, you little shark."

"Why should I listen to you?" she says. Then, a second later, she's leaning over and biting at my neck. The car sways barely a fraction of an inch, as I laugh and shout at her to sit back before we get into an accident. I curse the seatbelts for being so loose, but I can't say I'm not enjoying her mouth on my skin. She's having a laughing fit when I finally push her down and glare at her shortly, but I can't stay mad at her long, with her too-large blue eyes and adorable laughter.

"You are quite insane, Red Sylvetti." I pick up my beanie that fell onto my lap in the middle of her biting and plop it onto my hair. This amuses her, and she giggles and grabs it and pulls it over her curls. I would grab it back, but it looks too cute on her.

"Quite," she mocks me, baring her teeth in a terrifying way.

"Gross. Don't do that," I say, but I'm laughing. And she's laughing. And I swear there's an open laughing gas in here.

It took a few minutes to find parking, but now we're quieter as our date's about to officially begin. I get out first, then help her out, even though she grumbled that she could get out on her own. To that, I plopped kiss after kiss all over her face. After receiving several shouts of my name and laughter, I smile successfully and sling an arm around her, and we head to the venue.

"A boardwalk? Seriously?" She scoffs at the location.

"What matters is what's *on* the boardwalk," I tell her, and she mumbles something. "Don't be like that. Smile. For. Me. Red." I kiss her forehead with each word until she's beaming up at me. I playfully tug down the beanie, covering her eyes, and she punches me. But I chuckle and drop my arm to the back of her lower back, holding her close and tight.

There aren't many tourists out, since this is an event not many families would spend their night on. People wearing matching t-shirts, caps, and hoodies are milling around. I hope I didn't ruin the surprise, but I know it's shit when a lackluster guy holding a sign in front of a little shack that says: *'MERCH 20% OFF'* definitely ruined it.

"The Arctic Monkeys?" she squeals and actually bounces on her reliable boots. She looks up at me with a hung jaw, dilated eyes, and peachy pink cheeks. I almost don't realize she's actually talking until she pinches me back to reality. "How—what? I didn't even know they were coming here!"

"I have my ways." I flip my hair dramatically, and she grins wider. I chuckle and blush, shrugging my shoulders. "I kept a close eye out for pop-up concerts and stuff ever since I found out you liked them and their kind of music."

She looks stunned, brows dropping, smile hopeful. "Seriously? You did that for me?" She sounds so shocked, it makes my heart ache.

"Of course I did." I cup her face and smile. "I'd do anything for you, Red. *Anything*."

"Kill for me?" She raises her brows.

397

"Depends on who it is," I say.

"Trump?"

"Done deal. Bourne just got back to me earlier than Wick—that prick." I shake my head and make a rueful expression, mouth bunched up, brows curved. She grins a toothy smile and shakes her head, golden curls swaying softly.

"You're something else, prep." She's holding my waist now.

I'm so close to her, I don't even see it coming. "Hopefully yours…"

She grips, and I sigh.

"Oh!" I pull back, but she doesn't let go, still shocked about my intensive research. "And to top it all off, I've got dinner. Huge…wait for it…" I flick my wrists in the air, making a gesture like I'm drumming rapidly.

She laughs into her hands, and with her red cheeks bunched up, blue eyes lit up under the soft street lamps, I lose focus on the drumming and just throw my arms wide open.

"Churros!" I scream obnoxiously loud. People stare at me weirdly, but I don't care. I pay attention to my beaming girl.

"Dope! Where?" She looks around with wide eyes, like a bunny on the lookout for a sweet-ass carrot.

"Over there by the food trucks—which will be our dignified dinner on this fine night." I point over my shoulder, and her greedy eyes follow my thumb…only to frown and look back at me.

"I don't see one," she says, and I freeze.

A pause, then a shaky, "What?"

She bites her lip and checks again. "That's all right, though. Everything else is kinda perfect."

"Kinda being the keyword." I turn around and search with my own eyes. Yeah. Yep. The fuckers aren't there. "Huh." I scratch my head, and she stands next to me, head tilted to the side, hands tucked in her jacket.

"At least there are gyros. I love me some gyros." She's trying to lighten this horrible, terrible, *despicable* situation.

"But you also love you some churros," I huff out and stomp. "Damn it!" I throw my head and scream. Again, staring people. Drawing my chin down, I look over at her to find her nervously chewing on her lip and looking around with her bug-eyes. I smirk and nudge her, reaching inside my jacket. "I guess it's a good thing I bought some earlier when they *were* here." I pull out a pack of the large churros, and I swear I have never seen a light so bright in her eyes.

She reaches for them, but I hold them up playfully. She glares at me.

"I didn't hear a: *Oh my God, Noah. You are the bestest, sweetest, most devilishly handsome guy on this planet to ever exist.*"

"And you won't ever." She reaches again. I hold them up higher, pucker a hand around my ear, and lean down. Sighing, I feel her smile against my cheek before she says, "You are all that and more." Then she kisses my cheek, and I turn to her. She's not even staring at her supposedly favorite treats in the entire world. She's staring at me. Like I'm her world.

I stare right back because she's my entire damn *galaxy*.

"Red Sylvetti, I'm pretty sure I love you," I say it. And I damn well mean it. My heart's a gone sucker because she bats her eyes rapidly and steps back. My heart breaks, and I'm pretty sure I died a little inside.

A storm of regret and sadness begins to hurl its best at me when she steps forward and cups my face before pushing her lips against my nose in the purest way. I close my eyes and wrap my fingers around her frail wrists. Rubbing gently, I pull her even closer to me and listen to her soft voice say, "I sort of think I love you too, Noah Wells."

My heart revives, does a backflip, dances, throws an office party with my other organs, and I'm lifting her off the ground and spinning around. Cheesy romance novels and movies ain't got shit on us. We're the true ones. I feel it in every bone and muscle in my body. I spin her around and around, listening to her sweet, lively laughter, ignoring haters, and feeling my love for this one girl soar my feet off the ground.

When she's still and in my heart, we're staring at each other with this sort of expression I can't explain. I see bits of fright and admiration and elation and euphoria and relief, and I see it all in her golden-kissed blue eyes. And I'm kissing her and feeling the band start their set in my heart, under my flesh, and against her soft, graceful lips.

Chapter Forty-Five

"Thank you for coming out, everyone!" Alex says into the microphone, and a cluster of girls wearing their merch screams like the man just told them there is a sale at their favorite stores.

Their complete and utter adoration over the guy makes me a little frightened of him randomly choosing my girl as his; they'd ride off into the sunset, wearing all black and him flashing me a smile of his stupid charming British mouth.

But when I look over at Red, she's just smiling fondly, like she's remembering a good dream. Has she been in a dream state all of the concert? During it, I glanced over multiple times to make sure she was enjoying it. And she was. She was dancing and singing, but not shouting as if the guy threw the spotlight on her and declared her his rock band wife.

I paid more attention to her than the band; I'm sorry, Arctic Monkeys.

"Did you enjoy it?" I ask her as we're aimlessly walking around the boardwalk.

"I did more than enjoy it," she exclaims. "I freaking loved it! Like, a lot! That was the best date *ever*!" She stares up at me with wide eyes and a giddy grin.

I think it's safe to say I can relax about her being swept off by a British guy with luscious black hair and the voice of an angel. What? I didn't say he couldn't sing.

My heart aches, and I breathe out heavily in relief. "I'm glad you did, Red. You deserved it after our last shitty date." I run a hand through my hair, embarrassed, but she pulls my wandering hand away and frowns at me.

"Our last date was not shitty," she says.

I hesitate, biting the inside of my cheek. "Are you sure?"

"Yes, I'm sure." She's laughing, but not in a mocking way. I watch uncertainly for a few moments until she notices my unease and stops us. We're in front of a store that sells knick knacks and souvenirs. "Listen. Noah, no one has ever treated me the way you have. And I mean both date-wise and regular-wise. Ever. You..." She pinches her eyes and pauses, and I watch the words circle on her tongue. "You're by far the best thing—best *person*—I have ever come across. Trust me when I say that I love what you do for me. And I love...I love..."

"I know." I stop her from continuing before she bursts into tears. I can see it from here, the demolition I wreck on the barrier she holds inside of her. She puts up a good front, but it isn't strong enough to withstand my burning love for her.

I want to lighten this kind of tense moment, however fused with love it is.

My eyes flick to the empty shop behind her. "Want some souvenirs to remember our memorable second date?"

She looks behind her, then back at me with bright eyes and a smile. "Hell yeah." She grabs my hand and pulls me inside of the shop. I laugh at her high energy as she weaves us around the shop, under the watchful, but friendly, eye and commentary of the Asian man giving us facts about things she likes and things we should check out.

A few things catch my eye, like a keychain with my name that lights up when I press a button, and an intricate starfish. When I come across a twirling stand of jewelry, I grab two specific ones with a victorious smile on my face.

"All done, Red?" I call out to her as I'm at the cashier, pulling out my wallet.

She turns from a wall of colorful penny skateboards. "Almost," she calls back, and I nod. I'll give her some more time.

But while she browses, I have another idea. I have the man wrap one of the necklaces before she's done. As he slips the boxed jewelry in a bag, my others in a tiny one, she walks over with a few minuscule things: a light blue jewelry box that's shaped like a clam, obsidian earrings, and gray beanie with the words: *FUCK EVERYTHING.*

I smile at her but remain silent.

"What? I like beanies."

"I can tell." I reach down and tug at the one she's wearing, which is *mine,* by the way. She smacks my hand away but is grinning like the sun. I thank the man when he finishes ringing up our stuff and hands us our bags, grinning as he does so.

"You two are a cute couple," he compliments us.

I flush. "Oh, we're not...I mean that'd be great but..." I stammer over my words because I don't know what the heck to say. My heart thunders as I begin to overthink. Thankfully, Red steps in, bids him a good night, then walks us out of the shop.

"I'm sorry that I'm not ready to be a couple, Noah," Red says as we're walking down tall, winding stairs to get to the beach. It's mostly empty since it's mid-November, so I have no idea what's pulling us toward it. But I thank the force because the moonlight on the water is breathtaking.

She touches my arm. "Noah?"

"Why can't we just be a couple, Red?" I exclaim, and she sighs and looks at the ocean. "You just said I treated you better than any other guy you've been with."

"And I meant it," she interrupts, exhausted.

I grab her hands, stop us from walking. "Then why not just be an actual couple?"

"It's not that easy, Noah." She looks away to try and ignore my probing eyes. I try to lock my gaze on hers, but she just won't look at me.

"Yes, it is," I push.

"It isn't, though!" she snaps and yanks her hands away from me. They push into her hair, slipping off my beanie in the process. I watch with crinkled brows and a confused frown as she pushes the hat into her pocket and takes a step backward.

"I don't understand," I say earnestly. I need to

understand. I walk closer to her, and she moves to distance herself from me. But—goddamn it! I have had enough of the distance between us. So I close it and take her hands, and she finally looks into my eyes with a weary expression.

"Because good things don't...*last* in my life. Ever. When things get good, and I mean *really* good...I fuck up somehow. Or I mess it up myself because it just would never work. It never has before."

"You didn't know me before," I point out with a hopeful smile.

She shakes her head, hands loosening; I tighten, and she breathes out like I'm frustrating her, but her voice doesn't even raise when she speaks. "And I'm glad I didn't because I would have fucked you over even worse. But now...now I'm still hurting you. I am *going* to hurt you." She talks with finality that makes my heart flail desperately and wonder what happened to her that makes her resent commitment, relationships so much. Whoever or whatever made her this way, I want to punch it/whoever in the face.

"You will not hurt me." She sounds insane.

"But I will. I—I will hurt you, Noah. And you don't deserve it." She pulls and pulls, but I keep her hands stapled with mine. She grunts and leans back. But I pull her closer to me, bodies flushed, and remove a hand to push escaped tendrils behind her ear.

"You will *not* hurt me. I'm already in too deep. Whatever happens, I am sticking with you." I smile from ear to ear and crinkle my nose, cupping her face, smooshing it a little. "So get used to it. Get used to *me*. Okay?" I need her to say yes. I need her back.

She bites her lip and looks up at the sky, as if waiting for it to give her the correct answer, which is a definite yes. I stare at her taut lip ring and then her long, graceful neck. Without thinking, desperate to get her to see we're right for each other, I bend down and splash some ocean water on her legs. She shrieks and jumps back like two steps and glares at me, with anger and confusion and infatuation. I favor the latter.

"What the hell was that for?" she screams and stomps her foot. She looks like she pissed herself, the large wet spot on her upper thigh spreading through the dry parts.

"Would one of your lame old flames still be alive after doing that?" I inquire.

She points a finger at me. "*You* won't be alive much longer."

"Really?" I lean down again and splash her again. It lands on her band t-shirt, and she shrieks. "How about now?"

"You're fucking *dead*, prep!" she claims.

"I'm still breathing, Rossa." I grin.

Despite being pissed-mad, she races after me. Ducking and dodging her, I splash her from behind. Pretty sure I got her, I turn around and watch her gape at me, water splashed in her hair. Laughter bubbles out of my mouth, and I clap.

"Classic!"

"Your *funeral* will be classic! Come here!"

"I'd rather not—oh shit! Mercy!"

She runs after me with fury written all over her

face. Instead of praying for my life, I laugh and continue to back splash her. I feel icy cold water splash on my back, and I definitely feel her pain. But that doesn't stop me from retaliating. Splash after splash, we get each other soaked and are laughing like we're high on stolen laughing gas. People stop to stare, some smiling, some grimacing, none experiencing the pure joy I am.

Her laughter is contagious, and so is her smile, and her closed eyes are pure bliss. I kiss her several times before splashing her with a kick. Each time she draws in for a sucker kiss before I surprise her. I twirl her around and splash and splash, and she splashes back with twice the amount of ferocity.

I grab her waist and twirl her around, savoring her laughter and her resistance. I put her down and kick some sand at her. Her hands fly up to protect her face, but she's too slow and some gets on her jacket. Giving me I'm-going-to-murder-you eyes, I turn on my heels and she chases me around the empty beach. My legs burn and her screams are patchy as we run, but she doesn't ask to stop, nor do I.

We continue this playful chase and splashing and sand-throwing, until we grow exhausted and fall on our butts in the sand up near the patches of grass underneath the boardwalk. Our heavy breathing and the soft waves of the amused ocean fill my eardrums, and I can't stop smiling. My cheeks physically runs on fire, and so do my lungs.

I fall back and tuck my hands under my head. "I think it's safe to guess we can't ride back in your car like this?" I say and make one move, causing a squishing sound to ripple underneath my soaking pants. My toes are numb, and goosebumps cover my arms.

"Got that right." She drops her head on my chest. I like the pressure of her head against me. My body equalizes and feels complete. Finally, in my nineteen years of living, I'm complete. I close my eyes and rub her back gently.

"I think there are a few hotels around," I say in suggestion.

She takes a while to respond. "Okay."

I peek an eye open; she's biting her thumb, staring faraway. "We don't have to do anything. We can even get separate beds, *rooms*, if you want." I don't want to make her feel pressured or anything.

Her eyes gaze up at me through her lashes. "No, no—that's fine." She breaks into an easy-going smile. "That'd be perfect actually."

"Great," I said, relieved. "We could go now." I begin to push up, but she quickly presses me back down. "Red?"

"Just...not yet. Can we stay here for a bit longer?" she asks with wide eyes.

"Yeah, yeah—of course. I'd be happy to." I lay back down and continue to lazily draw patterns on her back. She relaxes into me and breathes heavily. I love this. Her. How easy it is for her to melt into me like I am her resting place, her home. What she probably doesn't know is she's my home too.

And then she's staring up at the stars.

And I'm staring at her.

Most people look to the sky for stars; I just have to look at her.

Chapter Forty-Six

When the wind gets too strong for us to stay any longer, we hike back to the top of the boardwalk, heading in the direction of the nearest hotel. It is about ten minutes away, but we walk fast enough to reach before we freeze into popsicles. People stare in shock and confusion, but I am too busy smiling at my Red to even notice much. And she knows I am staring because she nudges me a few times with red cheeks, embarrassed.

If she's embarrassed now, then just imagine if she could read my thoughts of painting her face with my kisses before worshipping her. Because she deserves to be looked at as a goddess, I think before I am embarrassed by myself, by how head over Converse I am for this girl.

The Crescent Hotel's interior is standard, not the fancy stature I've been used to most of my life. Actually, all of my life. You'd think being able to order all the room service a little kid desired and being alone to watch movies and bounce on the beds would curb my burning need for the love of

409

my parents, their attention. But no. Even then, I wasn't enough and didn't get their attention for more than two seconds. I was accustomed to hotels because of my father's frequent business affairs and conferences.

So why am I nervous to share a room with Red?

I wave the confusion question away as we reach the front desk. A young woman with platinum blonde hair and a perky attitude greets me.

She waves at us. "Hello, welcome to the Crescent Hotel!"

"Hello, Crystal." I read the name off her name tag.

Red's silently glaring at her.

"Anyway, can we get one room, a king? Or—or double?" I look over at Red and nudge her to get her attention. "Still sure about the one bed?"

She smiles softly as an emotion crosses her eyes. "Yes, very sure. Now book it and stop asking me if I'm sure."

"Okay, okay—put away the claws." I hand Crystal my card, and Red anxiously bites her lip. I take her hand and rub the back of it, drawing her eyes to mine. "Hey, you all right?" My voice is low so no one but us can hear. There's a couple with children behind us, and their look of disapproval of our soaked and sandy appearance is loud and clear. The kids hide behind their parents' legs.

"Nothing," she tries, but I give her a look, and she caves with a sigh. "You're just such a gentleman. Sometimes I think you're too sweet, like you're gonna go all Voldemort on me at some point."

I gasp theatrically and look around. "Shhh!"

"Why?"

"You're not supposed to say his name out loud or he'll appear," I whisper and hear one of the kids laugh. I wave at her before their mom pulls her behind her thigh. I wave at her too and chuckle when she blushes, causing her husband to glare at me.

"See? You even have bitchy moms falling for you," Red says with a pout.

"Don't worry, babe, no one can steal me away from your clutches." I wink at her, and she growls. I just chuckle and look at Crystal, who's trying to get my attention.

"Who is the room under?" she asks politely.

"Mr. and Mrs. Wells," I tell her, and she awws, murmuring "newlyweds" before typing in the computer.

"Noah," Red hisses under her breath.

"I know." I hold up a hand. "Just let me live in my fantasy bubble for a bit. Please." I sound pathetic, but I want so much more with this girl. I'm not upset she isn't jumping for more, but I want to bask in the *idea* of it. "Sorry," I say quickly, accepting our room key.

"No, I'm sorry," she says, head hanging as I walk us to the elevator. It's closing, but I quickly stick a foot out before it does. I slip inside and press the floor our room's on. Then I face her and cup her face, despite the few people in the car with us.

"Do not be sorry. I meant it when I said to take your time, think. I won't be going anywhere anytime soon," I tell her honestly. "I was stupid to play around like that. Don't mind me if I act too pushy. I'm not used to being told *no*."

Her eyes widen. "What? You're spoiled? I never saw that coming."

"Shut up." I lean down and kiss her, saying *screw it* to PDA. This girl makes me break rules from left to right. And I just need to kiss her lips. It's been a while, and she's my own personal dose of perfection. If I stick around her any longer, I'll overdose. But I. Just. Can't. Get. Enough.

"Get a room," a douche in a gray suit says behind us.

The elevator slows down. I plan on ignoring him, but Red has other plans.

"That's the plan; we're in a hotel, dumbass," Red snaps, lip snarling. "Come on, Noah. Let's go have rough, wild, passionate sex, while this *loser* jacks off to pay-per-view porn." She blows her tongue at him like a child before yanking me out of the elevator. His dropped jaw and the elderly couple snickering are the last things I see before the doors close.

"Wow, Red," I cough out.

"I didn't mean it; I just got pissed," she explains, hostility clear in her tone.

"I know." I raise my hands defensively.

We stop in front of our room, and I watch her in amusement. Call me weird, but I adore when she blows up. She looks like an adorable pepper bursting into flames, with rainbows dancing around her gleaming blue eyes.

"Stop with the staring, prep," she murmurs hastily.

I chuckle. "Okay." I raise my eyes, and she sighs. I laugh some more but attempt to calm her down by kissing the top of her hair. Sighing again, but more relaxed, she jams the key in the slot and pushes it open. The room is large enough, with the king bed in the center, two bay windows, and a study desk.

I follow her inside and instantly kick off my shoes. I desperately need a shower. She obviously wants the same, as she's down to her bra and panties by the time I slip off my t-shirt. My eyes travel down to her slim stomach and wide curvy hips, before she catches me, and I look away with heated cheeks.

"Mind if I go first?" she asks, thankfully not calling me out for checking her out.

"Um, no—course not. Go ahead." I gesture to the bathroom and turn around...to nothing. There's just a dresser and a mini fridge. I drop in front of the fridge to keep my eyes away from her. If I see her toned, tanned body...oh God, I'm already harder than a calculus test!

"Well, all right then." I hear the mockery in her voice, then the door shut.

Huffing out in relief, I raise to my feet. To pass the time as she showers, I sit on the floor to avoid getting the pristine sheets dirty and pull out my nearly dead phone. Damn. I wish I'd brought my charger. Maybe she has a portable one? Doubt it, but anyway, I check my messages while I still have some juice left.

In total, there are seven missed calls from both of my parents, a few check-in texts from Ty and Mike, and a worried voicemail from Rachel. It takes me about twenty minutes to get to them. I reply to them all, except for my parents. They can suck a raw egg. Rachel was nervous about Red suddenly showing "ugly colors," but I assure her that the date went extremely well and that I'm now staying in a hotel since we're both too beat to go back and just want to crash.

I'm really glad for tonight. I got to see more of Red's rocker chick façade, and I loved every second of it. I can still clearly picture her face during a song called "R U Mine?" How blissful she looked through another and pulled me into random dance sessions. My heart pumps to the energized rhythm it felt just hours before.

I'm smiling to myself and imagining her soft laughter when Alex made a funny joke between song changes, when his voice sounded more feminine, less British...*y*?

I open my eyes to find Red staring at me with an amused smile.

"Enjoying yourself, weirdo?" she says.

"Very much." I smile back and push to my feet. Call me crazy, but she seems stiff when I brush past her to enter the bathroom. I stop before entering and lean back to her weird expression. "You all right?"

"Yeah." Her voice is off, so she clears it and nods. "Yep. Everything's fine..." But she looks like someone's holding her hostage and is telling her to act normal.

Okay...

"Okay," I voice my thoughts, watch her, then enter the bathroom. That was weird, I think to myself as I drop my jeans and boxers.

A gust of chill from nowhere hits me, and I quickly get in the shower. Thank God, she left the hot water running. I think I half moan when I put my head under it and feel the water cascade down my muscular back. The water feels amazing, especially as I see clumps of sand swirl down the drain. I hope it doesn't clog anything. I feel guilty as I let the water run down my body and face for a few minutes. After a while, I finally use the non-scented shampoo and body wash.

When I finally feel like I got every particle of sand out of every crevice I didn't even know could hold sand, I step out with a towel around my waist. I stand in front of the foggy mirror and rub another towel over my hair. I do this for a few minutes before I feel mostly dry in both my hair and body. I step into my boxers that were thankfully saved from our playful encounter and throw open the door.

It's dark, and I feel a sense of déjà vu.

I don't even take one step out before Red materializes in front of me. She has this blank, sort of lusty stare, on her face, and I pause for a moment, worried.

"Red? Are you okay?" I don't even get to finish my sentence before her lips crash on mine. I sink into her soft lips and hook my arms around her. Our bodies grow flush, and I am painfully hard. *Fuck.* I pull back briefly and look into her darkened eyes. "What are you doing?"

"What do you think?" Her knee brushes my loosely tied towel. I hear the soft thud before I feel her hand around my aroused cock.

"Oh, Red," I hiss in her ear.

"I want you. Do you—do you still want—?"

I don't even let her finish that ridiculous question.

I smash my lips onto hers and moan as her small hand pumps me slowly. Teasingly. I have to be dreaming this, I think, as she moans my name. I grip her plump ass and bring her to me, skin on skin. Fuck, she dropped her towel. We're both naked. I am so close to coming, damn it! But that's what I get for not having sex in so long or anything remotely as intimate as *this*.

I want more. I need more. Or I will fucking explode.

Hooking an arm around her lower back with one arm, I raise her, and she moans like a wild beast. We pry apart for a hot second as she looks down as I walk us over to the bed. The desire spread across her face grows even more, if possible, and she's pumping harder. When we're close to the bed, I drop her on her back, me on top. She kisses my neck and doesn't stop as I roll over, letting her straddle me.

Oh. My. Fucking. *God*.

Her hand is so small yet capable of creating a storm of pleasure inside of my bones. It creaks and howls and I'm panting, gripping her hair. I nearly bust when she lowers her mouth on me, sucking. Hard. Kissing. Soft.

Oh fuck oh fuck oh fuck.

Her mouth is so gentle as she kisses up and down my long shaft. Tongue moist as it glides up and down, and around, and lays against my erratic, needy cock. I pump her head around me with my fist in her hair. And my head flings back as I feel an orgasm creeping up my toes.

"No. I need to feel you," I say and yank her head back. I realize I pulled too hard and begin to apologize, but she's grinning like a madwoman, pleased.

"But my lips—" she begins.

I tug her up to me by her hips. "Not those lips," I whisper haughtily. She's turning me mad for her. I couldn't have switched around and get in between her legs fast enough.

"Noah!" she cries out, back arching, as I kiss her soaking pussy.

I swirl my tongue around and enjoy her pleasant screaming. I kiss her like I would on New Year's Eve when the ball drops. I kiss her passionately and tenderly, and I add a little tongue. Then I'm cupping her thighs and burying my entire face in her. She screams so loud, I can only imagine how many complaints we'll get. But I don't give a single fuck.

"Please," she murmurs, voice shaky. "More."

And I know what she means.

I'm on the verge of coming myself, and I just started eating her out.

"Hold on. I want to make you come first."

"I will when you're fucking me too," she says breathlessly.

I just smirk and continue my slow, fiery pace. I kiss and lick and tug with my lips. I add two fingers and watch her react because it gets me even harder. It hurts by now, as I watch her thrash around, coming close to her release. I pick up the pace, curling my fingers and licking faster. And faster. And faster—

"Oh, Noah!" she screams as she releases on my tongue. I lap up her sweet juices that give me a sugar high. I smile against her and peck her. She giggles, and I crawl up quickly, getting in between her legs. I kiss her deeply when she pulls me to her lips.

This kiss now…this fucking kiss. We roll around and around and are laughing one second, serious the next.

"Wait a second." I jump off the bed and race into the bathroom. Adrenaline courses through me as I pull out a strip of condoms I bought a week ago in hopes of something like this happening. Good thing I thought ahead. I take one back to the bed and climb on top of her.

I roll us back to the middle, with the golden foil packet in my fingers. I tear it open using my teeth, then brush fallen hair back on my head. She watches with fascinated, wide eyes, and arches her back. Reaching for me. I genuinely smile at her nimble fingers in the air as I roll the condom onto me.

"Come on," she whines, and the sound is like heaven and hell. Heaven because it's like a choir, and hell because…just look at her. She's a little minx that knows how to tug at the strings of my heart and cock—she's got real talent. And the most beautiful face and body.

"Hold on." I splay my hands beside her body, letting my eyes get a taste of her. The moonlight crawls and rests on her creamy skin, hitting her stomach and breasts, lighting up her eyes like fireworks. I could suffocate in her effortless beauty for days without ever growing bored.

"You're so beautiful," I tell her as I lean down. I glance down to align myself with her. When I look back at her, she's smiling with her lips closed, a fond look in her dancing eyes.

"So are you, Noah. You are everything I could ever desire and want in the most innocent way possible." She cups my face and brings me closer. I nearly lose it when she kisses me slowly, passionately...lovingly. Then she slowly releases our lips and whispers, "Now please make love to me." Her voice breaks and I hear the purest need; it crackles beneath her eyelashes and crosses her flushed cheeks.

"I love you, Red. I love you, I love you, I love you," I whisper as I enter her in one swift go.

She breathes in sharply as if I stole all of her breaths but still manages to say, "I love you, Noah. So much it hurts."

Just hearing her say that feels better than being inside of her. But then I begin to move in her, and the confession of her loving me and her beauty and my movements collide, and I'm panting and feeling euphoria linger in my veins. The heavy mixture fills me up until I'm drowning in it, but I'm enjoying the slow burn of my lungs.

This girl. This damned girl means the world to me. Hell, she *is* my world. And I can't get enough of her. Everything about her makes my heart race, makes me soft, yet hard, and—and I can't even form a coherent thought. *God.*

She makes a throaty sound, and it drives me over the edge. And I'm falling, falling, falling…I don't see the bottom.

I kiss her deeply as I move in her in a steady pace. Her moans hit my ears as I repeatedly move in her, getting deeper, hitting sharper. At some point, I don't even hear her, but instead our heartbeats. Hers and mine the same. Both beating wildly and peacefully. Rocking against each other. Caressing each other. The feeling is a phenomenon that is overwhelming yet very comforting.

"Are you okay?" I ask her. My voice is barely audible behind my heavy breathing.

"Y-yes," she stammers, gripping my hair with both hands. "Oh *God*." Her head flings back into the pillow, and I smile and press tiny, dedicated kisses along her heated skin. I nip at it with my teeth, drag them along, eliciting a silent hiss and cry for more.

"Let me kiss you. *Please*," I say, and she nods frantically.

I plunge into her, and her mouth drops open. I kiss her open mouth, and she moans, almost like a growl. I take deep, wide plunges into her like I'm swimming—swimming in her. We don't part until we absolutely need to, and when we come back again, we're smiling and just teeth and touch and barely lips. I can feel her love for me in the way she's beaming up at me. And I can definitely feel my love for her as I gently caress her cheek. Her head moves to the side, and it's the simplest yet most beautiful thing yet.

She trusts me.

Full-fledged trusts me.

And my heart soars, and the pleasure is building.

I can feel it in my spine, the soles of my feet, my legs, my head, my *heart—everywhere.*

Her breathing is picking up, her nails digging into my arm. She's close.

"Noah, please—" she begins to moan.

I swallow her lusty moan with my mouth. I glide my tongue around hers, reach my hand in between us. "Come for me, Red." I lure her to her increasing pleasure, circling my thumb against her. I rub slowly, then faster—over and over until she's arching into me, panting for breath, for more, my name, nonsense.

"Oh fuck. Oh, *Noah*!"

I hit my pleasure as she grabs me tighter, latches a leg around me. I grunt through my teeth but continue my increased pace. I hold the back of her knee and kiss her heavy pants. I kiss her with everything I have, *give* her it all. I don't want it. I just want her, in my veins, my heart, my soul—I just freaking need this girl. So much. It hurts and I get slower and thrust harder faster, milking myself inside of her.

She screams my name, tears puddling in her eyes. I kiss them away gently, giving one last thrust, claiming her moan, before slowly withdrawing.

Neither of us move as we bask in what we just did—made love in its purest form.

Chapter Forty-Seven

A feather-light tickling sensation wakes me from my peaceful slumber.

I feel drowsy and dizzy when my heavy eyes bat open. Foggy circles of saturated golden light and a lamp are in my vision as I try to focus. I feel like I'm underwater until I yawn and things come into focus. One after another, everything falls in line, and I blink a few times.

Sniffling, I wiggle lazy toes and focus my groggy attention on the ceiling. It has a white popcorn detail that makes me smile for some reason. Which may have something to do with the lightness and elation I feel spreading through my idle bones.

Hearing a soft intake of breath, then feeling a warm exhale, I look to my right, then down. And my heart flutters like a cage of exotic butterflies. Red's puffy pink lips are smooshed into my side, a peaceful expression on her glowing face. I look further down at the crumpled white sheet covering us from the waist down, her leg thrown over my waist, feet intertwined.

I drop my head against the pillow with a joyous smile. A relieved breath escapes me as I think back on last night. Our perfect, sweet night. Her hot skin against mine. The sounds she made. Oh God. I could feel myself grow hard, but it's too early. We need to gather ourselves, calm down. Either that or I will combust. Last night was enough for a century. This one smile that curved her bruised lips from our passionate kisses makes my heart twist and lunge slowly, landing in a puddle of her contented sighs.

I've never *ever* experienced what I did last night with Red. And I don't think I ever will again, at least, not unless it's with her. It was just the feeling of being home in her arms, feeling like I hit the huge jackpot. I had my Red in my arms, under me, moaning my name, claiming she loved me—I had her yearning for me as I've yearned for her. The sensations were almost too much to understand. Too much to handle.

I am growing a headache, the kind that brings up memory after memory, filling me from my toes to the top of my head. I rub my forehead and yawn some more. I let my palm meet her back. So soft. I smile to myself as I rub her skin. I lean over and kiss her shoulder blade. I kiss her tenderly and gently and pull back and stare at her breathing softly against my skin.

This feels perfect.

I almost move to grab my phone to take a picture, when she stirs slightly. I stop rubbing her back, not wanting to help wake her up. I'll let her sleep on me forever if she asks me. She deserves her sleep, anyhow. But she stirs some more, and I brace for her to awaken.

A gush of warm breath fans against my stomach and her eyelashes flap softly. I smile and rub her back some more, gently luring her into the morning.

"Good morning, love," I say with a smile.

She grumbles and lifts her head. I can't help but chuckle at her scrunched-up face, sleep marks on her cheek. She begins to say something more, but a loud yawn cuts her off. I watch her in amusement before she calms down and is staring up at me with a sedated smile.

"Good morning," she rasps.

This is what I'd love to wake up to in the mornings, I realize, as she yawns, eyelashes fluttering, blonde hair wild and everywhere. I wonder what it'd be like if we lived together…no. I put up a roadblock and create a room made of concrete around it. We haven't known each other for *that* long. Usually, couples of a year or more move in together, not two people who don't even have a label. It'd just be insane, right? Right…?

"It's eight in the morning. What could possibly be going through your head?" She squints at the sun peeking through the sheer curtains that are blowing in the slight mid-November wind. Then, her inquisitive gaze rolls back onto me.

I'm sort of at a loss for words; do I admit to thinking about getting a place with her, risk her running away from me and blocking me indefinitely, or lie and avoid all of that? We had sex just last night, and she means a lot to me, but she's also very hesitant to commit. We're already testing *us* out, so proposing moving in together would surely push her over the edge.

I don't want that. I just want her.

So, pushing the thought behind closed doors, I smile and wave a hand. "Oh, just thinking about the game tonight. It's the last one of the season, and I'm kind of nervous."

"Nervous? But you're the football *god*," she exclaims, wide eyes and everything. "Or at least, that's what all the bimbos around campus are saying. You get checked out at least ten times a day, and you don't even notice. I'm surprised they haven't built a statue for you yet."

Blushing, I cover my face with a pillow. "I am not worthy of a *statue*. I'm not even that good, and there are other players on the team, you know." My voice is muffled, but I hear her laughter loud and clear. I peek over the edge and find her beaming at me in amusement.

"I know, but none of them are as adorable as you," she teases, but she sounds closer than before. When I tip the pillow down, she lunges at me and roars in laughter. I join her and am amazed by how light she seems, how bubbly she is. It's almost as if our night last night opened up light that was dying to burst out from inside of her, and I'm relishing in her light, basking in it, and coaxing it with open arms.

She settles down and lays her head against my chest, arms wrapped around me. Her hair tickles me immensely, but it sort of feels nice, reminds me that she's snuggled into me, and comfortable. I am comfortable. I have never felt so at ease, it's insane.

What's really ridiculous is how much I have fallen for this girl in such little time. I almost have the urge to pinch myself, see if I'm dreaming or not.

"What did you think when you first saw me?" she asks, and it's so out of the blue, I'm too stunned to do anything but blink. And when I look down at her, she's staring out the window.

"Well, I thought you were beautiful."

She looks up, confused. "Shut the fuck up."

"I'm not kidding," I say, laughing. "And I was a bit intimidated, not gonna lie. But also intrigued. By a girl that insulted me. Twice. When we first met." She was, admittedly, not my type at all, in my past life, anyway. But when I saw her, something crushed a little, and I found myself genuinely drawn to her, like polar ends of two magnets, and when we connected, an unexpected explosion ensued.

Her scrunches up guiltily. "Oh. I was a bitch, wasn't I?"

"Yeah, but it's okay. It's who you are and I mean this in no disrespect," I say, and she slaps my stomach with a mock-offended gasp. "But at least you're constant. No one likes a flip-flopper. And I've actually come to adore the snappy, will-punch-you-in-the-throat-now Red."

"Seriously?" she scoffs and sounds incredibly thrown off. But she shouldn't. If she thinks she's so horrible and I'm apparently "too good" for her, then why does she think I stick around? It isn't just because of the physical things, it's because I genuinely care for her. In the most innocent meaning of the word possible. I'd rather be able to talk with her than just be able to engage in the

426

sexual things with her. The sex is a plus, but being with her is the real jackpot.

"Yes, *seriously*." I take one of her small hands, grinning. "Believe it or not, you're actually fun to be around. Especially when you snap, like last night with that douche in the elevator." I rest her hand on my heart, and she laughs. "*Ugh*. Totally melted."

"Stop lying," she whines, covering her face with her hands.

"I'm not, though," I promise, and she finally removes them, tipping her head back to stare up at me. My breathing hitches, heart stammering in my chest, as last night's events replay in my mind. Her hands are on my shoulder, scratching my back. Her head is tilted back, back lifted off the bed. I feel her hips rolling against mine as I thrust into her gently, picking up the pace slightly.

"Thinking about last night?" she asks, reading my mind. I nod slowly, unable to form words. I'm still caught up on the sounds she made. Her eyes cloud and she bites her lip, and I momentarily lose my mind, imagining my own teeth tugging on her lip ring.

"Last night was…" I let out a huff, and she chuckles, nodding.

"Yeah. Wow." Her back presses onto my chest, eyes staring at my mouth. Her hand reaches up and I hold in a hungry growl as she lightly pinches my lower lip. "Kind of makes me want to go again. You were kind of an animal."

My hunger diminishes, and I grab her wrist gently. "I didn't hurt you or anything, did I?" I remember I was a little rough at one point. I was just so caught up in *everything* that my mind got sort of clouded with lust and my love for her.

"What?" She laughs but stops when I don't join her. She scrambles up, holding the thin bedsheet against her chest. "Oh, Noah. Sweet, sweet, Noah," she croons and reaches over to cup my cheek. "You are the best thing to ever inhabit this messed-up planet. I sort of want to bottle you up and ship you off to Mars," she jokes with a lazy smile, thumb rolling over my cheek.

I cover her hand with mine, brows furrowed. "Red, was last night, you know...okay for you?" I feel embarrassed. This is the first time I've acted so shy, asked a girl if she enjoyed us having sex. I never had to ask because they were making breakfast the next morning, proposing more in the shower. But with Red, it's different, because I can't tell what she's thinking sometimes, like now, unfortunately.

"Are you kidding me?" she says, and I look into her eyes, hesitant of her wide smile. "Last night was amazing, and I'm not just saying that to stroke your ego or anything. I genuinely haven't experienced anything like that before. Makes me...kinda makes me wish *you'd* been my first time." My heart sparks at her honest words. And I am, again, at a loss for words.

"Mine sucked," I admit, but she doesn't look like she believes me. "Seriously. It was with this girl named Abby. And it was awkward and in the back of her dad's car. I was fifteen and a lot lankier and nerdier than I am now." She begins to laugh, and I continue. "I'm pretty sure I stuck it in her ass at one point. Communication was *lacking.*"

"Okay, okay—stop." She waves her hands around. "Mine wasn't any better. It was in the bathroom of this warehouse. The band sucked ass, and so did he." I grimace and she chuckles, dismissively waving her hands again. "Not in the literal sense. *Weirdo.* No, um, it lasted about five seconds before he left me for some skank. Worst sex of my life."

"But I'm the best, right?" I tease, totally kidding because who could be that conceited? And she thankfully gets my humor and shakes her head. "What?" I mock gasp and grab her waist, yanking her on top of me. Her arms flail against me as I press kisses against her warm skin. I love her laugh, so I keep doing it despite her protests.

"Noah!" she squeals in a high-pitched voice, hands flapping with my grip around her waist. I smile and kiss her cheek before leaning against the headboard. She sighs and falls on my chest as if she is sedated.

A comfortable silence falls around us, and I kiss the top of her hair. Rub her back. Close my eyes in bliss.

"June 15th, 2009," I say in a bare whisper.

"Hmmm?" She cocks her head up with a puzzled expression.

I smile softly and repeat the date. "My grandpa's birthday. My parents and I went over to this cute little college he and my grandma visit on holidays. My aunts and uncles didn't produce many children, so there was really only me as the little kid around grown people.

"Anyway, he walked over to me when I was just standing beside my parents talking to this couple they knew who were passing through the town, bored out of my mind, when he led me into his study." I pause and gulp thickly, letting the memory bleed into my mind, creating a crystal-clear image.

"He showed me this easel that had a blank canvas on it. He told me he loved to paint when he was younger and even showed me a few paintings. Each were incredible and unique in its own way. I remember my heart leaping and wishing I could do the same. When he heard that, his eyes lit up, and he told me it was mine.

"I was shocked because, usually, people get gifts on their birthday, not give them. But I accepted it and thanked him with each shitty painting I made. I grew obsessed, staying up late, researching the greats and painting until my parents physically couldn't separate my brush from my hand."

I smile softly at the memory of my parents haggling over my new obsession. They'd promised Xboxes and toy cars and even a dirt bike even though I was only ten, but nothing they said or did could mess with my newfound passion. Even now in present time. They can push me into colleges and lock away my funds, but they can't shake my love for art.

"Hmmm," she hums again.

"Last night was the best night of my life, and that time was the best *day* of my life. Now I sort of feel balanced, you know. Complete." I wrap my arms around her to bring her closer, but she pulls away, sitting up. Her face has fallen and is harder than a few seconds ago. I reach for her hand, but she looks away. "Hey. Whoa. Are you all right?"

"Yeah, yeah—I'm fine," she lies, giving me a fake smile.

"You don't have to lie to me," I tell her, reaching for her hand again. But again, she pulls away. My heart falls a little, and I frown. "Did I say something wrong?" I quickly go over what I just said but come up with empty hands.

"No, you said nothing wrong. Everything you said was *perfect*." She pauses and grumbles something under her breath. "But I have to go."

"Go?" I question, taken aback.

"Yeah, I'm sorry." She jumps off the bed, and I watch her pull on her underwear.

"Can I ask why? I'm sorry, but I really feel like I did or said something wrong, and I'm sorry if I did." I move to stand up, but she pushes me back down and grins.

"You are in the clear, Noah." Something in her eyes makes her frown, and I hate the shiver that slips down my spine. "But I have to go." She turns around and yanks on her t-shirt, skipping putting on a bra. I feel dumb just watching her get dressed, but I don't want to press myself on her, force her to stop. I would feel even worse than I do now.

"But we were just talking." When I find the words, she's already fluffing her hair out from beneath her leather jacket and pecking my cheek.

"And we'll talk later. But right now..." She pauses, and I see the pure hesitance in her eyes. She even looks tortured for a second, but she covers it up with a soft smile and another soft peck. "I have

431

to go." I watch her jog over to the door and throw it open. She pauses. Over her shoulder, she says, "I'm sorry," before closing the door behind her.

And all I can do is blink and think to myself, *What the hell just happened?*

Chapter Forty-Eight

"She just left?" asks Mike.

Then, the ever brilliant Ty asks, "Did you feel like a cheap hooker?"

I just pause the game, dumbfounded, and rub my eyes. Regret seeps into my bones and makes me want to slap him. Ty, I mean. Mike has more of a leash on his words. But my roommate...the force is not so strong with him.

I just finished telling them what happened earlier. I briefly told them about Red and my...*activities* last night before revealing to them how she just up and left the next morning. And she left like she was in a rush to be somewhere else. What really sucks is that she didn't leave the moment we woke up. We were playful for a bit and just talking. Things were fine between us. Until I started talking about a moment in my life that meant the world, and she just suddenly had to leave.

I know I shouldn't have made assumptions, but what did you expect me to do after getting left, naked and confused in a hotel room? I started thinking the worst things, like her running off to Ian and/or Tanner. Both A-class assholes, but also her past fucks she admitted to seeing when we were starting out. Though she says she never slept with them, my overthinking mind jumped to a nasty image of her screwing them because maybe I wasn't as good as she said I was.

Maybe I'll never be the sleazy guy she seems to favor more than the nice guys. The disgusting thought sticks like gum unwilling to detach from the bottom of my shoe. Because I know that she loves me, that she never truly loved them. I heard it from her own lips last night, over and over as I made love to her, claimed her soul that intertwined with mine. Yet my freaking mind went there and attempted to downplay everything.

But I put a stop to it, because I know her well enough to know that she wouldn't do that. I begin to think of reasonable excuses. Maybe she forgot to turn off her stove in her apartment. She could have had an appointment she forgot about. Or maybe she agreed to meet up with friends to study for finals that await us after Thanksgiving break. All of them make enough sense, so I latch onto sense of reason and push away the other negative thoughts.

None sounds reasonable enough to justify the look of terror and sadness in her eyes, but they are enough to appease my over-imaginative mind.

"No, I did not feel like a cheap hooker," I gingerly answer Ty.

He shrugs and resumes the game, landing a cheap hit; we're playing Mortal Combat, and this loser keeps cheating. "Then maybe you felt like an *under-appreciated* hooker. You can always haggle prices. But what you cannot negotiate, my friend, is having your service genuinely valued."

"Shut up, fool." Mike throws a throw pillow at Ty's face, messing him up. For the few seconds he's bickering with our friend, I land a triple-combo on his ass. We all watch, Mike and me cackling, as my character whoops his character's ass.

"Oh, fuck you!" he yells as my character finishes him after the game's voice demands I do so. As I split his character in half, he mumbles, "Hooker."

I smack his head. "I'm not a hooker, idiot."

"I just think she had something to get to," Mike says with a shrug. Reaching over, he snatches Ty's remote. "Mind getting some chips from the kitchen, loser? Thanks. Means a lot," he teases, and I can't stop laughing, especially when Ty flips him off. He is such a grumpy, sore loser.

"Shouldn't you be laying off the carbs?" I ask as I'm scrolling over the characters, searching for the right one. "I mean, the game's in only a few hours."

"Don't matter," he says, patting my back with a grin. "We've got our national treasure right here. Mind staying grounded after you make the winning run to the end zone?"

"Stop that," I whine and try to hide my blush. I am not the only one on the team. So what if I helped assist many runs to the end zones, doing some myself? Being on a team means other guys have a hand in our wins, not me alone.

The bell rings, and Ty begrudgingly answers it.

He comes back with Rachel in tow, large papers wedged under her arms.

"Oh, hey, Rach," I say, distracted with beating up Mike's character. I dare a glance when he does whatever combo he wants; I'm saving mine till the end so I can finish him in one swift move.

"Hey, Noah! Mike, Ty." She smiles at them warmly, plopping into one of the armchairs in front of the dark, leather L-shaped couch.

"What do you have there?" I nod to the bright pink paper, then the green one under her other arm.

"Your posters," she says, absolutely beaming.

My brows furrow. "Posters?"

"Okay, I caved. I got the stupid chips." Ty sighs before shoving a handful of potato chips in his mouth. As he and Mike pass the bag back and forth, I focus on Rachel.

"Yeah. I thought, since tonight's game was the last of the season, I'd support you. Not that I haven't before," she begins to ramble. "I've been there for you for every game. More so instead of my brother, which is kind of messed up, but you get it. He's an ass most of the time." Her nose curls as she waves a disgusted hand. "Who cares 'bout him, right?"

"The point, Rachel?" I chuckle and lean back in the chair, returning my gaze to the TV.

"Right. They just have your name and jersey number on them. A few dabs of sparkle, but they're nothing serious." She rolls them both out, and I more than glance at her. The posters are actually sick and kind of cute.

"They're great, Rach! Thank you! You really didn't have to," I tell her.

She opens her mouth, but Mike's loud screaming

cuts her off.

"Oh, fuck yeah! Take that! Swallow it! Eat. My. Sword!" Mike shouts and dances all around the room as his character chops my head clean off.

Rachel gags. Ty rolls his eyes. And I just smile. He's sort of adorable when he wins at video games, which is all the time. I swear it gets him more pumped than winning a game.

Smirking, Ty says, "Hooker feels defeated once again."

"What?" Rachel frowns.

"Fuck you." I flip him off.

***

Hours later, it's game time, and I am more than prepared. I do a few pushups and jumping jacks in the locker room to get myself hyped up like the rest of the team. As I thought, the last game of the season is a big deal. We have a clean winning streak and we cannot afford to break it when it's our last game. All of us promise to give it our best shots, all we have.

"Ready for this?" Mike asks me as we're jogging up to the mouth of the tunnel that opens to the field.

I can see flares of white light and hear the screams from about fifteen feet away.

My heart thunders, but I give him a smile and a nod. "Hell yeah I'm ready for this!"

"There we go, newbie! Let's go get 'em!" He pumps his fist and we bump around in excitement and adrenaline, blending into the masses.

We break through and are running through a

banner. A horn blasts through the air, then trumpets, and soon enough, the school's band is playing and marching after we pass. Cheerleaders are running about, shouting and flipping and trying to hype up the crowd even more, when they're already pretty pumped, shaking the stands with their stomping and cheering.

I feel a thin thread of anxiety as we go over the plays one last time. I would feel a lot better if Red was here. I don't think she's been to any of my games. Well, there was *one*, but it ended ten minutes into it because a team player on the visiting school broke their leg. *Badly.* After that, I never saw her at any of my nine other games. I felt stupid looking for her in the stands, but I tried not to think about her and focus on the games.

But now, now is when I really need her.

"Did you hear that, Wells?" Coach barks, and I nod frantically. "Well, then why the hell are y'all looking at me? Get out there and win this shit!"

"Yes, Coach!" we all say before taking our places on the field.

"Don't screw up," Ian seethes as he brushes past me. I begin to storm over to him, but one glance at a glaring Coach tells me it's not worth it. So I ignore him, clench my teeth, and get in position.

To calm my raging nerves, I dare a glance into the crowd. There are hundreds of people wearing the school hoodies and shirts and even have paint on their faces. The commitment of the paint makes me smile. And it grows when I spot a pink poster with glitter.

Rachel.

She's so far away, but I swear I see her grin. And I do clearly see her waving at me frantically. She's even jumps up and down, stumbles, but rights herself and continues to wave at me. I chuckle and wave at her briefly before facing the other players.

A whistle is blown, and the game kicks off. Each pass is exhausting as I run it and tackle players who stand in my way. Our score starts off crawling close behind them, angering a naturally pissed-off Coach, but as we exchange glances and make gestures, we play tighter and faster. Tackle harder. Run widely, narrowly—any way that gets us to that damn end zone.

Thirty minutes pass, and I am an exhausted mess, but I keep my head in the game. This is one of the last plays before halftime. Thank *God*. That is if there aren't any more time outs.

Players numbers are called out, and I watch Ty signal behind his back. I nod to him and then to Mike, who winks at me before tossing the ball in the air. Ty tackles a guy coming to me, and I grab the ball as he pins him down. I weave through grubby players on the offense. My heart is pounding like crazy, so hard I can feel it drumming in my ears. I dodge a pair coming for me, do a last second turn, and take off as they collide into one another.

My legs are burning as I continue to do the same as I pass everyone. Causing them to trip or miscalculate their steps. I hold back my grin. I have to make it to the end or I'll look like a fool.

One…

Dodge.

Two…

Jump!

Three…

Run faster.

And… "Touchdown!" the man in the overhead observatory declares into his mic.

The entire stands go wild, and I do a little dance. Mike pulls me out of the end before I can embarrass myself, and I laugh and run over to the sideline. We have a little time to cool off and recuperate before the game resumes.

"That was so awesome, Noah!" Rachel shouts as she peers over the gate. There's about a three feet high difference between us, but her smile is apparent in the bright lights.

"Thanks, Rach. You and your signs gave me motivation," I tease, and she blushes.

"Oh, shut up." She waves a hand. "But seriously. The way you made 'em all trip and fall was hilarious. A little sad and mean, but funny nonetheless!"

"Thank you, I guess." I laugh, and she joins. We talk about how everyone else is doing and how we're ahead by a few points. I'm telling her how confident I feel about this game when I feel my skin tighten. My chest feels warmer, and I have cotton mouth.

Something's wrong.

I look around expectantly and freeze when I spot Red. She's sitting up in the stands, her eyes flitting around aimlessly, almost doe-like, *innocent*, when they find mine. She looks shocked as if I'm not the reason she's most likely here, and I chuckle. I wave her over. I feel less inquisitive than I did earlier;

now I'm just happy to see her here.

"Hey, what's up?" I say to her.

"Nothing?" She sounds unsure, and I chuckle, which makes her even more confused. "Mind if we talk?" she asks.

"Not at all." Then I remember Rachel's standing there. I am such a piece of shit. I turn to her and catch her wandering eyes, noticing how annoyed she looks. "Hey, can we talk later?"

Her eyes brighten again, and she smiles, nodding. "Of course." She rushes back up the stairs.

Red squats, her face close to mine. "I'm sorry for skipping out on you. I didn't mean anything by it; I swear it. I love you," she says in one quick breath. And as she pants, I wonder why she's acting so weird.

"It's all right, Red. You don't have to tell me, whatever it was," I assure her. As long as she's apologetic and not here with Tanner. I don't even do a quick sweep to where she was sitting because I trust her, I decide. Truly and honestly. "And I love you."

Her cheeks bloom, and she looks down, like she's embarrassed. "I saw some of the game. I just came because I had a...a thing. I'm sorry. But, um, yeah. You're doing great. I'm *p-proud.*" Her voice breaks, and I find it the cutest thing.

I lean forward and press my lips to hers. People notice and whistle, clapping. I ignore them and get lost in the softness of her lips. I'm not usually into PDA, but I couldn't *not* kiss her. A stuttering Red who blushes is my kryptonite. She tastes like Pepsi and licorice; she must be enjoying the concession stand.

"You taste delicious," I murmur as I pull away slightly.

She smiles at me and pecks me again. "And you taste like sweat."

"Do I?" I touch my sweaty cheek before tapping hers.

She peels away slightly, squealing, "Noah!"

I'm laughing at her adorable reaction when I hear a *very* loud and unappreciative voice. I look past her and stare up into the eyes of my parents. It takes a *very* long while to process this. What the hell are they even doing here? And why do they look so pissed?

"Noah? What are you doing?" my mother barks, clutching her expensive purse with a venomous expression.

I roll my eyes, and Red looks over her shoulder with raised brows. "Guys, this is my…" I pause, and Red looks back at me. I watch her for a few seconds. Her face softens, cheeks reddening. *Go ahead, say it,* her expression says. Grinning from ear to ear, I say, "This is Red Sylvetti, my girlfriend. Red, these are my wonderful parents, Richard and—"

"Are you Noah Wells?" someone asks. I look to my left. A tall older guy wearing glasses and a trench coat over a dark suit is staring at me tentatively.

"Um, yes." I raise a brow. "Who are you?"

"Now hold up now, I told y'all to—" Coach is screaming at a woman in a dark trench coat, with dark pin-straight hair, holding up what seems to be a badge.

"Sir, this is a serious situation—" she begins in a monotone voice.

"I'm gonna need you to turn around with your hands behind your back," the man instructs in a firm tone.

What? "What?"

"Excuse me, what is going on, sir?" I hear my mother demand above me.

"Noah..." Red trails off. I see the fear in her eyes.

"Do not say a damn thing, Noah! Fuck the pigs!" Ty begins to chant as the man walks over to me.

"Noah Wells—" he says, taking my hands and pushing me against the wall. The crowd grows silent and buzzes with hushed whispers as he loudly says the next part, "You are under arrest for the possession of crack cocaine. Anything you say can and will be used you—"

"Don't say anything, Noah! You hear me? Nothing!" I hear my father yell as I feel metal clamp around my wrist. I freeze, unable to say anything without my heart falling out my mouth.

"—There is a game going on!" Coach continues to badger the woman.

"Noah," Red says again, tears in her eyes.

"It's okay." He pulls me off the wall, ranting a speech about my rights. "I'm fine. Just...just you and my parents. Follow me to the precinct."

Before he pulls me in the direction of the exit, his partner behind him, I think I see her mouth form an, "I love you," before I am forced to face forward, under the humiliating stares of the entire school.

Chapter Forty-Nine

I can see my parents through the thin window in the door. My mother is screaming at a police officer who's just doing his job, standing by, my father silent behind her. Her dark hair and dark brown eyes are blurs as she shakes with a fury so strong, I can feel the heat and I'm far away. My father lets her be angry without exhausting himself as well. One of them has to have a cool head or I'll never be released…which doesn't seem likely with the charges I'm being faced with.

Apparently the cops were tipped off that I possessed and had the intention of selling crack cocaine, which can easily land me in prison fifteen years or more. The weight of the time I could get in prison for something I didn't even do pulls an inhuman sound out of me.

I can't go down for this. The drugs they found in my locker aren't mine. I don't even know where to get the drugs, forget about knowing where and who to sell them to. And why the hell *would* I? I don't need the cash. I'm not a freaking *drug dealer*.

I rack my mind for who could have possibly set me up for something as serious as this. Two guys pop up in my head, and I literally inwardly thank the officer who handcuffed my hands to this metal table. Either of those two—or both!—had to have planted the drugs there. They both dislike me enough to do it. For what reason, I have no idea.

To get back at me for stealing their girl? Because Red stopped showing interest in them and paid more attention to me...loves me? That's the only reason one of those stooges would do this. Other than them, no one else comes to mind. No one capable of getting hardcore drugs like crack cocaine, which is on the official list of one of the most dangerous drugs *ever*.

I'm planning their slow, torturous deaths when the door flies open. My mother eyes the guard in the corner, and he leaves silently. That's how intense and intimidating my mother is. She's a dragon that can unleash hellfire without even having to open her mouth sometimes.

"How could you do this to me, Noah?" she spits, and I seriously question her mental state.

"Excuse me? I think I heard you wrong," I say, and she rolls her brown eyes.

"You heard me correctly," she assures me, baring her pearly white teeth. "You know how immaculate your father's and my reputations are. And yet you pull this crap. Do you hate us so much for wanting you to have more than some silly passion for making stick figures that you'd do *this*? Stoop so far as selling *drugs*?"

I am truly at a loss for words. On the one hand,

what the fuck? How can she possibly think I'd get caught up in drugs? *Selling* them? I mean, what the actual *fuck*? And on the other hand, I totally saw this coming. She and my father are unhealthily obsessed with their reputations, my mother especially. So of course she would jump to me ruining how *she* would look rather than worry about her son in *handcuffs*.

"Wow, Mother. My wrists totally aren't on fire and sore from these *handcuffs*." I yank at them to prove my point. They sling right back to the table, feeling even tighter. These are so uncomfortable; I've never been in cuffs before.

She just rolls her eyes, huffing. "You wouldn't be in them at all if you hadn't done what you did."

"I didn't do anything!"

"Then what were the drugs doing in your locker?"

"Someone must have planted them there," I tell her, and she shakes her head. "Mother, I am serious. I would never do something like that. And keeping it in my locker? How stupid would I be?" I pause and look around for a camera, holding my fingers up. "Not that I'm confessing or anything. I had nothing to do with this!"

"Stop it, Noah!" she snaps. "You're lucky I have connections here. There will be no charges since this is your first offense. Luckily, there won't be any of this on your record." She pauses, and I can feel the disappointment without her saying—"I am very disappointed in you, Noah."

Spoke too soon.

"I know. I am too. For hoping you would believe

me," I say.

Her dark brows furrow, and she looks like she's about to say something but pushes back in her seat, waving the words away. "An officer will be by to unlock you. Don't move."

"Ha-ha, you're very funny, Mother." I dryly laugh as I watch her leave the room. A heavy sigh leaves my lips, and I have the urge to run a hand over my hair, but I am wickedly reminded of the handcuffs when I move my hands. They drag back to the table, and I let out a laugh. Not because this is funny—this is the least funny thing ever—but because of how quickly I ended up here.

Just a few hours ago I was playing football. I was the all-American college student. I was playing with two of my best friends, another in the stands cheering me on. Then I was kissing my girlfriend, who I'd made sweet love to the night before. And a second later, I had handcuffs slapped around my wrists and hauled off to jail for supposedly selling crack cocaine.

I think I deserve a scratch-record moment right about now.

A few moments later, a husky officer walks in. I avoid my parents' disappointed gazes as he works to unlock me. The second my hands are free, I stand and rub my sore wrists. They have red rings lapped around them, but I feel much lighter. I'll feel feather-light when I step foot outside of this freaking jail. Just sitting in that interrogation room, breathing air of past criminals, made me genuinely uncomfortable. I felt like I would jump out of my skin.

"I think we all know why you ended up here," Mother sneers when I step out of the interrogation room.

"And why is that?" I ask sarcastically, rubbing my wrist.

"That delinquent you were kissing when we showed up," she claims.

I look at her. "You can't be serious." She doesn't even know Red. How can she pin something this serious on her?

"Oh, but I am. She was dressed all…all…Richard, you know." She looks to my father for assistance, and I give him a look. He doesn't know her any better than my mother does. Neither of them has the right to blame Red.

"No, Richard does *not* know; neither of you *know* anything!" I snap.

"Hey, son—" my father says.

"Don't *son* me when you're blaming my girlfriend for putting me in jail!"

"No one is saying that—" he starts, but of course Mother cuts him off.

"We are most *definitely* saying that." Mother is glaring at me like I tried to poison her cup of tea.

I laugh incredulously. "You don't even know a thing about her, yet you're accusing her of landing me in jail. Newsflash, not everyone is who you think they are. You can't *judge* a person just by looking at them. That isn't fair or rational."

"Oh, we could see how bad she is for you. You stay away from her, Noah," she demands, and I seriously wonder if she heard a single thing I just said.

448

"You don't know her!" I cry.

"I don't need to!" she snaps and stomps on her right high heel. Her brown eyes are melted with rage, and I search for the mother who used to put Band-Aids on my scraped knees when I played too roughly with the other kids in the neighborhood. But all that stares back at me is a changed woman— a scorned woman who has no heart. Not for me, at least. And my anger fades into a tired sadness.

"She is a sweet girl, Mother. She's funny, and clever, and sassy, and beautiful, and…and I love her. I really do."

She stumbles back like she's been shot. "Then you're an even bigger fool than I thought."

"Mother," I whisper. She didn't just say that.

I look to my father, but he hangs his head and follows her out of the jail. I stay put and shake her words away. I've lost the warm mother I loved a long time ago. So why do I keep searching for her in those cold, brown eyes…?

"We will talk later," my mother hisses when we're exiting the jail. It's night time now, and the air is cold against my bare arms. Thankfully, I got to change into jeans and a t-shirt provided by my lovely father. Unluckily, he didn't have a spare jacket or coat.

"There's no need to, because I didn't do it—" I begin, but my father holds up a hand.

"Later, Noah." He gives me a pleading look.

I just roll my eyes and shut my mouth. There's no use talking because they choose not to listen to me, my mother especially. She's one of those people that, once they have their mind set, there's

449

no changing it.

I pull my phone out of my pocket and begin to text Red when I hear a car's horn. I look up from my phone and smile at Red peeking out of her car's passenger window. I jog over and slip inside.

"I would have waited inside, but your parents don't like m—" she starts to explain, but I don't need that right now. I need to hold her in my arms.

I lean over the console and wrap my arms around her. I pull her as close as we can get. She's tense for a long while until her body tells her to just let go, relax in my tight embrace. My body feels energized as I rub her lower back and inhale her scent that just smells like home to me.

"You're not mad at me?" she asks, and I pull back to see if she's serious. Her mouth is set in a firm line, and her brows are frowning dramatically. Oh, she is serious.

"Of course not. My mother hates you. I would stay away too," I joke but instantly regret it when her gaze falls to the ground. I grab her hands and tug; she looks up hesitantly, chewing on her bottom lip. "But it's nothing personal. She's just a very judgmental person. She'll warm up to you. My father too. I promise."

Fear passes through her eyes. "I don't think I can meet your parents. Ever."

"Why not?" I rub her knuckles gently.

"Because…" She stops herself, swallows, and pulls her hands away. I watch with a frown as she pushes the gear to drive and pulls out of the parking lot. "Because I'm not a very good person. They're right to not like me."

"Don't say that." I scoot over to her. What is wrong with her?

"But it's true." She bites her lip.

I hate my mother and my father, who doesn't seem to have a backbone around her. I hate how easily her words can mess with you. The moment she saw me happy with Red, she didn't like it or her. Just because of the way she looks, which is the dumbest thing I've ever heard in my life. A person's appearance does not value who they are as a person.

A few minutes pass uncomfortably. I want to turn on the radio, but I feel glued to my seat. And I need the silence to remind her that I'm still present and not going anywhere until she speaks to me.

Wanting to lighten the mood, I smile and ask, "So what are you doing for Thanksgiving?" When she doesn't respond, I ignore the uneasy feeling in the pit of my stomach and continue. "I was thinking we could go somewhere. Like, maybe London? Or anywhere you have in mind?"

She just tugs on her lip ring. Her hands are tight around the thin, large wheel. I don't like how tense her position is, how wracked with nerves she looks. Maybe she doesn't want to do anything with me. It's a family holiday. She probably has plans to spend it with her family. As much as she loves me, I don't think she'd give up time with her grandpa.

"We don't have to travel; I'm sorry for bringing it up." We're near my house. I feel silly for even bringing it up. I just wanted to make things better.

"No, it's okay. I would love to travel with you, Noah." She parks in front of the house and stares at the car ahead. Her skin is pale, and she's blinking

451

rapidly, then not at all.

My heart sinks, and I scoot over to her. "What is wrong with you, Red? Please tell me so I can make it better." I reach under her chin and bring her head to the side to look into my eyes. Hers are wide, and I think I see tears in them.

"Hey, don't cry. I'm sorry about my fucked-up parents and that I was arrested. If you think I'm some undercover thug, I'm not. Just an unlucky asshole who has a target on his back. Please. Don't cry." I thumb away the tears underneath her large eyes.

"I'm sorry, I was just…" Her voice wavers as she sniffles. She wipes a hand across her eyes and offers me a small smile that does nothing to soothe the worry I feel in my veins. "I just love you so much, Noah. More than I ever thought I could."

I beam. "I love you too, Red." I lean down to hug her before I head inside, when she leans up and smashes our lips together. I'm momentarily shocked because I usually initiate the kisses unless we're in motels or hotels. But I'm not complaining.

I kiss her with the same ferocity she does me. I cup her face and she holds my shoulders. Our mouths part and I feel her hum contentedly. I rub her back and bring her closer. I savor her strawberry-flavored Chapstick and cigarette-soaked tongue. I move to pull her on me when she pulls away quickly.

But before she can turn to the wheel, she stares deeply into my eyes and whispers against my bruised, parted lips, "I love you."

I smile and peck her puffy lips. "I love you too."

We kiss one last time, but this one is simpler. I give her one last concerned look over my shoulder but get out when she gives me a simple nod. I get out and glance at her. Something sad flashes in her eyes, and I move to console her again when she pulls off into the road. I stand back, still for a few moments, and watch her turn the corner.

Well, that was nice.

My fingertips are cold against my lips as I walk up to the house. Inside, it's dark and empty. Everyone is out partying at another fraternity, celebrating our win. They would have partied here, but I guess no one wanted to risk getting caught for smoking weed when one of their star players got arrested for selling crack cocaine. *Supposedly*, though. I swear I've never even seen the drug in my life.

Sighing, I jog up the stairs. I'm on the last step when I hear a creak in the floorboards. I stop and feel a pause in the air. That's strange…maybe someone stayed back. Jogging up the rest of the way, I call out, "Yo! Anyone here?"

I get no response.

Okay. Weird.

Deciding I'm hearing things, I flip out my phone and begin to text Rachel to see where she is so I can join when I feel a presence. My heart begins to beat, alerting me I am not alone. I turn around quickly, expecting to find someone. But there's no one there. I look around, craning my neck to squint in the dark. No one.

The hell…?

I turn around and see him before my brain can

453

function. There's a tall guy wearing all black trying to blend into the dark, but his clothes are a tad lighter than the darkness.

"Hey! What are you—?" I begin.

Something sharp crashes into my head before I can finish my sentence, and I collapse to the ground. I gasp for air as my vision swirls, and the person in the dark bends over me, staring into my eyes. His eyes are a...a color...I can't even...I think...

And then, nothing.

Chapter Fifty

Sharpness. Cold. Black.

Those are the first things that pop into my brain like popcorn as I become conscious. Or at least I think I am. Either that or I am sitting in a pitch-black room of nothing and am able to think like I'm awake. Oh, fuck. I just gave myself the sickest headache. I scrunch up my face as if doing so will relieve the aching pain in my head, but I don't think anything's happening.

I hear a sharp beeping, and it clashes in my head like cymbals. I try to groan, but I don't hear anything. I do smell flutters of chlorine and medicine waft into my nose. I try to wave it away, but instead of feeling which seems to be the annoying trend of the night or day, I feel the drum of fingers against my thighs. I attempt to do it again, but I feel nothing. I make another piercing grunt, and hear more beeping, and then a little drumming.

"I think…up…doctor…" I hear through an ocean of questions, muffled in one ear and too bright in another. I hear more whispers, an intercom, and sniffling.

"Son...me?" I don't quite catch the sentence, if there's even one.

I tense up in anxiety when I feel a hand squeeze my hand. I know it's my mother before she even calls my name in a shaky voice. I freeze up again, but not because I'm nervous, because she sounds like the mother I knew so long ago.

A vivid memory plays in my mind: It's Fourth of July and my parents have thrown a barbecue in the backyard. My very best friend Liv Westerfield is running away from me, her blue eyes wide, my wicked smile huge. I'm chasing her with the booger on the tip of my index finger when I run into the legs of my mother. She scolds me to be nice to my future wife.

And while I attempt to figure out what the heck that foreign word means, I spot a girl my age with golden blonde hair and a black dress, unlike Liv's white one, standing in the corner, scowling at everyone who passes by. A boy a few years older dressed in all black stands beside her and, despite their hostile appearance, I find myself running to the girl.

The memory/dream-like scene fades before she could punch me in the heart.

And I feel it.

The sharp tug.

Something's wrong. Something is *definitely* wrong, and I need to wake up. Now.

I take a deep breath—or at least I think I do— and reach for the hand that's slowly trying to draw away from me. But I grab hold like it's an anchor and wait for it to pull me out of the foggy sea storm.

"He's waking up! Oh, call the doctor! Call a nurse! Just do *something*, Robert, for heaven's sake!" a voice commands, and I instantly know who it is.

"Mother?" I force my mouth to move, shape words.

My hand is gripped, and the beeping I heard earlier comes back full-force.

"Noah, darling," she sobs, "don't move a muscle, you hear me?"

"Geez, thanks for the advice," I say sarcastically, and I think I see her smile. But it could have been her signature grimace, as I am slowly opening my eyes. Large white dots and balls of blurs contort my vision until I blink rapidly and shake my aching head a little.

"…Just woke up," I hear my father say.

"Noah, my name is Dr. Howard," a male voice introduces himself.

"Um, hey." Doctor? Why am I in a doctor's office? Why are my parents here? Why is there an impossibly bright white light dangerously close to my eyeball?

I cringe as he waves the light back and forth, mumbling as he does. When I look to the side, I see a petite young woman jotting down whatever he says.

Finally, after a while of *that*, he pulls back. "How are you feeling today?" I briefly study his lab coat and graying hair and assessing blue eyes before thinking of an answer.

"Um." I steeple my fingertips together, then

glance at him. "Fine, I guess. But—" I close an eye and reach to touch my forehead, but instead of skin, I feel a weird texture. A bandage, I think? "My head hurts a bit."

"How would you rate your pain from one to ten?"

"Am I in a hospital?"

"Yes. Your pain," he reiterates, studying me.

I flick my gaze to my worried mother and father, then look back at him and shrug. "Seven, maybe six and a half. There's just this really dull pain in the back of my head."

"Yes. That's from the impact of the vase," he says casually.

Vase? "Vase?" I voice my thoughts, looking to my parents when he doesn't respond. My mother's worry simmers into a burning rage. "Vase?" I repeat like a broken record.

"It was that damned girl! That poisonous girl you call *Red*!" Mother cries.

"Red?" My head feels fuzzy, then my heart sinks and that strange bad feeling comes back full force. "What about...what did...huh?" I can't even think straight.

"Do you remember what happened to you, Noah?" Dr. Howard asks, squinting his eyes.

I silently shake my head, watching my father take my mother in his arms. I return my gaze to the doctor, trying my best to ignore the sinking feeling in my stomach.

He pauses, then goes on to say, "You walked in on a robbery at your house a few hours ago. The looters fled the home, but not before one smashed a

458

vase over your head in what the cops think was an attempt to stop your interference with the robbery."

I feel like I'm going to throw up.

"What…what did they steal?" And why don't I remember any of…*wait*. The memories all come screwing back in my head like a huge corkscrew trying to push its way into a too tiny bottle. I remember walking into the empty house and being upstairs. I saw a person in the dark, called out, then…nothing.

"Are you feeling any other pains anywhere else, son?" He makes a move to retrieve his flashlight and shines them in my eyes once again. I wince and he steps back, eyeing me studiously. "You were hit pretty hard and received a concussion."

No wonder I feel slow as hell.

"What did they steal?" I repeat groggily.

"The watch I got you for your seventeenth birthday," my father answers, a heavy emotion hanging under his green eyes. "And everything else you had in your safe."

"But…my safe is locked." I rub my eyes, hating this feeling of not being able to catch onto what anyone is saying. I feel sluggish, two tiny steps behind in a million mile races.

"Yes…but they seemed to get in with no problem," the doctor says.

"No, but you don't get it. No one knows the code. No one but me and…no one but…but me…" I trail off, and my head suddenly feels like it's walking on a road of lava. "No one but…" The phrase is latched onto the tip of my tongue.

I shake my head, willing the pain and unease to

go away.

"Where...where's my phone?" I ask, shoving my palms over my eyes.

"Why, son?" I hear my father ask.

"I need Red. I need to tell her where I am." Did she get away? Was she there?

My stomach flips and splits open.

My mother cackles, and I remove my hands to find her shaking her head. "Boy, you have no idea who you let into your life."

"My phone. Please." I don't have time nor the energy for her antics.

"Why? She already knows where you are," she says.

"No she...so why isn't she here?" Does she know that I'm here? I feel cold, I want my Red.

She laughs again and sneers, "Because she *put* you in that bed."

"No. What are you talking about?" I am so confused.

"She ordered those *thugs* to rob you, or she did it herself. I wouldn't be surprised either way," she claims, her eyes growing larger with each accusation that slips out of her bold red lips.

"No, she wouldn't do that." It didn't make sense. "Please, can I have my phone?"

"Yes, here." My father pulls it out of his pocket and hands it to me.

I smile gratefully at him. "Thank y—"

"What are you doing, Robert? You know she did it! You know!" my mother continues to bark, even as he pulls her out of the room. I feel a surge of appreciation for my father as he asks the doctor and silent nurse to follow behind them.

I sit in silence for a while, unable to move or say anything. What my mother said is absolutely ridiculous. Red would never *ever* do something like that. How would she even know I have a safe or where I keep it? Even if she did know where it is, there isn't any way she would betray me like that.

If anyone did rob me, it was either Ian or Tanner. They wouldn't have known where it was either, but they could have been pissed that Red waited for me after getting arrested, still turning them down, and went over there and ransacked the place, waited for me to come home and take their anger out on me.

It all sounds farfetched, but it's better than thinking my Red would ever do something like that to me.

Sighing heavily, I dial her number and lean back. I close my eyes and expectantly wait to hear her sweet voice. She'll be surprised to know where I am and rush down here to see me, to hug me. Just thinking about seeing her after this has my heart thrumming like a drum.

She answers, and I sigh, hearing her soft breathing. I can practically smell her strawberry-scented hair from this hospital bed.

"Red, it's so great to hear you. You're just breathing, but still." I chuckle and pick at the itchy blanket covering my lower half. "Anyway, um, you will not believe where I am—"

"Noah," she interrupts me. Her voice is chalky, and she sniffles.

I sit up. Something is wrong. "What is it?"

No reply.

461

"Red, what's going on?"

A few moments pass before she speaks. "Noah, I..." She sniffles some more, and I feel the heartbreak before she says, "I am so sorry."

And then, the line goes blank.

Acknowledgements

First, I have to thank Limitless Publishing for continuing to offer support and belief in me and my books that are a little insane at times. Having my stories out in the world has always been my biggest dream, and you're helping that dream become true. Thank you, thank you, thank you!

My family, you already know how much I appreciate your faith in me. Each of you taught me something I'll always remember and treasure. Thank you.

Of course, I have to thank Toni for trying her darned hardest to shape these books into intelligible. I know they must be a headache to comb through, but you manage to better each one that lands on your desk. So, thank you so so much!

Last but certainly not least, I want to thank my readers for sticking around for the emotional rollercoaster. I know you must hate me after every cliffhanger and tearjerker scene, but you suck it up and continue on like a damn warrior. Here's to many more stories about messed-up characters with colors for names!

About the Author

Allison White is a writer spending most of her days creating stories when most people are asleep. She has always been a lover of stories, especially romance. From the very first word she typed, she knew writing was her passion and never stopped. And when she isn't creating stories that tend to break and mend reader's hearts, she's either listening to music or getting way too involved with fictional characters.

Facebook:
https://www.facebook.com/AuthorAWhite

Twitter:
https://twitter.com/AuthorAWhite

Wattpad:
https://wattpad.com/user/authorawhite

Instagram:
https://www.instagram.com/authorawhite

Join our Reader Group on Facebook and don't miss out on meeting our authors and entering epic giveaways!

Limitless Reading

Where reading a book
is your first step to becoming
limitless...

LIMITLESS PUBLISHING *Reader Group*

Join today! *"Where reading a book is your first step to becoming limitless..."*

https://www.facebook.com/groups/LimitlessReading/